A RELUCTANT HERO
ROUGH DARKNESS I

D.C. WALLACE

Clifford Tuttle in
SHADOW
of the PALE BOY

outskirts
press

This is a work of fiction. The events and characters described herein are imaginary and are not intended to refer to specific places or living persons. The opinions expressed in this manuscript are solely the opinions of the author and do not represent the opinions or thoughts of the publisher. The author has represented and warranted full ownership and/or legal right to publish all the materials in this book.

Clifford Tuttle in Shadow of the Pale Boy
All Rights Reserved.
Copyright © 2016 D.C. Wallace
v2.0

Cover Photo © 2016 Ian D. Wallace. All rights reserved - used with permission.

This book may not be reproduced, transmitted, or stored in whole or in part by any means, including graphic, electronic, or mechanical without the express written consent of the publisher except in the case of brief quotations embodied in critical articles and reviews.

Outskirts Press, Inc.
http://www.outskirtspress.com

ISBN: 978-1-4787-7653-6

Outskirts Press and the "OP" logo are trademarks belonging to Outskirts Press, Inc.

PRINTED IN THE UNITED STATES OF AMERICA

Chapter One
Clifford's Awakening

The time was 8:15 pm according to the ornate clock that sat centered majestically on the mantle above the fireplace in Dr. Camilla's darkened office. In its company were two small gold candelabras that held slim, cream colored candles never touched by flame, and a silver framed photograph of what Clifford supposed was her smiling family. In addition to these ordinary objects was a glass domed display case just large enough to hold a peculiar set of glasses or goggles. To Clifford, they seemed like something straight out of a science fiction movie and he wondered if the doctor had once been an actress and these were a memento of a different life. He remembered seeing the curious goggles before, but being nervous about the first meetings with his new doctor, he paid little attention to them. Tonight, however, their sight was compelling and distracting.

As the clockworks ticked their way toward 8:16 pm, their noise was the only sound in the room. Dr. Camilla sat patiently by as she waited for Clifford's response to her question.

Finally Clifford spoke, "I don't want to talk about it! I don't want to remember any of it!" His eyes pleaded from a ghostly pale face framed by a shock of pure black hair. "You all want to know, all you doctors. Why? I just want to forget! I don't want to bring it back…" His eyes dropped to his lap where his hands were clenched into fists. He fell silent again but eventually continued in a weak voice, "It scares me…" His voice hardened, "and it should scare you too!"

Doctor Camilla shifted in her chair so she could reach over and touch Clifford's clenched hands. Clifford relaxed his fists but drew away from her touch.

"I know this is difficult," she said, sitting back up. "You're making great progress though. Don't stop now. You'll see. This will help you."

Doctor Camilla said this with a confident voice, and inside she smiled. She was the seventh psychologist to be hired to help this strange boy. The previous six had predictably failed to break down the walls that Clifford had thrown up against the memories. But she held hope. In her first three sessions with the ghostly pale boy, she had crossed the point that had taken the others each a year to reach. Maybe his walls were finally beginning to crumble perhaps he recognized something familiar in her.

"Tell me about that day, Clifford. Just the good stuff, like what you had for breakfast, or what the weather was like… anything you can remember. It doesn't have to be big… small." She gave him a bright encouraging smile and waited.

Clifford exhaled an agitated breath, "It was my birthday."

"Did you have a party?"

"I didn't get a party."

"Presents? Can you remember any of your presents?"

"I didn't get any."

"Can you remember *why* you didn't have a party or get presents?"

Clifford rolled his head back and stared up at the plaster ceiling. He could not remember– never had, never will. "I told you, I can't remember!" Irritation colored his words.

Dr. Camilla smiled in the dim light despite it all. She spoke softly, "It's alright Clifford. Try to relax."

Clifford became quiet. He listened to her soft words and to the rhythmic ticking of the clockworks. Their combined effect was pulling him down from his height of emotion.

"Just relax. Take a nice deep breath and release it."

The clock ticked on but it seemed far away to Clifford now, or as if it was submerged in water. His body felt light, his eyelids heavy as he stole a sleepy glance at the strange goggles. In a blink of an eye, he slipped into a place of utter darkness.

Clifford's mind settled into the absolute tranquility of the place and he felt safe there until a pinpoint of light pierced the dark. The light began to grow until the whole picture came into focus.

Clifford's awakening memories hinted that he was outside in the sunshine but he was not afraid. It was in the Before Time. It was his sixth birthday. He had squinted up into the sun bedazzled sky before returning his gaze to the ground where his very short, dark shadow pooled like ink on the stony ground. There were other shadows all around him, but none as dark as his.

His mommy and daddy had told him about something called the equinox. It was the moment in the year, one of two that the sun moves directly over the equator.

As he watched his shadow shorten and darken still more, Clifford's nose caught the subtle smell of citrus mixed with something else he could not identify. *"Time, Cliffy!"* he heard his father exclaim. Suddenly the ground beneath his feet was gone.

To a normal child of six, a fall was not as terrifying as the dark. (Gravity by this time had not severely punished him, and he really liked the dark.) But, when Clifford found the fall through the dark place did not end, the terror of the moment set in. He had never fallen further than three feet and the impact with the ground was usually less than notable. But this fall was way further than four feet, and his primal instincts told him this was bad.

A terrified scream erupted from his throat as he fell from total blackness into the glaring brightness of the sky. There seemed to be no top or bottom to it, just endless sky. But even as a six year old, Clifford knew without a doubt that the sky was always above the ground and the sea. He also knew his accelerating fall would eventually take him there to be crushed or drowned.

He was screaming– the sound of it barely audible above the howling wind in his ears. His eyes watered as he fought to keep them open. He had to know, was it to be ground or water? It hardly mattered. He was dead– that was what his instincts told him.

His heart's death defying pulse whooshed in his ears, mixing with the deafening wind. The fall continued with no land in sight and this gave him a horrible lot of time to consider his ultimate fate.

Finally, he thought he saw movement through blurred visual focus. He stopped screaming and blinked hard to clear his eyes. The sky below him was moving, undulating like the surface of a giant soap bubble and suddenly there was a spot and it was growing. In the last horrifying moments of his awareness, he saw his own reflection in the bubble's mirrored surface growing, racing toward him. Suddenly, something caught him and his terror was severed by merciful oblivion.

When Clifford woke, he was staring up at Dr. Camilla's dark ceiling. His heartbeat raced unbridled in his chest and he felt soaked in sweat. Somewhere in the distance, beyond the thundering sound of his pulse, a clock was ticking.

The sound of movement in his left ear redirected his

attention to the concerned face of Dr. Camilla.

"What happened?" his voice rasped through a dry, scratchy throat.

The doctor smiled but Clifford could see the shadow of alarm around the edges.

"You were hypnotized," she said and took a deep, settling breath in an attempt to slow her own racing heart. "Are you alright dear? Can you remember anything?"

Clifford tried to wet his sore throat but he had no saliva. "Can I get a drink?"

He watched, still pinned by fear to the couch, as the doctor got up and retrieved a glass of water from an old fashioned, dark glass bottle. The wait, though brief, was agonizing. When the drink arrived, he took it gratefully. Smelling a familiar citrus aroma Clifford downed the drink in one gulp. The ice cold water, its flavor as familiar and strange as the scent, diminished the flames in his throat but did not extinguish them completely.

When he thought he could speak again he nodded, "I was falling through the sky like I was dropped out of a plane, but without a parachute!" Clifford swallowed back a sob.

Then an idea rose above the chaos swirling in his mind. "I was little again… like, six. I was with my mom and dad in a place with no houses or streets. There were mountains that smoked… volcanoes, I guess? The sun was really bright and right over our heads… and then I was falling."

Clifford looked up into Dr. Camilla's attentive face,

"I fell through my shadow like it was a deep hole… like a bottomless pit. I was falling through the dark and then through the sky! Then… something caught me just before I–" Clifford shook his head. I can't remember any more."

He thought about it for a minute, desperately grasping for the dissolving details of his hypnosis.

"I get bad dreams of falling all the time." He was silent for a moment before he continued, "I've heard that if you have a dream like that… and you don't wake up before you hit the ground, you'll die. Is that true?"

The doctor shook her head, "I've heard that too. But it's not true. Maybe if you were very old, and had a bad heart or something, the fright could give you a heart attack. But no fourteen year old boy has ever died from a bad dream."

"Are you sure?"

Doctor Camilla shrugged her shoulders admitting she couldn't be entirely positive about that.

Clifford thought some more and then went on, "There was no ground in that place. Only sky, forever and ever!" He swallowed and winced through the pain. "Why does my throat hurt so badly? I'm not sick."

The Doctor adjusted her position in her chair. "You were screaming, dear. You must have been very frightened. Can you remember any more?"

"No. Not really. Nothing," he shrugged.

"How do you feel?"

Clifford was silent for a while as he thought about her question. His expression brightened, "Like, I know. Like,

I've finally remembered a forgotten dream. Like, I know why the sun... and my shadow scared me." He looked up into the Doctor's eyes, "Like, it was real... not a dream at all! There *is* a place where the sky never ends and... clouds can move without the help of the wind? Where the clouds can... talk?"

This memory came out of nowhere. His brow furrowed.

Doctor Camilla smiled. Her suspicions where now confirmed. She had to be careful not to go too far because she knew Clifford Tuttle was in a delicate place. She had two choices: come right out with the startling truth or make Clifford find the truth on his own. Earned knowledge was precious and the process of gathering that knowledge would temper his transition.

She continued, "It may seem real Clifford but we still haven't discovered the real truth. Something *real* did happen to you. You disappeared for almost two days when you were six. When they found you, you were nearly a thousand miles away from where you had disappeared. There has got to be a plausible explanation still hidden in that head of yours, don't you think?"

Clifford thought some more, feeling very certain that she was wrong– feeling fairly certain that she was holding something back.

"But there isn't!" he cried. I *know* what happened now! I fell through my shadow!"

Chapter Two
Touch of Sunlight

Clifford Tuttle stood in front of the closed doorway that led to the outside of his home and took a deep breath. Although the door's window was shuttered to the outside, sunlight cut a bright frame around the shade's edges. Clifford's fingers fanned out and tentatively touched the light. He held his fingers there allowing the light to play over his skin for several seconds before he withdrew them. Clifford thoughtfully rubbed his thumb across his retracted fingertips, reached for the door lever and turned it.

Opening the door, Clifford faced the early morning sunshine for the first time since he was six. The brilliance and color of the day-lit world was surprising, having almost grown alien to his life over the past seven years. But, there was a price to pay for this rare view. Although he wanted to keep looking, or to even step outside, the brightness hurt his light sensitive eyes, so after another look around, he reluctantly backed away from the door's threshold. This, he realized, was going to take some time. He needed to be patient and feed his curiosity in small doses.

Clifford's heart raced with the thrill of his first attempt to fight off his seven year phobia. He took one more look before he swung the shaded door closed. The dark interior immersed him in its comfort as he promised himself that he would keep trying no matter what. Any notion of a permanent retreat back into darkness was totally unacceptable to him now.

Over the three following days Clifford's new found knowledge ate away at his brain until he could no longer bear the mystery.

The previous night had proven to be the turning point. He had not slept well at first. When he finally did, he dreamed of flying, not falling, through an alien world that was fantastic beyond all his Earthly experience. When he woke he was more convinced than ever that the sky place was real and that he had to go back, but how?

The September air held tight to the overnight chill, but the sun was warm on his face as he studied his shadow in the doorway– closely, obsessively. Clifford slipped a pair of his aunt's sunglasses on, stepped further out of the house, paused and finally walked out into the yard.

Moving through the yard, he noticed his shadow still eclipsed every other shadow, no matter what cast it. It relieved him to know that at least that part of the puzzle had not changed. What once had been a wonder, then a fearful thing, had become a wonder to him again.

Clifford's first leap of faith was now behind him. What lie ahead remained a mystery. As he strolled the yard Clifford did not fall through his shadow, but it was early morning and the sun was barely up. He would have to wait and return to the yard at noon to see if that made any difference.

Following this latest early morning excursion into the daylight, Clifford returned to the darkened portion of the house where he spent his days. His Aunt Gwen would be rising soon (She was a late sleeper.) and he wasn't quite sure how she would take it if she found him outside in the sun after all the years he had shunned it. Aunt Gwen was twenty-eight years old and had been his home school teacher for the last five years.

Clifford's parents traveled as much as they ever did– his disability had only slowed them down a little. In their absence, Aunt Gwen was his caretaker, teacher and his only and very best friend. She was still young enough to be fun, unlike his first and second grade home school teachers. Some times he considered Aunt Gwen more a mother than his real one had ever been. He had certainly spent more time with Gwen these days than with his own mother.

When Aunt Gwen finally wandered in, she was sleep tousled and groggy. There was nothing new about that. Clifford was seated at his computer researching dream analysis.

"Morning, Cliffy. You're up and at 'em early."

Clifford swiveled toward her and raised an eyebrow, "I'm always up before you, Aunt Gwen."

She smiled back, "What are you up to over there?"

Clifford returned his attention to the softly glowing computer monitor– the only light source in his room. "I'm doing some research on dreams."

"Dream research is it?" She turned serious. "Have you been having those bad dreams again, honey?"

Clifford shook his head, "No. They were good dreams this time. I think they must mean something."

"Oh, cool. Anything I can help you with?"

"I don't know. In my dream I was flying instead of falling. The place was strange, like a different world... and it seemed real!" he mused aloud, and silently, *It didn't seem real, it was real.*

Gwen fingered her mussed hair, trying to flatten it out a bit. "Hmm. Flying usually represents freedom in dreams," she remarked.

"Yeah, that's what I found out." He swiveled back to face her. "Do you think there can be other places like alien worlds that are real?"

"Who knows? There's a lot of space out there. Each star is supposed to be a sun. I just bet there is, somewhere."

"How 'bout right under our feet?" he wondered aloud.

"Wow, aren't we waxing philosophical this morning? It must have been a whopper of a dream."

Clifford spun a couple times around in his chair as he stared at his ceiling. His eyes were bright with wonder. "I think there is a world inside our world that you can only get to by falling through your shadow." He stopped the spinning to study Gwen as she absorbed this information.

"Whoa, that's a new one." Gwen cocked her head and chuckled, "You've changed since your last visit to Dr. Camilla. She thinks you've had a break-through. I think she's right. You might be getting better, Cliffy."

Clifford smiled wryly. "I went outside this morning," he said matter-of-factly.

Gwen's mouth hung open with disbelief. "Before the sun came up? You *know* I don't like you going outside by yourself at night…"

"The sun was up, *and* I went outside!"

Gwen looked dazed for a moment then smiled, "Well, that's great Cliffy!"

"I had to know… I had to see my shadow again," he said in a serious and somewhat distracted tone.

Gwen came over and gave her nephew a big hug. "I can't believe it! After all these years! What ever possessed you?"

"I had to know!" he repeated, smiled and shrugged.

"How do you feel about that? I mean… What did you find?"

"That it's not scary anymore… at least not much. My shadow is still darker than anything, you know. I'll show you."

He walked over to a window and peeled a pane size piece of black contact paper from his window inviting in a beam of sunlight. He held his arm in the beam and looked down at the shadow his arm cast. "See, Aunt Gwen?"

She knelt down and studied the carpet that was touched by both the shadows of the blacked out portions of the window and of Clifford's arm. "Whoa. That's so weird! You say that's how it's always been?"

"When I was six I fell through *that* shadow."

Gwen, putting aside the phenomenal shadow the pale boy cast, looked up with a skeptical look on her face, "Well that certainly would explain a lot." she said with a crooked smile and snorted sarcastically.

Clifford felt a pang of anger but brushed off the sarcasm. "When are mom and dad coming home?"

Gwen sat down on the edge of Clifford's bed. She was feeling a little lightheaded. This was entirely too much for her to absorb this early in the morning, *and* before she had her first cup of coffee. It was like the world she had known for the past five years had suddenly tilted on its axis.

"October, I think," she answered. You never know with them. Do you think I should call them and tell them they should get right home? Wait a minute! Darn right I should get them home! This is a big move for you Cliffy. They need to be here!"

Clifford shrugged and nodded his head. "Yeah. They need to be here. I need to ask them about something too."

"Okay, Cliffy. We'll SKYPE Dottie tonight," she said knowing it was the middle of the night in Australia.

At noon that day Clifford returned to the sunshine and crouched on the concrete driveway that ran along the sunny side of the house. His shadow spread asymmetrically beneath him. With all the new knowledge he possessed came a new fear no less powerful than the one that had held him a prisoner in the dark for seven years. His heart beat fearfully fast knowing what he was about to do.

Clifford remembered only bits and pieces of the hypnotized state Dr. Camilla had put him into. One of the clearest memories was how his shadow looked just before he had fallen through it– small, densely black, infinitely deep, like looking into the depths of space, but without the stars. He reached out and placed all ten fingers on his shadow. His pale white hands glowed against the darkness of his shadow below. He held his breath to stop himself from trembling and pressed his weight into the shadowed pavement. The ground did not budge.

With this definitive answer to a seven year old dread came an unexpected flood of emotion, fueled by a mixture of relief and utter disappointment. Crushed by the unbearable weight of emotion Clifford collapsed to the concrete and wept until Gwen, who had been watching from the doorway, tearfully swept him into her arms. They sat there embracing each other in the sun for a long time until their tears had been spent.

Chapter Three
The Plan

As nightfall approached, Clifford's uneasy mind began to feel trapped and helpless. As the sun set, he began to pace the house like a caged animal and his personality took on an edginess alien to his normal state.

As always, his Aunt Gwen tolerated this personality swing as she had his obsessive fear of daylight. She was truly a good and understanding person. Besides, she had a lot on her mind as well. It would be day soon in Australia, where Clifford's mother, Dottie and father, Ed were at the moment.

At 7:00 pm they connected on SKYPE with Ed and Dottie– 9:00 AM Australian time. Dottie's excited voice came across the internet as clearly as if she were next door, "That's great, Honey! I can't tell you how proud we are of you!"

Clifford leaned into the camera, "Mom? When can you come home?"

Dottie's small smile hardly hid her regret. "As soon

as I can... but not right away. Just a couple more weeks, honey. Gee wiz! I can't wait to see you again!"

Clifford slouched back into his chair. He was nearly crushed by the very response he was expecting. "I thought you would say that. Two weeks, huh?" he sighed.

What had he expected? His parents' work always came first, especially their field work.

"I really need to talk to you about what happened when I was six. I'm starting to remember a lot more stuff now."

"Ah, that's, er, great Honey," Dottie said carefully. "Is it bad? Do you remember how you ended up in Quito?"

Dotty had lived through years of wonder and worry regarding this unsolved event.

"Have you talked to Dr. Camilla about this?" she went on.

"Yeah! She hypnotized me! We both know what happened but she won't admit that it was all real."

"What happened, Honey?"

"I fell through my shadow!"

There was silence at the other end. Dottie seemed to physically deflate before the camera and looked uncomfortable as if she were searching for words. "You fell... through your... shadow?"

Ed, seated silently next to Dotty, had remained neutral in expression until he heard this. (Dotty usually did most of the talking. Ed was the listener.) His eyes went wide in an expression of sudden insight.

"Yes, into another world!" Clifford leaned in toward

the lens again. His words spilled out in a frantic rush. "I need to go back there!"

Dottie looked concerned on the screen, like she always did when they discussed his phobia of the sun and his shadow. It was as if nothing had changed after all. But it had! Everything had changed. Clifford's mental malady had just shifted to another track.

"We'll talk about this when your dad and I get home. I'll see if I can bump it up a few days. Have Aunt Gwen set up an appointment with Dr. Camilla in the first week of October. Can you remember that, Honey?"

"Yeah, mom." He was silent for a moment and his mother waited. "You don't believe me either, do you?"

Dotty tried to smile but the effort failed, "We'll talk about it when your dad and I get home. But… hey! This is great news… really, dear." This time she did smile, "Hey," she continued, "you should work on your tan in the meantime. See you soon."

They signed off and Clifford sat in silence for a long while before he finally got up to get ready for bed.

Clifford was the first to rise again the next day. His anxiety doubled as the day dawned heavily overcast. To settle his nerves he took to his computer and researched everything he could find about his disappearance.

He found that he was, of course, the only child of University of Pittsburgh Professors– Geologists, researchers. The couple had traveled to many exotic places and taken their young son along since he was an infant. They had been on Isabella Island, off the coast of Ecuador, South America when he disappeared on March 20, 2009. The expedition had been encamped at the base of an active volcano in the northern region of the island. (The place was also notable because the equator just happened to cross the very point where they had camped, but the newspapers hadn't picked up on that important detail. Why would they have?)

Clifford vaguely remembered his father scratching a long line in the volcanic soil to indicate the equator's estimated location. This, he felt, had some significance. The date marked that year's vernal or spring equinox for the northern hemisphere. (Was this more coincidence? Clifford guessed, yes.)

The records showed that he had vanished at around 2:20 PM in broad daylight. It was initially feared that he had wandered into an area of unstable ground north of their camp and fallen into some kind of sinkhole. The expedition team had searched the area in vain for two days and nights without rest. The child was not found and presumed dead. That was until he had popped up in Quito, Ecuador early on the third day.

Clifford sat back in his chair– the information glowing on the screen forgotten.

During this point in the equinox there would be very little shadow. The sun would have been directly above my head, he thought. It all made sense to him now.

"At high sun, could my shadow have become concentrated enough to create a hole?" he whispered beneath his breath. "No," he said shaking his head. The theory was impossible. A shadow had no substance.

The story of Peter Pan had been on his mind. In that story, Peter's shadow had escaped him and had taken on a life if its own. But that was complete make-believe.

Clifford slouched deeper into his chair and wondered, *Dr. Camilla couldn't be right. She said something "real world" had to have happened to me that day. That was not true.*

Clifford had no other memories of normal worldly events between the last moments he remembered of being on Isabella Island and when he found himself lost and confused in Quito. And besides, there were all the recurring nightmares of falling to consider.

The scenario unfolding in his mind made perfect sense. The sky place was real. What was really eating him was the missing time. He had been in that place for over 44 hours but he could not remember a thing about it.

As the days passed, Clifford's curiosity morphed into an obsession. The calendar glared at him from his bedroom wall. It was mid September. To exasperate his anxiety, he had not seen the sun since that first day, because Pittsburgh had been under a six day stretch of chilly, rainy days.

The shadow he had cast in his driveway the other day had not swallowed him up. He was now convinced it wouldn't, not in this latitude. He knew the equator had to have something to do with it. The only true fact he had to go on was the incident happened on the equator, on the very day of the spring equinox at high sun or at 2:20 PM. There were no other facts.

Clifford shut down his computer, moved to his window, looked out at the gray day, sighed and plopped onto his bed to think. One thought extinguished all others: He had to get to the equator, but the equator did not pass through Pittsburgh, Pennsylvania, nowhere near.

The morning passed without a realistic solution to his dilemma. To his credit, he had come up with a list of crazy schemes, a few that could actually work. But at 11:00 Aunt Gwen called him down for his daily lessons. The true answer would have to wait.

Following dinner Clifford and Aunt Gwen sat in front of their modest, outmoded analogue TV. The family wasn't big TV watchers but they had cable, and in the days since his awakening, he and Aunt Gwen had taken to watching old movies in the evenings. Tonight's fare was "Sleepless in Seattle." He had seen the movie before and was amused by the way Gwen bawled at the end every time. The two spooned ice cream into their mouths as they watched the boy's computer-savvy friend log onto her mother's travel agency website and reserve plane tickets to New York City.

Like the boy in the movie, Clifford had spoken incessantly not of New York City, but of Isabella Island, Quito, Ecuador, and the equator.

Gwen gave him the evil eye, "Don't you get any ideas, Cliffy!" she scolded. "You hear me?"

Clifford feigned incredulous shock, even though the

thought *had* crossed his mind more than once. "I wouldn't do that! Geez, I'm fourteen!"

Gwen released her glare, "OK. Just so you know… it would kill me if you disappeared again."

On the eighteenth of September Clifford sat cross-legged on his bed with a very large world atlas spread open before him on the rumpled comforter. With his chalky white fingertip he traced the path of the equator. He noted the location of Isabella Island from which he had disappeared and followed the equator east to the Ecuadorian city of Quito where he was found; the distance scaled nearly one thousand miles.

He got up went over to his computer and Googled Ecuador and then Quito. This was not the first time he had done this. Before, it was done simply to quench his curiosity. Today he had other things in mind. Popular tourist destinations for Quito included the Equatorial Monument to the Sun which was bisected by the equator and located 16 miles north of the city. He Googled "Travel to Quito" and found a flight. It would cost $1,400 for a last minute round-trip ticket. He tapped his fingers nervously on the keys of the keyboard. They made a comforting rattling sound. *I've got to do this. I'm running out of time,* he thought.

What harm would be done? he reasoned. He would go there and wait. When the time was right he would try his shadow again. If it didn't work, all he had to do is get back on the return flight. He would leave his Aunt Gwen a detailed note explaining his plan. It wouldn't "kill" her if she saw how flawless his plan was. Sure, he would be in big trouble when he got home, but Aunt Gwen was a softy when it came to discipline. He barely required discipline. How much trouble could a kid in his situation get into? Besides, he was getting better every day. That had to count for something. Just this one little thing and then he would know. In the long run, everyone would be better off.

He stared deeply into the screen, not focusing on anything except for what was going on in his head.

But what if it works? Really works? What then? he fretted. *Well, then I will deal with it.*

Gwen would probably be killed from worry. He was sure that wouldn't happen, but it would truly be sad if she was. On the other hand, his parents would be proud of him after they got done being angry. *This is research isn't it? Yes, field research.*

"I don't worry that much when Dad and Mom are off for months poking around in volcanoes," he muttered to himself. *But what happens if I can't get back?* "I got back before, I can get back again… some how," he said, giving the computer screen a nod.

His parents had left him a credit card for use in the event of emergency or for his Aunt Gwen to buy him things he needed in their absence. He had swiped the card from his aunt's wallet the day before and had hidden it in the drawer of his computer desk. He reasoned his aunt would not miss it unless she needed to use it for one of his needs. He knew for a fact that there was enough on the card to buy him and Gwen airfare to just about anyplace his parents might be in the world. His parents told him so.

He had a real need now, but it would be impossible to convince Aunt Gwen to use the card to buy him a flight to Quito, Ecuador. He commenced to rattle the keys nervously with light, noncommittal finger taps as he stared at the contraband card. His need to know the truth had, by now, far outweighed his common sense, so he reserved a flight for the twenty-second of September, the day before the Autumnal Equinox was to occur in Quito.

Chapter Four
Busted

As the date of Clifford's departure for Quito grew close, so grew his anxiety. Aunt Gwen's quizzical looks, whether real or imagined, sharpened the edge on his nerves even more. And today, as they worked through his lessons, Gwen suddenly clapped her hands and sat forward in her chair.

"Why don't we take a break?"

Clifford looked up from his sheet of algebraic word problems and was locked into her intense gaze like a deer caught in the glare of a car's headlights. He instantly saw something there that caused him to freeze, both physically and mentally. He swallowed hard with the guilt of all his secrets catching in his throat, "Ah… Sure… Why?"

Gwen held him in her stare. "What's eating you, Cliffy?"

Clifford held his shrug too long, like a turtle trying to hide from a threat while maintaining a careful watch. "Nothing."

Sensing his discomfort, Gwen relaxed her glare. "It's just... You seem distracted lately. Is there something I should know?"

Clifford shook his head but remained silent.

Gwen raised her eyebrows in expectation of further reply. The stare returned.

Clifford fidgeted with his pencil, avoiding eye contact. "I'm just a little antsy... that's all. I've got a lot of stuff to think about too."

"Ah, yes," she cast an exaggerated glance at the floor, "Other worlds beneath our feet?"

"Yeah," he said, relieved that she hadn't brought up the equator. Yet, her mockery had struck a nerve.

"Are you sure?" she asked. "There isn't anything else? Something you should talk to Dr. C. about? Are some of the old fears coming back, maybe?"

Clifford paused to collect his thoughts and to devise a response that would surely throw her off the whole Quito, equator thing.

"It's... it's all these rainy, dark days. I need to get out and see the sun."

Gwen turned and looked out the window. It was still cloudy but at least it wasn't raining.

Gwen smiled, "Good idea Cliffy. Let's wrap this up and go out somewhere."

Clifford's mind darted straight for Quito. That was the only place he really wanted to go to.

Gwen thought for a moment, "How about the zoo? You've never been to the Pittsburgh Zoo. It's really nice and I think the weather might be improving." As she spoke the sun broke through the clouds.

Despite the incredible stress Clifford was experiencing, it was amazingly fine to be out in the daylight again. Everything seemed bright and new to him as if he had been delivered into a brand new world.

As they walked the paths of the zoo, Clifford noted a handful of the caged creatures that he had actually seen in the wild on some of his parents' early research trips. The exercise and the fresh outdoor air did him a world of good, but by the end of the day he was utterly exhausted.

It was the twenty-first of September, the day before Clifford's scheduled flight. Clifford woke earlier than usual, partly because he had things to do before Aunt Gwen woke up, and partly because he simply couldn't sleep. He crawled to the back of his closet and retrieved a travel bag he had stashed there and tossed it on his bed. He went to his dresser and gathered several pair of socks and underwear, three shirts, one sweat shirt and a pair of shorts and placed them neatly in the bag. He threw in the sun glasses Gwen had bought him at the zoo and he added his Pittsburgh Steelers ball cap to protect his head from the sun. The cap was a present form a relative who assumed, since he lived in Pittsburgh, he would be a fan of the team. No one in his immediate family, however, followed sports and he had never gone outside to need a hat in seven years so it had remained unused until his trip to the zoo.

He tossed in his passport and wallet containing the credit card and about $100 worth of small bills he had squirreled away over the past year.(It was an impressively thick wad of cash, though was mostly ones, fives, and tens.) He stood and did a final inventory, zipped the bag up and shoved it back in his closet.

With that accomplished, Clifford moved to his computer and typed in the web address for the Weather Channel and found the forecast for Quito, Ecuador. His heart dropped a beat when he saw that there was an 80% chance of isolated thunderstorms mixed with sun and clouds on the day of the equinox. The high temperature would be 68. *"Pretty chilly for a place right on the equator"* he thought.

Clifford had researched Quito's weather and was surprised to find that Quito's altitude in the mountains combined with a steady wind off the ocean kept the temperatures comfortably cool throughout the year.

Clifford ran his hands roughly through his hair as he fretted, *What if it rains when the time comes? Everything would be ruined!* Worry raked his guts from the inside but it was too late to back out now.

Moving on, he went back to his dresser to retrieve the concealed folder that contained his research. He had stashed it beneath the paper drawer liner, and several layers of shirts. His fingers felt under the paper but the folder was gone.

Clifford cringed as he sniffed the air. The drawer smelled faintly of fabric softener, a smell he had not noticed before. And that was the only clue he needed.

Heat built up under his pajamas and he broke out in a cold sweat. "Ah, no!" he groaned. He gripped his head in his hands and tried not to panic.

He had to think fast. If Gwen had found the folder it would give her a very good reason to be suspicious. He tried to remember what incriminating evidence he may have filed there. Surely the printed flight itinerary was in her hands now and that would be all she needed.

"Ah, man! I am so busted!" he cried as he wiped the sweat from his forehead and plopped down on the floor in front of the dresser. *How long has Aunt Gwen known? Did I use the file in the last couple of days? When did she do the laundry? If she knows, why didn't she say something?* His hopes for success faded to a dim spark. *What do I do now? Confess? Wait it out?*

Clifford steeled up his courage and crept out into the hall. He listened to the house before he moved on. It seemed as silent as it usually was at this early hour so he descended the stairs, taking care to walk only on the outside edges of the treads so the boards wouldn't creak. At the foot of the stairs he stopped, cocked his ear to the ceiling above and listened. There was no sound.

Feeling less vulnerable, he treaded silently into the kitchen. The space was unoccupied. The countertops glowed dimly in the early morning light. And then he saw it.

Clifford's heart jumped into his throat. There, on the kitchen island counter, was his file folder. He swallowed hard against the raging panic consuming him.

"Ah, crap! This is bad," he said.

Suddenly the lights came on and he nearly jumped out of his skin.

Gwen stood in the doorway grinning. "Going somewhere Clifford?"

Clifford was stunned speechless with fear. Gwen never called him by his proper name unless he was in deep trouble.

Her face set sternly but her eyes sparkled with secreted mischief. "What? Cat got your tongue?" she growled. Her voice rose, "Come on, fess up, Mister!"

Clifford jumped again and backed up a step, cringing beneath her wild-eyed glare. He felt as though he were going to cry.

"I… just…" he stammered before he was cut off by her stern words.

"*What* were you *thinking*?! I *told* you. No more disappearances! What made you think you could pull this off? This is *not* TV, buddy-boy! Bad things can happen to kids!" she scolded as she sauntered over to the file folder on the counter. Her fingertips tapped a couple of drum rolls on the cover.

"Come on. Let's sit. It looks like you're going to faint or something." Her sarcasm was thick.

They both took a stool. Gwen continued, "What's all this, Clifford? I have my suspicions…"

Clifford swallowed what seemed like a wad of dry cotton. "My research," he croaked.

"Aaaa… huh," Aunt Gwen said and began to slowly, torturously, turn the pages. She studied the contents on each sheet as if she had never read the information before. She seemed to be enjoying the building suspense.

"Hmm, impressive," she said finally. "Taking after your folks, I see."

Clifford had just about had enough of Aunt Gwen's game.

"Okay! You *caught* me!" he said irritably. The tears were close but he held onto them.

Gwen smiled triumphantly and slapped both palms down on the open folder's contents. "Oh, boy did I! So where do we go from here, hmmm?"

"Nowhere, I guess," Clifford mumbled. The tears began to flow as his frustration grew. "I just thought–"

Gwen smiled. "Mmm hmm. Close, but no cigar… So you know. There were quite a few *flaws* in your plan. All this would have gotten you as far as the airport, and no further."

"What flaws?" Clifford muttered through his tears.

Aunt Gwen held up one finger. "Passport!"

"Got it!" he retorted.

She held up a second finger. "Shots!"

Clifford frowned, "What shots?"

"Honey, you are traveling to the tropics, in a different country. You need to be inoculated for all the diseases you could catch before they let you travel there. Daaa."

Clifford felt himself deflate. "Oh," he said.

"A huh…" She held up a third finger. "Documented

approval from a parent or allowing you to travel abroad, alone?" She wagged a finger on her free hand as she said this.

Clifford remained silent, and defeated.

Gwen held up a fourth finger. "There is a little clause attached to the credit card you *swiped* from my wallet that states 'because the card is in a minor's name,' that's you buddy, 'that any transaction over $100 has to be reported to your parent or *guardian*.' Didn't you read the fine print?"

This had gone way too far for Clifford to bear. "So now what? Are you going to *ground* me or something? *BIG DEAL!* I've spent the last seven years grounded!"

He took two great gulps of air to steady his anger. "I know it was wrong to try to do this, but you have to believe me! I have to go! I have to know!"

Gwen still patiently held up her four fingers as he ranted. "Shall I continue or should we get our selves down to Dr. Wells for our inoculations?"

Clifford's monologue fell silent and his mouth hung open in gaping surprise.

The rest of the morning evaporated in a flurry of activity. Their early morning, impromptu meeting concluded with a quick breakfast and Aunt Gwen's briefing. As it turned out, Gwen had already packed for both of them and had arranged their flight which was to depart from Pittsburgh International Airport at 1:05 pm, that day, a day earlier than Clifford had planned.

Aunt Gwen explained, "If we're going to Ecuador, we

might as well make a real vacation of it. I packed enough for two weeks. How about it, kid?" she growled as she roughed up his mop of hair.

Clifford was completely beleaguered despite all his preparation.

"Okay," he croaked weakly. "Already? Now?" His head was spinning from the emotional rollercoaster ride he was on.

"Hey, mister. You're the one that got this thing started. Now move it!"

Chapter Five
Return to Quito

They hit Dr. Wells' office for their shots then drove strait to the airport. It wasn't until they were in the air that the reality of the situation had settled in Clifford's mind.

"How come you're doing this for me Aunt Gwen?"

"Let's just say that this is part of your therapy."

"Therapy?"

"Sure. Dr. Camilla suggested it. When I found your research file I got worried. Now, don't get mad. I called Dr. Camilla and we had a nice long chat."

"About what? I thought she didn't believe me."

"She has her concerns, but she was so pleased with your recovery that she felt this trip would do you some good."

Gwen paused and thought to herself, *Yes. The Doctor was quite eager to commend the plan Cliffy had assembled despite the stupidity and danger of it.*

She shook her head absently in silent disbelief then

returned to the conversation.

"She thinks that the sooner you find the answers, the sooner this will all be resolved."

"I guess she thinks I'll find out how stupid I've been," he pouted, "then thinks I'll just forget the whole thing." He frowned out the window, "But I'm not sure I can. It's in my head. I know it's real."

"Well then, when this all shakes out, the truth will be known."

"What happens if it is real?"

Gwen turned to him agape, "Oh, God! I hope not! How would I ever explain this to Dottie?!" She said this just a little too lightly and knew immediately that it had stung him.

"I didn't mean for it to come out that way, Cliffy. It's just a *tiny bit* far fetched… don't you think?"

Clifford shook his head. "You said it yourself. The universe is a big place. I believe there's more to it than meets the eye."

Aunt Gwen smiled proudly, "Listen to you. You're so grown up for a fourteen year old! Let's just say for now, that the jury is still out. Hey, I'll believe anything is possible until the experiment proves a theory wrong. I've always had an open mind to the mysteries of the universe and I can honestly say I hope you're right." She reached over and ruffled his hair. "You're not the only one who has dreamed of another place, another existence. I was born with a fantastic imagination. Your mom was always preaching hard science to me. It used to really piss me off.

I guess I just kept on dreaming. Maybe that's why I went into teaching. Young minds are so imaginative."

Clifford turned to face her then repeated his question. "What if this is real and I actually *do* fall through my shadow into that place?" He shivered involuntarily at the thought.

Gwen bit her lip. "Wellllll. I guess we'll just have to deal with the consequences of our actions then." She reached over and touched his pale white arm, "We'll find out in a couple of days, won't we?"

Clifford remained silent for a time before he resumed, "Senõr Martinez will know what to do."

"Ahhh, yeah. The man who found you after you disappeared from Isabella Island, right? I read about him in your articles. Wasn't he regarded as an early suspect in your abduction?"

"No one could prove he was guilty. He's lived in Quito all his life, actually rarely left town. He found me wandering lost near that equator monument. There were no witnesses that could say otherwise..." he smiled a small but confident smile, "I have a feeling there's more to Senõr Martinez than meets the eye too."

"I'll have to hand it to you; you really know your stuff. Do you think he's still alive? He was pretty old seven years ago."

Clifford shrugged, "Bummer if he isn't. I can remember exactly where he lives though. I can see his house in my mind like it was yesterday," he paused, staring intensely into his aunt's eyes to emphasize his next words. "I can remember everything now. Dr. Camilla said there had to be some other explanation but I can't remember anything else. It wasn't kidnappers. If it was, wouldn't I remember at least something about that too? Everything else... the sky place... is so clear!" Clifford peered out the window and thought of that place.

The plane adjusted its course, bringing the direct sun in through their passenger window. Gwen looked down at the extraordinarily dark shadow Clifford cast across her lap and she wondered of fantastic possibilities.

Their flight arrived in Quito, on time, at 11:40 pm. Once through customs, the two weary adventurers hailed a cab and rode to the hotel.

Clifford gazed out into the dark night and wondered how he would have ever made the trip himself. His aunt was amazing and on that day, as he sat in the back seat of their cab, drained both emotionally and physically, he loved her more than ever.

The weather was warm for that time of night and humid, not unlike a mild early September night in Pittsburgh. Dark thunder clouds hung invisible in the night sky obscuring the stars and moon. Lightning flashed and thunder rumbled across the land.

Big drops of rain began to strike the windshield as the cab wove its way up the steep, crowded street and pulled up in front of the Hotel Viena Internacional. As poor luck would have it, the clouds opened up just as they were pulling their baggage out of the trunk of the car.

They screamed and laughed as they made the mad dash between their cab and hotels lobby doors. They were both dripping wet as they were greeted warmly by a smiling staff and shown to their room.

The air conditioner hummed as it pumped cool air into their room, chilling them more than they had been before. It was a decent size room with two full size beds and a sitting area. The room was time worn and old fashioned in a quaint kind of way, though the bathroom left much to be desired.

"Well, it's not the Ritz but it will do," Gwen said as she moved to turn the dial on the air conditioner to a warmer setting.

Clifford shrugged, "It's not that bad. I stayed in a lot worse places before, with Mom and Dad. Mom used to worry out loud about cockroaches carrying me away in my sleep. I think she was just kidding though."

Clifford moved to the window, pulled open the curtain, stared first out at the rainy night then focused on his own ghostly reflection in the glass. All he could think about was what if the clouds and rain persisted through the equinox? He sighed heavily.

As if Aunt Gwen had read his mind, she came over to him and put her hand on his shoulder and said, "At least we'll get a vacation out of this, Cliffy."

She sighed too, her thoughts hidden. "What do you say we get dry then try to get some sleep? I don't know about you but I'm exhausted. This has been some day huh, Cliffy?"

"Yeah... and this is just the beginning," he said, turned, and gave his aunt a long hug meant partly to thank her and partly to reinforce his shrinking courage. *For better or worse, this is really going to happen.*

Gwen latched the room's door behind her. She cradled a steaming hot cup of coffee in her hands. The sound of the door brought Clifford out of his deep slumber.

"Morning, Cliffy."

Clifford roused groggily from a dream of swimming in a glowing pool hidden deep in a stony place. He scooted his butt up and leaned his back against the bed's headboard. He blinked in surprise because this was something entirely new to him. Aunt Gwen was never up before he was.

"What time is it?"

"Almost 9:00. I didn't want to wake you. You seemed so tired last night."

Gwen set her cup down, pulled the curtains open, and regarded the day before sinking into one of the chairs. "The sun's out. You'll be happy to hear that."

Clifford's sleep blurred eyes blinked into the harsh light as he felt his stomach flip with anxiety.

"Are you hungry? There's a really cool courtyard with a fountain downstairs where we can eat. The food smelled delicious when I went down for coffee."

Clifford licked his lips. Despite the anxiety flipping his stomach like pancakes, he could definitely eat. Neither one of them had had anything big to eat since their flight's layover in Atlanta, Georgia. "I'm on it!" he exclaimed as he bounced up out of bed.

Forty minutes later, washed and dressed, the couple sat in the shaded courtyard eating enormous South American seasoned omelets. Gwen pulled out a map she had picked up at the tourist counter.

"So how do we find this Martinez?" she asked through a full chewing mouth.

Clifford leaned over the map. "We need to find the police station, and then I think I can remember the way."

The city was as he remembered it, big, crowded and old. The streets in some places were steep and narrow and clogged with pedestrians. At that time, he was a frightened, lost child, but despite the anxiety and confusion of that day, the important details had stuck.

Their first mission was to find the police station where Clifford had been held until his parents could arrive. Gwen had studied Clifford's articles and had been careful to find a hotel nearby. It wasn't far.

Clifford walked up to the police station. The memories were flooding in.

An old, grandfatherly man named Salvador Martinez had discovered six year old Clifford standing in the shade of Quito's Equatorial Monument to the Sun, utterly abandoned and bawling his eyes out. The man had been very kind, and made sure Clifford had been delivered to the appropriate authorities. In fact, he had remained stubbornly by Clifford's side until his parents arrived nearly eight hours later. They had talked about many things. The old man especially liked to ask questions about him and his family. He talked at length about Quito and of the marvels of Ecuador. Martinez had also told him many children's stories of fantastic journeys and fabulous creatures.

The old man lived close to the police station, so after all the official procedures were completed at the station Martinez had insisted that the family join him at his home for supper.

For a supposed bachelor, Martinez had managed to produce a wonderful dinner. He had explained, in an offhanded way, that this was no inconvenience. He received many unexpected visitors and he was used to this kind of thing.

He and Clifford's parents had hit it off famously like three world savvy travelers. Though the man never mentioned venturing outside of his home city, the intrepid traveler's spirit was there and the conversation that ensued was vibrant.

What a day that had been. Still, Clifford had been in the throws of harrowing shock and little of that day had recurred to him, until now.

Though everything in his memory was clear, it still took Clifford an hour and twenty minutes to find Salvador Martinez's house. They had walked almost every street in the old, historic part of town before Clifford's memory got a positive hit.

Finally, to Gwen's relief, Clifford cried, "This is it! I'm sure of it. Wow! It hasn't changed a bit," he said jogging forward. He hurried up to the door. Gwen hesitated, shrugged and finally followed him into the yard.

Clifford knocked. The house seemed silent and unoccupied. He knocked again, more urgently now, bouncing excitedly from one foot to the other. Still, there was no answer. Reluctantly after some time, Clifford turned to go only to find the old man studying him and his aunt from the garden gate.

Salvador Martinez was dressed in khaki pants, shirt and a sportsman's vest which was stretched so tightly over his pot belly that the buttons threatened to pop. He wore on his head, a wide brimmed Fedora hat that shaded his dark, round face. His chin and cheeks were covered in a thick iridescence of white whiskers. All in all, the man hadn't changed a bit since they last met.

"I know you?" The old man asked.

"Senōr Martinez?"

"Si? You are American?"

"Si, yes. You helped me once, Senōr Martinez. I am Clifford Tuttle. This is my Aunt Gwen, my mom's sister."

The old man's eyes smiled, "Si, Clifford Tuttle," he chuckled, "Of course I know who you are!" He gave Clifford a wink of the eye and then politely acknowledged Aunt Gwen with a shallow bow. He shortly returned his attention to the pale, dark haired boy he had rescued years before.

"Tell me child, are you lost again?" he asked with

another sly wink of his eye.

"No. Not really. I came here to see you. I need to know how I got here."

"So, you do..." The old man indicated the garden bench with a nod and a smile, "Here. Sit, sit. We will talk." He joined them with an aged groan. The sun was to their backs and their three shadows stretched out before them on the stone walk. Two of the shadows matched in darkness.

Gwen studied the three shadows, and it was true, hers was half as dark. "That is so weird," she breathed.

The old man nodded to her, "Si, shadows of this kind are very rare." He turned to address Clifford, "So, you are all grown up and want some answers now, do you?"

"Yes," Clifford answered with a confident nod.

The old man patted Clifford's knee, "I thought you would come to see me someday," Martinez said in a thoughtful tone. "I knew we would find each other again."

Clifford stared down at their shadows, "They're the same."

Martinez nodded solemnly, "Si. You have the gift, same as I do. This is how we found each other before. The dark shines brightest."

"'The dark shines brightest.' What does that mean?" Gwen put in.

The old man chuckled, moving the conversation forward, "What can you tell me of that time, Clifford?"

Clifford looked into the old man's eyes, "I couldn't remember for the longest time. I was afraid of the sun…

and my shadow, but couldn't tell why."

"You are very pale. I would guess you have discovered this hidden knowledge most recently."

"I didn't go out for over seven years. I was scared. Everyone thought I was crazy. I went to a lot of doctors. Dr. Camilla was the last."

The old man's eyebrows rose. "Ah, si. Dr. Camilla."

"Yes. She hypnotized me to help me remember."

"And what *do* you remember?"

"I remember falling through my shadow."

"Do you, indeed?"

"Yes. And there was endless sky. I fell a long way before something caught me. The next thing I know, I'm here, a thousand miles away!"

Gwen jumped in, "Excuse me, Senōr Martinez. Is there any truth to what Clifford is saying? I would hate to be wasting your time with this…"

Martinez smiled, "Time, I have. And, si, there is truth to what young Clifford is saying. He is a Traveler, and so am I."

Clifford let out a long sigh of relief, "I knew it! I'm not crazy. See Aunt Gwen?"

"I don't know what to say," she said feeling dumbstruck.

Martinez's demeanor shifted as he leveled his glare on Gwen but directed his warning to Clifford, "Reveal nothing of this. There are many who would think you loco, others who would want to use these powers you possess—some for good, some for bad. You have remained discrete, yes?"

Both Clifford and Gwen nodded, wide-eyed back at the old man.

"Who knows of this, Clifford?"

"Just Aunt Gwen, here, and Dr. Camilla… My mom and dad, sorta… but I don't think any of them believe me.

Martinez smiled a thin smile, "Come inside, I'll make us something to drink."

The two accepted his invitation gratefully. The heat of the day was growing and the sun's brightness seemed unnaturally close.

The interior of Martinez's house was cool and lit dimly by stray sun rays seeping in around the drawn drapes.

"Like you, Clifford, I find the dark comforting." He motioned to the island counter that divided the living room from kitchen, "Please sit. I'll get us all a cool drink".

Clifford and Gwen took their places on two stools as Martinez retrieved a large, old looking glass jug from the refrigerator. The image of the bottle was instantly recognized.

Martinez undid the stopper, a devise made of metal wire that clamped the stopper lid tight. As soon as the stopper was removed the water's citrus perfume filled Clifford's nose.

"Dr. Camilla had–" Clifford began.

Martinez smiled, "Si, Clifford. You remember now?"

Gwen was looking at Clifford. Her eyes were filled with a mixture of wonder and fear. "What do you remember? Wait! What!? Is she connected to this, this thing too?"

Clifford watched as Martinez chuckled knowingly

then poured the water into a glass made of heavy crystal. It looked like the kind of glass you would keep only for the most special occasions. He raised the liquid filled glass to his nose and sniffed like a wine connoisseur and smiled dreamily. He poured two more then passed them across the counter to his guests.

"Dr. Camilla gave some to me after she hypnotized me," Clifford sipped it. It tasted of citrus and something else he could not identify, which was not peculiar for a boy so young. He looked up at Gwen, "Have some."

She drank then examined the fine glass at arm's length. "It's good. I've had a lot of gourmet bottled water but this... this is out of this world! What brand is it?"

Martinez touched his finger to the tip of his nose, a universal charades signal indicating a correct answer.

Gwen wrinkled up her forehead, "What?"

Martinez lifted the heavy crystal goblet to his lips and sipped. A look of dreamy reminiscence mixed with sadness again passed over his face, "Out of this world? Yes and no... There are many worlds within 'The World'. He made quote signs with his fingers, "But si, this water does come from a place beyond the boundary of ours. Clifford has been through the boundary, and si, the essence of this wonderful fluid he knows well. There it exists in vast quantities."

Martinez sipped again then smacked his lips, "Ahhh, that's good. We are permitted to bring a few bottles of this back each time we go. Like fine wine, I preserve it for only the most special Travelers," He took another sip, visibly delighting in its flavor, and then set the glass down.

"That said..." he grasped one of Gwen's hands and one of Clifford's then squeezed, "This, is my retirement," he announced heartily. "Finally my replacement has come of age!"

He cast a long, relieved gaze into Clifford's eyes, "I am just too old for this business anymore. Traveling is best left to the young of heart, and mind... and body." He squeezed their hands again then with a solid nod, released them.

He raised his glass in a toast. Gwen and Clifford followed suite out of pure human response.

"It has been a most exhilarating gift... A shame this water doesn't promote eternal youth, though it does stretch it a bit. Clifford here, I am certain, will be a worthy heir." Martinez eyed Clifford thoughtfully as if assessing his abilities as a mind reader would. His eyes were intense and unblinking. He continued after a thoughtful pause, "And now there is much to do."

Martinez clinked the rim of Clifford's glass with his, setting both crystal glasses to tonal ringing. The sound was magical, and unnaturally sustained in volume. The sound waves sent vibrations deep into Clifford's body, exhilarating his senses. Gwen tapped in too, experiencing only a tiny fraction of the sensory stimulation Clifford felt. She felt it though. There was definitely something there, something her senses had never felt before.

They all drank and the sensual trance was broken.

Gwen looked at Clifford, not sure what had just

happened. Had there been some sort of unwritten contract closed between Clifford and Martinez? Suddenly she felt very hot and uncomfortable.

"Uh... Sir?"

Martinez shifted his pleasant smiling face to Gwen. "I understand your apprehension. You are charged with this boy's welfare." His smile remained, but a subtle darkness crossed his eyes. "I assure you, your fear is... justified." He rested on that word.

His frank remark, spoken off-handedly, took Gwen off guard. She hadn't expected any negative connotation, at least not now. Who came right out and said, bluntly, that a loved one was in danger, and that is how it has to be? No biggie? No problemo?

Martinez continued, softening his previous remark "...as any would, when sending a loved one off on an adventure into the unknown."

"Exactly what should I fear, Senōr Martinez?" she said, a bit peeved, ignoring his last words. She did not wait for his response.

"You're right," she continued. "I *am* responsible for Clifford's welfare. Up until two weeks ago, the only concern I had was Clifford's fear of sunlight. I'm used to that, but all this... this-" Her sentence cut for lack of a word to describe the madness she was listening to. "No," she said shaking her head, "I'm sorry but I can't subscribe to anything that would put Clifford in danger!" Her tone was caustic and final like a mother protecting her young.

Martinez was not surprised. Instead he applauded

her courageous sense of duty, "Si... Bravo, Miss Gwen. Clifford is fortunate to have such an advocate. My own mother was as much concerned as you, if not more," He smiled easily. "But, my mother possessed neither the youth nor imagination you have." His smile and eyes radiated the deep kind of understanding one would have if he had known her intimately for years.

"I am not Clifford's mother!" Gwen snapped.

"Si. But who knows Clifford better than you?"

He saw Gwen's stare remained flat and focused. To reassure her as best he could, Martinez took her hand and kissed it gently, "I assure you, in time, you will become used to this as well."

As his lips touched her skin Gwen felt the same sensual vibrations she had felt before. For now, her anxious need to turn the whole thing around before it was too late vanished in a golden cloud of excited expectancy.

Martinez knew this would buy him a short reprieve. Time would tell if Gwen would accept what she must accept. But time was running out.

Chapter Six
The Real Thing

Martinez prepared the hungry travelers a simple but delicious dinner of brazed achiote beef with sweet and hot peppers over a bed of saffron rice. Gwen had remained pacified. Afterwards he invited them out to the patio bench where they first compared shadows. The sun had dropped low in the sky on its journey west and the evening air had cooled to a comfortable 72 degrees. Clifford habitually checked their shadows that spread across the ground behind them. Something had changed. His shadow was darkest by far. The remaining shadows cast by Gwen and Martinez matched in depth while his was almost as black as a puddle of spilled ink.

"Your shadow!" Clifford exclaimed.

Martinez regarded Clifford with a kind, yet sad smile. He cleared his throat as if something had caught there, "Si, young one. I have passed on. My days as a Traveler are at an end. I have passed what power I had left to you, Clifford."

"Really?" Clifford asked.

Martinez sighed, and stared into the sun for a long moment, shrugged his heavy shoulders and chuckled, "At least, I no longer have to watch my step on the solstice… but you, young Clifford, must."

Clifford turned away from the shadows to stare into the deep orange sunset. Suddenly a strange sinking sensation caused him to jerk into a stiff resistant posture. It felt for a moment as if something beneath him had shifted.

"I'm not sure I like this!" Clifford said, speaking through clenched teeth.

Gwen stood, turned and looked at both of them, "What do you mean? Can Clifford actually… this is crazy!" she said looking up from the pavement and squaring her shoulders, "Clifford can *actually*, like, fall through his shadow? Really? Now? Right here?

"Si, Miss Gwen. Clifford is a Traveler. Of course he can." Martinez pursed his lips, looked over and searched Clifford's stricken face for an extended moment. "But, certainly not now. The sun is not positioned correctly in the sky," he continued matter-of-factly.

"What did I just feel then?" Clifford asked.

Martinez searched Clifford's face as if he were trying to read his mind before he said, "You're tired, child. Nothing else. This is a very big step for you. All so much happening in a short amount of time–" He gave Clifford's face another quizzical look then cast his gaze to what remained of the pale boy's shadow. He did not like what he saw. The very edges of Clifford's shadow appeared to blur with vibration. Suddenly he said, "We better get you inside. Come."

The moment had caught them fast. No one moved. It was as if they all sensed the ground could suddenly crumble beneath their feet. An edgy silence fell between the three. The very air seemed heavy and charged with apprehensive energy.

Clifford finally demanded, "What?!"

Martinez's gaze had remained frozen on the shadow. He suddenly looked up and locked eyes on to Clifford's face, "No," he said shattering his paralysis. He threw his arms up and blustered, "it's nothing... only the rarest and skillful Travelers can go anytime. It's complicated. In all my years, I have not even come close to that level of expertise."

Gwen's mouth moved in silent speech. Other than that, she had not moved a muscle. Finally she managed, "This really isn't just some weird made-up fairytale?"

"No, Miss Gwen."

"Geez, Aunt Gwen," Clifford said in a shaky voice. "Haven't you been paying attention? This is the real thing! Stop living in denial!"

Gwen regarded Clifford's scolding with irritation. The spell she had fallen under had shattered. She took a deep, steadying breath, exhaled then spoke her mind.

"I am very sorry, Senõr Martinez, but Clifford isn't going anywhere! He's only fourteen years old!"

"I'm almost fifteen!" Clifford interrupted.

Gwen scowled deeply, "He can't go traveling around

the galaxy, willy-nilly without his parental guardian! And that's me!"

She stopped, dropped to her knee in front of Clifford then looked him straight in the eyes but continued to address Martinez, "I can't let this blown-out-of-proportion fantasy continue," she said, breaking eye contact with Clifford. She gave Martinez a sideways look, "You can take that power, or what ever you gave him *right back!*"

Martinez placed a comforting hand on Gwen's shoulder. He could feel the fear trembling inside her.

"This is how it is," he said as gently as a man of his size could. "Clifford is a Traveler. He was born with the gift and he can not give it back." He tried to put on a reassuring smile but it faded quickly. "I watched my mentor and my mother square off in much the same manner. What is important for you to understand is that this power to travel is part of our worlds. It has always been here, and there is a reason for it. There is much beyond what you can see, and fantastic worlds you could not begin to imagine.

He turned to address the shaken woman directly, "Gwen, both of you will grow to believe this and respect its power and purpose. Most never experience this mutualism. But the few who do participate, assure that these places will always be here. I have been a part of these worlds since I was thirteen. They do exist!"

Gwen rose up. "The dangers, Senõr Martinez?" she asked in a stern tone.

Martinez nodded the affirmative silently then spoke.

"Do not misunderstand me, Miss Gwen," he said seeing the red flare up in her face. "Si. There is danger, but this danger is far removed from the young ones. Here, as in any world, danger can be anywhere, but the travels of the young are highly regulated."

Gwen began tapping her foot and crossed her arms across her breast. "He's been cooped up in the dark for over seven years! He knows nothing about the real world, let alone the invisible one! He is practically helpless!"

"Hey!" Clifford said, taken aback. His feigned bravado covering his own doubts.

"Clifford will find help wherever he travels. It is understood, in all six known worlds, that the Travelers are essential to their very existence."

Gwen's foot stopped tapping then she bent in close to Martinez's face. "There are six now," she said flatly.

"Si, Miss Gwen. Ours and five others," he said smiling timidly.

Gwen paced away turned and paced back.

"I should never have agreed to this crazy trip!" she cried, waving her arms around in a fit, "Clifford, your mom's going to *kill* me!"

Martinez spread his arms and laughed grandly, "See Miss Gwen? There are mortal dangers right here in this world too!"

Gwen regarded him with a stern look, but remained silent this time.

Clifford shifted nervously on the bench.

"I feel really stupid, Senõr Martinez. I don't know

what to do and the equinox is in a couple days. I guess I'm just a little scared. Maybe I better give you your power back."

"Can't take it back... It's yours now, Clifford. You were destined to this life from birth. It took you once before. You can not refuse its will."

Martinez sat in silent contemplation for a moment then continued, "For example, I find you here, now, right in front of my eyes, not five kilometers from the Temple of the Sun, do I not?"

"Uh huh."

Martinez raised his eyebrows, "This journey you have embarked on was no whim. You have pondered this for a long time, am I right? I ask you. What fourteen year old boy with his mind fully intact just wakes up one morning and decides to jump through his shadow into another world? They don't. All able-bodied Travelers eventually find themselves on the equator, one way or another, by purpose or by accident. You are standing on the brink of an incredible adventure few get to experience!"

Clifford scooted around on the bench so he could look at his shadow. It was late and the sun was about to set, but it was still with him, a dark and ominous smudge upon the pavement.

Clifford fell into deep thought before he muttered, "I need a lot of help."

Martinez pulled him around so he could look Clifford in the eyes, "So you will have it," he said, slapping the boy on the back. "Now let's go in."

Martinez tidied the kitchen while Clifford and Gwen rested on a comfortable sofa that sat before a large tiled fireplace. It was not cold but Martinez had lit a fire, and now its ambiance was lulling them into a tranquil state of mind. It was only 8:00 in the evening but their tired bodies and minds were urging them toward bed.

Martinez had insisted that they stay the night regardless of their protests.

"Despite my seemingly solitary life," he said, "I am rarely alone for long. I have many visitors, and I am happy for it," he concluded with a convincing smile.

He brought over a tray holding three wine glasses and a glass pitcher filled with a dark burgundy colored liquid afloat with small chunks of fruit. He placed the tray on the coffee table then poured them each a glass.

"This is a nice sangria. It will help you sleep," he announced as he handed them each their glass. He groaned as he sunk down into his chair.

Clifford looked at the glass in his hands then looked to his aunt for approval. She smiled and gave him a nod. And they all sipped.

Gwen smiled, "This is good. What's in it?"

Martinez swirled the liquid around in his glass, "It is red wine, mixed with fruit juice. I add some fruit, sparkling water and for good measure, a splash of brandy."

Clifford took another sip and grinned, "I like it."

Gwen gave him a look of good natured caution, "Just take it easy there kiddo. We can't have you getting drunk and staggering off the edge of the world or something."

Martinez's chuckle was steeped in nostalgia, "Oh, more than once, this has happened, si."

Gwen gave him a look. "Really?"

"Si. We are all human and prone to foolishness and folly. The fall usually does wonders in the sobering up."

Gwen snorted then took a long drink as if to force a return, though be it by chemical means, to her previous state of ease. "I imagine it would," she replied after she had come up for air.

By the time the pitcher was empty the trio were primed for retirement. Martinez showed them to their living quarters then bid them a good night.

Their quarters, decorated in earth tones of terracotta and cream with accents in turquoise, consisted of two small bedrooms adjoined by a study. Each bedroom had its own tiled bath containing a rustic wooden tub that looked more like an elongated and halved wine barrel. Their forgotten luggage, to their surprise, waited at the foot of their beds. The study, more fantastic still, was furnished with two comfortable leather chairs, a writing desk and bookshelves. The shelves were lined with dozens of leather bound journals.

Clifford ran his fingers along a row of the bound volumes. "What are these?" he asked, pulling one out.

The book cover was lined in heavy leather and inside the parchment pages were filled with notes, essays, and illustrations.

Gwen abandoned the urge to fall unconscious into bed for the more tantalizing possibilities the books might hold. This was a battle, for she had consumed the lion's share of the sangria, and her mind was currently floating away on the drink's intoxicating affects. In the end, for Gwen, books usually won out.

Despite their fatigue, the pair spent the next hour exploring the volume laden shelves. Clifford settled on a journal by Daniel Southerland filled with fantastic sketches and intricately detailed illustrations. There were maps that read more like vertical cross sections than ones of horizontally flat ground. There were drawings of strange creatures and architecture. Towards the center of the journal he came across the elements of a familiar world. He knew immediately that he had been there before.

"This is it, Gwen!" he shouted.

Startled by Clifford's sudden outburst, Gwen nearly jumped out of her skin then lowered her journal that read like a scientific dissertation.

"This is the place I was!" he held up the pages, "See! Flying Cloud People!"

Gwen smiled then bit her lower lip, "I don't know about all this, Cliffy. It's all so... unreal. You should read this stuff! It's like nothing I've ever known. This person is describing the physics of locomotion through solid rock. Here," she said, flipping forward through the pages, "flying inside streams of light waves from world to world! Who is this guy? Einstein? It reads like quantum physics!"

She screwed up her face, "How are you ever going to

do all this, Cliffy?"

Clifford came over and squeezed into her chair. "Maybe you should look at this book. It's full of nice pictures. All that other stuff will take care of its self. I want to see *all* these things, and like Senōr Martinez said, I'll get lots of help. Look," he pointed at a rendering of a man riding comfortably on a cloud-like creature. "See? I did this and I didn't die! I came back and I was only six! I'm bigger now."

Gwen put an arm around him and sniffed back the tears that were threatening to flow. "Oh yes, a grown man of fourteen. Oh Cliffy, what have we gotten ourselves into?"

Clifford helped his aunt into bed and lovingly covered her up. The combined forces she had endured throughout the day, emotional turmoil, travel fatigue and of course the sangria, had laid her low and listless.

Clifford changed into his pajamas then got into his own bed. He finally dropped into a fitful sleep, propped up against the headboard of his bed, with Daniel Southerland's amazing journal, still open, nestled in his lap. His sleep was haunted by the numerous illustrations he had observed in the journal's parchment pages. When he woke, Gwen was already up, her nose in one of the journals. She looked tired and above all, worried.

Clifford rubbed the sleep from his eyes and came over to her. He squeezed into the chair she was sitting in and gave her a hug. Gwen grunted from all the weight crowding in on her, "Morning, Cliffy. Did you sleep okay?"

"Yeah…I guess. I had some weird dreams. How are you?"

"Good… Tired. And hey, next time Martinez pulls out a pitcher of his sangria, remind me to take it easy. I've a bit of a headache," she added as she rubbed her forehead with slightly trembling fingers.

They fell silent and stared into the contents of the journal she was reading until they heard a soft knock on their door.

Clifford got up and invited Martinez in.

"Ah, I see you have discovered the journals," he noted with a bright smile. "Most Travelers keep journals, especially the ones more prone to scientific discovery. Oh, there are all sorts of people who travel. Some are drawn to the adventure of it all. There are artists and philosophers as well. Each journal is a unique expression of their experiences."

Martinez perused the shelves for a moment then extracted a leather bound journal that appeared to be newer than the rest. He handed it to Clifford then returned to the center of the room.

Clifford examined the cover and was surprised to find his name engraved there in gold leaf. He reverently opened the book to the first page that was of course blank. "When did you..?"

"Oh, I have had this journal ready since you were six." Martinez raised his eyebrows as Clifford looked up, "What kind of Traveler will you be, Clifford?" he asked as he returned again to the shelves and picked another journal from the ranks. "Ah, si. This one is Doctor Camilla's journal."

Clifford took the book and turned to the first page. The first date, he figured, would have put her at about his age, between twelve and fifteen years old. He wasn't quite sure how old she was but she looked like she was as old as his mother, Dottie. Her journal was filled with a mixture of words and pictures.

Gwen smirked, "Yup, there she is. My God they're everywhere. I'm surprised that there is anyone left here in the real world! A psychologist! Who would guess?"

Martinez smiled. "Si. There are many Travelers dispersed among you, but few compared with the Earth's total population."

"This is crazy," Gwen said then bit her lip. Her smirk was gone. She was suddenly feeling jealous as she was now totally immersed in this insane situation. "I wish I could go," she said.

Martinez lay his hand lightly on her shoulder, "Alas, I am afraid you will have to live vicariously through the words and illustrations of the chosen."

Gwen nodded then sighed, "Why are all these books still here? Why hasn't anyone, especially the intellectuals, published papers or written books about all this?"

"It's forbidden. All these journals must remain here or locked away… safe. If this got out and into the wrong hands, the result could tip the balance."

Martinez gave Gwen a stern look. "I trust you will

both be respectful of these laws." He softened, "I have trusted you thus far…"

"I just can't believe no one has ever spilled the beans," Clifford said. "I mean, this stuff is fantastic!"

"It has happened, and… in each case, no good came of it. Your secret is best kept a secret. It is an awesome responsibility. But we are all human. We make mistakes. We, as you say, 'spill the frijoles.' Unfortunately, the mess then becomes all of our responsibility. You will be watched and protected from here on out… as you have been for the past seven years. It is in everybody's best interest to keep this a secret."

Gwen wiggled her way out of the chair then began to pace the room. "Is there a purpose for all this traveling? Or is this all just some extreme, macho adventure quest?"

"Purpose, si… I believe there is a physical necessity for this. I suppose it is somewhat like breathing. As our bodies require certain elements from air, so do these worlds."

Clifford turned another page in Dr. Camilla's journal. He studied an illustration on the page and pointed at it. I've seen these at Dr. Camilla's office. What are they, some sort of special glasses?"

Martinez leaned in to look. "Si, goggles. That brings us to the next step in your preparation. We must go and see The Optometrist."

Chapter Seven
Not the Run-of-the-Mill Eye Doctor

They ate a quick breakfast of fruit, toasted rustic bread and coffee, and then made their way out to Martinez's garage where they found his Land Rover LR3 SUV.

Clifford was very impressed. The machine was decked out with all the off-road gadgets you could imagine: oversized tires, jacked up suspension, heavy custom bumpers with built-in winch and racks on the roof supporting carry cases and lights. All the windows were tinted with black film.

"Wow! This is great!" Clifford exclaimed.

Martinez smiled proudly, "What did you expect, a donkey cart?"

"Well, yeah," Gwen said feeling as surprised as Clifford.

"In the old days, si, the chasers used less sophisticated

modes of transportation, mostly horses. And in some extreme cases those are used still. Today's technology comes in very handy though. Get in. I'll show you."

Clifford climbed up into the plush leather front passenger seat and Gwen hopped into the back. With all the doors closed the exterior light was completely shut out. Soft LED dashboard and dome lights lit the passenger compartment. The windows were completely black.

Martinez pushed the button on the garage door opener that was integrated into a ceiling console. They could hear the garage door roll up but still, no light came through the windows.

"How do you see to drive?" Clifford asked.

Martinez touched the ignition button and the engine roared to life. The windshield and all the other windows turned on like super high definition flat screen TVs showing them the interior of the garage clearly.

"Awesome!" Clifford cried.

"No shadows, Clifford. I, like you, need to avoid the sun at this time of year. Now look here," he said indicating the large flat panel set into the center of the dashboard. "I have GPS tracking and satellite mapping with topography, infrared, night vision, seismometer and Sirius/XM Radio!" Each time he touched the screen the view from the windows changed from satellite topographical to infrared view with all of its hot and cool colors, then to glaring, green tinted night vision. Finally, the windows went back to regular TV view and the music came on through a fantastic sound system.

"What's all this stuff for?" Clifford asked.

"First and foremost, it is to find you!" he said as he backed the rumbling machine out of the garage and into full sunlight. The view was bright but it cast no shadows inside the Rover. "Your helpers on the other side are not always as precise as we would like. This is where your chaser comes in," he said indicating Gwen in the back seat.

"Me!?"

"Si. To recover your Traveler is your responsibility. Sometimes your Traveler can pop up miles from where he or she goes in, sometimes hundreds of miles away– worst case scenario, of course," he added, this time indicating Clifford with a curt nod. He chuckled, "It was lucky for you that you popped up in my neighborhood, Clifford."

"Many early travelers met with unfortunate ends if they popped up in the wrong place. There are desserts, jungles, mountain ranges. Over the centuries, we have gotten better at targeting specific rendezvous. Still," he indicated the Rover's technology laden dashboard, "this all becomes very handy in preventing unfortunate accidents. You and I, Gwen will be ready if the time comes."

The trip to The Optometrist was short, no more than two miles, garage to garage. The Optometrist, an extremely tall man with a lean figure and triangular shaped head greeted them in silhouette from a back-lit doorway. The scene from Close Encounters of the Third Kind, where the aliens emerge from their spaceship in foggy silhouette, leaped immediately into both Clifford and Gwen's minds, but this one was much larger. They looked at each other at the same moment and both smiled nervous little smiles.

The Optometrist beckoned them to enter, as he moved with fluid agility back inside.

The shop was nothing like any office of optometry Gwen had ever seen. The place looked more like the workshop of a metal sculptor and glass blower. There was an area dominated by a forge, another by a smelting pot. Between the forge and smelting stations stretched an enormous workbench. The air inside the shop was very warm and smelled like a foundry.

The Optometrist welcomed Martinez and Gwen silently with a slight bow of his head. That done, he turned to Clifford. He leaned in close bending down low and stared down into Clifford's upturned face. His almond shaped eyes were like nothing seen on Earth. Where the whites should have been, black sclera surrounded an iris the color of blue sky. Clifford blinked with surprise and The Optometrist blinked back.

"You're not from *here*, are you?" Clifford said in a breathless rush.

The Optometrist blinked again. A smile curled up on his too small mouth.

With out any further ado, The Optometrist slid a flat plate out from under the bench.

"If you please, Clifford, Stand here," he said in an accent that was punctuated in unusual clicks. These were his first words.

Clifford obeyed. Suddenly the plate, with him on it, rose up from the floor. Clifford stiffened atop the plate like a first time surfer. The plate, however, seemed very stable so he took a chance and glanced down. He found that he was hovering three feet off the floor. Clifford looked up and was met eye to eye by The Optometrist.

"Now, hold still, Clifford. I must determine your facial structure."

Clifford stiffened as he felt his face begin to tingle, and then sensed pressure as if his skin was being kneaded by dozens of tiny fingers. The Optometrist did this without actually touching him.

After a thoughtful pause The Optometrist clicked his tongue and nodded.

"Good. I am finished. Yes. Very good."

Clifford's levitation plate lowered him back down to the floor.

The Optometrist backed away in his strange fluid way, and turned to his massive work bench. The workbench's top was built four and a half feet off the ground to meet his extraordinary height.

Clifford had to stand on tiptoes and crane his neck to get a better look.

The Optometrist moved along the work bench's length, picking up a piece here and a piece there, until the tray he was carrying was full. He worked without a word for ten minutes then turned back to Clifford. The levitation disk raised Clifford up again. The Optometrist held out his creation and fitted it to Clifford's face.

For how large the ornate frames were, their weight hardly registered on Clifford's face. The Optometrist stared through the eye holes at Clifford's eyes for a long moment, blinked, nodded his approval, and lowered him back to the floor.

Clifford looked over at Gwen. "Well, how do I look?"

Gwen gave him a crooked smile and said, "Elton John would be envious!"

The Optometrist moved over to the forge and pumped the bellows. Dark coals glowed red as he began to work a globular piece of raw glass.

In the interim, Gwen had begun to pace slowly around the workshop (Gwen always paced when she was nervous.) She walked slowly like a shopper in a curiosity shop, hoping her condition wouldn't be noticed. She stopped and picked up a piece of metalwork from the work bench and examined it. It was the color of gold but weighed next to nothing.

"What kind of metal is this?" she asked.

The Optometrist answered her without taking his eyes off his work. "Treous tylithsian from Treous, of course. Treous is good metal, easily pliable when heated above 800 degrees. Cold tylithsian is harder and lighter than anything found on your world," He chortled with a high whistling sound that filled the room, "Wouldn't your engineers love to get their hands on some of that? Who knows, maybe some day I'll give it to them, just to drive them, how you say, bonkers."

Again, the whistling laughter filled the room. His tall,

slender body was just a silhouette as he worked before the glowing coals that seemed too bright and hot for safety.

Clifford, in the meantime, had removed the strange frames from his face and examined them as if they were a precious relic. In construction, the goggles didn't require the temples or the sides that would hook the ears like normal glasses frames. The frame's inner surface curved to the exact contours of his face. The glasses fit snuggly as if they were an extension of his skull and somehow were held in place like a magnet to steel. He wondered how this could be possible. Perhaps the glasses were attached by some organic means, or maybe by suction? He had no idea, but however they worked, it was amazing. He put them on again and gave his head a tremendous shake. The frames stayed put.

While Clifford was contemplating the goggles, The Optometrist had moved to another station and placed two fresh-blown glass pieces into a machine that reminded Clifford of a miniature toaster. Five minutes later the machine stopped and The Optometrist raised Clifford up again.

The Optometrist blinked then gently guided Clifford's face to a point where he was facing the piece of equipment then waved his slender hand in front of the machine. The side lit up.

"Now be still," he said holding Clifford's head in hands with a grip that felt as rigid as a vise.

To Clifford's horror, lit tentacles emerged from the device and snaked toward his eyes. He tried to move, to evade the threat, but was held tight. He tried to blink but found that defense futile as well. It was as if he had no eyelids to close. They kept coming. Clifford cringed inwardly in anticipation of their first impact.

The moment the lit tentacles touched his exposed eyeballs, his entire head lit up. The sensation was amazingly pleasant. After years of living in the dark, the light was wondrous.

A moment later the light went out leaving behind only darkness, and for a terrified instant, Clifford feared he had gone blind. But slowly, the light of the room seeped back into his eyes.

Again, Clifford found himself facing The Optometrist's strange eyes. And, if he thought things couldn't get much weirder, they did. Two antenna-like tentacles began to grow out of The Optometrist's forehead. The ends were lit like tiny flashlights or like the strange luminescent lures of the deep water angler fish. As the tentacles advanced toward his eyes in snake-like motion, The Optometrist's grip tightened. Again Clifford's eyelids were paralyzed against any defense.

As before, with the tentacle's first touch, Clifford's head lit up. The sensation was short lived. A moment later the light was extinguished casting him back into blinded darkness. Slowly, his sight returned.

The Optometrist removed the frames from Clifford's face and went right to work installing the finished lenses.

When he was done, The Optometrist placed the glasses on Clifford's face. Suddenly the room snapped into sharp focus. It was like comparing the resolution of a regular, old fashioned tube style color TV with a super high definition flat screen LED TV.

"Wow!" Clifford exclaimed. "I didn't think my eyes where that bad!"

"Poof!" snorted the Optometrist. "You *have* what they call 20/20 vision… perfect for *you* humans. Bah! Humans have no idea! But now, you do, yes?"

Clifford looked around. "Cool!"

At first, the detail he was absorbing through his eyes was so overwhelming that it hurt his brain to see it, but gradually the feeling subsided.

Again, The Optometrist put Clifford's head in his vise-like grip. The lit antennae grew out of his forehead and locked onto Clifford's eyes again, this time through the new lenses. Clifford's head lit up again, but the light had order and shown in a prism rainbow of color.

The Optometrist retracted his antennae then backed away a step. "Very good, Clifford. At least now your eyes can finally see as they should. Now, I will show you how to breathe."

The Optometrist went back to his bins, picking a part from one bin then another. He sat the lot down on a tray then moved to a large silver wall with a door. He entered what looked like a commercial walk-in refrigerator and emerged shortly carrying a cylindrical beaker filled with a cloudy substance. He sat that on the bench beside the tray of parts and commenced to work again.

Martinez finally broke the silence that had fallen over the group.

"It seems like it was just yesterday I was standing right here, in your place, Clifford. Oh, it was years after I had first begun to travel, though. This gadgetry hadn't been available in the beginning."

He chuckled, "My first time through was as Clifford's, unprotected eyes and all. The natives of the worlds we visited found ways to improvise life support as necessary. Many early Travelers died before a more precise understanding of our physical bodies was gleaned. It was a long period of trial and error for which I am very grateful I followed. By the time I came along things had been figured out. Still, in the mean time, we had to do some improvising of our own."

He dug into his shoulder satchel and pulled out a set of World War II era aviation goggles. He removed his ever-present wide brimmed hat and pulled them on. He blinked through the glass lenses and smiled broadly. He pulled his newer goggles from the bag and showed them to Gwen. They were much bulkier than the ones The Optometrist was making for Clifford.

The Optometrist turned briefly from his work. "I see you still stubbornly hold onto that old antique. I tell you, I can make you a new pair, Martinez. Better. Lighter."

Martinez smiled and pulled the WWII goggles off and placed his newer goggles on. "I'm retired now. I have no use for them anymore."

"Poof!" the Optometrist snorted. "Indeed." He sounded doubtful.

Clifford, who had been captivated by the Optometrist's

work, turned his attention to Martinez. "He *is* retired. He gave me his powers."

The Optometrist just shook his head and returned to his work. "Bah. You never retired, Martinez. Nobody retires until they're dead. I say, you need new glasses and that is what you will get. Poof!"

Martinez shrugged his shoulders. "Si. Suit your self, my friend. At least they'll make good reading glasses."

"No! You need!" The Optometrist snapped, and turned grudgingly from his work.

Even though Martinez was halfway across the work shop floor the Optometrist's arm stretched out, impossibly long, and with his finger, he poked Martinez in the chest. "You – must – be – prepared!"

"For what?" Clifford asked.

Martinez shrugged. "There are those who foretell a time when the balance will collapse," he said doubtfully.

"Really?" Clifford asked.

"My friend here is one of those," Martinez said giving The Optometrist a nod.

"It *will* happen, Martinez! It is inevitable. Poof! Mark my word. Between you humans with your primitive greed and the Horwrath soul eaters or their Trunjenn ilk, something will cause the collapse."

"Soul eaters! Gwen exclaimed. "What in the world is a soul eater? Cliffy won't be meeting any of them in there will he?"

"Nonsense!" Martinez said. "They were all but wiped out in the Great Convergence seven years ago. They have no power!"

The Optometrist reached out and poked Martinez in the chest again. "Perhaps… That just leaves the humans then, no?" He turned to Clifford and Gwen. Gwen again stood rigid in full protection mode.

"Vigilance, Clifford Tuttle," The Optometrist said, giving Clifford a curt nod, "First and foremost, vigilance must be the chief priority of every Traveler, and those," he turned his eyes on Martinez, "who aid the Travelers. It is the only way."

Martinez relinquished his combative tone, "My friend here is right. He most often is. Traveling is a great adventure full of wonder and surprise. But, as in our world, there are dangers. Evil is not restricted to our world. Evil is universal. In most of the worlds that we travel to, the mere strength of their advanced cultures has pushed evil to near extinction."

"There are worlds that harbor evil. These places are traveled to by only the most advanced travelers. My friend here and I have seen these places," He cast a wary glance to The Optometrist and saw he remained silently focused on his work.

"And then there is the inevitable influence of Travelers on the most civilized worlds to consider. One bad Traveler can act as a virus to an otherwise peaceful world. Trouble can ensue when a Travelers gift is discovered by non-travelers who act on their jealousy or their desire to travel. These events are more an annoyance than anything else and can be controlled."

Martinez regarded Clifford for a moment before he returned his attention to Gwen. "True evil can lie dormant for eons until the right time arises. And when it arises it is usually the result of some sudden, catastrophic event."

The Optometrist nodded silently then turned to Clifford, "Come, boy."

Clifford stood upon the levitating disk and rose up to the Optometrist's eye level. Clifford stood still as the Optometrist placed the glasses back on his face. Immediately the glasses, like a suction cup, adhered to his face.

"How do they feel?" he said in a kindly voice. His eyes blinked and he cocked his head back and forth as he examined his work.

"Okay... Excellent!" Clifford responded.

The optometrist nodded. There was a mischievous glint in his strange alien eyes. He blinked again and it was as if the disk beneath Clifford's feet had turned into a hole.

Clifford had one split second to scream before he dropped through the hole and into a deep pool of water.

In the precise moment that his face touched the water, the goggles' new accessory activated. Something that felt like jelly covered his nose and mouth, but it didn't stop there. To his horror, the substance, in one coordinated move, surged inward to fill his sinuses, mouth, throat and lungs. Clifford thrashed wildly as his fingers probed the substance covering his face. Seconds passed before

Clifford realized he still had air.

As the initial shock subsided, Clifford began to swim around in what seemed like a large cylindrical aquarium. He could see his reflection in the curved glass, but nothing outside.

Beyond the glass, Gwen, Martinez and The Optometrist were descending a curved stairway that wrapped around the wall of an equally cylindrical subterranean room. Gwen descended at a more urgent pace.

"Oh my God!" she screamed as she raced to the base of the two story high tank. "Cliffy!"

When Gwen saw how Clifford was thrashing about near the bottom, she feared he was drowning, but as she watched gape-mouthed in horrified wonder, he calmed and then began to paddle awkwardly toward the top.

Gwen was joined shortly by the other two. As soon as she felt their presence she rounded on them.

"What the hell are you doing?! He can't swim! He'll drown!"

"Poof!" The Optometrist said. "He looks like he's doing fine to me. Eh, Martinez?"

"Si, my friend, like a fish to water," he said pursing his full lips.

Gwen turned and stared in disbelief as Clifford paddled around inside the tank. She couldn't recall him going up for air since she had arrived at the bottom of the stairs.

"How!?" she demanded in a shrill voice.

He had never been swimming before. At least Clifford

couldn't remember doing so. He knew very well that people could drown in water. Aunt Gwen made a point of warning him every single time he went in to take a bath, which was annoying. Yet, here he was, in deep water, and he wasn't drowning.

He could breathe, but it really wasn't like breathing as he knew it. That part wasn't working at all, but he had air. His mind was clear and his arms and legs were working tirelessly as well.

He dogpaddled around the tank then took some strong, yet clumsy strokes. As a result, he shot off at an angle and thumped into the side of the tank. He tried again, this time balancing his strokes. He soon mastered his efforts, and started swimming in earnest.

Curious, he swam toward the top and shortly broke the surface. In an instant the stuff in his lungs and nose retreated back into the glasses. He treaded water, breathing normally.

When he began to tire, he sunk back into the water. Just as suddenly, the stuff in the goggles filled his airways and the muscle fatigue dissipated. He swam back toward the bottom, fascinated with his newly discovered gift. It was like being a merman. So cool! Everything was so cool.

"How can he do this?" Gwen repeated as she watched Clifford swim.

"Gelled oxygen, mated with a primitive, living organism. This organism is incredibly efficient in its one task… that is to keep another living organism alive. When

Clifford's goggles are submerged in any kind of inhospitable atmosphere, be it water, or even airless outer space for that matter, the organism reacts, filling Clifford's airways with its life supporting oxygen. The symbiotic relationship is much more efficient than the human's act of breathing. Poof! I dare say... if one of your athletes got a hold of this stuff he or she would be invincible! Clifford is feeling oxygen enhanced strength like he has never felt before!"

Gwen and the others watched in silence as Clifford swam tirelessly around inside of the tank.

Martinez said finally, "Well, it's time we got him out of there and dried him off. There is the gathering to attend tonight, and there are still some preparations for Clifford's big day tomorrow."

"Martinez is right. There is much to do." The Optometrist said and then moved away toward the stairs.

Before The Optometrist released Clifford out into the world, he presented him with a tubular object. Clifford examined it carefully.

"What's this?" he asked.

The Optometrist reached out and touched a point on the object's side and the tube slid open exposing what appeared to be two simple stereo ear buds without the wires. "This is how you communicate when you travel. Go ahead. Insert them into your ears."

Before Clifford inserted the buds, The Optometrist held up a finger. He began to speak in a tongue that

Clifford had never heard. While The Optometrist was still talking he nodded and Clifford inserted the ear buds.

As the ear buds slipped into his ears a tingling sensation commenced then settled. Simultaneously, Clifford's brain comprehended the Optometrist's language. Clifford could understand every word The Optometrist was saying.

"How do they fit, Clifford?" the Optometrist asked in his native Cygnus tongue.

Clifford cleared his throat and spoke back in perfect Cygnus. "Oh, my, God! That's so cool!"

Gwen stared stupidly at her nephew. "How can you just know his language!?"

The Optometrist chortled, "Poof! This is nothing. A mere child's toy." He reached out and poked Clifford's forehead with one thin finger, "Soon you will be required to learn the languages of all the worlds. The difficult way through study. By using your *own* brain."

Clifford remained unmoved by this threat and turned his attention to Martinez who was suppressing a grin. At once the Spanish language flooded into Clifford's mind. "Awwwwwesome!"

It was 3:00 P.M. when Martinez parked his tech-laden SUV back in his garage. Clifford and Gwen piled out as Martinez went around to the rear compartment and pulled out a large garment bag. They followed him back into his home and plopped down on the kitchen island stools. Martinez offered them cold drinks, nothing exotic this time, just Cokes and they took them willingly.

They had traveled back from The Optometrist's in mutual silence. Martinez allowed them ample time to absorb the information in silence – and there was much to absorb.

Martinez fixed them a late lunch of fruit, cheese and bread. The meal was small by American standards but he explained with a sly smile that there would be a better meal at suppertime.

When they finished, he cleared the plates away and sat back down smiling at them in silence.

"What?" Gwen giggled, breaking down under his jovial smiling eyes.

"Tomorrow is the big day Clifford. How do you feel?

Clifford lowered his eyes to his folded hands and breathed a ragged sigh. "A bit nervous, I guess." He really didn't want Martinez to know just *how* nervous he really was. Truth be known, he was nearly petrified with fear.

Si, Clifford, just a little nervous, eh? Good boy! I would be a nervous, too, if I were in your shoes! In fact, I believe I threw up once before *my* first time," He smiled knowingly.

"Okay, I'm a lot nervous," Clifford moaned. "What if I mess up or something? What if the whole thing just doesn't work? What if I go and can't find my way back?" He was nearly in tears. *Some great traveler,* he thought bitterly.

Gwen, her face all screwed up, looked at Clifford with concern for a moment, and, her attention drawn away, watched Martinez stand and walk around the counter. He took them both into his arms and gave them a great hug.

"The first time is always hard for both the traveler and their family. If I were to sum it up, it's like sending a soldier off to war for the first time. All the training in the world can not prepare you for what is to come. That is where instinct comes in. We are all wired for survival, some more than others. We are not fortune-tellers. We cannot see the future. You would be crazy not to be afraid," he said giving the two another squeeze before releasing them. "I suggest that we all take a little siesta. Try to get some sleep before supper."

"But you said that there are some more preparations to make!" Clifford said in a surprised voice that was embarrassingly high.

Martinez smiled, "Rest first. These things will come as they will."

Clifford tossed restlessly on his bed as Gwen perused another Traveler's journal. His lunch, as light as it was, sat in the pit of his stomach like a rock. Though the urge to disgorge was there, he refused to puke in front of Aunt Gwen. He rolled onto his side, a risky position to be in, in his delicate state, and looked over at her. She was like a mother to him and he loved her very much.

"You okay Cliffy?" she asked looking up.

"No," he said quietly. "I don't feel that great."

Gwen sat up, "You're not going to yak are you?!"

"No... I don't think so. How about you?"

"It's like having squirmy worms in my stomach," she

admitted with a weak smile. "Oh, Cliffy. What have we gone and gotten ourselves into?"

Clifford gave her a crooked smile. He felt better talking to her. "It's my destiny," he said in a breath. "It's weird…"

Gwen got up and sat on the edge of the bed, "Weird." she repeated.

"Are you too old to curl up with your aunt like when you were young? I think it will make us both feel better. It did back then." She lay down behind him and draped her arm over his thin, pale body. You should get some rest. I have a feeling Martinez has something big planned for you tonight.

They were both asleep in minutes.

Chapter Eight
A Night to Remember

Martinez woke them at just past 5:00 P.M.. "Come, you two," he said gently as he emerged from Gwen's bathroom. "We have a supper to attend tonight."

Clifford and Gwen sat up, drunk with sleep.

"I hope it's not fancy. I didn't pack for fancy," Gwen said blinking the sleep from her eyes.

Martinez smiled, "I have poured your baths. I have also put your clothes out. Why, this is an all inclusive holiday! Didn't you know that?"

Gwen looked at him suspiciously.

"For you two, I think this will be a very memorable evening," he smiled.

Gwen sat up on the edge of the bed and peeked into Clifford's bathroom. She could see the steam rising from the tub. "Wow. I must have been really out. I never heard you come in."

Martinez chuckled, "I will see you when you are finished."

Gwen held the gown up between herself and the antique mirror that stood in the corner of her bathroom. The gown was full length and elegant despite its simple lines. The fabric, however, was strange– so black that it seemed to be no more than a shadow between her and the mirror. She smiled at her reflection and tried to feign personal elegance to match. She gave herself a reassuring wink then said, "Not too shabby for a twenty-eight year old school teacher from the 'Burgh."

The garment was certainly finer than anything she had ever worn and to her surprise, seemed to be exactly her size. The gown was accompanied by a full length cloak of the same deep, black color.

"Weird," she said, regarding the cloak, and smiled.

She hung the gown next to the cloak, undressed and stepped into the deep elliptical barrel-like tub. She sighed contentedly and sank into the perfectly warm water. The bath smelled faintly of the water Martinez had served her and Clifford the day before. As she drifted in its comforting warmth, the water's gentle essence seemed to vaporize the anxiety she was feeling.

Clifford lie, fully submerged in his deep elliptical wooden bathtub, absorbing the water's warmth and silence surrounding him. He stared through his goggles into the gently undulating surface above and felt a keen sense of familiarity. How this could be, he did not know. He was never a swimmer, never anything except a frightened kid, troubled by his dark shadow and what lie beyond. *And now I'm supposed to be a Traveler. I'm only fourteen. I'm not ready for anything this important,"* he thought.

Everything seemed to be changing at once. He was on the move, yet again falling into the unknown. He could count three chapters in his life now: the before time, the dark time and now the time of the Traveler. Each shift in progression had been heralded by some upsetting experience. Birth, he supposed, must have been traumatic. The fall through his shadow, well, what could he say, horrifying at first but now, in light of these new revelations, fantastic. (It wouldn't be a far reach to compare that to birth, as well.) And now, from this day forward, he would be a Traveler. What earth shattering experience will mark this change? *For better or for worse I'll know tomorrow.* And then, he wondered, *what about tonight's big supper?"*

Clifford's mind moved to the strange clothes Martinez had set out for him. There was nothing odd about the shirt and pants, except of course the black fabric that didn't reflect light no matter which way he moved it. A cloak though? Really? Last time he looked, he wasn't a student at wizard's school.

As he pondered this immediate future, the light beyond the surface of the water brightened as if the ceiling had suddenly opened to the sky. At the same moment he felt that similar unsettling shift in the surface below him. Panicking, he closed his eyes expecting to retreat into the comfort of darkness. Yet the scene remained vivid, but much larger– an entire world made of water. A moment later he had broken the surface of the water, the life supporting goop had retracted back into the goggles and he was back in his bathroom.

At 7:00 P.M. Clifford, Gwen, and Martinez, dressed in their peculiar evening clothes, slid into the Land Rover and headed out into the twilight of the evening. Martinez drove north, out of town and then turned onto a highway that wound its way up into the mountains towards a town called San Antonio.

"We're going to the monument?" Clifford asked talking loud over the rhythmic Latin music that was pumping out of the Rover's sound system.

"Si," said Martinez. He smiled with a youthful glee that seemed to take years off his lined face. "We gather there twice a year for the equinox celebrations. Si, the equinoxes are very special."

"Experienced Travelers can, of course, travel most anytime while here on the equator, but the equinoxes are the most traveled days. It is like a holiday for us."

Martinez stared ahead, into the TV like windshield. "The equinox suppers are like send-off parties. Travelers are like the explorers of old, leaving on sailing vessels bound for uncharted seas. As I have said before, traveling is not without its dangers and sometimes a Traveler is required to stay for long periods of time," he said and chuckled, "but of course, *we* Travelers have been 'traveling' much longer."

As Martinez spoke they reached a large roundabout in the road. Taking it, he drove west. After a mile or so, he slowed the Rover, pulled off onto the shoulder and then stopped before they reached the large, brightly lit parking lot that served the monument tourists. Martinez shut off the headlights and waited in silence.

Gwen leaned forward from the back seat. "Is something wrong?"

Martinez shook his head and said in a hushed voice, "No, no. This is where it gets interesting, Miss Gwen."

A red light that did not seem to be given off by any physical device outside had appeared in the center of the windshield.

"What's that light?" Gwen asked.

Martinez smiled. "These meetings used to be less complicated before this monument was built and the tourists came."

The light turned green and Martinez shifted into drive. He turned off the road and headed cross-country. The windshield mode had switched to night vision, casting them and the world beyond in flat green light. "Here we go."

Without the artificial aid of the TV like windshield they would have seen the landscape before them quiver like the view through heat waves. The windshield mode changed again. This time the road before them appeared like a simulated runway lined with tiny blue lights. A moment later the windshield turned back to normal mode and they found themselves in a parking lot some 50 yards east of the brightly lit main lot. Martinez pulled into a space that faced the splendidly lit monument and shut the engine off.

"Dumb question," Gwen said, "but why didn't we park in the other parking lot?"

Martinez regarded her with a glint in his eyes, "This one is hidden."

They got out and looked around. They could see the tourist crowds milling around the monument grounds, seemingly oblivious to their hidden company.

"Cloaks on. Hoods up." Martinez said in a whisper. He waved his hand in an exaggerated good bye as he slipped into his own cloak then pulled the hood over his head.

Gwen let out a small squeaking gasp. Martinez seemed to have suddenly disappeared into thin air before her eyes.

Clifford, his mouth agape, breathed, "Oh, my, God! This is wizard's school!"

When Martinez spoke again it was in a disembodied voice, "In your cloak's pocket, you will find some spectacles. Put them on."

Clifford and Gwen felt around their cloaks and found their spectacles. The transformation was now complete for Clifford. He slipped on his round, wire-rim glasses which were the exact replica of a certain boy wizard. Immediately, Martinez's form came into focus. He appeared as nothing more than a flat standing shadow.

"Oh, man! Cool!" Clifford said being careful not to be too loud.

The shadowy form seemed to turn toward him.

"Hoods up," the disembodied voice whispered. "Now, Miss Gwen, Clifford… You must be silent. Our clothing hides us quite remarkably, but we can still be overheard."

Clifford and Gwen lifted their hoods in silence and joined the shadowy company of Martinez.

"Here, we are hidden from the people, but we must move through their population at certain points in our walk. It is most important we avoid contact with the tourists at all cost."

Gwen leaned into Martinez's form and whispered, "Why through them? Why can't we just go around?"

Martinez snorted, "It is The Optometrist. He likes to subject us to unnecessary excitement during our passage," He chuckled quietly, "It amuses him. And, to make matters worse, he has inadvertently created more exhilaration by attracting *more* tourists on *these* celebratory evenings. You see, some more observant citizen tourists *have* noticed us. To these, we appear as shadowy apparitions… ghosts. Thanks to the Optometrist's high jinks, a small tourist industry has been built up around these ongoing sightings. This, of course amuses him all the more." He snorted in annoyance, "I believe he owns at least one of these ghost tour companies himself."

"Has anyone ever caught one of us?" Clifford whispered.

"Almost. Si, many times. But he takes care of this, too, most flamboyantly, I might add." He grunted his amused disapproval. "Shall we go?"

They walked only five yards or so beyond the boundary

of the parking lot before they passed through the wavering barrier. The effect was slightly dizzying as they got closer. When they were past it, and back in the realm of the citizen tourists, Martinez put a shadowy finger to his lips.

The lot and the paths leading to the monument were full for this time of night. The air was free of clouds, allowing a crystal clear view of Quito which appeared as a bedazzling oasis of light below. The monument itself was lit spectacularly.

As they tiptoed along the least populated path they could find, Clifford noticed several different buses advertising ghost tours. He felt the nervousness creep back into the pit of his stomach and made his footfalls quieter still.

They successfully skirted a tour group that was making their way back to one of the regular tour buses. As they passed, Clifford thought he saw a young girl of maybe eight years of age turn and look at him. She tensed but said nothing to her parents. Ahead, a more menacing group of tourists, led by a tour guide dressed in a black cloak, trod the beaten path. The guide was speaking in Spanish to his rapt audience– one of the ghost tours, no doubt. Again, on the peripheral edge of the group Clifford saw one of the tourists turn quickly and point at a shadow moving further up the path. At first the woman was at a loss for words then she croaked in English, "There!"

The crowd turned in unison just as the shadow vaporized with an audible "pop!"

With the tour group's attention redirected, the three

upped their pace and slipped by unnoticed. They crossed over the line laid in white brick which lead to the center of the towering monument.

The sight of the line provoked Clifford's mind to travel back to the day of his sixth birthday, the day he had first fallen through his shadow. He remembered vividly, the line his father had scratched in the volcanic earth to mark the line of the equator. This was one of his last memories before…

Clifford intentionally did not step directly on the line but took an extra large step to avoid it.

As they moved into the midst of a more concentrated crowd, Gwen reached over and took Clifford's arm as a brace.

Clifford was amazed that they could pass within mere feet of a tourist and not be seen. He watched ahead as additional shadowy figures weaved in and out of the crowd. The others seemed to be converging on an unpaved foot path beyond the hustle and bustle around the monument. As the three merged into the line, Martinez's shadow figure nodded toward many of the others. They were still within hearing distance of the tourists and a careful silence held as they made their way up into the foothills beyond.

Clifford saw the world waver and felt the queasiness bloom once again as he passed through another boundary. At once, the others fell into more relaxed movement. There were many of them here now, all in similar cloaks. Some removed their hoods and spoke to each other in hushed tones.

They further passed in and out of two more non-boundary areas, which they invisibly shared with a thinner population of the more intrepid tourist hikers. They were now moving toward a narrow passage between huge stone cliffs. The way was tight and the three had to move into a single file line along with dozens of others.

As Clifford waited his turn to pass into the gap, he heard another distinctive sounding "pop" in the distance. Several of the others around him rolled their eyes and snickered knowingly.

Initially, the passage was very narrow and there were more than a few moments when Clifford didn't think Martinez would fit through, but the way became increasingly wider. Then, all at once, the crevice opened into a huge space filled with light and sound. The shock of all this noise and light, after such a clandestine journey, took Clifford off guard. Martinez noticed and put a hand on Clifford's shoulder to steady him.

Gwen removed her hood and looked around in amazement. Beneath a great roofed pavilion, dozens of large round tables covered in elegant satin tablecloths, each adorned with its own golden candelabra, formed islands of light throughout the space. Polished silver and glassware sparkled like jewels tossed across the tables' surfaces. Somewhere, beyond her sight, a band was playing lively Andean music. Uncloaked guests gathered in conversation everywhere. Waiters moved through the crowd with trays heaped with delicious looking hors d'oeuvres and liquid libations. Gwen moved to Clifford's side, and found him as awed as she.

"What is this? All these people can't be Travelers!" Gwen said in his ear.

Clifford shrugged. He was too overwhelmed to speak.

Martinez took each gently by their elbows and guided them toward the crowds. "Here you are Clifford, the great gathering place. Travelers and their families have congregated here for centuries. They come from all over the world." He looked around the open pavilion. "There may even be some from Europe and Asia from the looks of it." He guided them to a bar set up at the center of the great space and ordered them drinks: Coke for Clifford and for Gwen and he, beer.

Gwen was not much of a drinker, at least as far as Clifford knew, but she accepted the beverage as if it were the most precious drink on Earth. She took a long swallow then exhaled a significant amount of her tension. Clifford regarded her with a stern eye.

"What? Your auntie can't have a beer?" she retorted.

"Remember the sangria?" Clifford teased.

Martinez chuckled, "A well deserved indulgence! Your aunt has been through a great deal these past few days, Clifford." He turned to her, "Drink and eat your fill! Tomorrow will take care of itself. Ha, ha," he laughed and spread his arms as if to embrace the entire scene, "This is a celebration!"

Indeed, many in the pavilion were indulging themselves merrily. Martinez drew them into the crowd and began introducing them around to some of his old friends.

Some names Clifford and Gwen recognized from the library of travel journals.

Gwen shortly landed with a strikingly handsome gentleman who had been responsible for penning the overly technical journal she had been astonished with the night before. He ordered her another beer and they tucked in for an in-depth conversation of math and physics. Clifford quickly grew bored with the topics and moved back to Martinez's side.

Martinez had settled in with three gentlemen of his same age. Their raucous talk of past journeys held Clifford's attention briefly then his eyes began to wander. He had noticed other kids when they had first arrived but he could not pick them out now. Martinez noticed and smiled knowingly. "Mingle, Clifford. Go ahead. I'll find you before we sit down for dinner."

Clifford looked back at him, doubtful.

"Go on. Don't be shy."

Clifford reluctantly wandered off. He glanced at Gwen as he passed. She seemed swept up in conversation still. He went to the bar and ordered another Coke then turned to the gathered crowd. Still there were no kids to be seen. His curiosity was piqued. *Where are they?* Then he heard a familiar voice call his name. He looked around to see.

Doctor Camilla, his psychologist, was weaving her way toward him through the crowd.

"Clifford Tuttle! I see you have found us!" she exclaimed. "How did you ever persuade your parents to bring you down here?"

"I… I didn't. I'm with Aunt Gwen. She insisted she come."

"I am impressed. What has it been, a few weeks since we last met? How did you hit on Quito?"

Clifford shuffled his feet, "It just seemed right, I guess. I saw the monument was here. This is where Senõr Martinez found me when I was six."

"Indeed," she said with a raised eyebrow. So you've remembered everything?"

"Yeah… I guess. You hypnotized me. It came back in bits. Finally, I went outside but couldn't fall through my… you know, shadow?"

"So here you are, on the equator. Martinez is here as well?"

"Yes, I remembered his name from before."

Doctor Camilla gave him an exaggerated wink, "You have turned out to be surprisingly resourceful, Clifford Tuttle. And that is a very good quality to possess as a Traveler."

"Has Martinez prepared you?" she asked, shifting to the more serious matters at hand.

"Sure. I guess so. He explained some stuff and took me to The Optometrist."

"Fascinating creature, The Optometrist, don't you think?"

"He made me some cool goggles. I remember seeing yours on the mantle in your office."

"Yes. He's definitely the brains behind this operation,

in case you haven't noticed. Because of him, we are far ahead of Europe and Asia, technology wise."

"Is he here tonight?" Clifford asked, looking around.

She smiled, "He's always around. Right now he's probably attending to the unfortunate ones who were spotted on the way in. That vaporization and then 'pop!' It's enough to scramble one's entire being to the quick. Beam us up Scotty!" she chuckled. "I suppose," she sighed, "it brings him some perverse amusement." She noticed the concern on Clifford's face. "Oh, I'm sure they'll be okay."

"So. Here we are on the brink! How are you taking all this?"

"In big gulps, I guess. There's a lot to deal with, plus… I'm really worried, you know, about messing up."

Dr. Camilla regarded Clifford with an impish smile, "You would be *crazy* not to be worried, and believe me, *I* know *crazy*… being a psychologist and all." She snorted out a giggle like a young girl. "Oh, I'm sure you'll be fine!" She winked. "The first time is wicked gnarly!"

"Yah. I wouldn't quite describe it like that…" he trailed off remembering in vivid detail what it was like, as a six year old, to fall out of control into an alien world.

"In your case, Clifford, you've had a sneak preview," she beamed and then grew serious. She knelt down to be eye to eye with him. "You will be much better prepared and equipped this time."

Clifford slowly shook his head, "Maybe… I have my goggles, but I don't know a thing about where I'm going except for what I saw in the journals. It will take me a lot longer than a day to get through all of those."

"Oh, I think you will be ready. Leave that to The Optometrist," she said with a positive smile and nod. "So now you are wondering if you are the only kid here."

"I thought I saw some kids earlier," he craned his neck around to see, "but I don't see any now."

Dr. Camilla clasped her hands on his shoulders, "Seek and you shall find." She winked again and then stood. "Good hunting," she continued in a sing-song voice.

Clifford watched her back as she returned to the adult revelry.

"Crap! Why does everything have to be a game?" He looked around and seeing no other kids, began to walk the perimeter of the gathering place.

The hollow seemed to be completely surrounded by steep rock cliffs. He walked past the break in the rocks through which more cloaked figures were arriving. He considered that way but it would make no sense to go back out. He continued his walk looking for anything that might be a passage then suddenly, there it was, a crack in the rock barely wide enough to squeeze through. A hand painted sign printed in three languages including English, **DANGER: STEEP PATH. PROCEED WITH CAUTION.**

Clifford smiled wryly to himself. *What kid wouldn't be tempted by a sign like that?* He moved up to the crack and looked back over his shoulder to see if anyone was watching. To his distress, most all the adults *were* watching with knowing smiles on their faces. He blew out a stressed breath then squeezed through the gap.

Chapter Nine
New Friends

Clifford moved cautiously through the short gap in the rock wall and emerged unexpectedly onto a dark, forested ridge. He immediately heard the sound of rock music and voices drifting up from below.

"Well, this sounds promising," he said and then started walking down the trail.

The trail, as promised, was steep but worn down to bare rock by years of foot traffic. To either side of the path, the forest seemed impenetrable, clogged with low growing bushes and intertwined vines. A buzz of animal and insect life common to a tropical rainforest, mixing with the music, filled his ears. The air was warmer and more humid than the place he had come from.

If it weren't for all the growing things around him, Clifford would have guessed he was inside a mammoth cavern. He looked up but could see no sky at all through the dense tree canopy, but there was light.

As Clifford's eyes adjusted to his new surroundings,

he noticed an abundance of luminescent moss that hung from the forest's vines. Equally bright were the fireflies that floated around in the air like fairies in some magical wonderland. The effect was spectacular. He could have stood there all night but the youthful activity below drew him on down the path.

Clifford emerged from the forest onto a wide rock ledge. Above, the domelike tree canopy opened to a dazzling circle of night sky. Out on the ledge, dozens of silhouetted figures congregated, moving against a glowing backdrop. The light seemed to be coming from beyond and below the rock ledge.

Pushing aside his inherent shyness acquired through years of isolation, Clifford pressed forward toward the people. As he approached, he found, to his disappointment, that most of the kids were older teenagers. They all gathered in what Clifford assumed were well established cliques. Beyond, individual couples sat holding hands at the edge. Far to the right he could see a D.J. spinning tunes under a bar of flashing colored lights while a group of kids danced before him. Over the music he could hear the sound of excited, youthful voices, but he could not pinpoint the direction through the echoing distortion of the place.

As Clifford stood timidly assessing the situation, one of the teenage girls broke away from her group of giggling girls and sauntered over to him.

"Bon soir! Hi. Are you going to stand there all night or come and join us?" She appeared to be Asian but spoke in English accented with French. She looked to be about eighteen, but who could tell? Girls seemed to look older sooner, while boys kind of stayed geeky longer. She was taller than he was and pretty too, in a weird, emo-style way. Her alternating short to medium length, razor cut hair was dyed an unnatural shade of intense, coppery-red and was held in place with lots of bobby pins. She wore heavy black eyeliner that exaggerated her Asian eyes. Her eyelids were shaded in an amazing iridescent blue to green fade. Her lip color matched her eyelids. She, of course, wore the same black fabric as everyone else but the outfit was artistically styled in many layers, poufs, and textures. The whole effect was sexy, in a fashion model kind of way, which worked to sink his self esteem level even lower into the geeky category.

"I... I wasn't sure where to go. It's my first time here." he replied feeling more stupid with every word.

She rolled her eyes, "Yeah. The first time, jeez! You would *think* they'd give you a little heads up, non?"

Clifford nodded his agreement, "'Seek and you shall find' was all I got."

She gave a little snort of a laugh through her cute nose, "Oui. That is more than most get. I'm Shelly," she said holding out her hand, palm down, wrist slightly bent.

Does she want me to shake or kiss her hand? Man, I'm no good at this. "Cliff...Clifford." he stammered as he held out his hand for a shake. I'm from Pittsburgh... you know, in Pennsylvania."

"Nice to meet you..." she said and raised her pretty, pierced and metal studded eyebrow, "...Cliff." (She emphasized the word Cliff in a husky voice.)

Clifford secretly did an air punch in his mind seeing she had chosen the more grown up version of his name, not Clifford or heaven forbid, Cliffy.

"Oh, by the way, love your look," she purred, "are you wearing powder or are you just that white?"

"No it's just me. It's a long story."

She ran her eyes over him and cocked her head. "Hair's natural too, I suppose? Nice. I know people that would kill for that color."

"Thanks, I guess." He was not at all used to being complimented by a girl and he was sure he was blushing. *I like her.*

She continued to study him for a moment longer, and then continued, "Come on then, let me show you around."

She introduced him to the group of girls she had been hanging with and as she did so, some others took notice and joined them. Christa was dark haired with olive skin and was from Mexico City, Mexico but spoke perfect English. Tasha was African American with sharp wit. She was the giggler. Her hair was done in what seemed like hundreds of thin braids that terminated with colorful beads. Her dark-skinned face naturally seemed to smile always, and she wore no noticeable makeup. Her eyes were beautiful, dark brown, and shone with inner intelligence. She was from Chicago. (He immediately liked her too.) Andrea had long, perfectly strait blond hair. She was taller than the others with broad shoulders and a strong physical build to go with her nice looks. She was from Virginia and she seemed rather standoffish. Shelly, as it turned out was from Quebec, Canada.

The boys, who had come over to join them for introductions, were all well out of the "geek" stage and looked strong and intimidating. There was Dan from Encinatas, California. He had shoulder length bleach-blond hair and savage tanned skin. He reminded Clifford of a stereotypical surfer dude. Marco was from right here in Quito. He was dark, stocky and solidly built. Travis was from Austin, Texas. He had close cropped hair, ice blue eyes and a handsome chiseled face that just radiated arrogance. They all seemed so big and self assured that Clifford's confidence, having been momentarily strengthened by the girls, began to slip back again.

Travis was the last to shake his hand. He gave Clifford a cocky smile as if he could sense Clifford's uncertainty. He released his grip, regarded his hand with a grin, and then wiped it on his pants.

"Whoa, Casper… little nervous there?" he smirked as he waved his hand in the air to dry it. "So, first time, huh?"

Clifford had little contact with other kids, less so with teenagers, but he recognized a jerk when he saw one. He bolstered himself up, and then made his reply.

"No. This will be my second time."

Really? How old are you anyway, little dude?" Travis' voice was belittling.

"Fourteen."

"When?" Travis said making no attempt to hide his skepticism.

"When I was six!" Clifford shot back.

There was murmuring among the others.

Travis backed off a step and gave Clifford a good look. "No way dude. You're not *him* are you?"

Clifford was taken aback. "What?"

Shelly stepped forward to speak excitedly. "You're the kid that fell through when you were six?!"

"Yeah, when I was six." He said, and then thought to punch his reply up. "It was, uh, wicked gnarly! Yeah."

"Wow! No one that young ever fell through, and survived, that I heard of," Marco put in.

Clifford's confidence had started to rebound, "I had help, I guess. From the other side."

"Yeah, you *must* have," Travis snorted sarcastically, then turned and gave Dan a fist bump.

Clifford decided to ignore the insult for now. "Hey, Marco, how come you never fell through when you were young? I mean, you live right on the equator and all."

"Now that's the advantage of living here. They knew as soon as I was born. It was rough though, growing up that way. They had to keep me out of the sun most of the time."

Clifford nodded, "I can definitely relate to that. In case you didn't notice, I don't have much of a tan."

Dan bobbed his head and guffawed, "Dude, you have got to be the whitest white dude I ever saw!" He came over and gave Clifford a high five.

This was good. Most of these teenagers seemed to like him. "So how many times have you guys gone?"

Clifford noticed right away that some of them were shuffling their feet.

"Once," replied Dan.

"Zilch," Tasha said with not-quite-sad, downcast eyes. But maybe this time," she continued in her positively animated manner.

"Me too. Big zero" put in Christa. Most of us haven't gone yet. Shelly, Marco, and Travis have gone the most."

"Wait a minute. Not everyone goes, even though they can?" Clifford asked. He had assumed everyone went.

"Not everyone. The borders have the say in these matters. It's complicated but necessary I guess. It's 'the Balance.' It's all about 'the Balance.'" Marco said.

Clifford was thunderstruck. *Not everyone goes?! What if Gwen and I came all this way and nothing happens?* He cast about for some sign of this being a joke. None of them were smirking. The idea of there being no resolution to his dilemma was unthinkable. How could he ever just go back to Pittsburgh, normal and unfulfilled? *Normal. I can't do normal! How boring would that be!?*

"Are you okay there, Casper?"

Travis' voice broke through his thunder-tossed thoughts. Clifford took a deep steadying breath. "Yeah, sure. And my name's not Casper!"

Clifford's disappointment had turned to adolescent anger. He knew he was still immature enough to throw a respectable tantrum when he didn't get what he wanted. It took all his strength, but he managed to will himself away from that path which would be, above all else, embarrassing in front of these older kids. It was hard but he reigned in the anger and settled for moving forward. "So what's this place?"

The group had begun to break up. Apparently the novelty of meeting the new kid had lost its charm for the time. To his secret delight, Shelly and Tasha stuck with him as the others departed.

"It's kind of the kid's area," Tasha began. "Don't get me wrong. It's not a bad thing. Actually, it's pretty cool. Come on. We'll show you around!"

They walked to the edge of the rock ledge and looked twenty feet down on a glowing pool that rippled with the activity of silhouetted swimmers. To the right was a waterslide that cut a glowing serpentine line through the forest.

"Bummer. I didn't bring my swimming trunks."

"Doesn't matter," Shelly smiled, "You go anyway. We all do," she said, pulling him along by the arm. They stopped at the buffet table that was set with all sorts of delicious looking hors d'oeuvres.

"Hungry?" Shelly asked as they planted themselves in the queue.

"Starving!" Clifford said. He could feel his mouth water.

They filled their plates and made a stop at the beverage bar where they helped themselves to a glowing punch concoction. With all their hands full, they moved to a bench that overlooked the fabulous waterslide and dug in. Clifford smiled inwardly, happy to be sandwiched between the two attractive girls.

The food was wonderful and the punch was filled with tropical fruit flavor, the real flavor, not some industrially dyed artificial flavor.

Tasha finished chewing a mouthful of mini tortilla and turned to Clifford.

"So, how do you like this so far?"

Clifford smiled, "It's the biggest adventure I have had since…"

Shelly's eyes grew wide. "Since you fell through."

"Yeah. I haven't really gotten out much since. I guess the whole experience kind of freaked me out for a while," he said staring into his punch. He took a sip and swallowed. "Seven and a half years to be exact," he finished and shrugged.

"So, you've gone?" he asked after a moment of silence. He quickly glanced over at Tasha, worried that he might have hurt her feelings by reminding her that she hadn't gone. She seemed okay with it so he returned his attention to Shelly.

"Twice." She answered. "It was like what you said, wicked gnarly!"

"What was it like?" he asked.

"Don't you remember?"

Clifford shook his head, "not much of it."

"Well," she began, "it's not like here, that's for sure. I was fourteen too, when I first went, and it was a lot to deal with. I mean, one day you're just a normal kid, and the next, you're like some kind of freaking astronaut! The first time, I just kind of hung out with the adults. It's really a weird place, from what I could see. The people there have like bubble skin bodies. It was like, if their insides weren't so cloudy looking, you could see right through them. We stayed in this kind of space station, like in that old Star Wars movie. You know, where Lando Calrissian lived? The bubble people, I guess, live in the clouds. But there's not a lot you can pick up in a couple of hours. It seemed like it was over before it started."

The inflated imagery in his mind, wrought with great adventure, was slowly crumbling. He had hoped there would be more than what Shelly was describing.

"So you were in the sky place huh? That's where I was. I can't remember anything except for falling though-"

Shelly was shaking her head. "I don't know how you did it without the goggles."

"You must have been crapping yourself!" Tasha put in.

Clifford grinned, "I don't know, I can't remember if I did. I was sure scared enough to."

Clifford turned back to Shelly with an expectant expression on his face. "How about the second time you went? Was it more?"

"Nope. Pretty much the same but I was allowed to stay longer. Two days, I guess. I stayed in a sort of clinic with Dan and Travis. The bubble doctor did some tests on us and stuff," she said then noticed Clifford's crestfallen expression. "Oh, don't get me wrong, Cliff. It was way cooler than here. It's cool. You kind of feel important like you're helping out with 'the Balance' and all."

Clifford's attention was momentarily interrupted by a speeding body whooshing down the waterslide, and then returned to the conversation.

"Martinez, that's who brought me and my Aunt Gwen here tonight, and the man who found me when I was six, said stuff about the other worlds needing something from us. What is it?"

Shelly shrugged as if she didn't have a clue but Tasha moved in with an enlightened look in her eyes.

"I think it's some kind of essence or chemical our bodies give off. It's sort of like when we breathe in air, oxygen goes into all our body's cells and keeps us alive. You see? We could be like the oxygen to those other worlds. Just a hypothesis... I... I was never there–"

Clifford gave this some thought. "It doesn't make any sense though. We breathe all the time. Travelers don't go all the time. It's weird."

Shelly nodded her head. "It's *all* weird."

Tasha straightened in her seat. "Some day, I'm going to figure it all out!"

"Yeah," Shelly put, in smiling crookedly, "you're such a brainiac, I think you could." She reached behind Clifford and gave Tasha a good natured slug in the arm.

For a moment she let her arm rest on Clifford's back giving him an unexpected thrill.

"Hey, speaking about weird," Tasha said. "I think its time to show Cliff the pool."

Clifford followed Shelly and Tasha up a rocky path that led to the top of the waterslide. He was still worried about the prospect of getting soaked, but the girls had assured him that getting wet would not be a problem. At the top of the path a luminous, swiftly flowing waterfall fed into a huge funnel shaped depression carved in solid rock. Its shape reminded Clifford of those charity donation contraptions where you drop a coin into a slot and it rolls around and around inside, going faster and faster, until it drops through the hole in the bottom. Despite the volume of water that appeared to be flowing over the falls and into the funnel, the noise it made was as silent as a light breeze. It was almost as if he had suddenly gone deaf.

Tasha smiled knowingly at Clifford. "Weird, huh? And this is just the beginning!" Her eyes were wide with anticipation.

Clifford examined the funnel shaped depression. "We're going in there?!"

Tasha gave him a quick, confident nod, "Yep. Who's first?"

Shelly stepped up. "Me first, then Cliff." She gave Clifford a sideways look. "Tasha, make sure he doesn't chicken out. You look scared," she teased.

"I'm not scared!" Clifford lied. He was, on the contrary, quite alarmed. He was not a swimmer unless of course he was wearing his new goggles. He had never in his life voluntarily jumped into any deep water.

Before Clifford had time to think, Shelly leaped into the silent swirling drain, rode around the vortex's circumference three times then, with an excited squeal, dropped through the bottom and out of sight. He barely heard

Tasha say "jump" before he was helped along by a light kick to his butt. He had only a second to be angry with her before he was whirling around the dizzying vortex, through the hole and was washing along the waterslide's winding course.

The ride was so fast and invigorating that he barely noticed he was not getting wet. Twenty crazy, out of control seconds later, he was shot out over a five foot ledge and plunged into the glowing pool.

He barely saw the pool's surface recede before he had sunk deep into its contents. He had held his breath instinctively as he entered the pool but was now panicking and struggling to make it back to the surface when Shelly's face drifted into his point of view. She was laughing hysterically with her mouth open and seemed not to be drowning in water. He could hear her voice urging him to relax. Still he was reluctant to let out his breath until Tasha grabbed him playfully from behind and began to tickle him. This finally loosened his lungful of air.

Remarkably, his next breath was normal. Whatever he was submerged in was not water but something similarly buoyant. He took another chance and tried to talk. "What is this stuff?"

"Who knows? But it's awesome isn't it?!" Shelly said.

Clifford took a swim stroke up and broke the surface. Tasha and Shelly bobbed up a moment later. To Clifford's surprise, their faces and hair were perfectly dry. The three treaded as they would in water.

Clifford laughed nervously, "Well' just when you think you've experienced all the weirdness possible-"

The girls laughed then dunked back under the fluid plane. Clifford remained at the surface pondering yet another mystery.

Clifford's attention was drawn to the top of the twenty foot high ledge when he heard Travis' voice bark down at him.

Hey Casper! How's the water?"

To his left Dan and Marco made their boisterous entrance from the slide.

"Water… or what ever this is… is great." Clifford yelled back, "Are you coming in or what?" he added, wondering why Travis hadn't come down the slide with the others. Secretly he hoped that Travis was more afraid of water than he was. He also thought it would be good to have one up on the jerk.

Travis shattered Clifford's hope flamboyantly by making a perfect dive off the twenty foot ledge, breaking the pool's surface silently no more than four feet away from where Clifford was floating.

"Nice." Clifford muttered in utter disappointment. He already knew that he was out of their league when it came to hanging with Travis and his friends, but not *this* far out. He looked around and was further disappointed to find that he was the only one left at the surface.

With much trepidation, Clifford allowed himself to sink back down and began to clumsily paddle his way toward the others who had congregated far below.

He was feeling more like an outsider than ever and was seriously considering just ditching the lot of them. *I've dealt with enough anxiety for one day.* Then he thought, *Why stop there. I wish I could ditch this whole thing.* He was beginning to rue the day he let Dr. Camilla open his Pandora's Box of memories. *How great would it be to be home in my dark room, to be back in my more simplistic, isolated life?*

Even if I was cured, I would have been fine back in Pittsburgh. Conquering his seven year phobia had placed him back in the realm of normal fourteen year olds. He could go outside now, maybe even go to a real school. He would be thousands of miles away from the equator and never fall through his shadow again.

The home sickness flooded across his mind and heart. *Aunt Gwen was right. We should've never taken this trip,* he admitted as his tears began to flow.

It was amazing but when he went to rub the tears from his eyes, his hand came away wet.

Clifford slowed his progress toward the five silhouetted swimmers and felt a pang of jealousy as he watched Travis crack up laughing about something Shelly had just told him. Clifford was sure it was some mean joke on his behalf and that was all it took for him to decide. He needed to get out of there but where would he go?

Remembering the scene from the surface, Clifford recalled no way out of the pool. The ledge was twenty feet straight up and the rest of the pool was surrounded by shorter but equally insurmountable sides.

He was about to physically drown in his despair when Shelly's face drifted again into his point of view.

"A little overwhelming, huh?" Her pretty face smiled in total understanding.

Clifford made no attempt to hide his tears. He was too far gone now. "I feel stupid. I don't belong here."

Shelly reached over, pulled him in by the head until the top of their foreheads touched and held him there. "First time's a bitch. I know exactly how you're feeling. This pool has a strong effect on newbie's. It's kind of a bath for your brain. Every thing you feel feels stronger. You feel the worst you ever felt at first, then by the time you're done you feel better than you ever have. You just have to go with it."

Clifford closed his eyes tight then sniffed, "Okay. I'll be okay. I guess I'm still just a stupid kid. You guys are a lot older. More ready."

"Cliff, I'm not that much older! I'm only a kid too. I'm fifteen, almost sixteen, and it seems like I was just going through this stuff yesterday. Believe me, it takes some getting used to, but I bet you will be just fine."

"Wow, you seemed older."

"She giggled, "It won't be long before you catch up. Trust me. This stuff will put years on you in a hurry." She pulled back, looked him in the eyes then surprisingly reached in and gave him a quick kiss on the cheek. She pushed playfully away kicking at his face and beckoned him to follow her back to the group. "Come on! The real fun is about to start."

Clifford snapped out of his post-kiss trance and putting his feelings of despair behind him, followed her. *More fun?! Can I take any more?*

As the reassembled group swam still deeper into the glowing abyss, Clifford perceived the start of a definite tingling in his skin. It was nothing at first, but the sensation increased to a very noticeable vibration as they swam deeper. He was just about to bring this up to the others when they were suddenly pulled into a circular current.

The current's pull wasn't alarmingly strong, but enough that it started pulling them apart, dispersing them single file and into a large circular track. As he circled around with the others, Clifford noticed that many more of the kids from the ledge had joined them and were caught in the same current. They began to grasp each others hands. Shelly took Clifford's right hand and Tasha took his left. As soon as the final connection was made, the current increased in velocity and the centrifugal force began pulling their legs outward.

"Hold on tight Cliff!" Shelly called over to him, "And don't let go, okay?"

Clifford tightened his clasp on her wrist, "I won't! What's happening?"

"Are you ready?" She called back.

"Ready for what?!"

"Ready to flyyyyyyyy!"

They were suddenly freefalling through the sky like adjoined sky divers. The completed circle had grown to a total of twenty-two persons, and to see that they all were whooping and hollering in adrenaline-rush delight, reassured Clifford that he was, for the time, relatively safe. Shelly had told him "You just have to go with it". So he did.

The sensation of falling was real, but Clifford could feel no rushing wind or air to sting his eyes or resist his plummeting body.

The fall continued and for Clifford, there were many flashes of panic to follow. At one point electrical charges began to arc from the circle's clenched hands. As unnerving as that may have seemed, it wasn't until an ever thickening condensation of water began to coat his body that Clifford's fear of drowning returned. Even though he could breathe, instinct told him to panic. He attempted to shake the water from his face and hair but the wet layer continued to condense and thicken. Looking across the circle he could see the others were also totally cocooned in the liquid. When the volume of water apparently reached critical mass, they all suddenly plopped together in what Clifford perceived as a giant rain drop. Still they fell.

Clifford had an uneasy feeling that he knew what would come next and he was right. He saw their tiny reflection start to grow, coming ever faster in the same soap bubble, mirror-like surface that he remembered seeing when he was six.

Clifford tensed as their speeding droplet crashed unbroken onto the elastic surface of the planet. There was a disorienting moment of chaos, and then he felt the more organized sensation of what it might feel like to be sealed inside a super ball as it hit and bounced, hit and bounced, in ever shortening arcs. The bouncing soon ceased, but they were still in motion, rolling along the glasslike surface as if inside a clear marble. Once on the surface, their momentum slowed rapidly to a stop.

The group, who had all let go of each other, was now placidly floating around the inside of the large water drop like snow flakes in a shaken snow globe. Slowly they began settling to the bottom where they all piled on top of each other.

Clifford had one settling moment to recover his bearings and to try to ignore the fact that someone's butt was in his face before they were all absorbed like a drop of rain water into a pond.

The new place was a vast ocean of deep blue. They had all drifted together and turned toward a pinpoint of wavering light that seemed miles away. Clifford could see other lights of different hues and brightness floating distantly as well, but he felt, as did the collective body of the group, drawn to this one light.

"Wait 'til you see this," Tasha said in Clifford's ear. Her voice sounded completely normal and unaffected by the weight of water around them.

They all swam eagerly toward the light and when they arrived, Clifford found that the rainbow colored light they had followed was emanating from a giant crystalline prism. He watched as others reached out and placed their hands flat on the glowing surface. Clifford followed suit.

All of a sudden Clifford's eyes filled with the same brilliant light he had experienced when The Optometrist's antenna touched his eyes. The light changed from flat, brilliant white to a prismatic array of 3-dimensional colors.

The water world was gone and now Clifford perceived a vast space filled with hundreds of out-of-focus glowing crystals. It was as if he were inside a fantastically colorful kaleidoscope.

Clifford and the others had landed on a flat, dry, brilliantly lit glasslike surface. The vast crystalline space around them was filled with a tonal vibration that worked its way deep into their bodies.

To Clifford, the sensation was like mild electricity, passing through and around him. His aura crackled with energy as he looked around to find the others. To his shock, all of their eyes were shining like super lit crystals.

The experience lasted another minute then ceased. For a moment they all just stood frozen and awestruck by the prismatic beauty of the place. Suddenly everything went black.

Martinez and his friends Richard Gardener, Felipe Montrose, and Eugene Franklin, all men well into their late 70s, sat about one of the large round tables that had been set for dinner. Gwen and her new friend Scott Fillmore had joined them. They were listening to a speech by a very tall man who bore an uncanny resemblance to a 1980s version of Leonard Nimoy. He introduced himself as Diminutive T. Little, an obvious play on words considering his dimensions. The "Spock look" was pretty witty too. Gwen guessed that the man, who appeared in every way human, save his extraordinary tallness, was really The Optometrist in disguise.

Regardless of the man's charismatic draw, Gwen was having a very difficult time concentrating on the speech. Ignoring the others' attempts to assure her that she had no need for worry, every minute or so her eyes searched the place looking for Clifford. The unsettling thought dawned on her that she hadn't seen him since she had first sat down to talk to Scott Fillmore.

Gwen scanned the room one last time with no luck then returned her attention to the podium just as a brilliant array of prismatic light exploded thunderously up from the floor to either side of the podium. The affect was quite unexpected and startling to the gathering. Their shrieks and gasps filled the place. Gwen, herself, cringed and yelped in terror, nearly falling backwards off her chair. When she opened her eyes finally, the bewildered children, twenty-two of them, eleven on each side, stood flanking the speaker.

The room took a while to settle from the sudden chaos. Some, Gwen noticed, had actually fallen out of their chairs and were picking themselves up and trying to regain their composure. Accompanying the regrouping was a great deal of hushed, expletive-peppered muttering.

Diminutive T. Little simply paused in his discourse. "I see our young Travelers have joined us. Please," he addressed the young ones, "sit, sit. Our suppers will be served soon."

Clifford picked out his Aunt Gwen immediately because she was the only one standing, waving her hands, and calling his name. He was happy to see her, but she was being kind of embarrassing. He moved off the platform with the others to join their families.

Gwen and Scott Fillmore moved over one chair to allow Clifford a seat between her and Martinez. Clifford, still a little dazed, took his seat.

Martinez leaned into Clifford. "You found the other children I see. Did you make some new friends?"

"Yeah, I met a few." he said absently as he picked out Shelly across the room. Apparently she had found him too, because she had been watching him and smiled when their eyes met.

"Well, you will have to introduce us later," he said following Clifford's gaze. "For now, these are *my* friends. Clifford Tuttle, this is Senõr Richard Gardener, Senõr Felipe Montrose, and Senõr Eugene Franklin."

The men each gave Clifford polite nods of greeting in turn.

"We have known each other from the beginning," Martinez continued. "You, Clifford, I hope, will find such excellent friends. Si, we had a fine group, some sadly have departed including my beautiful Annette." He paused for a moment of thought.

The other three men nodded in agreement.

"It is important," he continued, "to be a part of a

group. You become a team of sorts. If you are as lucky as I am, your group will be diverse, each with their own special strengths. You will travel together in adulthood."

Clifford thought about Shelly, Tasha and Marco, and wondered again if he would have the chance to travel with them this time. Martinez had said, "In adulthood," hadn't he?

Clifford had not learned much about what strengths they had. Tasha, he thought, was the smart one or as Shelly put it, the "brainiac". Marco? Sure, he fit in. He seemed strong and confident. And Shelly, absolutely! She was very kind, and really pretty. He wasn't quite sure of anything else about her or the other two. All he knew was that he liked them.

"I think I found three really good friends tonight. I don't know much about them yet, but they seem to like me."

"Excellent, Clifford!" he said and he patted Clifford's knee.

"So, where did you run off to, Cliffy?" Gwen asked when Martinez had finished.

"It was a really cool place in the woods. I wish you could have seen it. There was this awesome waterslide and pool."

Gwen reached over and touched the fabric of Clifford's shirt sleeve then ran her fingers through his hair. "You didn't go swimming though?"

"Sure I did," he said with pride, "And the water was way over my head," he added. *It had been over my head, all right. Way, way over my head.* But he decided to keep that part of the story to himself.

"Really, Cliffy?" Gwen asked with a concerned look on her face. "Was there a lifeguard?" she prodded, and then bit her lower lip.

"Aunt Gwen!" Clifford replied, taken aback, "No, but there was a bunch of bigger kids there," he said finally, realizing she wasn't trying to embarrass him, but just showing concern. "It was perfectly safe," he concluded with a smile.

"Oh… good then. Ah, what about how you got back here? Whew! I almost fell out of my chair!" Gwen said as she took an apprehensive glance at the now vacant podium.

"Why?"

"Well, there was this big explosion," She said shifting her glance to the podium and back again.

"Really? What explosion?" Clifford said a little too loud. "I didn't hear an explosion. But it *was* kinda strange. One second I was swimming, the next I was here."

Martinez leaned in, "Just more of The Optometrist's hocus pocus. A shame you missed it," he said, chuckling, "it was a good one."

Their appetizers arrived, starting off a wonderful five course meal of local cuisine. They all ate until they were stuffed. Afterward, the Disc Jockey from the stone ledge entertained with some lively dance music. Their table broke up, Gwen and Scott headed off to the dance floor,

Martinez, with his friends, retired to one of the numbers of sofa and chair groupings that had appeared after the tables had been cleared.

Clifford approached his three new friends who had regrouped around a high cafe table with stools. In the center of the table a fat candle flickered, casting a warm glow on all of their faces.

"Hi. Can I hang with you guys for a while?" Clifford asked.

"Sure dude. Have a seat," Marco said. He offered a fist bump and Clifford took it.

"Thanks," he said as he sat. "My Aunt kind of ditched me. She's out there dancing with that Scott Fillmore guy. I think she found herself a new boyfriend," he smirked. "He's some kind of scientist or something. My aunt and I read some of his journal."

Tasha's eyes brightened with inspiration. "*The* Scott Fillmore? Oh, my, God! I've heard of him! Wow! Do you think I could meet him?"

"Sure, I guess," Clifford said. "He seemed pretty cool."

"So, Cliff, how do you feel now?" Shelly asked.

"Confused… but good, I guess. Yeah, better," he replied.

"I thought you would be, ah, better, and confused. We all are."

"I don't get it," Clifford shook his head. "I remember swimming in that weird pool and talking to you– (He wished he could put the crying part out of his mind. He definitely remembered the kiss.) And then, we were back here. But, I feel like there was a whole lot more. It was like when I was six. I only remembered some of it."

"Si, mi amigo." Marco put in. "You're not the only one. I've done it four times now, and it's always the same."

Shelly and Tasha nodded their agreement. "Yeah, it's weird," they said in perfect unison.

Marco looked suddenly deep in thought. "Sometimes when I traveled, stuff came to me, stuff that I could never have known."

"Like what?" Clifford asked.

Marco shook his head. "It's hard to say. Sometimes I get flashes, you know, like memories of things I never did? It's like remembering a dream that seemed real. My mind tells me I was never in that place or situation, yet there it is! But it never happened in the first place!" Marco shrugged, "I don't know... its just crazy, man.

Clifford nodded his head. "I've had stuff like that happen since I was six."

"It's all so maddening!" Shelly said.

Tasha inserted her theory, "If you ask me, there's a conspiracy to shield us from something. As far as my own personal experience goes, I think the weird water does something to our brains. It, like, puts us into a trance or something then inputs knowledge. So, then, guess what? We immediately forget it! And, whoa... then, sometimes we remember it at random times? And then, we forget it ever happened. Whew... Maybe the water, like, tweaks our basic instincts to deal with life on different planes of existence. It's all stored there in our subconsciouses for our use some day."

She looked into all their rapt faces. "The adults all go, right? Are they ever a part of your clinic time? Are they always there?"

Shelly nodded her head. "They are there, some."

"All of them?"

Marco shook his head, "no."

"There must be other places they go then."

"Senōr Martinez said there are five worlds."

"Well, yah, we *all* know about *those*," Shelly said rolling her eyes.

"Why have you only gone to Skyloumia and not anywhere else?" Tasha asked.

Marco shrugged his shoulders. "Beats me."

Tasha fixed Marco with her bright-eyed stare. "Maybe you *have* gone other places and *that's* what they're hiding from you. *That's* where your residual memories are coming from."

"It's possible," Marco said. "It surely puts traveling into a more interesting light."

"If there was only a way to keep you from forgetting," Tasha said stroking her chin and looking out over the crowd of older Travelers. "When's the cut-off age for finally being aloud to remember?"

"I hope soon," Marco said. "This shit is driving me crazy."

Clifford rested his chin in his hands and rubbed his tired eyes with his fingers, then stared down at the tabletop. "Is this what I have to look forward to, if I even *get* to go?"

"Oui, Cliff. *If* you get to go."

Clifford sighed, "It will just kill me if I don't."

"You went once before! Why wouldn't you go again?" Tasha encouraged.

Clifford squeezed his eyes shut, "I'm terrified," Clifford said finally through his fingers, "if I go, or not."

Marco reached over and gave the boy a jostle. "I hope we all go! Then we can work this thing out together."

"Me too?" Tasha asked.

"Especially you!" Shelly said. "We could use a brainiac like you along to help us figure this all out."

"Sounds like we have a team!" Marco announced and gave each of them a high five. "Tomorrow, we stick together!"

The gathering dispersed its revelers at around 12:30 A.M., Tuesday morning. There had been a brief ceremony at midnight to christen the Autumnal Equinox and then the weary company began to make their way home.

By that time of night the monument was closed and the parking lot empty of cars and tour buses so the walk back to their cars was less clandestine.

Clifford had volunteered to take the back seat when they reached Martinez's SUV and was asleep before the vehicle pulled out onto the main road. Gwen remained determinedly awake for the ride back, despite her exhaustion. She was used to late nights because of Clifford's previous schedule, but the combination of travel time differences and the considerable amount of food and drink consumed and the dancing after, had just about knocked her out.

"So this is it, the equinox," Gwen said more to herself than to Martinez.

"Si, the big day," he replied simply.

Gwen bit her lip, "Clifford. He'll be okay, right?"

"Si, Miss Gwen. Clifford will be okay, unless…"

Gwen turned to him. "Unless what?"

Martinez turned to check the back seat to make sure Clifford was asleep. "Unless, he doesn't go. It will be very disappointing to him, I am afraid."

"You mean there *is* a chance he wouldn't be able to… fall through his shadow? After all this?"

"Si. Many times the borders deny passage for the young ones. It's all based on maintaining the balance between worlds."

"My God! After all Cliffy has been through?"

"Si. I'm sure he has an idea by now. His new friends have probably let him in on that part. I noticed he seemed very thoughtful at dinner."

"I don't know whether to be upset, or happy about this," Gwen said.

"We will know soon enough," Martinez concluded.

"So, today, what can we expect? I assume the Travelers walk outside at noon and 'poof,' they disappear?"

"No. That might be a bit unnerving to passing bystanders," he chuckled. "There are places, hidden places, we go to."

"I see. Are they far?"

"No, very close. Not far from the monument there is a small museum located directly on the equator."

"You mean the monument isn't actually *on* the equator?"

"No. The monument was constructed before modern global positioning technology, and in a place that was most convenient to development and tourist access. It is close enough though to pass for legitimate. The museum is most accurately placed thanks to modern GPS and, of course, input by our friend The Optometrist."

"This is a big tourist time, with the Equinox celebration and all. Isn't this an official holiday here? Any way, won't the museum be packed too?"

"Si. But we have a private wing, secluded from the tourists."

"Okay, that's good then," Gwen said, "Does this museum have a gift shop?"

"Si, Miss Gwen… of course. Why?"

"Because," she sighed, "I'll have to buy Cliffy a really nice gift to soften his disappointment if, you know, he doesn't go."

Martinez just chuckled.

Gwen had guided the half asleep boy into his bedroom and tucked him in. She now sat, propped up in her own bed, crushingly tired but not ready for sleep. She recounted the evening's stirring events. It had been a marvelous evening, good food, drink and company, especially

Scott Fillmore. She had never spent time with any man who had stimulated her quite as much as Scott had, both mentally and emotionally.

Sure, she had boyfriends in the past, the best one when she had been attending college. At least that one had more of a scholarly edge to him. The rest had been more about physical attraction than intellectual enrichment. Those relationships had been brief though. Then there came her years with Clifford.

For five years Clifford had been her life, and her selfless focus. There had been no romantic relationships since then. She hadn't even been out on a date in all those years.

And now, her life was about to change drastically. Clifford was cured of his shadow phobia, for now. (Who knew what she would see at the day's conclusion. A very bad experience could put him right back in the dark.) There was a very good chance that, option one: he would want to attend regular school back in Pittsburgh or, option two: resume traveling the world, our world, with his parents. In option two, would she remain his private teacher? The former option would most certainly put her out of a job.

She had begun teaching Cliffy as soon as she had graduated from Duquesne University. Where could she go if Clifford opted to attend public schools? Pursue a career in public education or something more dramatic like a total relocation?

If Clifford did become a regular "Traveler," he would need to live near the equator wouldn't he? Where would that leave her? His part time chaser and of course teacher, that's where. That wouldn't be so bad. Quito, from what she saw of it, seemed a nice enough place to live. She would have to brush up on her Spanish. And the best part of this scenario was that she would be close to Scott Fillmore. Scott had told her that he lived here in Quito, hadn't he? Yes this would be nice, but what about Clifford's mother, Dottie?

Her momentary reflection of life with Clifford crumbled to ash. Clifford was her sister's child, not hers. Wouldn't Dottie insist on having her son back? Sure she would. And then, there was this business of "traveling." How would Dottie take that?

Gwen could just see her sister inflicting years of intense therapy on Clifford in order to cure him of this latest malady. Dottie worked in hard science. This stuff would never be accepted without a major battle. This scenario, she concluded, would bring her right back to Pittsburgh.

Suddenly this outcome became unacceptable to her mind. How could she... no, both she and Clifford, go back to that life? Nope, going backwards just seemed impossible at this point. But of course, if this thing didn't happen today, where would *that* put them?

Gwen got up from her bed, walked across the darkened study, and leaned on Clifford's door frame for a moment watching him sleep. *The child was so dear to her. How could they ever separate?* She blew him a kiss, returned to her room and turned out the lights.

She slept for about two hours before she was awakened by the distant rumble of the Land Rover's engine and the sound of the garage door opening.

Chapter Ten
Voices of Concern

The call had come at 3:45 A.M., waking Martinez from a deep sleep. He had been summoned to an emergency meeting at The Optometrist's house, which was not a frequent occurrence. In fact, he could remember this happening no more than three times in the past seven years, all in close procession following Clifford Tuttle's first journey. The first was to alert him to Clifford Tuttle's imminent arrival in Quito, the second to brief him of the aftermath of Clifford's untimely visit, and the third to brief him of the outcome of the short lived war that ensued. He was certain that, given the timing of Clifford Tuttle's recent return to the equator, this was again going to be about this remarkable boy.

The Optometrist lived in a converted five story commercial office building in the center of Quito. The building itself was unremarkable. You would forget it in a minute if you had even noticed it at all. Inside was a different story. The subterranean floors were made up of a small parking level and the Optometrist's workshops. The street level housed a tired looking souvenir shop and the offices of the ghost tour business. The second and third floors held his living quarters. The fifth floor, where Martinez now stood waiting, was decked out like a futuristic starship. For all he knew, the entire fifth floor could just lift off from the rest of the building and shoot into outer space. He could see The Optometrist working at a control panel inside a secure glass room in the center of the space, but the tall alien had to this point, rudely ignored Martinez's arrival. Shortly he beckoned him in.

"Buenos dias, my friend," Martinez greeted as he was finally admitted to the secure room and sealed in.

"Martinez. Good you could come."

"Did I have a choice?"

"No," The Optometrist said flatly.

"And this is about?"

"Clifford Edward Tuttle."

"Si, of course," Martinez said as he suppressed a yawn.

"The Consortium knows that Clifford Tuttle has become aware of his powers. They are… watchful."

"Certainly, they don't think—"

"They do! And for good reason, Martinez!"

Martinez scoffed, "Seven years ago a six year old boy fell through his shadow. He was *a child*. He is *still* a child. The consequent disturbance could not be assumed the responsibility of this one child. It was mere coincidence, my friend."

"Maybe yes, maybe no. It was a sudden, significant

insurgence in a time of protracted peace. Of this 'one child,' there have always been suspicions."

"What power could this child possibly hold that would draw out such a thing? I still believe this to be coincidence."

"Believe what you may, Martinez. The Consortium believes what they may. They win!"

"What do you believe, mi amigo?"

"Poof! What I believe makes no difference," The Optometrist said waving him off.

"On the contrary, what *you* believe makes *all* the difference."

"So be it," The Optometrist relented. "The facts, Martinez: The boy fell through at a remarkably young age. The boy was astonishingly rescued far from any mecca. The boy was recovered by *and* lost in *three worlds* before he finally was expelled into your hands. The boy was last detained in the very mecca on Arris in which the insurgency erupted *exactly* seven and a half of your years ago. Coincidence? Maybe. Does the Consortium have need for caution? YES!"

"As always, mi amigo, you have a point."

"Of course I do! I tell you, Martinez, vigilance! Poof! We will see today if history repeats itself."

"The boy may not even go. Few of his age do."

At that moment the light in the security chamber dimmed as the surrounding transparent glass became opaque. At the same moment the Optometrist was bathed in laser light. Martinez stepped back to the glass wall.

The air above the large, round glass table that dominated the center of the room flickered to life and four nearly full size holographic figures stood before them. The first, from Earth, Johanna Rassahmie, was human. The second, Sackus Rhue, was of Skyloumia, the air world. His balloon-like form, resembling a giant sea flea, hovered above the table. The third, Teunnept, was of Aquan, the water world. He had the head of a seahorse, the torso of a man and below his waist, the tail of a fish. Merman jumped instantly to mind. And finally the fourth, Sedent O, was of Arris, the crystalline world. His appearance was most disturbing as a large, disembodied head. All were the four worlds' top Consortium leaders. The Optometrist or as he was called on his home world, Optomeetruss, was the representative of Cygnus, the fifth world. Notably absent was the representative from the sixth world, Drake 2, the boycotted planet that gave birth to the insurgency seven years ago.

"Greetings Consortium," The Optometrist began, "Before we start, I have here, the boy's mentor, Martinez."

The four nodded, indicating that Martinez may stay.

"That said... how may I be of assistance?" The Optometrist asked with uncharacteristic humility.

Sedent O spoke first. "It is understood by the Consortium that the Earth child, Clifford Edward Tuttle has become aware. Am I correct, Optomeetruss?"

"This is correct, O. He is aware," replied The Optometrist.

"He will travel on this equinox, yes?" Sedent O continued.

"The borders hold sway in this determination, as always… But travel, he most likely will. His shadow has proven able."

Teunnept, from Aquan spoke up. "As this boy may travel to Skyloumia, he must be contained there, Rhue. Clifford Tuttle must be studied to determine his future as a Traveler. He has already demonstrated powers beyond all others his age. Does the Consortium have your guarantee? Will Tuttle be contained?"

Sackus Rhue nodded, "He will be contained, by all means. I might suggest Clifford Tuttle enjoy a very, shall we say, *brief* visit, if indeed the borders allow him through in the first place."

Sedent O spoke in. "That may not be enough to settle the voice of the Consortium body. How speak you, Johanna? Can this boy of Earth be deterred from your equator?"

Rassahmie held out her arms and shrugged, "Yes, I can demand this today," she said and dropped her arms and clasped her hands before her breasts, "But forever? No." She shook her head. "Clifford Edward Tuttle is aware and the equator offers an infinite circle of possibilities. I speak on behalf of the Earth body. Here, now, we see him. There is a degree of control. Let him go, if the borders permit, watch him, study him… make it a short visit and put him off the equator for another six Earth months. We will see what Sackus Rhue's Skyloums can glean from this boy's examination. We will see if Clifford Edward Tuttle should be put off the equatorial zone permanently… or *neutralized* all together."

Martinez staggered backwards, "What?!"

Chapter Eleven
The Equinox

Gwen was seated at the island counter in Martinez's kitchen when he arrived back home. It was 5:10 A.M.. He looked extremely tired. His normal smile was absent, and that missing piece made him look much older.

"Miss Gwen. Buenos dias," he said with as much brightness as he could manage. "I did not take you for an early riser."

"I'm not, if I can help it. Would you like some coffee?" she asked as she poured.

"Si. Gracias," he replied and took a seat across from her.

"I heard you leave very early this morning," she said. "Is everything all right?"

"Si, it is now. I went to see our tall friend. There is nothing to worry about," he lied. Just last minute preparations–" he trailed off, revealing some hidden information with his tone."

"Is this about Clifford?" she asked pointedly.

"No," he lied again with a dismissive wave.

Gwen eyed him with growing suspicion. She knew he was hiding something but could tell by the tone of the "no" that she would get nothing more from him, at least for now.

Martinez sipped his coffee, "Clifford is still asleep?"

"Yes. The poor kid was knocked out last night."

"Si. Swimming in the pool has lasting effects. I expect you will have to wake him before he misses the high sun."

Gwen smirked. "Not Cliffy. He is an early riser. I imagine he will be up any minute. So, what is this pool? Cliffy mentioned taking a swim last night but he was dry when he came back."

"The pool is one of our tall friend's creations. The waters hold knowledge, and as our young ones swim, the knowledge is absorbed. I can say little else about it. The pool was conceived long after I could consider myself a youth."

"Wow. The perfect teaching tool." Gwen thought aloud.

"Si," he agreed chuckling. "A tool like that could put all you teachers out of a job, wouldn't it? But its instruction is not what you would call practical learning in the sense of reading, writing, mathematics and science. The knowledge is more on the primal end of the learning scale. You see, Miss Gwen, we are of the Earth. Thousands of years have instilled in us a certain amount of primal instinct. We are born with it. What the pool teaches are those instincts native to other worlds. This is deep knowledge. These lucky children have an advantage over us older travelers. I suppose in your terminology, you could call this a 'head start program.'"

"That's pretty amazing," she said at a loss for more words. Her silence lingered as she watched Martinez finish his coffee.

She spoke again, leaving the last line of conversation behind. "You look tired, Martinez. You should try to get some rest."

"Si. A few hours will do," he said getting up. His spry manner of the days before had deserted him. "Wake me at 9:00 if I am not up."

At 8:45 Martinez stood in the doorway of the adjoining guest study, clean, dressed and looking more like himself. Gwen, who was immersed in the writings contained in the journal of Scott Fillmore, looked up, startled by his silent arrival.

"I see Senõr Fillmore's study has captivated your fancy, Miss. Gwen."

Gwen smiled. "He is a fascinating man."

"He is more than that I suspect, if you don't mind my saying so," he said with a wink. "You two seemed to get on quite well last night." His eyes twinkled with delight.

"Well, yeah," she said, blushing. "in an academic sort of way."

Martinez chuckled knowingly, "It is time to rouse our young Traveler. We must get started."

Clifford had a very difficult time getting started despite the looming events of the day. He remained dazed and blurry right up to the time they climbed into Martinez's Land Rover. His curiosity was finally roused when he saw Martinez place magnetized signs on the front doors of the Rover, identifying them as the Global Geotechnical Research Institute.

"What's that for?" Clifford asked.

"Cover, Clifford," he replied with a wink and a smile.

When they arrived at the museum Martinez drove around to the back of the complex and parked under a wide shading canopy. There were other vehicles too, similarly equipped, and marked as their Land Rover. Also parked there was a tour bus that looked a lot like one of the ghost tour buses Clifford had seen at the monument the night before, except the Global Geotechnical Research Institute logo covered all evidence of that.

"Here we are, Clifford. Are you excited?" Martinez asked.

"Yes, and a few more things," he said swallowing hard. "Is there a bathroom here?" Clifford could feel the cold sweat breaking out all over his body. "I really have to go!"

"Si, Clifford." Martinez's expression was serious. "Let's get you inside."

Clifford stepped out of the Rover with the apprehension of someone testing the temperature of a cold pool. To his relief, he did not feel the ground shift beneath his feet.

"Come, Clifford. This way."

Gwen slipped a supporting arm around Clifford's

back and they followed Martinez into the building. Inside they found a comfortable lounge area where others gathered and snacked on the refreshment provided on a buffet counter.

"Here you are, Clifford." Martinez said handing him a black gym bag. "Inside are your goggles and some appropriate clothing. Your restroom is over there. Take care of what you need to take care of and get dressed. We will wait here."

Clifford wove his way through the now familiar attendees on his way to the restroom. He picked out Scott Fillmore -Aunt Gwen would be thrilled- and Dr. Camilla. Some of the older kids he had seen the night before were pigging out at the buffet table. Somehow the idea of eating anything made him feel queasier, if that was possible. The butterflies were dancing with wild abandon inside his guts.

Tearing his eyes away from the piled food, he turned to enter the youth men's restroom and ran flat into Travis' chest.

"Whoa there, Casper! Watch where you're going, dude," he said and smirked. "What's the hurry? Got the pre-race runs?"

Travis, who seemed even taller and more intimidating this morning, was dressed in a sharp looking jump suit.

"Sorry. I didn't see you there." Clifford excused himself and moved past quickly but not before noticing the jerk's green pallor.

Clifford met Marco inside. He was in the process of

slipping into his own jumpsuit.

"Hola! Hey Bro! You ready?"

"Yeah, I guess as ready as I will ever be." Clifford said as he shot an involuntary glance at the row of three toilet stalls. Two, he noticed were occupied.

"I'd give that one a minute or so to clear. Travis just dropped a bomb in there." Marco warned.

Immediately, Clifford's stomach anxiety diminished. "Really?"

"Oh yeah!" Marco grinned, and then grew serious. "It's okay to be nervous. I don't care who you are. Don't take anybody's crap. We all get it." The smirk returned to his face. "I feel sorry for the dude in two," he concluded, poking a thumb at the second stall.

Clifford felt a new vitality wash over him. This wasn't so bad, knowing that everyone else was in the same boat.

Avoiding the first stall for the moment, on good advice, he set his mind to getting dressed. He hoped that Martinez had packed him one of the cool jumpsuits and he was not disappointed. Inside the gym bag he found the jumpsuit, socks, shoes, gloves and a small back pack that held his new goggles and ear buds. There were other supplies in there as well: Three Cliff Bars, two bottles of water and several packets of what looked like flavor powder. The meager supplies gave him pause. Not much for an extended period of time. He reluctantly remembered Shelly's description of her first trip. *"It seemed like it was over before it started."*

He put this thought aside and got undressed. The

jumpsuit was nice, unremarkable except for the cloth which stretched from the inside of his arms to the side of his torso. He immediately thought *wings* and that did make sense, considering the inevitable flight through the sky place. "This is so cool."

He finished dressing and moved in front of the mirror. He slipped the goggles out of their pack and placed them on his face for the full effect.

"I look like a superhero," he said beaming a confident smile.

He hit the john for a quick pee (that was all) then headed out into the lounge area where the majority of the attendees were now dressed in similar jump suits.

Shelly and Tasha found Clifford before he found them. If it weren't for the startling color of Shelly's hair, he would never have recognized her. She was plain faced, still pretty, but looking much younger, more like a fifteen year old. Also absent were her pierced studs. Her shocking copper red hair hung straight without the support of the numerous bobby pins.

"Bonjour, Cliff! Looking good!" she sang in greeting as she looked him up and down.

"You too... I don't think I would have recognized you-"

Shelly suddenly looked hurt. "Disappointed?"

Clifford shook his head vigorously. "No! I mean... just... with out your makeup and all... Don't get me wrong you still look great!" He said this with so much sincerity that Shelly brightened immediately.

"Yep. This is me, in the raw. My mentor disapproves of 'my look' and there's something about my metal studs. They might fry my brain on reentry or something." Her forehead wrinkled in thought and then she smiled mischievously. She patted her back pack. "I'm packing though."

"How are you doin', Cliff?" Tasha butted in. Her ever smiling eyes shifted back and forth between Shelly and Clifford.

"I'm good. Really good," Clifford nodded.

"Not at all nervous?" Tasha asked, raising an eyebrow.

"Oh, yes I am," he admitted freely. "But not as nervous as Travis though." He said and nodded toward the men's lounge and pinched his nose with his fingers.

Shelly and Tasha looked confused.

Clifford smirked, "I won't go there."

The light of understanding suddenly went on in their eyes and they both laughed, Tasha, of course more energetically.

"So what's next? he asked them.

"Well, we wait." Tasha replied. "They'll tell us when to go out in the sun. We go outside and wait some more."

You mean it doesn't just happen as soon as the sun casts your shadow?" Clifford asked.

"Some time passes first. I don't know why, but when it does happen—"

"Sometimes it doesn't happen at all," Travis interrupted. He was looking right at Clifford. He was flanked by Dan the surfer dude and Andrea, the blonde babe. Marco and Christa moved past the three and joined Clifford, Shelly, and Tasha.

Clifford straightened up with pent-up resolve. "We'll all see when it happens," he said with a flat but strong voice.

"Oh, we'll see *you* when we get back, Casper."

Clifford felt his rage grow exponentially but before he could say or do anything, Martinez was at his side.

"Come on Clifford. It's nearly time to go."

Gwen ripped herself away from Scott Fillmore and came running over. "Look at you!" she exclaimed, "You look so cool in that jumpsuit! You look just like an astronaut!"

Suddenly tears welled up in her eyes. She looked pleadingly at Martinez. "Is it time?"

"Si, Miss Gwen. It is almost time."

Gwen fell to her knees and looked tearfully up into Clifford's face. "You come back, you hear?" She gave him a wet faced kiss on the cheek.

"Aw, Aunt Gwen! Cut it out! You're getting me all wet!" He reached in and gave her a big hug. "Don't worry. I'll be back before you know it." Then Clifford got a mischievous look on his face. "You better hurry. I bet Scott Fillmore could use one of those wet kisses before he goes too."

The short wait that followed seemed an eternity to Clifford. He followed Martinez into a dark, curving corridor with heavily shuttered windows on the inside wall. He was trailed closely by Shelly, Tasha, Marco and Christa along with their mentors.

Martinez was the only mentor not dressed in a jump suit and this made Clifford feel a stab of regret for the old man. They stopped when they met the group coming around from the other side of the circular corridor.

"This is it, Clifford, the moment for which you have waited."

"Or dreaded," Clifford replied in a weak and shaky voice. His entire body seemed to be trembling involuntarily.

Martinez kneeled down in front of Clifford so he could look him straight in the eye. He studied him closely before he finally spoke. "What ever happens now, you will be all right. Do not forget, my young Traveler, you have done this before and you have *no* idea of what jeopardy you surmounted then... *and* survived."

There was a mechanical sound accompanied by the rolling up of the heavy window shades. The brilliant sunlight flooded in around their feet then grew in strength as the shades completed their recoiling cycle. Clifford was blinded at first and then the scene of a large round inner courtyard surrounded by arched openings filtered in. Clifford could see the others waiting in the shadow of the covered corridor across the way. Slowly the adults and mentors began making their orderly way out onto the sunlit ground. Their goggles gleamed magnificently in the sunlight. Clifford's eyes were immediately drawn to their feet where he could see the stunted pools of their dark shadows. They stopped and crouched, one knee down, in what looked like a runner's ready stance. Still they did not fall. They all nodded indicating that the younger Travelers could come forward.

Martinez gave Clifford's shoulders a reassuring squeeze from behind and backed away.

Clifford turned and gave his mentor one last confident nod then turned toward his other four companions. "Let's do this!" he said. They all placed their goggles on their faces and spontaneously took up each others hands in a show of mutual unity. "Yeah, let's do this!" they all repeated.

Clifford watched Travis step boldly into the sun, march out to his place and kneel. His group, now diminished to Dan and Andrea, followed on his heels.

An instant later Clifford and his friends, hand in hand, stepped out onto the glowing earth. The five had a second's time to look wide eyed into Clifford's dark and wildly vibrating shadow before all light was extinguished.

Chapter Twelve
Catastrophe

The ground inside the courtyard rippled violently, radiating in fluid, concentric rings outward from where the five children had been standing seconds before. Those standing staggered and fell. The kneeling adults toppled from their stances. The rolling concussion struck the foundations of the circular walkway with structure damaging force. Plaster ceilings cracked and rained debris onto the remaining people in the lounge area.

Gwen had been watching the proceedings through a large plate glass window when the shock wave hit. The glass exploded into millions of diamond size shards before her startled eyes.

Martinez saw Clifford and the other four vanish seconds before he was blasted into the wall behind. He now lay stunned on the floor.

Back in the guise of Diminutive T. Little, The Optometrist, who had been observing from his private room, gained his balance quickly and raised an iconic

Spock eyebrow. He watched the others pick themselves up off the ground then he turned to a console that had automatically folded out of the wall. He put his large, but slender hand, palm down on the screen. A green light flashed and he removed it. Almost instantly a doll sized hologram of Sackus Rhue hovered above the screen.

"Rhue. We have a problem."

A stunned silence followed the catastrophe, and then mild panic set in. The adult Travelers and the mentors began to rush the younger ones out of the sun. Most of the young ones, still in shock, complied, but Travis held his ground. He checked his shadow and to his dismay saw that it had lightened considerably.

"What is this shit?!" Travis shouted. He stomped the ground violently three times before he gave up and knelt on the ground.

Travis' mentor, a man named Dominic Holden, strode back out into the sun and knelt along side his pupil. As he knelt he too saw that the depth of his shadow had diminished. "Come out of the sun Travis."

"No, I won't!" he snarled.

"Son, it's over." he looked around, "Apparently for all of us."

Shortly, many of the others ventured back out into the sun. It was the same for all of them. Their power of travel had been stripped away.

Inside, Gwen frantically shook the glass bits and plaster debris from her hair and clothes as if she was being attacked by bees. Feeling something wet on her forehead she wiped at it with the back of her hand. It came away smeared with blood, but that was the least of her worries.

"Clifford?" she called. Her voice, at first, held little power. "Clifford!" This time her voice was back. She scanned the chaotic scene at and around the court yard. Clifford was nowhere to be seen. She stepped quickly through the opening that once was a window and jogged across the courtyard to the place where Clifford and his friends had vanished. She spun around in dizzy circles looking into all the arched openings to no avail. Her eyes finally lighted on Martinez who was still reclined in a daze against the far wall. She ran to him shoving stunned Travelers out of her way as she went. When she reached him she pulled him forcibly up into a seated position.

"Martinez! Are you alright?" she shouted into his face.

"Si. I think so." He replied.

"Good! Now where's Clifford?" she growled.

"Gone," he said simply. "He and his companions went through."

He looked befuddled as he said this and Gwen could see his eyes fluttering as if he was going to pass out.

"I *know* they're gone! I saw them disappear!" she shouted in his face. "Stay with me, Martinez!" she snarled.

His eyes fluttered open again. "Yeah, yeah, I'm here. Jesus, my head-" he muttered. His eyes fluttered shut again.

"Wake up, Martinez, and listen to me! I'm looking around here and I'm seeing a lot of confused people! What happened just now?" She shook him by his collar. "The way I see it, this isn't normal! This is something bad!"

Martinez roused himself enough to take a look around. "The others… they are still here?"

"No one went except for Clifford and his friends! And get this: the rest are all talking about their shadows. It seems they've lost them!"

"Extraordinary," he said as he tried and failed to stand.

Suddenly Gwen sensed a presence behind her. She turned and looked up at the soaring figure of Diminutive T. Little. Gathered behind him were the mentors Gwen had seen escorting Clifford's friends.

"Are you quite alright, Martinez?" The Optometrist asked.

"Do I look alright to you, mi amigo?" Martinez groaned.

The Optometrist kneeled down then bent further over to touch Martinez's face. He held his hand there for a moment, and then pulled back. "You will be all right. That is more than I can say of my wall. Your head must be as hard as a bowling ball. Now get up. Your head has been fixed."

Martinez, with Gwen at his elbow, got stiffly but steadily to his feet.

Gwen waited a moment to make sure Martinez was truly stabilized then turned on The Optometrist. "Maybe *you* can tell me what's happened here," she said stormily.

"My dear Miss Gwen, that is precisely what I intend to find out," he said in a calm and confident tone.

"You mean *you* don't even know?! Aren't you supposed to be the mastermind here?!"

"I will have to confess my… puzzlement." he replied simply.

Chapter Thirteen
Free Fall

They burst into the wide open air of Skyloumia after a protracted time in pitch darkness. Christa, who had not stopped screaming since they dropped into darkness, suddenly ceased, momentarily struck dumb by the vast emptiness of the place. It took only moments before this new terror set in. Miraculously, (and to the relief of the others) Christa's gel goop had deployed from her goggles, silencing her for the time.

Clifford took a quick count and found that all five of them had made it. Marco and Shelly, having experienced this several times before were relatively placid and Tasha, who had never been, seemed to be holding it together. None of their goggle gels had deployed. Christa however was flailing wildly and falling behind.

Marco had taken notice of this and was using the wing flaps in his jumpsuit to slow his momentum. Soon he had her. He wrapped his arms around her and got them into a more aerodynamic posture. Soon the two caught up with the others. Holding Christa with one arm he motioned to the others to fly in closer.

Clifford, who had been dropping without the aid of the wing suit, tried to readjust using the flaps and immediately began to cork screw. Shelly, attached to Tasha, adjusted their course with practiced agility and cruised up next to Clifford. She grabbed his arm to steady him then did a quick, silent demonstration for the two.

It took the two some time to master the rudiments of the wing maneuvers but soon they were able to control the falls on their own.

Marco, with Christa who had regained her fragile composure, floated in to join the other three. He pointed to a place on the side of his goggles, and then pushed a hidden button there. In an instant three lines of the gel deployed from the goggles. Two reached and engulfed his ears and one reached his mouth and covered it with a solid looking bubble. Clifford and the others did the same. Now they could communicate.

"Is everyone alright?" Marco asked in a commanding voice.

They all nodded, Christa more weakly.

"Good. Now we all need to slow down. Easy, now. Spread your arms until you just begin to feel air drag. If you open up too far we'll lose you. Got it?"

They all nodded.

"Okay. On my mark... Now."

There was a moment of total disorganization then they all began to stabilize and slow.

"Awesome, mi amigos! Now we need to slow more. Open up further now." They all did in a more controlled manner this time. Soon they were all fully extended and catching plenty of air drag.

This accomplished, Marco turned to Clifford. "Cliff. What is up with that shadow of yours, bro? You opened up way to soon, man, and I think you dragged us all in with you."

Clifford shook his head, "I don't know. It just happened."

"All I know is that we went through way too fast. We usually have to wait. It never happens that fast."

"I don't understand." Clifford said.

"This is how it always happens: first the adults go out, then us. We wait while the sun begins its pass. There is a metal line that cuts through the courtyard following the equator exactly. You see this gleam start to move along the metal as the sun comes overhead. It takes minutes. As the gleam comes across people start to fall through. The thing has to be timed perfectly."

"Or what?" Clifford asked.

"I think it has something to do with the position of the Terminal."

Clifford had a moment of pure dread as the reality of the situation dawned on him. "So, we are too early."

"Si," Marco said with grim voice.

Since she had calmed some, Christa's gel had retracted and she was breathing normally. "What does this mean?!" she shrieked.

Marco searched the sky. He shook his head. "I don't know. I think we're screwed."

Shelly, who had been silent thus far, spoke up, "Where are the others? I mean, shouldn't they be right behind us?" Her voice shook with anxiety.

"Oh my God! We're going to d-!" Christa shrieked. Her last word was cut short by the redeployment of the goggle gel.

Marco did a quick maneuver to turn his back to the fall and Clifford, less gracefully, did the same. Both boys searched the space from which they had fallen.

Clifford was awestruck by what he saw. The border from which they had emerged appeared like an endless dome of white and blue flame, like looking at the sun inside out but not as bright. It looked very hot but the apparent radiance did not register in his skin.

"Wow! I don't remember seeing that before!" Clifford exclaimed.

"Si. You were focused on what you were falling toward. I know. I didn't look up on my first fall either," Marco assured him as he continued to search the flaming expanse for the telltale peppering of the other flyer's forms. "I can't see anyone! Cliff, you?"

"No! Where are they?" Clifford replied after a long search. The goggles, he knew, produced inhumanly good eyesight. Despite this he could not pick out anything.

"Jesus, Cliff, we're the only ones who came through."

Shelly's voice shrilled, "I can't see the Terminal anywhere! Where is it Marco?!"

Marco and Clifford readjusted their flight position to face down again.

They all searched. There were intermittent cloud groupings far off in every direction.

"Look," Marco said. "Each one of those big cloud banks is what they call 'mecca's'. That's where they live, like in cities."

Clifford somehow knew this, though he had never been told.

"The Terminal is near to one of them, but there are so many!" Shelly said as she shot glances in every direction. "Which one is it?"

Suddenly Christa shouted, "Look! Over there!"

They all followed her stare. There, before the backdrop of a great, distant cloud bank, was a pinpoint of black.

"That's it!" Marco shouted.

"It's too far away!" Shelly screamed. "We're going to miss it!"

"Come on! Follow me!" Marco barked.

He readjusted his trajectory toward the tiny spot. The others followed, a bit more clumsily.

They were really moving now– the speed perceptible by the way the skin of their faces pressed tight against their skulls. The space between them and the tiny speck was so vast that their progress toward it seemed indiscernible. Still, they cut through the sky like projectiles.

The black dot was now nearly parallel with their trajectory.

"This isn't good!" Marco shouted. "We're going to

miss it if we don't level out! But that will slow us down! We slow down, we drop!"

Clifford's eyes searched the place below, fearful of the first glimpse of their reflections off the mirror surface he knew awaited them. Still, to his tentative relief, he could see nothing.

They followed Marco into a more level trajectory and noticed the slowing immediately.

"How much longer before we-" Clifford asked.

"Before we hit the ground?" Marco finished. "I don't know. I never got close enough to even see it," Marco replied, "if there is any," he concluded, somehow knowing there was something but having never been told of it.

"There is something," Clifford said. "I've seen it."

They all looked at their target point that was now rising above their parallel then looked down.

"We have missed it," Christa's voice sounded hopeless. "We are going to die…"

"No we aren't!" Clifford said with feigned certainty. "They will catch us. They won't let us die."

They continued to fly, still aiming at their target, or now the empty space below it. The point of darkness had grown perceptively but they were still far off their mark. They continued to fly, each holding on to their silent hopes that Clifford was right about an impending rescue.

Christa was the first to see the pin point of darkness below them. "Look!" she shrieked, "I see something! There!"

They followed her gaze.

"Is that another Terminal?" Tasha screamed with relief.

Clifford's heart seemed to drop dead in his chest. "No. That's the ground."

Tasha and Christa wailed miserably as Shelly moved in and touched shoulders with Clifford. She didn't have to say a word. He knew she knew they were going to die and she wanted to be close to him. They looked into each others eyes then cast their gazes to their fast growing reflections below.

Suddenly, five arcing vapor trails on an intersection course raced in from the vicinity of the Terminal. They were moving so fast that the five despairing young Travelers never saw them until they were caught.

Chapter Fourteen
Action Must Be Taken

Gwen paced the second floor bedroom in the Optometrist's home. Martinez had reclined on the bed with his head propped on an uncomfortably, lumpy bag of ice. The Optometrist had repaired his concussion damaged brain but the superficial wounds were what pained him now. He had closed his eyes to block out Gwen's relentless movement– this and the broad array of pains his body was experiencing had raked his nerves raw.

"Adverbio por favor, Miss Gwen. Rest your self," Martinez groaned. "He is doing all he can."

Gwen paced back to the comfortable chair in the corner, crossed her arms across her chest, and sat. "I'm sorry, Martinez. I can't seem to help it. Why is it taking so long? It's what," she checked the screen on her cell phone, "an hour since Clifford disappeared?" She rose up out of the chair again.

"Gwen, sit por favor," he growled.

She sat. "An hour! There has to be something wrong!"

"An hour, Si, but you must understand that we are dealing with travel between different worlds. Clifford is not just lost in a mall. Besides, this event is unusual."

Gwen snorted. "Unusual? That's putting it lightly."

The Optometrist stood before the holograph table inside the safe room on the fifth floor. The holographic images of the four Consortium leaders flickered before his alien eyes. He addressed Sedent O, Arris' Consortium leader, "This boy, we know, possesses extraordinary traveling powers, O. At age six he falls through alone. At age fourteen he falls through, this time he takes four young Travelers with him, and much more. There is no way of telling for certain if all four would have fallen as individuals. Perhaps they would have anyway, fine. Perhaps, not. The ramifications are serious. Non Travelers could possibly travel with the aid of this boy's shadow. More serious yet is Clifford Tuttle's ability to disable other Travelers around him. All who were within 250 square meters of this boy's shadow were affected."

Sedent O spoke, "Is this affect permanent?"

"It has been one hour, Earth time. None of the affected Travelers have recovered yet."

"Very serious indeed," Sedent O mused.

At that moment Sackus Rhue bent as in covering with an unseen entity then straightened. "We have Clifford Tuttle and his four companions!"

"Excellent, Rhue," Sedent O said curtly. "Take Clifford Tuttle and his companions into Consortium custody. Lock them up in a very dark place.

Chapter Fifteen
On the Terminal

At last, Clifford, Marco, Shelly and Tasha had their feet on solid ground. Christa had moved beyond feet on the ground to entire body on the ground. She had fainted dead away as soon as her rescuer had deposited her safely onto the Terminal's flight deck. Clifford was the first person she saw as she woke. To her traumatized mind Clifford's pale white face, haloed in dark hair, before a backdrop of flaming blue sky, looked like an angel.

"Am I dead?" she asked with a tremble in her voice.

Clifford smiled. He could definitely relate to her condition.

Shelly's face floated into her vision. "No. You just fainted, silly," Shelly said.

Christa looked around. Her deep, brown eyes had, for the time, come back into focus. She found one of the strange creatures that had rescued her, floating off to the side.

It was large and looked like a weird, insect shaped

water balloon. Its skin appeared to be a translucent membrane over a bluish green milky interior. Its head was tucked on its shoulders and elongated by what appeared to be an integrated crest that molded into its back. Its face came to a point where its mouth was. There was nothing resembling a nose on its smooth face. Its two eyes were made up of a cluster of nine luminous spots each, which seemed to float just under the thing's translucent membranous skin. Its fat arms protruded from where a human's ears would be and terminated in human like hands that held five fat digits each. The palms of its hands appeared to be hollow and expelled a constant hiss of air that stabilized its posture as it floated above the deck. The torso was large on the top then tapered gradually down to its hips. The torso was unproportionally long for the length of its stunted legs. Despite the leg's relative dimensions, they were still as long as an adult human's legs. The legs ended without what you would call feet. Instead, there were five tubular extremities that merged out from the shins and calves, pointing downward. The extremities seemed to work in harmony like booster rockets to keep the thing afloat. Its body was completely naked but the translucent skin was decorated in tattoos.

Suddenly, Christa felt the faint returning.

"You're going to be fine Christa," Clifford said and helped her up to a seated position.

From this vantage point Christa could take in a bigger picture. There were, in addition to her four friends, five Skyloums. Beyond them, towered the huge cylindrical

Terminal with many protruding structures. Beyond the structure was the vast sky, powdered here and there with large, static cloudbanks. Thin vapor trails crisscrossed the space between them like filaments in a giant spider's web.

Christa saw that one of the Skyloums had come forward and seemed to be speaking to her but its voice came out sounding like puffs of air.

Shelly pulled Christa's backpack open and produced a small silver tube, unscrewed the lid and slid out two ear plugs.

"Oh, sorry. You need these," she said as she gently placed the plugs in Christa's ears.

Suddenly the puffs turned into words.

"Can you walk, young Traveler?" it spoke.

Christa looked dazed for a moment then got her facilities back on-line.

"Sure… I think I can," she nodded. There was a short delay as she contemplated some sudden, alien thought. She pursed her lips and made a series of puffing noises.

"Very good." The Skyloum seemed to smile and bowed his head in understanding.

Clifford and Shelly helped Christa to her feet.

"Are you okay?" asked Shelly.

"Yeah… Yeah, I'm good," she breathed once she felt she could stand on her own.

"You must come with us now. We must get you inside," it said. Despite the light puffiness of his voice, there was a note of demand there.

A door had opened in the side of the tower and the

Skyloums quickly led them to it. As soon as they entered and the door closed behind them, all hint of an alien world, aside from their escorts, was eradicated. The corridors were bland grey and white with standard Earth familiar finishes. There were no windows to let in the natural light so all illumination was of stark white LED glow.

The five were led along a corridor and up to a bank of elevators. Once inside, the elevator car shot silently upward, stopped and opened up onto a large lobby. The room was furnished spartanly, and to Clifford's disappointment, it was very much like any drab waiting room you could find on Earth.

"You will wait here," the Skyloum puffed briskly, regarding each of them in turn with what appeared to be a stern look. Its strange alien eyes settled on Clifford for a long, uncomfortable moment. Then it turned and floated away, taking with it the two others. The two remaining Skyloums took up their stations at the elevator doors.

Clifford was beginning to feel uneasy. This was nowhere near what he had expected. Admittedly, he had no idea what to expect. How could he know? All he knew was that this didn't seem right.

When he looked at Marco, Marco gave Clifford a confused shrug back.

"Is this right, Marco?" Clifford asked.

"No, Cliff. I never came here," Marco said and shot a glance over at the two Skyloums at the elevators.

"Me either," Shelly put in. "It's like they're guarding us, or something."

"Si," Marco said, "It's like we're in trouble."

"Why would *we* be in trouble?" Tasha hissed, "*They're* the ones who should be in trouble for letting us *almost die* out there!"

Clifford studied their unadorned surroundings. "What's different? You know, from when you were here before?" he asked Marco in a whisper.

"Well… there were always adults with us. That's different. Maybe this is where they bring you if there are no adults," Marco paused in thought. "I remember we came in a different way before. Up near the top of the station, I think. It was fancier. Kind of like the lounge back at the museum. There was a big domed ceiling too so you could see the sky. There were a lot of the Skyloums around too. It was really cool. There was even Earth food and drinks if you wanted. When we stayed, we had rooms close to the clinic. Everything was nicer than this. This is more like, I don't know… before, I just felt more welcome.

Shelly nodded her agreement. "This is nothing like before."

"It's creepy," Christa said. They were the first words she had spoken since they arrived, "I don't like it. I want to go home."

"Soon, Christa," Marco said. "I never stayed here more than a couple days. I think my first time was just a few hours," he smirked, "Talk about disappointed."

"Me too, Christa," said Shelly. I'm sure they'll send us right back because we didn't come with our mentors," she assured her.

Just then a nondescript door opened and two more of the Skyloums came out.

"Come with us," one spoke simply.

If these creatures had the ability to inject warmth into their voices, there was none in this creature's voice. All of a sudden Clifford thought *this is how on duty military personnel would act.*

Clifford and his friends looked at each other. They all wore worried expressions. Even Tasha's normally happy face looked tense. Her eyes focused, and grimly cautious, like those of a trapped animal.

After a guarded moment they slowly got up and obediently followed the two Skyloums back through the nondescript door.

Chapter Sixteen
Clifford is Safe

Gwen rose from her chair as The Optometrist entered the bedroom. "Well?"

The Optometrist blinked his alien eyes at her abrupt tone. He couldn't blame her, of course. Her remarkable nephew truly was in trouble. The Consortium had made its decision. Clifford Edward Tuttle was a danger to the precise balance that existed between the six worlds and beyond.

"The boy is alive and safe," he announced with a small but reassuring smile.

Martinez struggled to an upright position. "When will they send Clifford back?"

There was an unnaturally long pause before The Optometrist spoke again. This gave Gwen pause to think the worst.

"He and his companions are with the Consortium now. I know not when they will release them."

"The Consortium? What is that?" Gwen snapped.

"It is an organization comprised of the leaders of the six worlds, Miss Gwen," Martinez replied. "You could compare it to our United Nations," he added.

"It is a large body of individuals, and, as is the nature of such, there may not be a speedy resolution to this problem," The Optometrist put in.

Martinez scoffed. "Certainly, the Consortium cannot suppose that this one boy is worth the commotion that is being raised."

"I can say nothing for that. Clifford Tuttle is safe for now. This is all I can say," The Optometrist said and turned to leave.

"Excuse me! We are *not* done yet!" Gwen surged forward and grabbed The Optometrist by the arm, but quickly released him as if she had been jolted with electricity. "I need to know exactly where Clifford is. I need to know now!"

"Poof! I can see I will have no peace– Very well, Clifford Tuttle is on the Terminal. It is what you might call a space station. There is no danger there. He is safe." The Optometrist simply stared at Gwen. She appeared to be working herself into a bad temper.

Gwen was just about to launch an attack on The Optometrist when suddenly she received a vision of a large cylindrical structure floating placidly in a vast blue sky. Unexpectedly, her anxiety lessened and she felt compelled to apologize for her outburst. "I'm sorry. It's just that I'm very worried about Clifford. Thank you."

"You are welcome, Miss Gwen." The Optometrist said

in a polite voice. He gave a courteous nod to Martinez, turned to the door and paused. "I will keep you both informed. That is a promise."

After the Optometrist was gone, Gwen turned to Martinez who had remained in an upright position and was looking much better. "I think he put a picture into my mind, of the Terminal. Is he telling the truth? Is Clifford really safe there?"

"Si, Miss Gwen. He is safe there, if not very disappointed." Martinez assured her.

"Disappointed, why?"

"I am afraid the Terminal is not quite the adventure Clifford was hoping for. There is nothing exotic about it. The Terminal is just another piece of Earth, I fear. The views from the reception level are excellent, but considering Clifford's trip down, he has seen plenty of the sky."

Gwen sat back down in her chair. "I can't believe, from what Clifford has told me of this sky place, that it's safe to go there without a parachute or something."

Martinez chuckled merrily then grimaced as if the movement had hurt him. "You would think. But they do have a retrieval process in place. It is what you would call a tractor beam. It is very effective in most cases."

"In most cases?"

"Si. Its range is limited."

"Clifford spoke about being caught and carried by some kind of creature when he was six. I assume this tractor beam was not effective then?"

"No. It was operational then. Timing is important, however. That world, like our own, revolves. The Terminal is in static orbit. It is a small target to hit in a very large world. When Clifford was six, he traveled unexpectedly. He fell far outside the abilities of the tractor beam."

"Jeez! No wonder the poor kid was so frightened. Even at six, he would have known he was falling to his death."

"Si, Miss Gwen."

Gwen paused, deep in thought and then continued, "Clifford and his friends went through early today, didn't they? I mean, the rest were still getting into position. My God! Do you think those poor kids would've been out of range?"

"I believe there is a good chance that they were. But, they are alive and safe," he said brightening. "Why, at this very moment, Clifford and his friends are enjoying the views and experiencing the Skyloum hospitality. I am sure we will be summoned soon to retrieve him. And," he held his finger up, "I am positive, considering what he has been through today, the Consortium will take great measures to return Clifford and his companions in the most accurate way possible."

Chapter Seventeen
Waiting

Clifford and his fellow Travelers were escorted to yet another dreary waiting room and left under guard again. The feeling of the place was becoming more and more like a military base considering the number of staunch sentries they were encountering.

Shelly was biting her lower lip in worry. "Marco? Why are they treating us like this? I'm really starting to get scared."

"I don't know. This is definitely not right," Marco responded.

Christa took in a deep, shaky breath and it was apparent to the others that she was trying very hard not to cry. Tasha slid over and put her arm around Christa's shoulders. She herself was very near tears.

"What have we done wrong?" Christa sniffed.

Clifford had been silent since they were relocated. "It's my fault," he confessed.

He had been pondering their situation and had

landed on the only viable reason he could think of. *My shadow was at fault, somehow.*

Gradually, Clifford had come to realize he had vague memories of being here before. *There must have been trouble back then as well. I had been missing for nearly forty-eight hours.* He recalled Martinez mentioning that time was slightly different in this world. Time moved slower here. *Still, considering this, I could have spent longer here than necessary. That amount of time wouldn't make sense unless something had gone very wrong.*

"Why would this be your fault, mi amigo?" Marco asked, just a little too insincerely.

Marco had had his suspicions. As far as he knew, traveling on the equinoxes always went without a hitch. Three years had passed since he first traveled. He had come and gone three times since, without a single glitch.

Now there was Cliff, a kid who had traveled at an unheard-of age and survived. Clifford Tuttle, the legend.

Before he and his mentor had left for the museum that morning, Marco had asked him about Clifford Tuttle. His mentor had told him that the strange boy was rumored to have had something to do with the short war seven years ago. He had assured Marco, however, that this was all speculation and that it was a sheer coincidence that that visit and the subsequent war correlated chronologically.

This tantalizing speculation had been enough to move Marco to reconsider his alliance with Travis' group. He had been on three uneventful journeys to the Terminal with Travis. The prospect of risk and uncertainty this time appealed more to his reckless side. He had made a solid decision that morning to move over to Clifford Tuttle's side. Now here he was.

Clifford shook his head, "Just a hunch, I guess."

"There are stories about you, Cliff." Tasha interjected. I asked my mentor about you."

The others had huddled in, and all nodded their agreement.

"What stories?" Clifford asked, perplexed.

"That you started a war seven years ago," Shelly said smiling mischievously.

"What war?" Clifford asked as his stomach clenched.

"Something having to do with the Horwrath Soul Eaters," Marco answered.

Clifford frowned, "Martinez mentioned them the other day. My Aunt Gwen almost went ballistic."

"That was just a story, right? Christa said. "Just a co-incidence… that you were there, at the same time, right?" Her pleading eyes settled on each of her friends in turn, and then shifted to Clifford.

Clifford shrugged. "I don't know… I can't remember any of it. It's like my memories were taken away… sort of like after the swim in the pool. There seems to be more to it-" Clifford's voice trailed off.

"Then maybe that's what this is all about," Tasha said. Her eyes were wide with wonder. "Maybe the stories are true!" She shook her head, "Wow, are we in deep crap!"

"Well, mi amigos, at least this isn't boring," Marco remarked.

"I think I would rather be board," Christa said while wringing her hands.

There was renewed movement from the Skyloumian centurions guarding the exit door. It was as if they were preparing for something big. A third Skyloum entered the room. He pointed to Clifford's ear indicating they should reinsert their translator ear buds. The five complied and awaited his orders.

"Come. Sackus Rhue will see you now." The centurion announced, and then moved in closer to the huddled group. It regarded them sternly and continued in what appeared to be hushed confidence. *"Remember this. You must be reverent in the presence of our world's most esteemed Sovereign Leader. You are honored by his audience."*

Clifford stood. The others followed suit. "We will," Clifford agreed. "Is there, like a custom… Should we bow or something? Some cultures on Earth require that, you know."

The Skyloumian appeared to smile. *"If this is a gesture of respect on your world, it would be appropriate here. Yes, very good Clifford Tuttle. Come. We will all join Sackus Rhue."*

Chapter Eighteen
The Sentence

They convened in a well appointed conference room that had no windows. Five chairs had been placed along one side of the table. Five Skyloums hovered on the opposite side. Apparently these beings did not sit. Their escort floated around to join the others. One looked vaguely familiar to Clifford.

The conference table top was like a giant computer screen which shown what Clifford supposed to be the emblem of Skyloumia. Where the others hovered, smaller windows had opened presenting information that Clifford could not read. Suddenly the room came to attention. Clifford and his friends stood in reaction. Shortly Sackus Rhue was introduced. He entered through a hidden panel door that hissed shut and sealed behind him.

Sackus Rhue was as tall as the rest but far broader through the middle. His membrane skin was covered in wrinkles giving him a less translucent appearance than the others. Clifford assumed he was quite a bit older.

Clifford, Shelly, Tasha, Marco and Christa all bowed awkwardly but it appeared to please Sackus Rhue. He gave each a hand gesture that was similar to what a priest would do to bless his faithful. As he did this, gentle puffs of air from his palms ruffled their hair.

Sackus Rhue took a moment to study the five Earth children across the table. His eyes finally lighted on Clifford Tuttle and he thought *such a small child to cause such a stir.*

He had just come from a closed meeting of the Consortium leaders. He had been disturbed by the severity of their discussion. This pale child did indeed have abilities beyond the norm when it came to the Travelers, but to lock the poor child away was far too severe a decision. Certainly Sedent O had reason to be cautious. It was his world that had been affected by that short lived war. Still, the further consideration of using the child as a weapon had gone too far.

"Please sit," Rhue said, indicating the five. *"I believe I speak for all in this room when I say we are sorry for the inconveniences you have suffered here, but considering the circumstances, the Consortium has agreed to err on the side of vigilance. Therefore, it is the Consortium's opinion that Clifford Tuttle be detained until a full evaluation of his abilities can be concluded."*

Clifford's mouth dropped open as his friends gasped.

"Excuse me, Mr. Rhue," Clifford said as politely as his panicked mind would allow, "I haven't done anything wrong. Neither have my friends. All we want is to go home."

"Please, young Traveler, sit. I have not finished," Rhue said evenly.

In a show of defiance, Clifford remained standing. "At least let my friends go. It's not their fault," Clifford pleaded in a voice of mixed anger and fear.

Rhue seemed to puff up and turn a deeper shade of blue-green color than was his normal tint. *"Clifford Tuttle! Please take your seat and hear me out!"* his voice scolded.

"Yes Sir," Clifford relented, and sat.

"Thank you. I will now tell you how I feel about this sentence that has been given you, young Tuttle," he said as his coloration returned to normal. *"Here is where I part ways with the Consortium's harsh decision. I feel the conviction is far too inconsiderate."*

Clifford felt a wave of relief wash over him. Shelly and Marco, who sat on either side of him, reached over. Shelly touched his arm and Marco patted him on his back in gestures of mutual assurance.

"I wish to express my sincere apologies to your friends, Clifford Tuttle. They are, of course, free to resume their typical clinic schedule and will be escorted immediately to the observation deck," he continued, designating each of the four with his priestly hand gesture.

Christa let out a pitiful mew of relief as the other three released their stress less audibly.

"Now, as for young Clifford Tuttle… I am sorry, but I must comply with most of the Consortium's recommendations."

Clifford stiffened feeling a sense of total confusion, fear and a great deal of anger. He began to stand but Rhue locked him in such a stare that his legs simply refused to comply with his wishes.

Rhue released his glare, and a sympathetic expression fell over his strange face. *"Regrettably, I must keep you here for a time. We have to be sure that you pose no danger to our world."*

Clifford had begun to feel as though this conversation was running in a big loop. First he will be detained, next, not detained, and now yes.

"But what to do with you?" Rhue continued contemplatively.

The familiar looking creature floating directly across the table from Clifford had been studying Clifford intensely. He puffed slightly. *"My sovereign, may I speak?"*

Rhue regarded this interruption for an uncomfortable moment and then made the hand gesture. *"Sackus Ishtabar, what have you to say? Please, speak."*

Sackus Ishtabar nodded his thanks to Rhue. *"I know this young Traveler from before,"* and turning to address Clifford directly, he continued, *"In fact, I was the one who caught you that day,"* he said regarding Clifford with a nod. *"I recall the events of young Clifford Tuttle's last visit. The Consortium has its rights to be on guard in this matter. However,"* he said addressing everyone in the room, *"I agree with my sovereign leader. Locking this innocent boy away in a dark prison cell seems very callous. We are a peaceful world and know little of the consequences of violence and war that the other worlds know. I move that we should offer this remarkable boy a more hospitable solution."*

Sackus Rhue nodded in agreement and the others convened on that side of the table followed suit.

"*What do you propose then, Ishtabar?*" Rhue asked.

"*As a former Centurion, I feel that I can be trusted to take this remarkable boy in as my guest. As you know, I keep an apartment here on the Terminal. It is quite comfortable, more so, I dare say, than a black prison cell.*" He held a pause before he continued. "*In compliance with the Consortium's wish to keep this boy in the dark, I can arrange to have the windows shuttered. It is my belief that this matter will not soon be resolved. Why not allow young Clifford Tuttle to live as comfortably as possible throughout his ordeal?*"

Rhue appeared to smile and nodded his approval. "*So be it. Have the apartment furnished to suit this amazing boy of Earth's needs. Spare no expense,*" Rhue spoke grandly, obviously glad of an amiable solution. "*If they wish to join their friend, the others may stay with Clifford Tuttle in their interim.*" Rhue decreed.

Ishtabar nodded his acceptance of Rhue's decree. "*Very well, my Sovereign, I will make it so.*"

Clifford was glad of the fact that he would not be spending time in a dark cell, but hated the fact that he was still a prisoner. What could he do, though?

"Excuse me again?" Clifford asked timidly.

Rhue puffed again, "*Yes?*"

"Will I be able to talk to my Aunt Gwen? She'll be worried sick."

Rhue appeared to shake his head. "*We will communicate the situation to your aunt through Optomeetruss. It is all*

I can offer for now, and you should be grateful for this," he puffed tersely.

Clifford was not satisfied, but again, what could he do? He watched helplessly as the room came to attention and Sackus Rhue retired through the hidden doorway.

Chapter Nineteen
Not the Best News from Skyloumia

The Optometrist stood, staring down at the silent holograph table. The proceedings from Sackus Rhue's conference room on the Terminal had just concluded and he could not say whether he was happy about the outcome or not. Rhue had decisively disregarded the recommendations of the Consortium. He could spare a small degree of favor regarding Clifford's upgrade from a dark, isolated prison cell deep within the Terminal to a comfortable apartment suite. But it was a risky move. Of course, The Consortium had not witnessed the conference. He had made quite sure of that.

Sackus Ishtabar interested him. The former centurion had made a startlingly rapid rise to power over the past seven Earth years. It was a curiosity that this very same centurion had been in place to save Clifford Tuttle those same seven years past. And once again, this same Skyloum was in possession of Clifford Tuttle. Interesting.

The Optometrist pushed away from the table, paused in thought and walked out of the secure room. Time was growing short. His sabbatical on Earth would have to be cut short. Unfortunately, his trip back to his home planet would have to be delayed further to make one last visit to Clifford's annoyingly emotional Aunt Gwen. In his opinion, the woman had nothing to worry about. Clifford Tuttle seemed to be handling the ordeal with impressive resolve, thus far.

Gwen and Martinez had moved from the bedroom to the Optometrist's expansive living room. The room was furnished with a scattered hodgepodge of different styles and size pieces, some Earth scale some Optometrist scale. Gwen could see the Optometrist spent little effort on aesthetics and probably little time here in this room at all. If he had, she was sure, the creature would have been compelled, by good taste, to do some rearranging. She now stood at the window looking out on the view of Quito. The time was 3:30 P.M.. Clifford had now been gone for over three hours.

"I presume it would be a waste of breath to remind you to relax, Miss Gwen." Martinez said from his veritable throne of an overstuffed chair, Optometrist scale.

"It's been three hours, Martinez. Two, since that bean pole of an alien has bothered to let us in on the situation," Gwen griped.

"Si, Miss Gwen," Martinez said with a heavy sigh. "You must be patient. Time moves slower where Clifford is. He has only experienced two hours there. I can assure you, not a lot has happened since the last report.

At that moment the Optometrist entered the room.

"I see you have made yourselves at home," The Optometrist said with a small smile.

"Yeah, nice place. Love what you've done with it. Who's your decorator?" Gwen said sarcastically.

The Optometrist scanned the room with his strange eyes. "Poof! I have no need for aesthetics. It is a shame I have to have this at all, but alas, occasionally I must entertain guests."

Gwen smiled wickedly. "So, is there any word from 'beyond' or are you going to serve us tea and crumpets?"

The Optometrist looked confused for a moment then broke out in a fit of whistling laughter. "Oh, Miss Gwen, you slay me!"

He continued, only after a purposefully long pause. This exasperating woman deserved some bit of mild torture. It amused him to watch her wait.

"I do have news. Clifford and his friends remain in the capable hands of the Consortium. They have had an audience with the Sovereign Consortium Leader, Sackus Rhue. You will be glad to hear that Rhue, shall we say, went lightly on the Consortium's decree. He is a fool, but it worked out much better for Clifford in this case."

Gwen could feel her blood begin to boil. "What decree? Why in the world should there be a decree?!"

"Please, Miss Gwen," The Optometrist said, restraining his temper. "First, the decree. It was decided, unanimously, by the governing body of the Consortium, that Clifford is to be kept out of the light for a while. This is an important precaution, taking into account Clifford's last trip. That said, Rhue took it upon himself to have Clifford moved from a darkened prison cell to a luxurious apartment suite," he concluded with a smile.

"Am I hearing you correctly? Is Clifford being held prisoner?"

"Correct," The Optometrist replied.

Gwen felt a knot of fear bunch up in her gut. This was turning into a nightmare. What must Clifford be feeling? "How long?" she inquired flatly.

"There will be an evaluation period," The Optometrist replied.

"How, in the *world*, do you evaluate a thing like this?! Tie a rope around the poor kid, throw him out in the sun and see what happens?!"

The Optometrist retained a calm demeanor as he rode out Gwen's rant. He knew his next words would push her over the edge. "Not quite," he replied simply, and waited for the explosion.

"Listen, you, you, whatever you are! I want my nephew back *right now*! Go! Get your arse, or what ever you have, down there and bring him back! Once I take Clifford away from this insanity and back to Pittsburgh, there will be no reason for your bloody Consortium to worry! And I swear, I will *never* allow Clifford to come within a thousand miles of this God forsaken equator again. EVER!"

"I would tell you a lie if I said I could do this for you,

Miss Gwen. Please understand. This is not about you... or Clifford. This is about keeping peace on six worlds, *including* Earth," he said darkly.

"He is a fourteen year old child! What difference could he make?

"Much." The Optometrist said, now dreading more what he had to tell her next. "In light of this upheaval, I must return to my home world. There, I am my planet's Sovereign Consortium Leader. If there is trouble, I must be in place," he said, then cringed.

"Oh! Great! You're leaving us? Heh, heh, heh. Just great! What are we going to do now?"

"Wait," he said as kindly as he could. "Clifford will be fine. Besides, your Earth's Sovereign Consortium Leader, Johanna Rassahmie will arrive here soon. She will be your liaison from this point on." *Lucky woman.*

"I have never heard of her."

The Optometrist smiled coolly. "I have no doubt," he scoffed. "I trust you will show *your* Sovereign more respect. Rassahmie does not share my... sense of humor.

"What? You think this is funny?" Gwen blustered.

The Optometrist was no longer smiling. "No, I do not."

With that he turned and left the room.

Chapter Twenty
Imprisoned

Clifford could not tell how many hours he had passed inside the darkened prison cell before he was lead to the apartment Sackus Ishtabar had generously offered. Clifford's escort was a Skyloum named Bags, for short. Bags was not like the more oppressive centurions, but rather a chatty fellow, if you could call these Skyloums fellows. He seemed genuinely fascinated in Clifford and why wouldn't he be. In this place Clifford was an alien from another world. Bags, Clifford guessed, was assigned this task only to make him feel at ease. In any case, Clifford remained uneasy because he had noticed two centurions a distance back and knew those were his real guards.

When they arrived at the apartment, Bags gave Clifford a tour, showing him all the amenities while apologetically promising that there would be further modifications made to better suit his human needs. It was funny but the parallel to earth's occupations was uncanny. Bags was a real estate agent, or so it seemed.

The main room of the apartment was a large place, lit only by the harsh LED lighting. Where there had been windows, which undoubtedly looked out on the bright, open sky, shutters had been sealed tight so that not even a leak of daylight could make it through. Bags had purposely avoided any mention of such a view and Clifford knew it was killing him not to. The two bedrooms were small and had been rigged with roomy looking hammocks. There was no other furniture. No dressers or desk. Clearly, the Skyloums required few possessions. The kitchen was much the same as the rest of the place. It had only a few cabinets and the shelves were clear of any contents. There were no dishes, pots or pans. This made Clifford wonder if, in fact, these creatures even required such things as well. The counter surface was clean and smooth as glass. There was a vague hint of a stove top integrated into the shiny surface, that Bags demonstrated and there was a sink and faucet. The small room, that Clifford assumed had to be the bathroom, was a mystery at first. Its surfaces were seamless and immaculately clean. There was no toilet, sink or shower. Bags showed him the three panels that operated the toilet, shower and sink.

First, the toilet was nothing more than a hidden panel that slid back to expose a grated opening in the floor. Apparently the Skyloums required no sitting to do their business. This was not an entire surprise because he had seen this kind of toilet on a trip through Europe with his parents. With the touch of another pad a sink folded out of the wall. The shower turned out to be nearly invisible holes in the ceiling that poured a misty, fine rain of water. The tour concluded back in the main room.

All in all, Clifford was not impressed. The apartment could not be described as cozy by any means. The walls were pale grey, the floors, hard and devoid of rugs or carpet. There was furniture, but it looked as if it had been hastily scavenged from various lounges and waiting rooms on the Terminal. Bags instinctively noticed Clifford's disappointment, as any good realtor would, and assured him that modifications were on their way. He then shortly excused himself, leaving Clifford quite alone.

The silence inside the apartment was maddening. Clifford had hoped to be jubilantly greeted by his four friends but that hope had been dashed. He had been separated from his friends immediately after their meeting with Sackus Rhue adjourned, and had not heard from them since. By this time, as far he knew, they could be back on Earth, safe from his fate. For having only known them a day, he missed them bitterly.

With nothing else to do, Clifford scrutinized the small buffet that had been set out for him and filled a plate. Judging by the way his stomach was growling, he figured it must be far beyond his dinner time, and he had totally missed his lunch. He took a comfortable chair, sat, and stared at the shuttered windows that wrapped the room. He could only imagine the view they might offer. This increased Clifford's depression still more.

During his time in the darkened isolation of his

previous cell, Clifford recalled his prior life in his parent's Pittsburgh home. It seemed now that he had merely woken up from a dream of life in the sun, only to find himself back in the dark.

Clifford ate slowly in dead silence and wondered how his Aunt Gwen was doing. She of all people would be fighting tooth and nail for his release. She was just that way. He recalled many other battles she had fought for him over the years. This gave him hope, but what could she do? She was away on another world, and that suddenly seemed very strange and frightening to him.

Clifford had been so wrapped up in the adventure, so sure of a smooth, controlled passage to and from this world, that he had not even considered the distances he had traveled. To his perception, it was as if he had just fallen through the earth's crust into another layer of reality, but what he knew from books and most assuredly from his parent's research, the Earth was not built that way. Skyloumia was not just miles beneath the earth's surface; it was a completely different world or planet. *But, how far away could it be from Earth?* All of a sudden his appetite was gone.

Clifford abandoned his half finished plate and paced around the perimeter of the room. The silence was growing more oppressive.

"Well, now what?" he said to himself. (It was good to hear a human voice, be it his own.) "Don't they have a TV or a computer in here… anything?" He searched for other panels like those in the bathroom that would operate something or even open the shutters, but his search was to no avail.

"Sure," Clifford said aloud, "this apartment has more rooms, but really, it's no different than the prison cell I was in before."

There *was* one control panel by the entrance door. He studied the flat glass touch-screen. It was without markings, and about six inches square. "I wonder–" he murmured, shrugged and reached out and touched it. The screen lit showing a fisheye view of the corridor on the other side of the door. He was surprised to see the corridor empty.

"Hmmm. No guards,"

Just to see, he carefully tried the latch. To his shock the latch turned. He checked the screen again. The view, though enhanced for best coverage, couldn't show everything. He took a deep breath, pulled the door inward, and peered out into the corridor. As far as he could tell, there were no guards stationed anywhere.

Emboldened, Clifford moved out into the corridor and worked his way toward the main entry lobby. There he met his first resistance.

The security desk was manned by an oppressive looking Skyloum who Clifford assumed was one of the two centurions who had followed him and Bags earlier. To his fortune, the centurion had apparently not noticed him there.

Disappointed to finally be stopped, Clifford eased back around the corner and out of site of the desk. Not wanting to risk giving anyone the idea that his door should be locked, Clifford surrendered his folly, and decided to beat a hasty retreat back to his room. He turned, and then he froze in his tracks.

The second Skyloum centurion had silently floated right up behind him. Startled, Clifford retreated back a couple of steps. The centurion followed, talking urgently with that puffy voice they all had.

Making sure not to make any sudden moves, Clifford carefully fished the translator ear buds out of his pocket, showed them to the centurion, and inserted them into his ears.

""*Clifford Tuttle. Why are you here? You must return to your room.*"

It took Clifford only a second to think up an excuse. "I don't understand the bathroom. I have to go," Clifford announced in a meek voice.

The centurion puffed and colored, "*Go where?*"

"What? Oh... Not go where, go to the bathroom."

"*Your bathroom is not here. It is in your apartment.*"

"Yes, I know that!"

"*Then, why are you here?*"

This conversation was going nowhere. "I came to ask how to use the bathroom."

"*You said you have to go.*"

Clifford groaned and raked his hair with his fingers. "I said I have to go *to* the bathroom!"

"*Your bathroom is in your apartment, not here.*"

"Ug! I have to *pee*, *urinate*, take a *leak*!

The creature looked confused for a moment and then smiled what appeared to be an irritated smirk. *"Bags didn't instruct you? Worthless, he is! Come, Clifford Tuttle."*

Back in his apartment, the Skyloum centurion led Clifford into the bathroom. *"Here, touch this,"* he said indicating the small touch pad integrated into the smooth wall surface.

Clifford touched the spot on the panel that Bags had shown him, and a louver grate opened in the floor.

The centurion pointed, *"Urinate there,"* he said, poofed irritably, and glided silently out of the doorway.

The centurion was hovering in the main room when Clifford came out.

"Thank you," Clifford said as politely as he could.

"Will there be anything else, Clifford Tuttle?"

"Yes. The others I came with, there were four of them. Have they gone back yet?"

"No, not yet."

"Will they be allowed to come see me before they leave?"

"Yes. That is what was agreed to. If they want, they may come."

"Is there any way to get in touch with them?"

"Yes, I will send word," he said with a nod.

"Why can't I go back with them? Wouldn't that be better?"

"Sovereign, Sackus Rhue has made his determination. You must stay."

"Has anyone from Earth come yet? I'm sure they

would want to find me and bring me back."

"I know nothing of this. I know only of your four companions."

"Then are there any other humans here on the Terminal?"

"No one of authority is here at this time. They had been expected today."

"There has to be someone!" Clifford insisted.

"No humans are here besides the service staff," he said, and appeared to smirk. "You could talk to the cook, but I doubt he could help. Please, Clifford Tuttle. You must be patient." He regarded Clifford for a moment then gave him a small bow. *"I understand this is difficult for you and I am sorry,"* he concluded, turned and left the apartment.

Chapter Twenty-One
Sack

After an indeterminate length of time, a buzzer woke Clifford from a deep sleep. He shook the sleep induced fog from his head and found that the screen next to the door had lit up showing four familiar faces. Clifford thrilled and hurried to his door to let them in. For all his excitement, his friends all seemed very subdued.

"Hey Cliff! Are you in the mood for some company?" Tasha asked.

"Hi! Yeah. I was hoping you'd come see me before you left," Clifford said.

Tasha snorted. "There's no way we could just ditch you without thanking you for this *wonderful* experience," she stated with a bright-eyed smile.

Shelly, on the other hand, looked as if she were near tears. "Oh, Cliff, what are you going to do?" she whined.

"I don't know. I guess I just have to wait it out," Clifford replied, trying to put a strong face on it. "So you're all going home tomorrow?"

"Si. That is what they're telling us," Marco said as he stared at the floor. "This sucks, Bro. They should let you go too."

"Yeah, I wish they would."

"Aren't there laws that prevent keeping someone from Earth prisoner here?" Tasha suggested. "Isn't there, like an Earth embassy?"

"I think were floating in it." Marco said.

Tasha frowned. "Haven't you talked to anyone from Earth? I mean, there has to be someone in charge here. Duh," She rolled her eyes, "this is an *Earth* Terminal, right? So, where are all the Earthlings?"

"The guard, who was here before said the cook was the highest authority. The ones they were expecting didn't show today," Clifford said shaking his head. "There would have been someone with authority from Earth at that meeting if they were here, right?" Clifford added.

"I think it's weird that no one followed us from the museum," Shelly said.

"Si, that is strange, but then there is the timing issue, you know, in order to hit the Terminal at the right time? Maybe they had to wait or they dropped somewhere else in Skyloumia and have to travel to get here," Marco suggested.

"Yeah, I suppose your right," Clifford agreed. "Maybe tomorrow," he said with some hope. "So what have you guys been doing all this time?"

"We had some food and just hung out until they let us come for a visit." Shelly replied.

"There is nothing else we could do. They haven't even taken us to the clinic yet. We always go to the clinic… It's like, *here we are!*" Shelly said rolling her eyes.

Bummer trip, huh?" Marco put in.

Clifford shook his head. It sure isn't anything like what I expected. I just can't see any point to any of this," he said, and then fell quiet.

"So," Marco said. "This is where we're all staying tonight?"

"Yeah, I guess so. There is this room, two bedrooms and a really weird bathroom."

"Yeah, the bathrooms here," Tasha snorted.

"So, how long have we been here? It's hard to tell with these stupid shutters closed off and all," Clifford asked. "Do they have actual days here or does it always stay light?"

"No. It stays light here pretty much all the time," Marco said.

"How do they tell time then?" Clifford wondered.

Shelly cast a glance at the shuttered windows. "There is a giant spot, like on Jupiter that comes around. I guess when it passes that is their night. It doesn't get dark, dark, like on earth though. It's like the sun's been blocked out by a heavy cloud. As for how long we have been here, about seven hours now."

"When the spot comes again, that is when we go," said Marco.

While his friends discussed other things and explored the apartment, Clifford sat alone, deep in thought. If he had any chance to escape it would have to be with his friends. If the dark spot blotted out the sun or what ever they had here, he could move outside without his shadow.

The problem was he had no idea how his shadow worked here. He could tell from his descent that there was no high sun, just a uniform light. But he had to assume that any outside light would have its affect.

"Where do you go to travel back?" Clifford asked Marco finally.

"There's a main Terminal deck. To get there you have to pass through the same kind of customs area like you find in Earth's airports. The deck is the same place we usually land." He replied, and then studied Clifford's face. "Forget it bro. You think U.S. Customs is tough–"

Clifford felt himself deflate. "I've got to get out of here! I've got to get back to my Aunt Gwen. I can't stay here indefinitely!" Clifford moaned.

"Easy, mi amigo. I'm sure it won't be more than a couple of days."

Clifford shook his head. "No. Look around! Why would they go to all the trouble to fix up this apartment if I was only going to be here a couple of days? And you should have seen the prison cell they moved me from. I mean, it was a *real* prison cell!"

Marco looked around and shook his head in agreement. "You do have a point there, bro."

The others had rejoined them in the main room.

Christa came in and sat close to Marco. "Clifford's right. He's not leaving here anytime soon." Her voice was flat and resigned and she appeared to still be in shock.

Marco looked down at his feet. "What can we do? Nothing."

Clifford bowed his head and closed his eyes. "There's nothing to do but wait, I guess."

Seeing that everyone seemed to be withdrawing into their own troubled thoughts, Marco decided to take charge of the would-be team. He had stowed a deck of cards in his pack and quickly got a game of Screw Your Neighbor started. This, he hoped would take their minds off the dilemma and it seemed to be working.

They had played for about an hour. It was Christa's turn to shuffle. She tapped, split the deck, and gave the cards a quick shuffle. Astonishingly, the shuffle noise was echoed by what sounded like a fart. Immediately all eyes turned to Christa.

"What? That wasn't me!" Her dark Hispanic skin glowed with a blush.

Tasha's face lit up with a smirk.

Christa ran the shuffle through her thumbs once more. Again the flatulent sound echoed.

"Really, girl?" Tasha teased.

Christa's forehead knitted. "Really, *no!*" she squeaked. "It wasn't me!"

"She's right," Clifford said. It sounded like it came from down the hall," He took a quick inventory of his friends. All were present.

Yet again the sound came sputtering from beyond.

Marco got silently to his feet, followed by Clifford. "Some one's in here with us," Marco whispered.

Clifford could feel his heart pounding in his chest as he followed Marco to the hall that connected the bedrooms and bathroom to the living room. He jumped when the rude sound came again and jumped a second time when Shelly, who had crept up behind him, touched his back.

Tasha had pressed in behind them while Christa remained seated, frozen in mid shuffle.

"Why would someone who's hiding be farting so bad?" Tasha hissed after the sound flapped offensively again.

"Shhhh," Marco hushed irritably as he began to carefully work his way down the hall. Despite his signal for them to stay put, the rest piled along behind him.

Marco stopped at the first door which was the bathroom. Slowly he pushed the door in and peeked through the opening. The room was unoccupied. That left the two bedrooms and a hall storage closet. He had looked into the closet earlier and it was fitted with shelves loaded with cleaning supplies and a vacuum hose. It was his opinion that it was too small to hide someone so he moved past and up to the bedroom doors.

Both doors stood wide open as they had left them. The three others huddled in front of the closet door and watched breathlessly as Marco looked into the boy's bedroom.

As they were standing there, Clifford's hearing began to pick up a strange wheezing sound nearly covered by their collective breathing. To his horror the sound was coming from the closet.

Suddenly, a violent explosion of flatulence sounded from inside the closet. Tasha and Shelly shrieked and threw themselves against the opposite wall. Clifford, with his heart in his throat, flanked the right side of the door while an equally nervous Marco flanked the left side.

In one quick movement, Marco took the door lever and yanked the door open.

The Skyloum floating at the threshold was about 5 feet tall and thick through the middle. His color was the same blue-green as the others but more vivid in hue. His skin was mostly clear, free of the tattoo-like markings the adults wore.

Clifford immediately guessed that this was a juvenile. "Hello?"

The creature seemed to color still more and pressed back as far as it could into the now empty closet, all the while, emitting fluctuating sounds from his hand jets.

It began to speak quickly in its puffy language.

"Quick! Who has their ear buds?" Marco said.

They all dug through their jumpsuit pockets for the tube containers. Tasha was the first to install hers.

"Is Clifford Tuttle still here?" the small Skyloum asked urgently, looking around her.

"Sure. What do you want from him?" Tasha asked still blocking the doorway.

"I am… I am an old friend of Clifford Tuttle," his voice raced.

"I didn't know Cliff had any friends here, especially old friends." Marco said as he shouldered Tasha to the side.

"Please, may I see Clifford Tuttle?"

Clifford had moved up behind Tasha. "I am Clifford Tuttle," he said gently as he moved Tasha aside still more. "Do I know you?"

The creature hesitated as if it weren't sure what to do, and then spoke, *"My apologies to you, Clifford Tuttle. I am Sack Earnestus, son of Sackus Ishtabar. This is my father's apartment. We met last time you came here,"* he said eagerly.

Clifford racked his brain but could not recall meeting anyone that time. "I'm sorry. I can't remember, but, hey, that doesn't mean we didn't meet. I really can't remember much of anything from that time," Clifford conceded.

"We were both younger then. We played some before you..." he said settling a bit.

"Before I went off and started a war?" Clifford said lightly. "So, how long have you been hiding in this closet?"

Sack Earnestus seemed to grow uneasy and the puffs of farty sounding air had increased. *"Not long."*

Clifford studied the creature for a moment before he spoke again. "Well, you might as well come out of there," Clifford said. "These are my friends: Tasha, Marco, Christa and Shelly. Guys, this is Sack Earnestus.

They all nodded their hellos, remaining silent otherwise. There was an awkward silence that followed.

"Let's go into the living room," Clifford offered and led them all out of the hallway. Marco held back and paused at the empty closet. After a quick study, he followed the rest.

"So you say we met before?" Clifford started once they were gathered in the large room.

Sack Earnestus appeared to be frozen in wonder as he looked from one to another. Finally he replied. *"Yes, yes. My father rescued you and then was charged with your care until your Earth men were to come for you. We were both the same age so we were put together to play. That was before your trouble started, Clifford Tuttle."*

Clifford felt a thrill well up inside him. Finally, this was a chance to get some real information about those washed away days seven years ago.

"What trouble? I'm sorry but, like I said, I really can't remember any of it."

"You and I played, and then some centurions came and took you away. I was not happy with that because we were having so much fun."

"That's it? Can you remember anything about the trouble?"

"Yes. It is a great story! The grownups lost you. You fell through your shadow and they lost you. It is said that you traveled between many worlds before one of your Earth men found you and brought you back."

"Wow. I wish I could remember. You say that a *man* found me and brought me back?"

"Yes. His name was Mitchell. He was a hunter. This is what makes a great story! Two legends, Clifford Tuttle and Mitchell, in one tale!"

"Tell me more about Mitchell," Clifford insisted.

"He was a Traveler like all of you, but the story goes that he decided to stay away from his Earth home. He traveled all the worlds never staying anywhere for long, so I am told. He was a shabby specimen, what you call a homeless drifter, but he could hunt and catch anything in the six worlds."

"You talk like he is gone."

"Yes. No one has seen him in six of your years. The story says he went bad after the war and went to the fifth world."

"Have you traveled to any of the worlds yourself?"

"No. There are those of my kind that can, like you, travel between worlds. Me? No. Not even my father can."

"Do they teach you about the six worlds?"

"We learn of these other places mostly through stories, but I know they are not just stories now that I see all of you! Only the Travelers know for sure, but what they truly know must be kept secret."

"Yeah. They are like that with us too. There are balances or something like that to protect."

Sack Earnestus moved in further toward the group and appeared to be more at ease.

"There are six worlds: Your Earth, ours that is called Skyloumia, a world of nothing but water called Aquan, a crystal world called Arris, Cygnus and a sixth… Drake 2, the forbidden world.

"Forbidden, why?" Clifford probed.

The story goes that like your Earth, there is much evil there, only much worse."

Tasha cleared her throat to get everyone's attention.

"Who says the Earth's evil?! We're not evil!"

Sack Earnestus pulled back as if he had been struck, and as he did, his color changed and his jets let of a round of flatulent tones that nearly brought everyone to tears trying, out of politeness, not to laugh.

Finally it was Tasha that lost it. She rolled off her chair and sprawled on the floor.

Seeing this strange and sudden reaction, Sack Earnestus expelled a copious detonation of rude sounding air. This was all it took to drive the others over the edge.

Sack was beside himself in confusion. *"What is wrong? Have you all been taken by fit?"*

Christa, who was more couth than the others and who had retreated slightly with embarrassment, was the only one capable of speech. "They are fine. They are just laughing."

"Laughing? Is it painful to them?"

"No, not painful, *but very rude!*" she scolded.

"What causes this laughing?"

"Funny stuff... like jokes or certain sounds. It's just that," she cleared her throat, "the sound you make, from your hands... well it sounds like flatulence."

"What is this... flatulence?"

Christa blushed super red, "Oh, my God. I...I-" she could not bring herself to describe it.

Sack appeared confused beyond words. Finally Marco managed to pull himself together.

"It is called a *fart*," he declared, wiping tears from his eyes. "We humans have touchy digestive systems.

Sometimes we get gas and the gas has to escape through our... butts," He said pointing to his posterior.

Meanwhile Tasha was killing herself on the floor with laughter. Clifford had barely gotten a hold of his laughter and was trying hard not to let Marco's description start him up again, but when Marco pointed at his butt, peals of laughter overtook his short-lived composure.

Christa had her head in her hands and her shoulders were shaking. It couldn't be told whether she was laughing or crying.

Marco continued. "Sometimes the gas is noisy coming out, like the sound your, hand-jet, things make. Only, most of the time it smells really bad and that is what we call a fart," he shrugged, "On Earth it's just really funny... I don't know..."

Sack just stared at the five humans each in turn. *"I think I understand... you have your propulsion ducts in your... what you call it... your butts?"*

This absolutely brought the house down, and it was many minutes before the five had silenced themselves once again.

Once the room settled, Marco became serious. He studied the small Skyloum with hard, skeptical eyes. "So, are you going to tell us how you got in here?"

Chapter Twenty-Two
Rhue Laments

From high in his vapor habitation, Sovereign, Sackus Rhue looked out upon the massive cloud cluster that was Skyloumia's capital mecca. The proud cluster consisted of over one thousand beautiful, voluminous, vapor habitations of varying sizes and shapes. From there he could also look down on the tiny cylindrical Terminal.

Compared to Skyloumias' majestic vapor habitations with yielding airy spaces, this rigid minuscule object was like an irritant to the eye. Before, there was nothing as alien in his world, and today he wished more than ever that it had never come.

Rhue glided around to another point of observation that expunged any sight of the infuriating Terminal. Here he could look out on a pristine scene of tranquilly floating vapor habitations with their delicate webs of interconnecting bridges. Here they required no solid boundaries such as floors, walls and ceilings.

All Skyloums lived in near complete harmony. There

were rules of course, all civilizations required this, but in all the history this world knew, there had never been a war. The Most Superior Skyloumos made certain of that. Under her absolute will, the population gladly went about their business with a single minded synchronism. He, for one, wished he had never parted from that way of life.

Sackus Rhue regretted having agreed to the Consortium appointment. What the other worlds showed him was a completely opposite mind set. Earth and the Sixth world, Drake 2 in particular, troubled Rhue always. He now possessed too much knowledge of these other places to know serenity in his personal life again.

Rhue turned away from his musing as he sensed the arrival of another presence.

"Ahhh. Greetings, Sackus Ishtabar. Join me, please."

"My Sovereign," Ishtabar said as he nodded his head in respect.

"I never tire of the view from here. What a wonderful world we live in," Rhue announced, having turned back toward the Terminal-blighted sky.

"I concur, Sovereign Rhue. It is a marvel," Ishtabar said and glided up next to his leader.

"Thank the Most Superior Skyloumos for that," Rhue said and he made the obligatory reverent hand gesture.

"Indeed." Ishtabar said making the same gesture. He paused to admire the view and waited for Rhue to speak again. When his leader remained silent, Ishtabar turned to him.

"Excuse my saying so, but you seem troubled, my liege."

"Yes," he replied, bowing his head. "It is this Clifford Tuttle mess. It is my wish that this child of Earth was off our world. But, I have no choice in this, so it appears… Yes, this troubles me, Ishtabar."

"Excuse me, if I might ask. How went the latest conference with the Consortium?"

"Troubling as well, my friend… Troubling as well," he conceded as his gaze remained fixated on his beloved world. "For now, I fear, Clifford Tuttle is ours to keep. Why this troublesome child can not be contained on his own home planet is beyond me." He glided absently back to the place where he could view the Terminal, and fell silent.

"If I might say so, our world has been chosen for the very reason that we are incapable of the unchecked ambitions and weaknesses rampant on the other five known worlds. Clifford Tuttle is hidden to all eyes but those of the Consortium. Nowhere else could this child be safer."

"Yes, but how long before the others let slip this wearisome secret? How long before our very own people get wind of his existence?"

"The Terminal has been quarantined for the duration of this boy's stay, my liege. Not even our Skyloums may communicate beyond, or leave the Terminal. Clifford Tuttle's existence is contained within those fortified walls. I can promise you that."

"If this is true, why do I not feel safe, Ishtabar?"

At that moment, both observed a bright flash at the top of the Terminal.

Chapter Twenty-Three
The News is Broken

The arrival, in Quito, of Earth's Consortium Representative, Johanna Rassahmie offered Gwen and Martinez little relief from their worry about Clifford. Thus far, the Sovereign Leader had refused an audience with the two, no doubt having much greater issues to deal with. One of the many issues being the remaining Travelers inability to go through.

It had now been over eight hours since Clifford and his friends had vanished from the inner courtyard of the museum and four hours since their only Consortium contact, The Optometrist, had departed for his home planet Cygnus.

Following The Optometrist's departure, Martinez had driven Gwen back to his home. With nothing to do but worry, Gwen's thoughts turned to the guilty knowledge that she had lost her sister's only child, and to the dread that she would eventually have to call her sister with the news. For some reason, when making the decision to travel to Quito with Clifford, Gwen had totally taken her sister's opinion out of the equation.

Gwen finally broke down and called her sister, Dottie, who was still on expedition in Australia. Her heart pounded in her chest as the phone rang once, twice...

Martinez placed a tall water glass filled with his special sangria on the counter next to Gwen's free hand as the phone continued to ring. Gwen grabbed up the glass and took a huge swallow at the same moment Dottie picked up. The combination of swallowing and throat constricting fright caused her to choke.

Dottie on the other end: "Aaa, hello, who is this?"

Gwen continued to choke but managed to croak out, "Me, 'cough,' Gwen."

Dottie: "Are you okay? What the hell's the matter with you?! Is there a fire?"

Gwen, who thought at the moment a fire would be much better, managed, "Yeah, I wish... NO! I just choked, that's all. Hold on," She took another swallow and continued with a more lubricated throat. She spoke lightly, "I, just, wanted to let you know, Cliffy and I are in Quito!"

Dottie: "Quito? Ecuador? What the hell are you doing there?!"

Gwen: "Aaa, here's the thing... You know Cliffy had a breakthrough the other day-"

Dottie: "Yes, try nearly three weeks ago, when we SKYPED."

Gwen: "Ah, has it been that long?"

Dottie: "Get to the point Gwen!"

Gwen: "Yes, well... Quito. Cliffy wanted to come back to the place it all happened, him disappearing and un-disappearing, you know, here, in Quito-"

Dottie: "Gwen! I know what happened there! Is this going somewhere? Concentrate!"

Gwen: "Okay. Therapy... Clifford thought it would help, so we, I talked to Dr Camilla. She thought it would be good for him too."

Dottie: "Are you all crazy?!

Gwen: "No."

Dottie: "I would have expected some kind of consideration in this decision. I am his mother!"

Gwen took another drink, "You sure are," she nodded. She was suddenly feeling light headed, but couldn't determine whether it was the sangria or panic.

Dottie: "Gwen, you sound guilty as hell," she said in a flat, toneless voice, "What's going on? Is Clifford okay?"

Gwen: "Cliffy... Sure... Fine, he's doing... fine. Just fine..." she trailed off.

Dottie more frantically: "Gwen! You're lying! I always know when you're lying! Now if you don't tell me *right now* what's going on, I *swear*, I will *crawl* through this phone and *beat* it out of you!"

Even though Gwen knew perfectly well that her sister was clear on the other side of the world, she drew the phone an arm's length away from her ear just in case Dottie's fist came through it. "I *swear* that *everything* is under control. Why, Doctor Camilla even came along!"

she yelled into the distant phone.

Dottie: "Now let me tell you this! *I* am Clifford's mother! *Not* you or that *quack* doctor! You have absolutely *no* right to take my son *anywhere* outside of Pittsburgh with out my permission! Who the *hell* do you think you are?! Quito! Shit! Gwen! You have really crossed the line here! What, has, happened?!" she growled enunciating each word.

Gwen retorted defensively, "I did it for Clifford! He needed this!"

Dottie: The hell he did! What's happened, Gwen?!"

Gwen: "Nothing!" she screamed.

Dottie: "Put Clifford on the phone."

Gwen shook her head, "Can't"

Dottie: "Why?!"

Gwen: "I can't!" she cried.

Dottie blaring: "Gwen, put Clifford on the phone this instant or I swear–"

Gwen: "He's out with... Martinez!" she wailed.

Dottie: "Martinez? Who the hell is Martinez?! Gwen!"

Gwen felt as if she were going to faint. Her voice went weak. "Martinez. The nice old man who found Clifford that time."

Dottie: "You mean the nice old man who might have *kidnapped*, (she shrieked) Clifford?! Have you gone out of your frigging mind?!"

Gwen was in mid faint, "Martinez wouldn't–"

Dottie: "PUT, CLIFFORD, ON, THIS, FRIGGING,

PHONE, RIGHT, NOW!!!!"

All of a sudden, phone interference, a blood curdling sound like a thousand fingernails being scraped across a chalk board, cut them off.

A half an hour later, Gwen woke on Martinez's sofa. (Apparently, she concluded, she must have actually fainted). As she emerged from peaceful oblivion, her eyes fluttered open and the whole mess flooded back in. Still reeling from the tongue-lashing her older sister had given her, she could only imagine what rage would be wrought against her if Dottie knew the whole story.

Later, racked by terrible guilt, Gwen tried to call her sister back, but only got the same screeching phone interference and dropped calls.

Gwen had cried for a long time after the calls and Martinez did his best to console her.

Chapter Twenty-Four
The Secret Shaft

Sack Earnestus sputtered away from Marco's hard-eyed gaze.

"Please... I can not tell you. My father would be most displeased!"

Marco paced Sack's retreat across the room. "Don't worry. Your father is not here," he said with a conspiring smile. "I know that closet had shelves before. I checked it out when I first arrived. So, what is it, some kind secret passageway?"

"Yes." Sack said with marked caution. *"My father uses it to come and go secretly. I am not supposed to know about it, but once I followed him. Please, I am forbidden to be here. All Skyloums are forbidden. I will be in terrible trouble if anyone finds out, and not just from my father! I just had to see Clifford Tuttle once again."*

Marco paused, deep in thought. Finally he talked. "Do not worry. We will not tell. It's just good news for Cliff. Now Cliff knows he has a way out, if worse comes to worse." The smile faded. "Your people should not be holding him prisoner, do you understand? Cliff needs to go home with the rest of us."

"Yes I know, and thank you for your promised discretion."

Clifford had remained silent during Marco's interrogation. This new development offered a realistic ray of hope. "How much longer do my friends have before it is time for them to leave?"

"I did not know they were to leave. I know nothing of that."

Shelly spoke up. "There is a dark spot in the sky that comes around once in your day. That is when we go. How long do we have before that time comes?"

"That will come in three of our time increments," Sack replied with confidence.

Shelly did a quick translation in her head. "That gives us around two hours. Please," she said addressing Sack Earnestus, "Can you show us the passage?"

"I do not know. I could get in terrible trouble!" he reiterated.

Tasha smiled a wry smile. "It took a lot of balls-" she paused to examine Sack's physique, "I mean *courage* for you to come here in the first place. Do you know what that tells me?"

"No, I do not," Sack shyly admitted.

"That tells me that you are an adventurer like us!" Tasha encouraged.

"Like you? No," he said shaking his head in doubt. *"I could never be like you."* Sack's color faded.

"Like I said, you've already come this far. You're committed now." She watched as Sack seemed to shrink. "Don't get me wrong," Tasha apologized holding out her hands, "we're not asking you to help us escape–" she continued. A gleam came to her eyes, "not now, anyway. We just need a quick look at your father's secret passage."

"I don't know." Sack repeated, paling still more.

Tasha smiled sweetly. "You love the 'stories' you have told us, don't you? All of the adventure, the danger," she winked. "Do you know what I think? I think *you* could be in one of those stories. Yes, you!"

Sack appeared to smile. *"It is true. I have dreamed…"* he confessed, returning more to his natural skin tone.

"So. Just a little peek? For Clifford Tuttle's sake?" Tasha urged making big puppy dog eyes.

Sack swiftly turned an aggressive color and the sputtering sounds turned to the smooth hiss of his elder Skyloums. "Yes! I will do it for Clifford Tuttle!"

"Aaallll right! That's what I'm talking about!" Tasha exclaimed. "Is everyone ready?"

Sack's color abruptly faded and the sputtering commenced again. *"Everyone?!"*

"Everyone?!" Christa echoed meekly.

Clifford stood up. "Yes, everyone. We need to stick together. We're a team, remember. It's all or nothing!"

Sack colored again. *"Can I be on your team too?"*

Marco stepped up to face Sack with a large toothy smile. "Absolutely, mi amigo! Fist bump!" he said offering Sack his fist.

Sack backed away, momentarily confused.

"Like this, bro." he said demonstrating the move on Clifford.

Sack appeared to smile and made a fist and held it out. Marco gave him a bump. On contact, Marco's fist became completely submerged in Sack's water balloon like flesh.

After he pulled it back out, Marco examined his fist with a look of disgust. "Whoa! That was really weird, dude. Don't you have any bones or anything?"

"What are bones?"

Five minutes later all six intrepid explorers were stuffed into the small room behind the misleading broom closet. Clifford had insisted that they all bring their backpacks, just as a precaution. The added gear made the space even tighter.

Sack now stood in front of an open panel that exposed a vertical air duct that measured about 48" square. *"This is it,"* Sack said proudly. *"Now, we go back?"*

Clifford squeezed between Shelly and Sack to get a better look. It was weird feeling the difference between Shelly's solid body and Sack's totally elastic one. "Where does this go?" he asked looking down into the dark and seemingly endless shaft.

"It travels vertically from top to bottom of the Terminal structure. There are many such panels like this one leading to different rooms. Up goes to the clinics, human living quarters and the observation room on top. That is where I have seen humans before."

Marco stroked his chin, "That is where we usually go as soon as we arrive. That's where they took us after we were separated earlier. Where does down go?"

There are meeting rooms on three levels, the Terminal Centurion quarters and the jail level.

"Hey, you're okay Sack!" Tasha commented. She was impressed with the intel he had provided. "I take it you come here a lot, ay?" she concluded with a wink and gushy nudge.

"Yes. I know it is wrong, but I have an insatiable curiosity," Sack admitted with pride filled honesty. *"Now... we go back?"* he asked with less certainty.

Marco ignored this and continued his line of thought. "We do not want to go down. That is for sure. No. We need to go up."

"Not go back?" Sack's coloring was fading still more.

"No. dude. You got us this far, why should we stop now?" Marco asked in a false, harsh tone.

"No?" Sack replied weakly.

"We just want to take a look, that's all, mi amigo." Marco assured him.

After a thoughtful silence, Sack nodded reluctantly.

Shelly leaned carefully into the shaft. "In case you didn't notice, there doesn't seem to be a lift," she remarked.

"We don't need a lift. We have Sack here," Clifford said patting Sack's blubbery back. "Just get us to the clinic level. From the sound of it, there are no other humans here, at least not of authority. The clinic should be empty."

Marco stroked his chin deep in thought. "But, wait

a minute. You said that there is a service staff here? Why don't we go to that level? Maybe we could get you some help there."

Clifford had a strong feeling to the contrary. "No. Let's just keep this in 'secret recon' mode, for now. Okay? I say the clinic level. No one will be there. It's safer."

"I say we go to no other levels! We must stay here," a very pale Sack worried aloud.

"Come on Big Sacky. Where's that sense of adventure?" Tasha prodded and then addressed the room, "Now, who's first?"

Reluctantly at first, Sack transported each, individually, up the shaft and deposited them into a room of similar proportions. With each lift came greater compliments and encouragement. This helped to push Sack to a level of confidence he never experienced.

Until the day Clifford Tuttle dropped into his life, Sack had followed passively in his father's wake. At his young age, Sack had heard very little of anything from outside of his world. Then, suddenly, he had been faced with this strange alien boy.

Sack had been immediately enthralled with this strange human from the far away Earth. Of course there were certain obstacles to overcome, but once resolved they managed to get on just fine. For example, because Clifford Tuttle's body was heavy and could not float on air, he had to be supported by a cloud-hover, an old device his father had gathered shortly after Clifford's arrival. It was a funny thing made like a Skyloum body but not alive. It could float Clifford Tuttle freely on its own and could be redirected with as little as a breath of wind.

With this apparatus in place Sack and his new friend spent one very unforgettable day together. (At least it was unforgettable for Sack. He wasn't sure why Clifford Tuttle could not recall a thing about it.) Despite the fact that he and Clifford Tuttle had not been able to talk with one another they discovered many similar interests in age appropriate activities. Sack remembered fondly, that they had both enjoyed a rousing game of bubble catch.

However brief their friendship was, Sack's life had been changed forever.

After that encounter, Sack had become obsessed with knowing more about Clifford Tuttle and his human kind. This fixation was what had motivated Sack to disregard the rules in order to find ways to explore the human made Terminal. He had followed his father and learned the ways of traveling the shaft. Over the years Sack had spied on many of the human travelers. He had especially followed the young ones, knowing that some day he would witness Clifford Tuttle's return.

Sack had one last lift to make. The dark skinned Tasha who was fast becoming his favorite human despite his long lived admiration for Clifford Tuttle. There was something about the way she always smiled.

Once they were all together, Sack undulated through the crowded room and placed himself in front of the closed passage panel. *"Are you sure you want to go out there?*

"What if there are Skyloums there?"

"If Cliff is right about no other humans being here, there wouldn't be any reason for Skyloums to be about. At least not on this level." Shelly reasoned.

"I hope I'm right or we are all screwed," Clifford said more to himself than to the others. He had to stop and think for a moment before making his final decision to proceed. He turned to Sack. "There aren't any windows out there are there? It's just… my shadow, you know."

Sack considered this for a moment. *"No, there are walls all around, I think."*

"Okay." Clifford said deciding finally to proceed. "Just in case, Sack, you go first. If there are Skyloums there, your appearance would be unexpected but more explainable. We'll wait here."

"Me, first?!" Sack exclaimed and then let off a barrage of foul sounding air.

Tasha scoffed. "Thank Goodness he doesn't stink when he does that!"

Sack colored. *"What is stink?"* he asked innocently.

"Keep us penned up in here long enough, and you'll find out," Marco said, as he cautiously moved Clifford by the shoulders, toward the back. "Just to be safe, bro," he told Clifford then gave Sack the go ahead.

"Having fun yet?" Tasha said, addressing Sack who was looking very pale at the moment.

All Sack could manage, in response, was a small, grimacing smile. He then placed a finger on a touch pad next to the hidden panel and the door slid silently open.

As promised the panel opened up on an empty, unlit room. With the first indication of Sack's movement, the overhead LED light fixtures blazed to life causing them all to jump. Clifford had to grab onto Shelly's waist to keep from being knocked backwards into the yawning shaft.

"Hey, watch it!" Shelly teased him.

"Sorry," Clifford said embarrassed, "I didn't want to fall."

"Uh huh," she replied sarcastically.

Once inside the empty room, a cautious listen at the exit door revealed no other sign of life beyond. Sack again was pressed to be the first through the exit door. Once the hall was deemed safe, the rest followed allowing the door behind them to click softly shut. Several nondescript doors lined the curved hall that disappeared in each direction.

"Do you know where we are, Sack?" Marco whispered. All these corridors look the same to me, man."

Sack hovered in place trying to get his bearings. *"This does not look like the Clinic level,"* he said in an unsure tone, *"This looks more like–"*

All of a sudden there was a sound like escaping gas approaching from just beyond the blind curve of the hall.

Clifford moved quickly to the door they had just exited and shook the lever only to find it had locked behind them. "Oh crap! It's locked!"

They all shot wide eyed looks in the direction of the

approaching sound.

Sack exclaimed, *"Centurions!"* then blasted noisily off in the opposite direction.

Reacting just as fast to Sack's flight, the five followed closely in his wake. Within twenty feet they met a set of doors at a dead sprint. In their panic, they all burst through the doors and into the blazing daylight of the glass domed observation room. Clifford's jet black shadow immediately stained the floor beneath them and just as suddenly, they were falling through space again.

Chapter Twenty-Five
Mitchell

The ancient stone structure stood in its dilapidated state at the intersection of three steep and unbroken mountain ranges that symmetrically ringed the Planet Drake 2. Each ridge marked the equatorial tracks of the three distant suns that gave Drake 2 light and warmth enough to sustain life. Each ridge also traced the scars of ancient wounds inflicted by terrible weapons of war–weapons so powerful that they once physically shattered the fragile structure of the planet's outer shell. By whatever control, divine or natural, the planet was repaired, but the great ridges thrown up in that catastrophe worked to separate forever the three distinct civilizations that now populated the planet. Within the dank stone walls of the structure a man roused from a fitful slumber.

His aged body protested as he rose from the primitive bed. He swept aside the protective fur blankets and shivered in the chilly air. He remained there for a time and pondered the vivid visions he had witnessed in his dreams.

A boy, human and somehow familiar, played at the outer margins of his memory. This meant something but the fog of the previous day's inebriation worked to smother those recollections.

Relenting, he stood and walked unsteadily to the toilet chamber and relieved his straining bladder. That step accomplished in his day of typically few activities, he moved on to the makeshift counter that held a corroded, but still watertight bowl.

The rain had come in the short Drakin night, depositing, through the unfaltering leak in the roof, an ample amount of water. First he drank just enough to quench his tortured thirst and then poured the remainder into a battered canteen. Tipping the empty but still moist bowl, he let the remaining drops fall onto his upraised face. He replaced the bowl to its spot beneath the leak and then returned to the main room where he sat back down on the edge of his bed.

The sun was up barely three hours after its sibling sun had set. Its radiance fought to penetrate the heavy window coverings that draped the room in darkness. He would go out but not until the rite of the Shielded Shadow was successfully preformed.

He spoke the ritualistic words he spoke three times, each succession of the three sun day, crossed himself in the Catholic tradition of his life on Earth and rose from his squalid bedside. Cringing before the inevitable effect of harsh sunlight on his sore brain, he pulled the heavy drape aside.

Light simultaneously bathed the interior of his rooms and assaulted his sensitive eyes. The same outside view opened up before his squinting eyes. Three nearly perfect, linear mountain ranges receded into the hazy distance.

He turned away from the magnificence of the view and went to find the fragile glass mirror he kept safely swaddled in thick fabric. He took the mirror reverently from its wrapping, held it up before his face and studied his reflection.

His face, surrounded by a faded mane of tangled red hair, was grey with filth and a considerable growth of whisker stubble. What little exposed bare flesh remained was rutted and pocked. His eyes, once bright with intensely blue irises, reflected back at him. The gleam was still there, but was half concealed behind heavy, drooping eyelids and bordered in the lower regions by puffy bags of darkened skin. That residual glimmer of life was all he could recall of his former self and it granted him a certainty that he was still alive.

"I know you," he spoke to the reflection in his native Australian accent, "You are Mitchell."

Chapter Twenty-Six
In the Void

Clifford had to yell to make him heard over the auditory chaos of the group's terrorized shrieks and Sack's constant, violently sputtering fart sounds. They were still in the dark but for how long? "Everyone! Goggles! Get your goggles on!" he shouted.

As he plummeted through the pitch black of the realm of transference, Clifford fumbled blindly with his pack being careful not to lose his grip on the strap. Finally, after many panicked moments, he had the goggles and slapped them on his face. The screaming had died away as the others who had them, groped for their own goggles. The flatulent rumble continued, however. This gave Clifford a startling realization. Sack had fallen through with the others. A worse thought yet eclipsed the first and that was that Sack would have no life sustaining goggles. Still worse, Sack's noisy expulsions seemed to be growing fainter as if he were falling steadily behind.

As if Tasha had read his mind, Clifford heard her yell,

"I'll go after Sack!"

A flapping of fabric sounded in the growing silence and they all sensed Tasha's departure.

The communication feature in the goggles had deployed and now they could talk between themselves.

Marco performed a quick roll call.

"Tasha! Have you got Sack?"

"Yes, I am with him, but we are falling further behind! He's too light!"

"Okay, stay with him!"

"Christa! You okay?"

"Oh, God!" Came her weak reply.

"Shelly! How are you doing?"

"Roger! All systems go!"

"Cliff, you son of a-"

"Sorry, "Clifford replied humbly. "I 'm still here. We need to stick together though! We have to go back for Tasha and Sack."

"Okay. Tasha?!" Marco yelled.

"Yah, we're still here and still slowing."

"It's gotten quiet. Is everything okay? Is Sack still breaking wind back there?"

"No he seems to have fainted or something!" Tasha's tense voice yelled back.

"Great!" Marco groaned sarcastically. "Wake him up! We need to know if he can propel himself like those centurions that rescued us. If not we will have to slow down to let you catch up. You still need to wake him up so we can hear him!"

"Okay," Tasha said. "I'll do my best!"

"Everyone else, let's try to find each other. We can't get separated!

Suddenly there was a beacon of light off to Marco's left.

"What's that light?" he called.

Clifford's voice sounded, "In the packs… little flashlights. They work!"

A short moment of pack rummaging followed and one by one the tiny flashlights blazed to life in the blackness. What this revealed was that they had drifted far apart. Marco floated around putting his back to the fall. In the distance above he could see Tasha's tiny point of light.

While Marco performed this maneuver, the others began to move in closer.

Soon Clifford was at Marco's side. "How long do we have?"

"I don't know, I think this is about how long the first drop was. There's no way to tell. I've never fallen through twice!"

"We need to get back to Tasha and Sack!" Clifford said urgently.

"I know!" Marco replied as Christa and Shelly floated in to join him and Clifford.

"Everyone here?"

Oui, Shelly said.

Okay, we need to slow down. Remember how we did it before? We have to stay on course though. We can't direct ourselves anywhere but down. If we shoot off horizontally we'll loose them for sure. Now... on three. One, t–"

At that moment, the sensation of momentum abruptly stopped and they found themselves totally immersed in endlessly deep, blue water.

As soon as the initial shock passed, Marco called out to Tasha but there was no response.

Chapter Twenty-Seven
Clifford Tuttle Has Vanished

Though Sackus Rhue remained unaware of the precise meaning of the flash, Sackus Ishtabar was struck with the dread of knowing what it meant.

"No," Ishtabar breathed.

Sackus Rhue turned slowly to meet Ishtabar face to face, and at once noticed his pallor.

"Have my fears been realized so soon, Ishtabar?"

Sackus Ishtabar remained silent a moment too long and this told the wizened leader all he needed to know. He bowed his head in utter frustration. "So it is as it was before."

"Yes," Ishtabar said absently as the sudden chaos in his mind began to take over all reason.

The holographic image of two imposing centurions materialized before their eyes.

Sackus Ishtabar dutifully pulled himself together.

"Report, Centurion!"

"Commander. Clifford Tuttle has vanished from the observation level."

"And, the others?" Ishtabar pressed.

"We caught sight of them just before they traveled. There were five and—"

"Speak Centurion!" Ishtabar barked.

"With them was one of ours. A Skyloum youth."

"What?!"

The holograph of the centurions faded as the realization sunk in to both Ishtabar and Rhue.

Rhue was the first to speak, "A Skyloum youth, Ishtabar?"

"I can't imagine... how?"

"How, indeed, Ishtabar?"

Sackus Ishtabar summoned the two Centurions who were charged with guarding Clifford Tuttle's apartment. Instantly, their holographs materialized where the others had just faded. As soon as they appeared, the two snapped to attention as if taken totally by surprise.

"Commander?" the desk sentry replied to Ishtabar's unexpected summons. The holograph image of the hall sentry appeared as surprised as the first.

"Clifford Tuttle has just traveled from the *observation level*, Centurion!"

"No! Commander. This is impossible! He has not left the apartment since my last report! The door remains secure on your orders!"

Following the arrival of the four young Travelers at

the apartment, Ishtabar had ordered the door locked. The hall sentry had now arrived at that door and checked the status panel. He found the lock remained in service as well as the security alarm.

"Commander, the door is secure!"

A creeping panic had begun to fog Ishtabar's senses. It was impossible. How could Clifford Tuttle have found the shaft? The Skyloum youth? But, who? *Earnestus!* He could feel the color draining from his body and knew Rhue had noticed.

"Search the apartment! Report back immediately! Go!"

The holograph blinked out leaving the two Skyloum leaders alone.

Sackus Rhue studied his pale, momentarily silent centurion commander with hardened eyes. "Is there something I should know, Ishtabar?"

Ishtabar's bowed head came up to meet his leader face to face. "Yes, my Sovereign Leader. There is a secret shaft I use to move unobserved when I am on the Terminal. But I am the only one who has knowledge of this and the codes to gain access, unless—"

"Ishtabar?" Rhue urged, as his coloring radiated his immense displeasure.

My son, Sack Earnestus. He is very bright and can be very determined," Ishtabar revealed, feeling suddenly very weak and frightened.

Sackus Rhue nodded his head. "Ah. So now we have discovered the guilty Skyloum youth."

"My apologies for my son's part, Liege."

Sackus Rhue did not reply right away, rather fell silent as he pondered the situation. Secretly, he applauded Ishtabar for his indiscretion, and ultimate failure to contain the troublesome human child. Ishtabar had unknowingly eliminated the dilemma of Clifford Tuttle. Outwardly, Rhue retained an angry stance.

"Leave me, Ishtabar!" he said with all the frustration he could feign.

Sackus Ishtabar bowed his head, "Yes, my Sovereign," and turned to leave.

"Ishtabar!" Rhue barked.

"Yes?"

"Keep me informed!"

"Yes, Sovereign."

When he was alone, Rhue erupted in joyous laughter. Now all he had to deal with was the Consortium but this did not bother him. He had grown weary of their petty issues and intended to register his resignation as soon as the Clifford Tuttle debacle was resolved.

He turned his sight away from the hated Terminal, gazed lovingly at the floating clouds of his realm and imagined an unspoiled Skyloumia without the Terminal, the alien Travelers and most of all without the interference of the Consortium.

Chapter Twenty-Eight
Adrift

They were alone and slowly falling, if at all, in the pitch black void between worlds. Tasha knew this first because her auditory contact with the others had abruptly ceased, but more so because she could no longer feel their presence. Tasha was like that, a social being, a people person. When faced with seclusion, she felt its affects like an ache in her soul.

Tasha tried, with all her might, to move Sack's listless body on through the blackness without luck and had finally given up. Now she and Sack were essentially marooned, cast adrift in the dark nothingness of the void.

Sack had not yet regained consciousness and this worried Tasha more than being lost. In the void, her goggles did their part to sustain her life. Perhaps Sack was not so lucky. Maybe he was dying. Who but another Skyloum could tell? With one more desperate effort, Tasha tried to rouse Sack by smacking what she supposed was his face. It was hard to tell in the complete darkness what part of him was what. He was equally squishy all over. She shouted his name again and then in utter frustration gave him a hard kick. This immediately registered as a terrible mistake because now they were separated. It was at this point of despair that Tasha finally heard Sack sputter to life.

Sack's distressed cry came off of her left hand side. Tasha immediately called his name and frantically probed the nothingness with her small flashlight beam. "Sack! Sack! I'm here. Tasha… I'm Tasha. I'm here!'

At that moment she first felt the air displacement and then was hit from behind by his soft balloon-like body. He was whimpering incoherently as his air jets sputtered out his their nerve conducted tunes.

"Its okay Sack, I'm here!"

"Where is Here, Tasha?" he cried.

It amazed her how this completely alien creature could exhibit such human emotions. Somehow, she always pictured aliens from other worlds to be more cold and calculating, more like the Optometrist.

"We are in the space between worlds. This is how we travel," Tasha explained. The lame description was all she could offer this being only her second travel experience. She knew it wasn't enough to calm Sack's worried mind. Heck, it wasn't enough to calm *her* worried mind.

"It does not feel like we are traveling, Tasha," he whined.

"You're right. It doesn't feel like we are moving at all," she agreed as she thought, "I think you're too light to be effected by the gravity or whatever makes this work."

"Where are Clifford Tuttle and the others?" he asked

with concern in his voice.

"I think they're through already. I came back for you when you started slowing down."

Sack was silent for a moment then continued, *"What can we do to get through?"*

"We need to get moving again, but in which direction? I've lost the way, Sack.

"Oh."

She pointed her small flashlight at Sack's face. "Can you fly... like the others... you know, like the centurions who rescued me and the others?"

"Yes, I can fly. All Skyloums can fly."

"Good. I'm going to try something," then she stopped. "First though, I can't predict what world we will come out in. We all know there are six. Five, I don't worry about. The world you call Aquan... It's all water," she lowered her flashlight. "If we go there, there will be no air, just water," she raised the light beam and aimed it so both their faces were illuminated from below. In most cases this type of illumination would create a sinister appearance, but there in the dark, it was comforting for both to see that each was not alone. "Your stories of Travelers. Is there anything about how Skyloum Travelers survive in water? You see," she said pointing at the metal apparatus she wore on her face, "we have these goggles. They help us breathe in water."

Sack floated silently and seemed to be deep in thought. Finally he seemed to brighten. *"Skyloums are made of air. The stories tell of this water world, Auquan. All the stories say that our Travelers go there and come back. I think I will be okay, for a while at least. What is your idea, Tasha?"*

"Okay. I am going to let go of you. I hope I will begin to fall again. If I do, follow me. I will hold this flashlight. If this works, fly as fast as you can in the direction I am falling. I will grab onto your back. Just keep flying straight. I don't think the border is that far away."

"Okay, Tasha," he said with a brave nod of his head.

"Good. Are you ready?"

"Yes I am ready."

"Here I go," Tasha said and pushed off.

Tasha allowed herself to drift. To her surprise she seemed to be drifting head first. Up from down was impossible to tell, and she hoped she was going the right direction. Her acceleration was gradual at first, and then began to increase. "Come on Sack! Don't loose me!"

Sack sputtered in place for an indecisive moment as he watched Tasha's point of light accelerating away, and then thrust off in pursuit. In only a few seconds he had caught Tasha and together they flew headlong through the barrier and into the water atmosphere of Aquan.

Chapter Twenty-Nine
Aquan

Clifford instinctively knew the water would have no surface or floor so there was no need for a panicked swim to the top. His three other friends knew this too, but how, none could say. Their goggles had unfailingly deployed the life sustaining gel. For the time, the four reluctant Travelers were safe.

Clifford, Shelly, Christa and Marco reunited shortly after they entered Aquan. The distances between their entries were spread no more than one hundred yards apart, but what of Tasha and Sack? If they had even breached the Aquan barrier, at the rate they were falling, they could be miles away.

For the time they ignored a distant point of light that could be a safe haven for the more pressing need to locate their lost friends. Without the hint of communication the depleted group began to swim. They all seemed to have the same idea, to swim outward in increasing circular tracks using the distant glowing light as a reference point.

Their swimming seemed effortless thanks to the gel's ability to grant them nearly tireless strength and to the less resistant viscosity of the Aquan water. When compared to Earth's water, swimming here was like swimming through the air. At first, there seemed to be subtle differences in resistance, but the longer they circled the easier the swimming became. They were creating their own current, like walking in circles around a circular swimming pool. Soon the group had increased the speed and circumference of their laps to at least a mile. Each lap also brought them closer to the mysterious light source.

Time seemed to drop away from their minds as if the circular movement of their swimming had tranquilized them. The current they had created was now doing most of the work which added to their collectively relaxed state of mind. This tranquility would soon be disrupted by two events.

Clifford's worry for Tasha and Sack had calmed considerably as the mere physical act of swimming circles took over. Not only could he feel his own rhythmic strokes but soon could feel the others' as well. From time to time he would look over to see Shelly, Christa or Marco keeping pace and marveled that their strokes matched his exactly. Occasionally, he would get a sudden urge to accelerate or decelerate. He would notice the others do the same as if they were all swimming in complete synchronization. Then an analogy dawned on his swimming consciousness. They were behaving as a school of fish would. He turned to see his friends watching each other with equally knowing expressions in their faces. In that instant Clifford heard the thoughts of the others say at the same time. *Yes. We are like a school of fish!*

They swam into the section of their lap that brought them into view of the light source, now an extreme distance away. Suddenly the light was eclipsed by a very large object moving perpendicular to their course. A moment later the current they had created was interrupted, throwing their bodies into abrupt chaotic deceleration.

Alarm registered from their collective mind, and then instinct triggered their rapid regrouping. For the time, all they could think to do was to clasp hands forming a ring with each facing outward.

Clifford, who at the moment was facing the light, was the first to see the immense shadow as it moved the opposite way across their path. Though huge, it still seemed far away and indistinct. At that moment, he also felt the collective alarm of his friends join with his fear. *If that thing looks that large from this distance, how large would it be up close?*

Almost immediately on the heels of that concurrence, Shelly, who was facing the opposite direction in their protective circle witnessed a bright flash of sparkling light. To Shelly's mind, this registered as significant. Instantly the group turned and swam with her toward the spot of the flash. This was good in that they were swimming away from the ominous form. Instinctively, this seemed the right thing to do.

Though it felt like swimming against a growing

current, it also felt like they were moving very fast. They unconsciously formed a straight line, constantly rotating shifts at the front to maintain their momentum, but the current was growing stronger. None of them thought to look back.

Chapter Thirty
Drake 2

Kyle Mitchell pushed out through the heavy skin that draped the doorway to his stone shelter. Before he ventured too far out into the sunlight, Mitchell looked down at the smooth trodden stone at his feet. His diminished shadow mingled with the camouflage netting's spotted shade. Having completed the rites of the sheltered shadow, he was now free to live in the sunlight for the present sun cycle.

Mitchell walked stiffly toward the waist high parapet– a great ring of stone masonry that topped the convergence point of the six nearly symmetrical mountain ranges. These natural, stony ramparts, running pole to pole, divided the planet into six equal sections. From his vantage point Mitchell could view all six cribbed sectors that alternated land to sea. Instinctively, Mitchell's eyes always moved to the disquieting lands that expanded to the sunward horizon. This was the realm of the dreaded Horwrath or Soul Eaters. To either side of the Horwrath region stretched two equal sectors of unbroken sea that effectively isolated the Horwrath from the rest of the planet.

Mitchell began his habitual walk around the circumference of the parapet. His view shone to the east now, the segment of the Trunjenn. Two distinct species of humanoid life forms survived the planet's prehistoric beginnings, the Horwrath and the Trunjenn. Unlike the Trunjenn, the Horwrath had not evolved far beyond the very point where the humanoid masses split into the two distinctive types. The Horwrath remained primitive and vicious, and as deadly to each other as they were to the rest of Drake 2's population. The Horwrath scourge had, in the past, moved out into the universe, given their disproportionate numbers of born Travelers. Their terror was felt on every known world up until three earth years ago.

Mitchell frowned deeply. He had taken a large part in the methodical elimination of the far flung Horwrath Traveler population.

On the other hand, the Trunjenn race had moved on to become a mighty font of culture and invention. Despite the Trunjenn's intellectual supremacy, they were far more dangerous than their Horwrath cousins.

Mitchell studied the distant gleaming metropolis of Trunjenn 3 then returned his gaze westward where he could just make out the earthen mounds of the closest Horwrath hive. From his viewpoint, the hive appeared deserted, but Mitchell knew better.

The Horwrath population was divided into hundreds

of these isolated hives. For eons the Horwraths viciously hunted the Trunjenn's souls, souls of which, by evolutionary fate, the Horwraths had been denied. Once consumed, the Trunjenn soul would live for a time within the eater, rendering him or her one with the Trunjenn population. From there, the disease spread to corrupt the bloodline of the Trunjenn society, instilling an ever growing faction of violent minded Trunjennians. The evolving culture began to move ever more aggressively toward a militarized way of thinking. But there were those who resisted this path.

Mitchell turned away from the West and continued on the circular path to the point where he could see the third populated division of Drake 2.

Before the great cataclysm, the population most isolated from the influence of the Horwrath insurgency, moved steadily away from changing Trunjenn dogma and toward a more passive existence. The movement called themselves the Phlock or Enlightened Ones. City size communes sprouted up across the planet, each ruled by a high priest. Land was seized and boundaries redrawn.

The Phlock's charismatic leaders went forth as effectively as the Horwraths and gleaned hundreds of thousands of pureblood Trunjenns from the general population. This, in the end, left behind mostly the Horwrath tainted Trunjenn blood lines.

Mitchell smiled to himself as he looked down on the patchwork cropland that encompassed most of the Phlock's region. He then turned his attention to the sheer walls of the mountain ranges. How else could three more diverse groups coexist on a planet this size without nature's spectacular method of segregation? But, it was not always like this.

As the pre-cataclysm Phlock and Trunjenn societies evolved, the Horwrath's Soul Eater hives continued to grow and turned to feed increasingly on Phlock souls. The Phlock was easy prey but no Horwrath foot hold in Phlock society could be gained. Once infected, the hybrid individual was quickly identified and aptly put to death by the high priests.

The attacks continued on the Trunjenns as well. The Trunjenns implored their Phlock brothers to join them in a full scale military invasion of the Horwrath sector, but the teachings of the Phlock had led them away from that destructive path. The collective body of Phlock leaders unanimously refused. This infuriated the Trunjenn leaders and led to the Phlock's complete isolation by force.

Mitchell studied the impassable geologic fortifications that now cut sharply away in six directions to the horizon. He could only imagine the horrific power of the Trunjenn weapon that had physically shattered an entire planet. More awesome was the invisible force that moved the planet's very soul.

Some three-hundred earth years in the past, the Great War erupted, spawning this catastrophic outcome. In the aftermath, the planet Drake 2 had been physically shattered into six equal sections. As if by divine design, the planet's molten core erupted up through the fissures to form the mountain ridges that now ringed the planet of Drake 2. One hundred years of darkness followed. In time the three distinct societies emerged, diminished, but intact, each in their own sectors, segregated forever by Drakin divine intervention.

Mitchell turned away from the parapet and strode off along the two-hundred year old ridge trail that was built by the Trunjenn survivors after the Great War. From atop the ridge's watches they had kept tabs on their segregated Drakin cousins. As the centuries fell away, so too did the necessity for the manned watches. Trunjenn technology had developed and secretly deployed satellite surveillance into space.

Thus far, Mitchell's presence had not been discovered. He took no chances though. He remained inside at night where Trunjenn infrared technology could not catch his heat signature. A nearby thermal spring presented him with added protection and provided him with hot water and heat.

Super-heated water warmed the surrounding stones. From space, infrared surveillance would predictably detect a large area of heat that would be warmer than Mitchell's own body temperature. Still Mitchell took no chances. He built no fires and did not often venture outside of the camouflage net's covering during the day lit hours.

His habitual morning surveillance completed, he now planned to set out on his morning errands.

Mitchell sustained himself on the meat of the numerous species of native birds that, over the nights, unwittingly became entangled in the camouflage netting. He would harvest them once every three sun cycles, keep what he could eat in a day and throw the rest over the cliff. He would pluck and gut the carcasses and then cook them over the thermal steam until they were cooked through.

Next, he would go in search of the sparsely growing vegetation of the high altitude ridge. There was a variety of berries and greens that he gathered. When ground and boiled, bush nuts rivaled coffee in taste and effectiveness. And then there was his most sought after prize, the plant he had named grog pod. Three times in a Drakin year the grog plant produced fleshy pod fruit that once mashed and left out, fermented into very strong liquor. The affect of its moderate consumption was quite pleasant, but when consumed in greater amounts, the beverage induced strong hallucinations. Today Mitchell would risk aerial detection and embark on that very harvest.

The harvest marked the most dangerous exposure Mitchell would risk these days, but over the years his addiction to the liquor mandated the continued risk. The plant grew in thick, but isolated patches along the cliff walls. For years, Mitchell had attempted to cultivate the grog pod plants but it seemed the plant chose only the places it particularly liked. He would guess that the plant would grow in the same spot season after season, but he would be wrong. The plants moved, and each term he would have to search for weeks to find their small chosen gardens. He had finally located five growths, enough to sustain the needed production. The window of opportunity for harvest was very small, just six solar cycles.

In this sun he had only three earth hours before darkness fell. The growths were far outside the covering of the camouflage, one of those locations, a difficult two hour hike, round trip. There was no time to loose so Mitchell ignored the bulk of dead or trapped birds in the netting, pulled on his day pack and headed off down the trail.

Chapter Thirty-One
Hostile Welcome

Tasha and Sack had only a moment's time submerged in the Aquan water world when they perceived an enormous, dark form bearing down on them at an alarming rate of speed. As the goliath object closed in, Tasha willed her limbs to action but her traumatized brain had locked down all effort. The only things working were her eyes and they seemed to be frozen in the wide open position. (Right now she could have easily traded vision for a good set of kicking legs for the horrific view could not be turned off.)

Before the menacing backdrop of racing death she could see Sack had apparently been inflicted in much the same manner because he had gone ridged with fear. His entire body had also gone completely black in color. Simultaneously, the line of swimming friends materialized. At once they all collided in a frenzied storm of air bubbles and then everything went black.

Time seemed to slow down as Tasha's eyes recorded

every detail of the calamity. The formally indiscernible menace came into ultra sharp focus, or at least its mouth and eye parts did. Wide open jaws sprouted a ring of razor sharp teeth that framed a tunnel of throat that could have easily swallowed a semi tractor-trailer. Its large, bulging eyes glowed white and lifeless like the headlights of a car. In the same instant, a straight line of goggled swimmers led by Clifford Tuttle, seemed to materialize out of the blue, just in front of the horrific maw. Sack, in slow motion time, began to silently scream, exhaling a copious cloud of air bubbles. The swimmers, unable or unwilling to slow or deviate in course, collided with Tasha and Sack's petrified bodies. The impact forced from Sack's every orifice, an inconceivably massive emission of black ink. At the same moment, the power of that noxious release jet propelled the entire group just out of the blinded monster's path. They tumbled chaotically about in the strong wake of the passing beast and then everything went silent and dark.

Clifford and the rest could sense the additional presence of the two wayward friends but as yet, could not see them. Slowly, the water cleared and they were revealed, Tasha and Sack had returned.

There was no time for jovial reunions. All eyes turned toward the diminishing form of the sea monster. With their hearts in their throats, they all anticipated the thing's return but its form continued on and away.

At last, the five reunited friends came together in a big gang hug. Their collective mind registered elation and then, as suddenly, a sense of alarm. One was missing. *Sack!*

Where is Sack?!

Sack's body appeared to drift lifelessly in the deep, blue, watery abyss. Their communal mind screamed out in anguish as they spontaneously turned and swam toward their fallen friend. *No! He can't be dead!*

They reached Sack as a group and engulfed him in a desperate embrace. *Is he… gone? How can you tell if he is? He can't be! Please, he can't be.* In a coordinated motion the five all started rubbing his listless body with their hands and feet. Still there was no spark of life. *That light! We need to get Sack to that light!*

In the distance the tiny beacon still glowed bright. *We'll take Sack there. Hurry!* But as they all turned to swim, the light was eclipsed once again. *Oh no! That thing has come back!* they exclaimed in unison. *We must try anyway!*

At that, they all began to swim toward the light using only their legs to propel them forward as their hands were employed holding firm to their friend. Surprisingly, the going was slowed very little.

The light was eclipsed four more times as they closed the distance. *It is circling the light source again! Its pace is steady. If we time this just right, it may not notice us. We can get past it. We have to get past it!*

Timing was everything now. They could see its mammoth form circle to the far side of the light source. As it came back around to face their direction the group stopped still in the water until its tail was to them, and then they accelerated forward until it began its next round.

They could see its profile clearly now. It was like

something right out of the deep oceans of Earth, but on a more enormous scale. The huge mouth hung open as it gulped what ever edible life happened into its path. It had a shape like an angler fish but without the lighted fishing tackle. Its eyes glowed from the side of its head, white and pupil-less, giving it a ghostly, lifeless appearance. Its body was huge around but too short in length, almost as if it's entire mid section had been removed giving it the image of a creature with only a head, mouth and tail.

Beyond, the light of their objective shown invitingly as the giant moved past again. Once it had passed and it was a safe distance away, the coordinated group darted forward carrying with them the still, silent body of Sack. With this final effort the group moved through the thing's turbulent wake and inside the perimeter of the creature's course.

Although the light was getting closer, its source had still not been revealed. If anything its blinding light conspired to hide its very shape. *This is a good thing… right?* the group's mind worried. *We don't know what we are swimming towards. But if there is a chance to get help for Sack, we have to take it.*

It then occurred to their collective mind that, once inside the radius of the circling creature's track, they would become fully exposed. The mammoth fish was nearing its furthest distance from them. In an instant, the light source would be directly between them. With a concerted effort the group pushed off toward the light. They knew this was their last shot.

The light ahead was blinding, the mammoth fish to their right. They should have stopped but they were too close to their destination now. The behemoth's lifeless, white, glowing eye blinked recognition as the group took their last desperate strokes. In reaction, its body twisted in towards them. They were there, just yards away, swimming fast, abandoning all caution regarding their destination. Then a final, horrible scream erupted from their collective being.

Chapter Thirty-Two
Action Must Be Taken

Having returned to his home planet, Cygnus, The Optometrist stood in silent contemplation alongside his two Cygnus colleagues, Hornest and Doneenah. They had just received the troubling news from Skyloumia.

Composing himself with great effort, the Optometrist whose Cygnus name was Optomeetruss, finally spoke.

"So, it begins again," he breathed. "Sackus Rue was a fool to disregard the Consortium's orders! Or... I suspect he had, from the start, no concern for this. Poof! Rue has no idea how dangerous this child can be to the balance!"

"What action do we take, Supreme, Optomeetruss?" Hornest asked.

"Clifford Tuttle must be retrieved at all cost. Of course, we must locate him first. A monumental task considering the boy could have traveled to any of the six worlds, or perhaps, beyond," The Optometrist ominously ventured.

"This child, he has such power?" Doneenah asked. She appeared startled by this possibility.

The Optometrist shook his head slowly. "I have suspected this boy's abilities for some time now. He is special. I know this now."

"This is indeed disturbing news." Hornest said, shaking his head. "Such ability is most rare in these six worlds."

The Optometrist smiled ironically, "Rare? Indeed. We have discovered this anomaly, as of now, to exist only in Earth Travelers, and to the Consortium's knowledge, to exist only within Clifford Tuttle."

The two colleagues frowned in silence before Doneenah brightened and spoke up. "The goggles? They can be traced?"

"Indeed, they can, but still this takes time. Alas, to complicate things further, Clifford Tuttle possesses this most rare ability to travel at any time. He is new and has not been trained in the ritual of shielded shadow. For now, we can only hope he has traveled to Aquan. Aquan's orbit around its sun is slow, its nights long."

Doneenah looked into the Optometrist's eyes. "Then let us hope this is so."

The Optometrist's short lived smile had long since faded. "Aquan is the logical place to begin our search. It was next in the natural progression of Clifford Tuttle's first travel. With this boy though, who can predict." He paced slowly around his control room. "In the water of Aquan, there is much danger," The Optometrist said as he stroked his narrow chin. "Clifford Tuttle's likelihood to survive hinges on where he might have entered Aquan. If he is lucky, he will have entered near Turritopsis, the Aquan center of population. However, the odds of that fate are quite slim considering that world's vast size. Much of Aquan is unpopulated by the Aquanamen. There are regions too dangerous for even the most intrepid to explore. There are outposts, of course. But the Aquanamen who populate these places are less than cooperative, and can be very treacherous."

Hornest offered his opinion. "Then one of two outcomes can transpire in this perilous scenario: Clifford Tuttle will miraculously find his way to some civilized populous center or will be killed by the dangerous nature of Aquan." Hornest smiled dryly, "If he *is* killed, this dilemma will be eliminated. Poof!"

The Optometrist's frown darkened. "Yes, this is true. But even at age six, Clifford Tuttle exhibited great resourcefulness of character. I say his chances are good. He will find some Aquan populous. Let us hope he does not find the wrong type… If in Aquan, he truly is."

Hornest looked up from a deep thought. "Aquan… Indeed, this boy *is* phenomenal. How did Clifford Tuttle survive his *first* trip to Aquan? He possessed no goggles! Surely he would have drowned the moment he arrived there, no?"

"No." The Optometrist said. "In that there is an anomaly… or doubtful accident.

Honest cocked his head. "A conspiracy?"

The Optometrist smiled wickedly.

"So, Supreme Optomeetruss, what can we do?" Doneenah ventured, having woken from an introspective muse.

The Optometrist had migrated to the large control console and was also deep in contemplation. He finally looked up. "We follow the same strategy we engaged the last time this remarkable child traveled."

Doneenah's lips curled into a sarcastic grin. "Certainly, Supreme. You cannot mean– Mitchell!"

Hornest scoffed. "That human has not been in his right mind for a great span of time. He is as reclusive as they come… and an addict! I hear he lives in a nearly constant state of inebriation on Drake 2! Poof! Of all the worlds to choose! Knowing this, I say he must be mad!"

The Optometrist nodded his head slowly. "You, of course, are correct, Hornest. But, he alone has the rare ability to follow Clifford Tuttle's steps. Mitchell is a supreme seeker. He brought Clifford Tuttle back before and he will do it again."

"Mitchell will not cooperate, Supreme!" Doneenah scoffed. "He is a broken man. He hides on Drake 2 for a reason."

The Optometrist smiled knowingly. "You underestimate my powers of persuasion, my dear Doneenah."

Her face wrinkled up in a grin of understanding. "There is that…"

Chapter Thirty-Three
Duty Bequeathed

The grog plant harvest was never easy considering the plants tended to choose the most inconvenient places to grow. Mitchell was half way down his third and final descent of the day. Wiping his profusely sweating face with a filthy rag, he looked over the view of sky, cliff and water. Far below his dangling feet, the sunlight reflected off of the sparkling surface of the third sector sea. Again, he wiped his brow to clear the stinging sweat from his eyes.

"Crikey, a cool swim would put me right about now," he muttered as he checked ropes to make sure he was secure. He still had a ways to go.

Mitchell dropped another ten feet onto a rocky ledge just large enough to sit on. Once seated, he carefully pulled off his battered day pack and pulled out two water skins, one filled half way with warm and unappealing water and the other, a quarter full of his homemade grog. He needed to hydrate badly but thus far, the torturous descents had put his nerves on edge. He dropped the water back into his pack and uncorked the grog. He took a good size tug on the sweet, fiery liquid, his fifth of the morning, and then closed his eyes until he could feel the liquor's tranquilizing effects leak into his nervous system.

His brain floated on the tide of increased inebriation as his ears listened to the actual waves of the sea crash against the cliff's rocky base far below. Suddenly he wished he had taken the water.

"Easy now, Mitchell. The cliff's no place to be flying off with the pixies."

With a great effort Mitchell forced his eyes open. For an uneasy moment, the world before his eyes swam in liquid undulation and then thankfully, cleared.

Mitchell placed the grog skin back in his pack then pulled out the water. He gulped a large mouthful of the warm sulfurous liquid, and then almost gagged it back up. His world went into a swoon again, but he held tight to his consciousness.

"One more drop," he muttered and looked down.

Ten feet below, the fat clump of grog pods protruded from a crevice in the rock.

"There you are me bonnie beauts."

Always mindful of the danger in getting caught outside at night, he checked the height of the sun and blinked. It should have been higher in the sky. A cold sweat broke out on his skin.

"I couldn't have buggered out that long," he muttered and looked up toward the top of the cliff he had descended. Already he could see starlight struggling through the deepening dusk sky. His worry, somewhat numbed by the grog, deepened.

"I best get on with it."

Despite the drunkenness he would now gladly give back, he turned and dropped the final ten feet. He quickly filled his harvest sack with the pods and as he prepared to climb back up, took another swig of water. He hitched up his rope harness and began to climb.

The bare and rocky surface of Draken cliffs were full of convenient foot and hand holds and were normally easy to climb, but his legs and arms felt like jelly. Slowly he pushed himself up another step. The pack and harvest bag felt too heavy for what they held and he barely achieved his previous perch before total exhaustion halted any further progress.

Mitchell squared himself on the small ledge then leaned his back against the stony cliff wall. From there he looked out over the sea that was just beginning to take on the reflected color of the sunset. All at once, as if captured in time lapse photography, Mitchell's mind comprehended the sun's accelerated drop to the horizon.

Night had fallen unnaturally fast, casting Mitchell's wavering consciousness into a darkness deeper than night. His vision alternated between his real world and hallucination. He rocked his head back and stared in wonder as the star bedazzled sky wavered and then solidified into the all too familiar face of Optomeetruss, The Optometrist.

"What do you want, Mate?" Mitchell slurred.

"Clifford Tuttle." The Optometrist replied.

"Who?" Mitchell lied. He knew Clifford Tuttle alright. He could never forget. Not that one.

"You remember Clifford Tuttle, Mitchell? Troublesome child. Dark shadow? You and he, two of a kind?"

"Yeah, yeah, that'd be right," he groaned. "Splinter in the foot, that ankle biter."

"Clifford Tuttle has traveled again," The Optometrist announced.

"That'd be right," Mitchell breathed, knowing very well that he had, and then angered, "I am retired, Optomeetruss! Now, rack off!"

"Tut, tut, Mitchell. You know, as well as I, that this can not be ignored."

"Nah, nah, nah, NAH! Find someone else! Leave me alone! Leave me alone… This is my life now." His voice had at once, lost its strength.

The Optometrist smiled down from the heavens. His celestial voice retained a quiet, persuasive tone, "There is no one else, old friend. The sooner you find Clifford Tuttle the sooner you may return to your, so called life… such as it is."

"I'm slaughtered. I can't find the strength to scale this bloody cliff, let alone fossick the six worlds for one lost nipper," he moaned and finally shut his eyes in an attempt to extinguish The Optometrist's face. The face did not disappear.

"One child? Did I not articulate? There are four others of Earth, and apparently one Skyloum child," The

Optometrist added.

Mitchell exhaled a ragged breath, "Oh, noice."

"There is strength in you… you have just chosen to forget, Mitchell. I think it is time you remembered."

Suddenly the sky began to brighten. Mitchell's eyes snapped open as if he had been abruptly roused from a deep sleep.

"Crikey! Optomeetruss! You dunny rat!"

Chapter Thirty-Four
Same Predicament, Different Planet

By all rights they all should have been dead. In the final seconds of their desperate swim toward the light, their collective mind first discovered that the light source had in fact been the phosphorescent lure of a real, giant angler fish. Their swimming momentum had all but delivered them right into the fish's terrible mouth. At once the behemoth they had been fleeing closed in on them, and in one tremendous gulp had delivered them from the jaws of the angler. Instead of finding themselves in the belly of a monster fish, they found themselves floating inside a ship of some kind. Though organic in shape, the interior walls were solid not flesh.

At first, a collective blind panic held sway on the engulfed group, and then, little by little, each separated from the school mentality and realized their unexpected predicament. Well, almost all. Christa remained in an agitated state of utter panic. Sack was still catatonic.

Clifford and Marco quickly restrained Christa despite her desperate attempts to break through the place where the supposed mouth had clamped shut. Though she continued to blindly thrash, Clifford and Marco held her bloodied arms and hands pinned to the wall.

Tasha in the meantime was trying in vain to bring Sack back to life.

Though her face was cloaked in goggles and life support gel, they could all tell she was sobbing. Sensing Tasha's distress, Shelly immediately collected her composure and swam to the aid of her friend.

Tasha resisted and then reluctantly turned away from the poor, stricken Skyloum and finally accepted a consoling hug from Shelly.

At that moment the water level inside the chamber began to drop. Their heads broke the surface and the goggle gel retracted. All at once their stressed voices echoed throughout the holding chamber.

Clifford released Christa's arm and began to feel around the sealed opening they had been swallowed through.

"What is this place?" Clifford asked

Marco reacted to Christa's renewed thrashing by wrestling her to the floor. Had he an extra hand, he would have clamped it over her screaming mouth. He was having a very hard time focusing, partly because of Christa's screaming and partially from the residual effect of the school mind meld.

"Some kind of submarine, that's my guess," Marco yelled over Christa's incessant shrieks. He turned back to Christa and gave her a rough shake. "Christa! Stop it! Get a grip! You're safe!"

Christa stopped screaming and shook her head. "NO! Mouth… Eat! No! Monster! Fish EAT!" She blathered.

Marco steadied her, "No. *Submarine* eat. We're okay, I think," he said as he loosened his grip and took an inquisitive look around.

Christa remained still except for her eyes that continued to dart about.

Tasha could now be heard weeping. Clifford moved to join them at Sack's side.

"Is he dead?" Clifford croaked as he tried to swallow the growing lump in his throat.

Marco had followed him over. "How can you tell?" Marco wondered aloud.

"He's still his normal color… maybe-" Shelly said, trying to offer some shred of hope.

At that moment they all felt the vessel make a sudden course change.

Clifford looked around, "Who's driving this thing?"

Marco shrugged, "Don't know, bro."

Clifford stood and yelled, "Hello! Hello! Is anyone there?"

They all listened but no answer came.

"Hey! Is anyone there?" Clifford listened, and then snapped his fingers. The translator ear plugs!" He felt inside his ears but they were not there. "Funny. I had them in when we... wait a minute!" He removed his goggles and inspected them. "Nothing, but where? He searched his pockets and shortly discovered the ear plugs stowed neatly away in their carrying tube. He snorted in disbelief knowing darn well that in the panic of the sudden passage, removing the plugs would have been the last thing on his mind. He shrugged and inserted them as the others discovered the exact same phenomenon had occurred with them.

Again Clifford called out. "Is anyone there? Hello!"

A low rumbling sound accented with clicks and ticks came in through his earplugs. The sound reminded him of the sounds that dolphins make.

"Hello?"

The sounds came again, this time forming distinct words. He could tell that the voice was not directed at them. It was more like a conversation overheard, filtering down from above their heads.

Clifford took a deep breath and shouted, "Hey! Down here! We're down here!" and waited.

The conversation hushed and shortly the ceiling above slid back to expose, through a glass-clear floor, the full height of the vessel. Three creatures peered down on them from their water filled control deck.

Suddenly Clifford felt like he had fallen into some mythological story. The three observers looked just like mermen. Their bodies were elongated and covered in what appeared to be scales. They had the lower body of a fish and an upper body that looked like a hybrid of fish, human and seahorse. They had muscular human-like torsos and arms. As would be expected, their five digit hands were webbed. Their faces diverged from human features to those of a horse. Though elegant in shape, the three looked rough and life worn. One looked as if he were missing an eye.

Clifford, Marco and Shelly stood together and looked up at their hosts.

Marco spoke first. "Ah, Hola? Gracias… Thanks for getting us out of that mess."

The three mermen remained silent as they continued to study their catch.

Clifford stepped up. "Can you understand our language? We are Travelers… from Earth."

The one-eyed merman leaned in, *"What is Earth?"*

"Earth is a planet… our planet. We have traveled to Aquan by mistake. We are lost. Can you help us?"

The three mermen turned away and rejoined their previous conversation.

Tasha, who had remained at Sack's side stood and addressed the three. "Hey! We need help! Our friend is injured!"

One Eye turned and peered down at Sack's unmoving figure. *"Is it of Earth as well?"*

"No he is from another place called Skyloumia," she cried.

"I see… It seems we have intercepted an all out alien invasion," he seemed to scoff. The others appeared to be laughing among themselves.

"Your comrade appears to be dead. Would you like us to flush him out?"

Tasha seemed to shrink. "No!" Tears welled in her eyes. "He is not dead! He just… won't wake up," she sobbed as she sunk back down to Sack's side.

One Eye turned to one of the large domed windows that had appeared as white glowing eyes from the outside. A soft pink light glowed in through the window.

Sawren! We are here. Wake this Skyloum if you can."

The one called Sawren appeared to smile maliciously. *"Right, Sir. And if I can't?"*

One Eye grinned. *"Then we will be rid of his rotting corpse. Ha, ha, ha."*

Sawren swam over to a control panel and touched a button. Instantly the holding chamber began to fill with water. Quickly the five replaced their goggles.

Once the chamber had completely filled the one called Sawren passed through the clear barrier that separated the control deck from the hold as if by osmosis. His height was now apparent. As was everything they had encountered in their short time in Aquan, Sawren was huge. He, measured, at the very least, twelve feet tall. Sawren roughly pushed past Clifford and Marco, who had taken up a defensive posture in front of the girls and Sack. The third merman sunk down through the barrier and joined Sawren in the chamber. He easily grabbed up Clifford and Marco in one of his large arms and Tasha, Christa and Shelly in the other and held them tight.

Sawren lifted Sack off the floor and began to laugh as he tossed him back and fourth between his hands like a balloon.

"Open the hold Kross!"

One Eye complied and the huge maw began to drop open.

The five Earth children gasped in awe. What appeared to be a gigantic jelly fish filled the view outside. Its domed body glowed bright red-orange before a backdrop of blackest sea. Thousands of dangling tentacles, each with a glowing tip, swayed hypnotically in the gentle currant below its body. The vessel had not slowed its approach suggesting that there was still a ways to travel before they arrived at the outermost tips of the dangling tentacles. The scale of the thing was more than enormous seeming large enough to encompass a small city.

Some minutes later the vessel arrived at the furthest extent of the tentacles. The body of the jellyfish hovered somewhere above and out of sight. Its glow bathed the chamber in red light.

Tasha thrashed in silent protest. Sawren pushed past, playfully bouncing Sack about like a ball, and went outside.

Once outside, Sawren clutched Sack in one enormous hand and approached the outer most tentacles.

Tasha and the rest watched helplessly as the merman studied the small Skyloum and then, to their horror, let go of Sack, allowing him to drift toward the forest of glowing tentacles. As Sack contacted the outer line of tentacles, electricity began to arc into Sacks body from every direction. With every zap, Sack's body bucked and twisted in what appeared to be painful contortions.

Tasha suddenly twisted violently out of the merman's

hold and swam for the opening. As it seemed she would escape, Tasha encountered an invisible barrier and was knocked backwards into the chest of the grinning Aquan brute. He only laughed and gave her a quick slap from his tail that sent her violently adrift bouncing off the vessel's walls and floor. Clifford and Marco tried to twist free but the big merman was ready this time.

Meanwhile, Sack jerked and writhed as he continued to be shocked by the electrified tentacles. Then, all at once, Sack became immersed in a cloud of bubbles, a second later he jetted away like a shot. Stunned by Sack's sudden resurrection, Sawren hesitated as if deciding whether it was worth the effort to chase him down or to just let him go. In the end he decided on the chase.

It took some time but eventually Sawren returned with poor Sack tightly gripped in one hand. Sawren had opened a hatch door and with a gush of water shoved Sack into the hold.

By then the hold had been drained and the five had taken seats on the floor. The sight of Sack alive and kicking both caused elation because he was alive, and disappointment, because he had not escaped. Seemingly no worse for wear, Sack, looked confused and overjoyed all at once. Tasha shrieked with joy at the sight of him and rushed him into a tackling hug.

Abruptly the vessel churned into motion and seemed to rise upward through the glowing tentacles.

Chapter Thirty-Five
Hoodwinked

"Optomeetruss! You dunny rat!" Mitchell's voiced curse resounded through the blackness of the void of transition as he tumbled out of control and wrestled the pod filled harvest bag to his chest simultaneously.

"Crook! If this ain't the biggest load of barker's eggs!" he cussed as he searched the pack for his goggles. Of course he hadn't thought to pack them. Who knew?

"Buggered!" he spat.

The border presented his hurling body into the Skyloumian heavens as suddenly as it had taken him from Drake 2. Through squinted eyes he checked the vast space for a reference point. As luck, or, the will of the Optometrist would have it, the great cumulus clouds of the Skyloum capital floated just off his left hand. He squinted further straining his tearing eyes to pick out the proverbial needle-in-the-haystack Terminal.

"Still too far away," he muttered and aimed his fall trajectory toward the big cloud habitations. "I hope those ning-nongs at the tractor aren't out on a smoko."

Shortly the tiny, gleaming Terminal came into view. Mitchell was flying fast and blind.

"Don't mind if I lob in, mates? Any time now!" he shouted as if that would matter.

All at once his direction adjusted and speed slowed.

Mitchell was gently deposited onto the deeply shaded landing deck and urged quickly through a set of windowless doors. Once inside, he took a moment to let his eyes adjust to the internal lighting and then moved a little wobbly-legged toward the Skyloumian customs paddock. There a very stout Skyloum centurion awaited his arrival.

"G'day mate."

The Skyloum studied Mitchell head to toe, frowned and pointed at the harvest sack filled with grog pods. *"Mitchell. You know you can not bring this here,"* the centurion said as he touched a hovering control pad. Instantly a cylindrical receptacle rose out of the featureless floor. The flat lid hissed open.

"Auh nuh," Mitchell protested and clutched the bag to his chest. "G'arn. You wouldn't take a bloke's tucker!"

The centurion scrutinized Mitchell's pleading facial expression silently for a moment. *"What is tucker, Mitchell?"*

"You know… grub, food?"

"There is Earth food here." the Skyloum assured him.

"Nah, not like these beauts, mate. C'mon, give a bloke a fair crack. They're harmless, bloody oath!"

The Skyloum called up another hovering touch pad and then held out his hand. Mitchell refused at first then wilted under the centurion's stern gaze and handed him one of the pods. The Skyloum scanned the pod with a laser scanner, worked the touch pad for an uncomfortably long moment, dropped the pod into the open shoot and then looked Mitchell in the eye.

"This is a Draken 2 fruit possessing very strong narcotic characteristics, Mitchell. I can not allow this illegal contraband past this station. Now, drop those into the waste chute, if you please."

Mitchell mulled this over in his head for a moment then smiled. "Right, then! No drama, mate! I'll just chuck a yewy and be nickin' off."

"I can not allow you to leave, Mitchell. Sackus Ishtabar is expecting you."

Mitchell sighed, "That'd be right. He's got tickets on himself, that one. A right, bloody show pony. What does he want?"

"It is important for you to know that Ishtabar is quite anxious to see you. But first, this is for you," he said and produced a key card.

Mitchell eyed the card and reached out to take it.

The centurion pulled it away before Mitchell could grab it.

"Auh… 'Tucker' goes into the bin first, Mitchell."

"Bloody hell," Mitchell hesitated and then after a long and brutal inner battle, dropped the full sack down the shoot. His hand was shaking as he reached for the key card again.

The Skyloum pulled it away again and with an obvious grin of sadistic pleasure. *"Mitchell... Your pack?"*

Mitchell blew out an agitated sighed and handed over the pack.

"Maybe you'd like to take me to a backroom waltz and have a fassick about in me bloody daks!" Mitchell raged, bluffing the beginning process of removing his pants.

The centurion appeared to ignore Mitchell's remarks as he dredged through the pack. He pulled out both skin flasks, sniffed each, dropped the water back in the bag and dropped the grog into the shoot.

Mitchell cringed, "Ah nah!"

The centurion took out the object wrapped in cloth, found the small mirror inside, and handed it to Mitchell. *"That will not be necessary, Mitchell."* he replied, finally addressing Mitchell's threat to remove his pants. The Skyloum considered the shabby pack and, after a moment's thought, threw the entire thing down the chute.

"Hey! That was my swag, you bloody bushranger!"

The smug Skyloum centurion handed Mitchell the card and smirked, *"You may now proceed to your objective, Mitchell."*

Mitchell was furious. A grog hangover was beginning to knock about in is head and he was completely depleted of all the patience he might have had to begun this journey with, which wasn't much. He hadn't asked for this.

"This is a right dirty hoodwinking for certain,"

Mitchell growled as he pushed past the grinning centurion and exited the paddock.

The observation lounge was uncharacteristically empty when he arrived. Normally there would be several Earth Travelers there at any given hour. Mitchell didn't want the company anyway. But what was worse, the complementary buffet table was empty as well. He held the card key up in front of his eyes and examined it.

"Key to a locka?"

He pushed on to the men's lounge and entered the locker room. Here too the rooms were empty of Travelers. He found the locker and swiftly opened it.

Inside was a full Traveler's kit including jumpsuit, trainers, fully stocked operations pack and a shiny new set of goggles. There was also a small locked safe box, but no obvious place to insert a key. Mitchell pulled out the spotless jumpsuit, snarled and threw it on the floor.

"I haven't used one of these daggy things since I was a kid."

Mitchell had, through all the years of travel, managed to maintain a certain Aussie form: Croc leather boots, leather pants or daks, denim shirt and leather vest. He found these garments to be functional on most worlds except, of course, Aquan. He sighed knowing well that he would be going there and knelt to pick the jump suit up.

Next he examined the contents of the pack with a smile. There was a holographic map pod, communication translator ear buds (military style) a variety of survival and cooking tools, a gleaming new buck knife in a leather sheath, climbing gear, back packer's food, water containers and a light set. This stuff he could use, seeing as the customs centurion had tossed just about everything he had left from his previous life into the chute. Truth be told, his belongings were pretty much worn to near worthless condition.

He tried the goggles on next. He was surprised how much lighter and more precisely fitting they were than the old set he had left behind. He removed the goggles and packed them away in their case.

His stomach, at that moment, growled viciously so he took out a protein bar, tore open the wrapper, and shoved it into his mouth whole. The sweetness of the bar surprised him. He had subsisted primarily on bland, steamed fowl flesh for the past five years. His saliva glands immediately went into overdrive and the wash of drool was not able to be contained.

He wiped his whisker-stubbled chin with the back of his hand and pulled out the safe box. The weight of it was surprising. At this point he could only imagine what the contents were. Was it money, gold or weaponry? He hefted the weight of it and gave it a shake. Whatever was inside was packed solid. He slid it back into the locker and then stuffed the scattered items back into the pack. He shut the locker, pocketed the key card and made his way to the bank of sinks where he stopped to stare into the mirror.

"Crikey, Mitchell. You look a right bonzer swaggie."

When he emerged from the locker room two Skyloum centurions were waiting. Mitchell purposely ignored them and headed toward his next planned destination, his tiny apartment on the next level down. Thanks to his exceptional abilities, he had once upon a time been an elite Traveler. This prestige awarded him private living quarters on all five worlds. He hoped it was still there because there was something he needed. The centurions however had different plans in mind.

The two hulking centurions moved to block Mitchell's way. *"Mitchell, come with us,"* the larger of the two ordered.

"Nah thanks, mates. I'm off to my bedsit for a kip. Nackered I am… dead cert."

The larger centurion floated in closer. *"You have no choice in this matter, Mitchell. We are to deliver you immediately."*

Mitchell shook his head. "C'mon, give me a fair crack o' the whip here, boys. I kid you not, blokes, I'm fairly dead."

"You will come with us freely or not! This is important. I have my orders."

Mitchell didn't have the energy to fight. He was hungry and fully hung-over now. "Okay… Let's be on our way then."

Sackus Ishtabar was waiting for Mitchell in the same conference room where, just the day before, he had met Clifford Tuttle and his friends. He watched bemused as Mitchell was rousted into the room by the two centurions.

The two saluted Ishtabar and left, closing the door behind them.

"Mitchell. It is good to see you again."

Mitchell eyed Ishtabar for a moment. "I wish I could say the same. Ow ya goin'?" he said as he eyed the Skyloum's tattoo-like markings. "Well aren't we the tall poppy now, Ishtabar. Made you boss, now have they?" Mitchell scoffed.

"Yes," he nodded, *"Now you can find Clifford Tuttle, and… my son, Ernestus."*

"So, that's what all this is about. Clifford Tuttle take him off on a little walk about, has he?"

My son is not important. Clifford Tuttle is. He must be found."

"Why me? I was done with this dog's breakfast seven of my years ago. Go find someone else to suck in."

"I am afraid you are it, Mitchell."

"Says who?"

At that moment the hidden panel door slid open exposing the elevator's delegation. Sackus Rue and Johanna Rassahmie stepped into the room.

Mitchell was stunned. "Yer, highnesses," he said bowing his head.

"Kyle, good to see you are still with us," Johanna said with a raised eyebrow and sarcastic smile.

"That'd be right mum," he responded as sharply as he could. The shock of coming face to face with two Consortium top leaders at once had cleared his muddled head. "Lucky, that."

Johanna gave Mitchell a nod. "I trust you are aware that Clifford Tuttle, along with five others, has traveled.

Mitchell nodded. "That'd be right mum."

"You are also aware of what is at stake here?"

"That'd be right… Can't have the lad fallin' into the wrong hands now, can we?" he said with feigned enthusiasm and much secreted regret. "Do you know where he's gotten too?"

"If history has repeated its self, he and his company are in Aquan."

Mitchell bobbed his head in agreement, "Aquan is a big place."

"We have a plan in place. We know the exact time and place at which he traveled. You are to follow his steps precisely. This should put you into the general Aquannian region."

"And what if he's diverged?" Mitchell wondered aloud.

"We will start there," she said with a decisive tone. "You have exactly five of your hours to prepare. You will meet us on the lounge level then. In the mean time, get yourself cleaned up. You look terrible… and smell worse." She sneered, wrinkling her nose.

Mitchell smirked. "No worries mum. I'll be getting a fair to better bath on Aquan."

Chapter Thirty-Six
In The Box

"Ever get the feeling that we've done this before?" Clifford voiced aloud, what he was thinking. He and Shelly were sitting shoulder to shoulder on a short, make-shift bench. They were sealed inside a box that measured no more than six feet wide by eight foot deep by six feet high. The only light inside their room was provided by an object that resembled a glow stick, but squishier, like a fat worm.

Though the remainder of the undersea outpost had been in water, somehow this box contained breathable air. It seemed to them that these Aquans had entertained humans or air breathers before, despite One Eye's feigned ignorance of their origins.

"Excusez moi?" Shelly replied as Clifford's voice pulled her out of her own thoughts.

Clifford shook his head, "It's like we keep getting captured and locked up. I'm beginning to feel like an outlaw or something," he shook his head, "This is so wrong!"

"Oui? A pattern is definitely emerging," she smiled wryly, "Perhaps you *are* a fugitive, a *bad* boy."

Clifford cast his gaze around the space, purposely avoiding eye contact with his flirting cellmate. The tight space seemed just a bit too intimate for his fourteen year old taste. "Four days ago I was just some kid living with my Aunt Gwen in Pittsburgh. Sure... I supposedly went through this all before but I can't remember one single thing about it."

Shelly turned toward Clifford's face so he could not avoid her eyes. "You were too young, perhaps. You said you were freaked out by what happened–what you *did* remember of it. Just think what would have happened if you had to deal with the whole thing– even a situation like this one."

Clifford smiled. "You're probably right. I would have gone crazy... I guess. Even more than I did."

Shelly broke off her gaze and returned to the study of their holding cell. "I wonder how the others are doing."

"All I can say is I'm glad they didn't stuff us all in here. It's kind of small, don't you think?" Clifford said.

"Oui." She said raising a pretty eyebrow, "It's definitely cozy."

Clifford blinked back at her, "How come they split us up like they did... you know, boy, girl, boy girl... Sack, girl?"

Shelly smiled mischievously, "Perhaps they want us to mate," she said giggling.

Clifford could feel himself erupt into an all out blush. "What?! Really?"

"Just kidding," she giggled again.

Shelly then turned serious. "I wonder what they want."

Clifford got up and pretended to stretch. He turned and leaned against the far wall that was the door. "They're probably curious. Maybe they never saw anything like us before. But these cells… and the ship. They know about air breathers or they wouldn't have air."

"Possibly they are waiting for one of their leaders to make a decision. Oui… That is it," Shelly suggested with a nod of her head.

Clifford slid down to sit on the floor. "I hope it's someone who can help us get back. Still–" He broke off.

"Still what, Cliff?"

Clifford's brow knitted as he thought, "I didn't get the feeling these… Mermen or, ah… whatever they are, are very nice. I don't know. I guess I've watched too many pirate movies. That's what they remind me of." Clifford rubbed his face roughly, "All I know is I didn't get a good feeling about them. They seemed a little too forceful. On Skyloumia the centurions were stern, but at least they showed some discipline. I think we really need to find a way to get out of this place, and soon. I keep getting the feeling that… we are running out of time."

"But how do we do this, my friend?"

Clifford buried his face in his hands, "I don't know. I wish Marco was here. If we only had our goggles," he lamented.

Their equipment had been confiscated as they were incarcerated in their boxes. It had been a terrifying moment for each. First, one of the mermen had produced head sized bubbles of air which he had pressed to their faces in order to trick the life gel into retraction, snatched their goggles away leaving them airless and finally shut them into the small boxes. In that panicked moment Clifford and Shelly were sure they would drown but the boxes quickly drained and filled with air.

"I sure hope these boxes don't spring a leak," Clifford added as he studied the interior seams.

Shelly was silent for a time then looked up, "Remember when we were in the water? It felt like we could actually communicate, you know, without actually talking? I wonder if that was the goggles or something to do with this place," Shelly wondered and took a chill in the damp air.

Clifford noticed and automatically got up and moved back to the bench. The two scrunched up close and the chill retreated, both mentally and physically.

"I assumed it was the goggles," Clifford said in response.

"Come, my friend." Shelly said turning to Clifford. "Give me your hands."

Clifford complied. There was a moment of uncertainty on Clifford's part then he let his forehead touch hers. More unexpected warmth washed over him as he picked up a sampling of Shelly's intimate thoughts and then the rest were there.

Hey you two! It's about time!

Their collective mind registered three identical cells and the exact fact that escape, without their goggles, was impossible. Outside their boxes flowed infinite quantities of drowning water. It was no surprise then that Marco had discovered that the box's door latches were not locked.

The collective mind churned out one unattainable solution after another until Tasha landed on an incredibly brilliant idea. *Sack is essentially a big bag of air, isn't he? Can we use him to breathe?*

The collective mind knew this was true. *But how to do this? That's another question isn't it?* And then this solution would be a temporary one at best, considering Sack's past fainting spells. *Our confiscated goggles will have to be located quickly and there is no telling where they are stored.* It seemed they were right back to where they started. The collective mind contemplated still, but it kept returning to Tasha's idea.

In the end it was decided that it would have to be Tasha and Sack who would make the dangerous escape since they had been confined together. *There will be only one chance. If we are guarded closely, we will be found out. The boxes would surely be locked then.*

Inside their box, Tasha was thinking of how she could tap Sack's air supply. He emitted strong jets of air from the palms of his hands and then there were the ten air tentacles down below.

"Okay, Sack, how do we do this?" Tasha asked knowing, since her communicator earplugs had been taken as well, that Sack could not understand her and she him. Sack seemed to understand though.

"I'll start with your hand." She took Sack's squishy hand and studied its physiology. She swallowed back a wretch as Sack's palm port farted out some nervous air. Carefully she put her mouth over the air duct and was immediately overwhelmed by the velocity of escaping air. Not only did her lungs fill too quickly but her stomach as well. In reaction she let out a gargantuan burp. Sack, startled by the sudden explosive sound, himself erupted in a short chorus of rude air flow. In any other circumstance, the nasty sound effects would have been a crackup.

Tasha wiped her tearing eyes, "Whoa! I guess that won't work," she said and burped again, less violently.

Sack seemed to smile shyly and then nodded to indicate his lower tentacle like air jets.

Tasha's eyes grew wide and her upper lip curled up into grimacing snarl as she regarded the wiggling members that emitted constant sputtering air as they kept Sack aloft. "Uuuuh… right," she stammered. She felt at once, the communal response of the others. Their emotions ranged from downright amusement, to utter disgust.

Reluctant to do so, Tasha finally reached out to take one of the tentacles in her hand. It would, she thought, be the equivalent of sucking on someone's gross toe. She swallowed back another belch, this one threatening to be a wet one, and carefully put her mouth to the end. The air flow through the tentacle was strong at first but she found she could manipulate the flow by squeezing it like a hose. (Or a cow's milking teat, she imagined.) The whole process was beyond disgust, but the result met her needs.

Whatever came next would be a breeze in comparison, despite the real possibilities of capture and resulting punishment, or drowning.

The communal mind of the school urged her on, sensing suddenly that time was of the essence.

Tasha and Sack looked at each other and nodded their willingness to proceed. Tasha with one hand on Sack's tentacle turned the box's door latch. The latch turned easily on her hand. With racing heart, Tasha gave the door a shove but the door wouldn't budge.

Chapter Thirty-Seven
Back in the Hunt

The apartment was as Mitchell had left it nearly six earth years past. The three rooms showed evidence of his hasty departure. In the main room, storage bins had been rifled through and their contents scattered on the floor and furniture. The kitchen refrigerator held containers of food long spoiled. The sink was filled with carelessly rinsed dishes. In the bedroom, articles of clothing covered the bed and floors. Several pint liquor bottles stood empty in silent ranks on the nightstand. It was as if he, the occupant of this apartment, had been absent for only days rather than years.

Everything was how Mitchell had remembered with one exception. His secret stash of unopened contraband liquor was missing.

Mitchell cussed the empty cabinet and stroked his rough, whisker-stubble chin with an unsteady hand. Of anything he would have returned to his apartment for, the liquor was the most important. He had a need, a very serious need for a little taste, just a small snort to calm his nerves.

As if in answer to his want, Mitchell's roving eyes focused on a single glass of liquid sitting in plain sight on the kitchen counter. Mitchell rubbed his eyes with his filthy fingers and reopened them in an attempt to erase this unexpected hallucination, but the glass was there, on the counter where it hadn't been on first inspection. Mitchell approached the glass as one might approach a hazardous object.

The glass glimmered, sparkling clean on the grimy countertop. He took the glass up carefully in his hands and smelled the liquid contents. His senses confirmed the liquid was his own grog concoction from Drake 2. An underlying scent hinted of its origin inside his musty skin flask.

Mitchell smiled, took a sip and smacked his lips. He raised the glass in a solute then emptied the remaining grog down his throat.

"Ah… That'll do," his voice horse with the burn of the liquor.

His mind began to clear as his nerves calmed. Now the weight of his appointed duty became apparent. He checked the watch that had been included with his new equipment. The watch was set to Skyloum time and was counting down to the exact moment in which he would depart from the lounge deck. He now had approximately four and a half Earth hours to kill in the count down to departure.

To pass the time, Mitchell spent the next hour showering and shaving. He cleaned the rooms for the next two hours then dropped into his chair. He felt exhausted and wondered how he would find the physical strength to pursue Clifford Tuttle across the known worlds. The answer to that question was easy, he wouldn't. As he closed his eyes Mitchell's mind swam with the fatigue and soon he fell into a deep sleep.

Mitchell woke an hour later to find himself standing in the middle of his apartment, soaked in sweat, and trembling with anxiety. His lucid nightmare had seemed so extremely real that he had flown out of his bed, and clawed at the air expecting to part the animal pelts that were his door on Drake 2. He needed to see that the Horwrath plains were empty and dead as always. Only drab white walls met his eyes.

For nearly six years, he had lived in very close proximity to a massive Horwrath hive containing hundreds, maybe thousands of the dreaded soul eaters, but he had never had a nightmare of them, as well, he should have.

Following the war on Arris, he had been assigned to an elite team of Travelers whose job it was to hunt down and destroy every Horwrath Traveler known to the Consortium. Inside his disjointed, yet very real nightmare, one Horwrath Traveler had eluded him, and was now on Aquan.

Whether Clifford Tuttle was truly on Aquan or not, and no matter if he particularly liked the idea or not, he was going to Aquan. The thought of it knocked what little life he grasped onto out of him. Letting out a long sigh of pain, Mitchell dropped into the nearest chair and remained there until the time had come to leave.

Bright sky light washed the Terminal's glass domed Traveler's lounge where Sackus Rue and Sackus Ishtabar waited, with no small apprehension, for Mitchell's appointed arrival time. Mitchell had been less than cooperative when they had last met. Both Skyloums expected the human not to show so, as a precaution, Ishtabar had sent two of his centurions to assure Mitchell's timely arrival. As it turned out, this had not been necessary.

Spurred by the uneasy feeling that there might be a Horwrath Soul Eater on Aquan, Mitchell left his Australian wardrobe behind and changed into his jumpsuit which was better suited for life on Aquan. Mitchell hated loose ends, although he could honestly say his own life was one big loose end.

What worried Mitchell most was the knowledge that seven years ago a great army of Horwrath Travelers had pursued Clifford Tuttle through the void and onto the crystalline world of Arris. The majority of the Horwrath had been terminated there in a short violent war. The rest had retreated to the wide encompassing realm of the known worlds.

Mitchell arrived at the curved corridor that opened onto the sky lounge before his Skyloumian escorts had left to gather him. Mitchell's watch was counting down to the exact moment, one Skyloumian day cycle after the time Clifford Tuttle had vanished along with his group of four humans and one Skyloum youth, Sackus Ishtabar's son.

Mitchell hitched up his weighty backpack, tightened the straps, and for a protracted moment examined his new goggles. Mitchell had been an active Traveler for over forty-five years, yet he was feeling as nervous as a first timer. He turned as the nearly silent Skyloum centurions floated up behind him.

"G' day. Noice of you blokes to come see me off," Mitchell greeted.

The Centurions nodded politely but remained silent otherwise. Mitchell knew this wasn't a sociable send off but a forced one if he had decided to lark off.

"No worries, mates. I'm well on schedule for my tee-up," he said indicating his wristwatch that had just then started beeping. "Right, then… I'll be nicking off now," Mitchell said with a confident nod. After a silent pause, he installed his new goggles, took a deep breath, pushed through the double doors, and stepped into the sun flooded brightness of the observation lobby. With a flash he was gone.

The deep blue world of Aquan greeted Mitchell as he plunged out of the void of transference. To his great relief the new and untested goggles did their job flawlessly. This, he feared, would be a terrible time to discover a glitch, but knowing The Optometrist, there were no *unintended* glitches.

Mitchell paddled around to take in a 360 degree view of where he was. One thing was for sure, he was deep in the Aquan woop-woop or boonies. On previous visits he had transferred close to the major population centers but today none of these glowing cities were in sight.

That'd be right, Mitchell lamented in his mind. *This Clifford Tuttle isn't an easy bird to catch, not even at age six. Why in the world would he be any different now? Bloody bother.*

Then the nagging question resurfaced, *out here, in the nowhere, what's the boy's chance of survival? Bloody hell… what are my chances?* He asked himself this as his instinct for survival alarm began to chime in his aching head. *There's something out there.* There was *always* something out there on Aquan, especially out in these woop-woop territories. He was not sure how he knew this. Maybe his sodden mind was playing tricks on him. Perhaps he had detected a slight change in the currents or seen a nearly imperceptible shadow pass in the distance. He swam around in a 360 turn again and wondered, in all this nothingness, which direction Clifford Tuttle had swum off to. What mark had drawn the boy's attention and got him moving? Then he saw it, a tiny spot of light.

Mitchell's instincts, though assuredly dulled by years of neglect, had not failed him. He had swum toward the light but stopped short of a direct approach. Instead he swam circles around the thing until he was close enough to recognize it for the danger it was, a giant angler fish dangling its glowing lure above its hideous mouth.

Blimey! If those kids swam into this, they're buggered cert.

Mitchell had learned some about this world from his short stint with a crew of Aquan outlanders after the war on Arris. Together, they had hunted down a pod of Horwrath Travelers who had escaped the other's fate of near annihilation on Arris. He found that these angler fish were extremely territorial, and rarely ventured far from the center of their region. While extremely deadly, their luminescent lures acted as the most reliable beacons in a world with few landmarks. He also knew that if this giant was here, any major civilization of Aquan would be far away, for the fish tended to avoid those places. Knowing that, Mitchell held little hope that Clifford Tuttle could have survived even one Aquan day cycle.

As Mitchell contemplated Clifford Tuttle's most certain demise, he was not aware of the speeding menace bearing down on him.

Chapter Thirty-Eight
Reconnaissance Mission

Leverage was a real problem for Tasha. She let go of Sack's tentacle and put her entire weight of ninety-eight pounds into the effort of pushing the container's door open. Still the door would not budge.

Panting with frustration and a fair amount of anxiety, Tasha looked at Sack who hovered helplessly against the back wall.

Tasha exhaled, "I don't suppose you have anything to offer here, do you?"

Sack shook his head slowly, clearly at a loss.

Sure, Tasha thought as she looked around the small cell, *what could a bag of air do in a situation like this?*

She couldn't use any of the walls. She was too short. Even stretched to her maximum length with her hands on the door, her feet couldn't touch the opposite wall.

Her gaze fell on the bench. If she could get the door open a crack she could use the seat as a lever. The trick was getting the door to open even a crack.

She had deduced that it was the pressure of the water that was holding the door shut. She figured if she could get a flow of water coming in, the pressure would slowly begin to decrease as the compartment filled.

Moving into action, Tasha squeezed past Sack and gave the seat a yank. The cobbled contraption was held tight, but was made from some kind of shell or flat fish bone. She raised her foot and stomped down hard. The bench seat cracked but did not break through. Again, she stomped with more force. This time the bench shattered into three pieces. She picked one of the shards up and examined its sharp edges with a smile.

Sack, who had been looking over her shoulder, saw the sharp edge and gasped.

Tasha turned and gave Sack a reassuring smile, pushed past him again, carefully concealing the sharp tool, and then worked the sharp fragment into the door jamb and pried hard. The piece broke.

"Crap, too brittle!"

She sat deep in thought for a minute. Shortly, she snapped her fingers and turned to retrieve the longest part of the broken bench. This piece consisted of the longest part of the seat and a leg. She wedged it against the opposite wall and tested her length.

By bracing her feet on the bench and stretching her reach, she would have just enough length to push the door out a couple of inches. She grabbed the broken piece of bench she had tried to pry with before and turned to Sack.

Sack recoiled as he stared down at the sharp object in

Tasha's hand, winced and let out a blast of farty sounding air.

"Hmmm," she said as she tapped the bench piece absently against her chin. Tasha arrived at a decision, smiled, then frowned, and finally exhaled.

Tasha unzipped her jumpsuit and stripped it off. Thankfully she was wearing reasonably modest brief panties and a camisole over her bra. She wrapped the jagged pry piece in the fabric jumpsuit and carefully held it out to a seemingly dumfounded Sack.

"What? Never seen a half naked girl before?"

Sack colored. *"No– Why, Tasha?"*

"Oh… I don't know. I'm a girl, you're a boy," she raised an eyebrow, "I guess."

Sack appeared to shrug, *"Is there a difference; boys and girls? You mostly look the same to me."*

Tasha looked down on her less than voluptuous figure. "Thanks Sack… You really know how to make a girl feel good about her self," she said with wanton sarcasm.

Sack shrugged shyly and smiled.

Moving beyond the uncomfortable moment Tasha thrust the jumpsuit wrapped pry piece into Sack's unwilling hands. "This is what I'm going to do," Tasha began.

Sack seemed to be off somewhere else in his mind as he stared dumbly at her.

"Are you listening, Sack!?" Somewhere in the recesses of her mind she picked up some chuckling from the collective mind.

Sack seemed to snap out of his reverie, *"Ah…*

Listening? Yes, Tasha."

Tasha rolled her eyes and exhaled irritably, "Stick with me, big boy! Now, I am going to brace my feet on that piece of broken bench. I will then push as hard as I can on the door. As soon as I get this door open a crack you are going to stick that piece into the crack to prop the door open. The water will begin flowing in through the crack. The more water that flows in the easier it will be to push the door open further."

Sack nodded his understanding. He floated up to the door as Tasha positioned herself. She nodded and flexed her leg muscles in a strong push. The door began to open and a slow but steady trickle of water began to seep in. When she had stretched as far as she could, Sack shoved the bench piece into the crack. Tasha relaxed and Sack backed away from the leaking door. Slowly at first the water covered the floor, and then deepened. The process was slow but it was working.

Many nervous minutes later Tasha was dressed and chest deep in water. Every minute was spent with the fear that the escaping air bubbles would be noticed, but still nothing happened from beyond their confines. When the water had risen to more than half the depth of the box, Tasha got up and gave the door another try. This time it began to move easily. More water rushed in as the air rushed out. The time was soon at hand for Tasha to reconnect to Sacks's toe.

Sack and Tasha were now totally immersed in water. Tasha was working blind, hindered by her unprotected eyes and the fact that most of her face was buried in Sack's squishy flesh. She had held little hope that they would get even this far because surely the great calamity of escaping air bubbles would have been noticed by any nearby Aquan guard.

Sack, however, could use his eyes because they were naturally protected by his outer skin. Slowly and cautiously, the two moved out of the box. By his lack of reaction, Tasha could tell they were safe for the time.

Unable to stand the uncertainty any longer, Tasha forced her unprotected eyes open and saw, for herself, that the space outside of the holding chamber was not occupied. Above, the escaped air bubbles had collected into a huge air pocket on the ceiling. Tasha spit Sack's toe from her mouth and swam up to the air.

Safe for the moment, Tasha guessed that they would get only a few more minutes before they were discovered. But as the minutes ticked by, no alarms sounded and no alerted guards burst in. Only then did Tasha began to relax, as much as an air breathing person could, fully submerged in water and forced to suck air from a Skyloum's toe!

Feeling an increased sense of urgency from the collective mind, Tasha dove back down and reattached her mouth to Sack's bubbling toe. Together the two explored the chamber.

The space was not furnished as you would expect on Earth. There were no tables or chairs. The only thing that did seem out of place was a row of coffin-like boxes standing on end against one wall. The wall was soft and organically formed like living tissue and radiated a soft red-pink glow.

As her eyes adjusted to the slight sting of the water and dim light, Tasha noticed along another wall six large glass cylinders that looked like giant upside down test tubes. Each was large enough to hold one human being. The boxes, however, looked like the best place to start.

Tasha pointed and Sack moved them toward the boxes with careful bursts of air from his hands. When they were there Tasha braced her mind against what she hoped was not some gruesome content.

Slowly Tasha opened one of the coffins. If her mouth hadn't been full of Sack's toe, Tasha would have yelped with joy. Inside was one of their backpacks which had been opened and rummaged through, but otherwise intact. Most importantly the goggles were there. But, the set wasn't hers so she moved to the next box and examined its contents, but again, they were not hers. On the third try she hit pay dirt.

Tasha quickly found her goggles and with one last inhalation and a repulsive mind spit, she released Sack's toe from her mouth. The gel quickly did its thing but having been submerged already she was forced to take in a burning lungful of water. She struggled with the deadly discomfort for a long, uncomfortable moment before she recovered normal goggle induced respiration. She turned to Sack and, with tearing eyes, smiled.

Sack looked very relieved.

Next, Tasha repacked her backpack and zipped it up. The contents would be sopping, but, for all that, she felt very lucky to be reattached to her own personal life support.

Now that she was free of Sack's toe, Tasha could get a better look around. The chamber that housed their containment boxes remained, apparently, unguarded. She could see the row of six containment boxes two of which she supposed held her friends.

Tasha closed her eyes and concentrated on the communal mind and was relieved to find everyone was still alive. She sent the message of the situation and received back Clifford's instructions to investigate the area further.

Clifford radiated a certain cautious urgency that immediately put Tasha on alert. She looked around and noticed an organically formed passage that led away from the room. Reluctantly, Tasha moved on Clifford's instructions.

Tasha found that the connecting artery-like passage followed a serpentine route and contained strong currents. The whole experience reminded her of an old movie called The Incredible Journey where a group of scientists and a submarine were shrunk down to a microscopic scale in order to navigate through a human's body. Being in these passages was just like swimming through a body's arteries.

Rather than move in a single direction, the currents that flowed through these arteries fluctuated in direction at precise intervals. After several failed attempts to swim through, Tasha figured out the rhythm and she and Sack moved on.

Eventually, the passage ended at another chamber, this one free of hard sided containment boxes. As on the strange ship, one wall had a clear membrane window that looked into another room.

As she started to swim out of the passage and into the chamber, Sack shook his head vigorously and reached out to grab Tasha's leg with his free arm. Tasha stopped and gave Sack a nod and a confident wink through her goggles even though she felt far from confident. The current suddenly shifted and she was pushed into Sack's arms. Their eyes met in embarrassed wonder for a moment before the reverse current made the next move by washing them out into the chamber.

Once inside the chamber, the currents were gentler and Tasha was able to follow the perimeter of the room making sure she kept an eye on the transparent opening.

As Tasha approached the edge of the opening, her ears or mind perceived voices. (Who knew anymore where the information was coming from?) The voices seemed distant so she ventured a peek through the clear membrane. That is when she first laid eyes on a Horwrath soul eater, though, at the time, she didn't know it.

He was in the middle chamber that obviously contained air. The Horwrath possessed a very human-like body, but on the larger end of normal human proportions. His hair formed a long, black mane and his skin was dark toned and despite the reddish cast of the place, seemed an ugly reptilian gray/green. He wore tight leather clothing the exact color of his own skin. If not for the tailored shape of the clothing the man would have looked naked. There was something unnerving about those clothes. Beyond, a second membrane separated two Aquan mermen from the Horwrath's air filled chamber.

The conversation was muted through the two membrane partitions and even if Tasha could hear the words, she was not able to decipher them. The need to understand the conversation was very compelling so she dug out her ear plugs and inserted them in her ears.

Tasha listened with her ear pressed against the very edge of the clear membrane that she found, acted like a giant ear drum. At once their voices, angry and threatening, came through clear as day.

The Horwrath was speaking, addressing One Eye, the leader of the vessel she and her friends had come in.

"They are here, Mikkaw!" he snarled.

Mikkaw swam up to the membrane and appeared to stare angrily back at the dark man. *"What would I do, Kak? Just hand them over to you? Ha, ha. No! Not without some… substantial compensation– compensation too rich for you,"* his horsy facial features appeared to sneer.

Kak ran his fingers slowly, calmly through his black mane of hair as if he were idly preening in a mirror. However, his yellow reptilian eyes revealed his volatile mood.

"You will be compensated with your , Mikkaw! I am rich in the ways of death. In this, I am wealthy beyond your comprehension," he said as he moved to the point where

his nose nearly touched the surface of the membrane. He and Mikkaw were now nose to nose. Slowly Kak began to undo his shirt exposing something to Makkaw that caused the imposing merman to startle and back away.

Makkaw shortly recovered his composure and his bravado returned, *"You do not frighten me, soul eater! You are one, we are many! But the many, I do not need. I have my own wealth in death ways too,"* he chuckled and moved to a panel. He held his finger over it and shouted, *"One touch and you drown, Horwrath scum!"*

Tasha's hand went to her chest as the shock hit her. *A real Horwrath soul eater! How can a creature like that exist outside of a terrifying tale, or nightmare?* Her mind screamed.

Sack seeing Tasha's sudden distress moved to her side and tried to pull her away. Tasha resisted as the conversation between Kak and Mikkaw resumed.

The Horwrath did not back down. *" Mikkaw, and I will have your Aquan soul before I die! I assure you, you will not survive, but I most certainly will,"* he said continuing to open his shirt.

Mikkaw jerked his hand away from the panel. His eyes had locked onto whatever he could see inside the Horwrath's open shirt. Suddenly Mikkaw twitched and fell into a stunned condition. Like a dead fish, Mikkaw began to drift toward the membrane.

Sawren, who was floating off to the side, quickly moved in to grab Mikkaw before he could hit the barrier.

Mikkaw woke with a start. His eyes were wide with

terror as if, in that brief interval, he had experienced a horrific nightmare.

Sawren steadied him.

Laughing wickedly, Kak pulled his shirt closed but did not button it. He paced away from the membrane, and, as if something had caught his attention, paused facing the opposite membrane. A sly grin spread across his face as he turned to face Mikkaw and Sawren again.

Tasha had quickly ducked beyond the clear membrane's edge, but held a terrible fright that the Horwrath soul eater had, for a second, locked his eyes on hers.

Kak continued in a dangerous voice. *"I trust you get my point, Mikkaw. Now I want what I have come for!"* he demanded.

Mikkaw wrenched himself out of Sawren's grip and stared angrily through the membrane at the Horwrath.

"My answer is still no! They are mine to do with what I want," Mikkaw replied defiantly. This was *his* Aquan outpost, *his* chiefdom. *He* was supreme Chief here. He wielded great power. *No one* threatened Mikkaw and lived as they lived before. He hurt his rivals and dissenters. He would never be witnessed backing down to this Horwrath scum or any other enemy. His honor was at stake, not to mention a considerable ransom for the Earthling Travelers. *"Now soul eater… you will."*

Kak's smiling, reptilian eyes met Mikkaw's unblinking single eyed stare,

"I think not," he said, and smiled brutally. *"Give me the boy, Clifford Tuttle. He is all I have come for. You, of course,*

can attempt to ransom the rest, but I warn you Mikkaw, the Consortium will destroy you before you get your ransom." he declared with a slight retention of his previous humor. *"If I were you, I would free the rest and be done with it. Give me Clifford Tuttle, forget this folly, and you will live a long and potent life."*

Mikkaw's facial expression morphed through a succession of emotions: anger, fear and finally shrewd suspicion before he spoke, *"What is so special about this one boy?"* Greed radiated from yet another facial expression as he spoke.

Kak's cruel smile faded, *"There is nothing special about this boy at all,"* Kak lied convincingly. *"Clifford Tuttle took something very precious from my people. What he took, my kind can never have back. This boy eluded me once in the past and I have been pursuing him ever since,"* Kak smiled a conspirator's smile. *"I have, as you do, my honor to defend. That is that is special about Clifford Tuttle, to me."*

Mikkaw's eye roved over the Horwrath's face as he searched for a chink in Kak's armored persona. He could not find one.

"I will consider your request and advise, Kak," Mikkaw said, then turned and abruptly left the membrane chamber.

Sawren hesitated for a moment catching Kak's fearsome stare and then turned to follow his leader.

Tasha quickly swam for the shelter of the passageway. Her progress was hastened along by Sack, who out of fear, protective instincts, or both jetted them out of harm's way and back into their own chamber. He did not stop pushing her until they were safely inside their containment box.

Sawren and Mikkaw swam directly to Mikkaw's habitat that doubled as his official office. The two had remained silent until they were behind closed doors. A strikingly beautiful mermaid was waiting for them there. She swam to greet them.

"Chief Mikkaw. There is news."

Mikkaw had been deep in thought when he had entered his habitat. The mermaid had startled him out of his funk.

"Yes, what is it now, Sinnsie?" Makkaw replied wearily. He had far from recovered from his clash with the despised Horwrath. Moreover, he had the very uncomfortable feeling of barely eluding death, and this gave him real reason to fear his days were numbered. He despised himself for this weakness. He was, after all, the chief of the outlands: bold, strong and deadly. And he was not accustomed to looking his own fragile mortality in the face.

He would give the Horwrath this Clifford Tuttle and quickly. The sooner Kak was off Aquan the better.

"Yes, Sinnsie?" he repeated.

She was studying him, and Mikkaw knew she was seeing his vulnerability. Something would have to be done about this before long.

Sinnsie cast her stare downward, and bowed her head respectfully, sensing Mikkaw's irritation.

"The Elder has had another vision, Mikkaw. Another

Traveler has come to the Outland. And, it is Mitchell, your old friend."

Mikkaw's face dropped, *Mitchell*, he mused. Their paths had crossed before.

Mikkaw replied with a snarl, "I suspect we must go retrieve him now? Go now, Sawren. I will wait here," he said, waving the big merman away.

"That will not be necessary Chief Mikkaw," Sinnsie reported. "There is a vessel already in that vicinity. The pilot, Knotrauf, has been alerted."

Sawren hid his feelings. Inside he was smiling. The plan was coming together most excellently. He would be the one to rescue and deliver Clifford Tuttle and his crew safely to Mitchell and the Consortium. He would then permit the coming events to expose Mikkaw's deceit, and eliminate the Horwrath in one swift move.

Sawren cast a glimpse up at the translucent, fleshy ceiling of Mikkaw's habitat and noticed it was growing lighter. The sun was coming to illuminate the short period in the Aquan day when all things hidden in the dark could be revealed. Mikkaw's days in power were few now. He, Sawren, would be Chief before the next sun.

Chapter Thirty-Nine
On the Move Again

Back in their water filled box, Tasha and Sack could not see the brightening glow of the chamber outside, but the communal mind of the six instinctively knew that the sun was coming up. The sun light would only last one quarter of the Aquan day cycle. This too, instinct told them. Despite the fact that they had just returned, it was time for Tasha and Sack to make their next move.

In order to travel, all six of them had to be well out in the open sea. The easy part would be getting the supplies from the coffin-like lockers and distributing them to the four other captives. The hard part would be finding their way out of the giant jellyfish outpost and past the thing's electrified tentacles before the sun was lost for another day. If the tentacles held the power to shock Sack back to life, they also had the power to shock them all to death.

The escape seemed impossible, but the alternative was much worse. Tasha knew, in her heart, that Chief Mikkaw would surrender Clifford to Kak. He would do it quickly too, if he wanted to live.

Tasha looked Sack in the eyes. "Are you ready for this, Sack?"

Sack rose up to full height releasing just a minimal amount of nervous air bubbles. He was feeling more prepared for peril because he knew that he was not alone. The humans were good and he, Sack, was now part of their team. He felt proud knowing that he had already helped Clifford and his team in ways he would never have imagined he could.

"I am ready, Tasha," he replied confidently. *"We must save Clifford from the soul eater."*

Tasha smiled and gave Sack a squishy fist bump which he returned now with practiced grace.

They pushed through the door, checked for signs of guards, and satisfied there were none, moved quickly to the lockers. They sorted the equipment, Sack took two sets and Tasha took the others. Clifford, Shelly, Marco and Christa were alerted through the strange telepathy and had begun to push their doors out. As soon as the doors were opened wide enough, Sack and Tasha pushed the captive's goggles through and urged them to put them on before the water became too deep. The transition from air to water went smoothly for the four and soon they were all gathered in the main chamber.

Clifford motioned them into a huddle and there they put their minds together.

We need to get out of here! Do we remember the way?

Collectively they gathered individual memories of the

way in. Once all the bits of information were compiled they had a clear understanding of the way out.

The way leads down that passage. But we'll have to pass the room where the Horwrath is being held.

At this point they had no idea what degree of freedom Kak had been granted by Mikkaw. Tasha knew one thing for sure, One Eye was afraid of the soul eater.

Kak will be locked securely, but we can not chance being discovered even if he is locked away. We have to silence our minds just in case he can tap into our thoughts.

How?

By concentrating on the remembered face of One Eye, Mikkaw, that's how. The Horwrath'll be fooled into thinking we're Sawren or one of the others in Mikkaw's company.

Can we do this?

We have no choice.

Tasha and Sack contributed their visual memories and soon Mikkaw's sneering horse-like face filled the group's collective mind.

The six fugitives moved with urgent haste through the currents and past the large membrane enclosed rooms. As they passed the center room, they knew Kak was there because every one of them felt the terrible evil radiating from within. With miraculous determination, the six held their mind together, but just barely, as a reversing current washed them backwards toward that dreaded room.

Once through the passage, they found themselves in the next large chamber. To their surprise and relief this chamber was unoccupied as well.

There had been many Aquans here when we arrived. Maybe it was because they knew we were coming. There were fewer guards than there were the curious. Still it is strange that we haven't encountered one single Aquan. Let's hope our luck holds out.

They gathered in a mind melding huddle again and reviewed their next steps.

There will be another passage leading to that huge open area where we came in. Then we have to move down toward the bottom of this organism.

They swam quickly across the chamber then into the next and last passage. Still they encountered no resistance aside from the whooshing currents.

The passage opened on to the enormous interior of the jelly fish dome. They were high up and could look down on the outpost's main center of population. Glowing sunlight, pink in color, filtered through the jellyfish's translucent body and fell on what seemed like hundreds of dwellings cobbled roughly together with a hodgepodge of materials. Multitudes of Aquan mermen and mermaids swam the corridors between the tightly spaced buildings.

The group's collective mind gasped. They had not perceived this thriving community on the way in.

It was darker before. We had been focused more on where we were being taken than where we were coming from.

Caught by surprise, the six remained stock-still as if they had become frozen in the very water that surrounded them.

In this light we will be seen for sure! Look at that lightning coming from those tentacles! There are hundreds of Aquans here! We can go no further! Then a single voice of reason sounded through the panic. It was Clifford.

What do you think will be worse, sneaking through that mess down there, or going back to the horrible wickedness we felt in the proximity of that soul eater? We can't go back to that! I won't be handed over to that monster! I say we make a plan and we move forward. We'll all die if we don't!

The communal mind collected its wits and studied the scene that spread out before them. Toward the outer boundary of the domed area, the buildings were spaced far enough apart to allow glimpses of meandering street and alley courses, but toward the center, the structures grew so dense that any path below roof level was buried. The passage to the open sea, a circular hole the size of a city block, pierced the center of the thriving village. The sea beyond the opening was black against the glowing violet-red tentacles that they had seen on their way in. Arcing sparks, like lightning bolts, flashed sporadically through the tentacles. All the while, vessels of many shapes and sizes rose and fell through the shaft. The approaching sun glowed brightest through the fleshy dome across the open space. On their side of the dome, the living walls of the jellyfish flexed and contracted and remained in shadow.

We will swim down along the surface of these walls. They're darker and the thing's movement will hide us. If we're careful, no one will notice us.

But, the curve along this side will take us further away

from the center where we want to go. We will end up deep into the habitats.

Yes, but we need to keep moving. The buildings below can give us lots of cover. Are we ready? As we go, try to remember the streets. Make a map in our mind. We need to find a good route to the center before we reach the street level or we will be lost forever in that maze.

They all felt their resolve toughen.

Okay, let's go, slow and careful.

The group swam as one with an economy of coordinated movement. Again the school mentality seemed to have taken control. Their mind focused on a spot on the edge of the central core where arriving and departing vessels passed through a bottleneck check point. One path below them clearly snaked its way toward that point.

We will follow that path and then figure out a way to use the routes that those vessels are using to get to the outside.

The six landed and hunkered down on the roof of one of the outermost dwellings. The structure was built to a maximum height allowed by the curve of the giant organism's fleshy dome. Its jagged edges rubbed against the jellyfish's scarred and inflamed tissue. The dwelling was constructed with a hodgepodge of naturally accruing materials such as seashells and fish bones. Pearlescent fish scales of fantastic size were lashed together and served as shingles and siding. Looking toward the center core, they could see dozens of like structures crowding in on their chosen thoroughfare. A mosaic collage of shimmering color bedazzled their eyes where the sunlight touched the buildings' scaly surfaces.

Moving on, the group stuck to the shaded side of the corridor and close to the tops of the structures as most of the Aquans tended to swim close to the floor of the great floating island. The going was slow. Many times they were forced to avoid the eyes of the higher swimming inhabitants in what ever nooks they could find. All the while, time continued to tick away, the sun continued to ark overhead, and the mood in the school became more frantic.

Finally they reached the congested area close to the core's edge where the tight buildings nearly touched over the passageway they were following. The numbers of Aquans moving about below had grown considerably.

The group gathered at a hidden vantage point overlooking the checkpoint and watched the traffic move through the routine inspections, and was relieved to find that the posture of the inspectors remained casual, if not lackadaisical. This could only mean that they had not yet been missed back at their containment boxes.

They waited with growing anxiety for what seemed an eternity until their chance finally came. An exceedingly bulky transport concocted of a chaotic assemblage of storage containers listed along at the end of the line. There were many sizable nooks and crannies between the haphazardly attached boxes in which to hide. To the Earth born, the vehicle was reminiscent of the shabby, over loaded contraptions driven by junk and scrap metal collectors back home. The opportunity was perfect for their needs unless the operator was as unsavory in character as his vessel looked. A person like that would certainly attract more suspicion, but that was a chance they would have to take. High sun was nearly upon them.

As no additional vehicles were approaching to depart, the six fugitives quickly swam for the concealing vessel, tucked into the deepest nooks they could find and, with racing hearts, waited to see if fate delivered them safely away.

After what seemed another endless wait, the vessel slowed to a stop at the checkpoint. Clifford had purposely chosen a tight gap close to the front of the vessel where he could pick up the translated conversation between the driver and inspector through his earplugs.

"Foulstik! We have warned you and here you are again with this wretched wreck!" the inspector scolded.

Clifford's heart dropped. He braced himself against the inevitability of an extra close inspection, or of the vessel being turned back altogether.

As the inspector began his work, the driver, feigning good humor, spoke back in a rough, crass voice, *"No, no, no…This vessel is good to go, inspector."*

Clifford felt the water shift as the large merman swam past the opening of his hidey-hole. The vessel commenced to sway as the Aquan inspector tested one lashing after another.

Breathless with escalating dread, Clifford waited for the inevitable shout of discovery, but miraculously, none came. So far, the plan was working.

The large inspector had nearly finished his round of

the vessel when something caught his eye. A large silver bubble rolled out of a space between two tipping containers and floated lazily up into the open dome. Momentarily amazed, he paused to watch the bubble float away like you would a loose balloon on Earth. Then with an audible growl, the inspector returned to the place he guessed the bubble had originated from. He looked into the dark gap, paused as he thought he saw something, then snorted an angry jet of water from his gills and swam directly to the place where the driver waited.

"What are you carrying, Foulstik?!" the inspector demanded.

"Nothing now! I am empty… I will fill these boxes at the flotsam as I always do. You know this," he said projecting his irritation. *"Why be interested in me?"*

"I saw air bubbles rise up from this excuse of a vessel!" the inspector said and waited for Foulstik's guilty reaction, but the driver only appeared to be confused. *"And… I asked myself,"* the inspector continued, *"where would Foulstik find air? What would Foulstik need with air?"* he insisted, looking sharply into the driver's eyes. Still there was nothing there but blank befuddlement.

Foulstik searched his less-than-brilliant brain for the word *air*. There were rumors of visiting creatures from other worlds that could not live in water. Was it *air* that they breathed? He had never met one and was always suspicious of those Aquans who claimed their existence. *"Air? No! What would I be doing with air? I don't even know what the stuff is!"*

"A...huh." the inspector snarled before putting on a smirk, *"Of this, I have no doubt, Foulstik."* He knew, very well, that Foulstik was a complete idiot, but sometimes even the most innocent dimwit could be tempted into doing things that weren't quite legal in the eye of the Chief. Of course, they, the outlanders, were all outlaws in the eyes of the enforcers of the GACB or General Aquan Code of Behavior, but, here on the outpost, the Chief's rule was paramount. If the fool was smuggling air, or more importantly, smuggling air breathers, the Chief would need to be informed. They would all be made fish food and dumped in the flotsam if it was discovered that they had let a thing like that pass.

The inspector did a mental shrug. Traffic had dwindled to nothing, so what else did they have to do at the moment?

Noting the delay, two more inspectors roused themselves from their relative idleness and joined the first at the driver's cab. The inspector turned to the two. *"Search this miserable excuse of a vessel top to bottom!"*

Clifford stiffened at the sound of these words. Seconds later, the rest who were out of earshot of the conversation, got the telepathic message loud and clear. The time had come for flight. But where would they flee to?

Clifford cast a desperate look to the edge of the core that was bounded by a sheer cliff of tightly spaced buildings and crowded with Aquan pedestrians and knew they were hopelessly trapped. Reaching out for advice, Clifford searched the telepathic airwaves but found he was alone.

Apparently, the sudden panic had once again shattered the mental cohesion of the group.

As Clifford had guessed, the group was indeed in shambles. Christa was paralyzed with fear and Marco was in kill or be killed mode. Emotionally, Shelly and Tasha where somewhere in-between those two reactions. Sack, for some reason, was not connected at all.

Foulstik shrugged. *"Ah... Go ahead. Knock yourselves out... but I'll have you know you're going to ruin my day's chances for good salvage, and for no good reason! I might as well call it quits if it gets too much later,"* he griped.

Clifford had hoped for more resistance from the driver in order to buy the extra time needed to regain contact with the others, but that wasn't going to happen now. He had to think of something and fast, some kind of diversion.

As it was, Marco had already made his move. He had slipped out of his hiding place and had found Christa. Christa's first reaction to seeing Marco's shaded figure was to think he was one of the inspectors. Blinded by terror, she violently clawed her way past Marco and swam across open water toward the imagined safety of the buildings crowding the edge of the great opening.

Marco, after a very short, stunned pause, went after her. Their flight would have certainly been noticed if something else hadn't already drawn the inspector's attention away.

As the menacing anglerfish-shaped vessel arrived at the outermost boundaries of the giant red jellyfish,

Mitchell, who had been conversing casually with the pilot Knotrauf and his crew, was strongly urged to move to the holding chamber below. Mitchell had complied.

As soon as he settled and became quiet, Mitchell began to notice a familiar tug on his mind. At once, he stiffened as an increasingly clear flow of telepathic bits and pieces began to arrive. Great relief was replaced by concern as most of the transmissions he was picking up were more chaotic babble than quiet presence. There was no doubt that Clifford and his friends were in some kind of trouble.

Mitchell released his mind from deep concentration and sat with his back leaning against the wall of the water filled holding chamber located in the belly of the angler fish vessel. He had to get to them fast but at the moment that was not possible.

From his vantage point Mitchell could see through the vessel's windows. The constant color of deep water had long been replaced with the red glow radiated by the enormous jellyfish.

As he pondered one escape scenario after another, the vessel moved into the forest of tentacles that hung from the underside of the huge organism. Electric charges arced through the hanging mass, sporadically filling the ship's windows with blinding light. They would be through this danger soon and then he would have to make his move on whatever opportunity arose. First he had to get into position.

Ignoring the crew's orders, Mitchell swam back to the

control deck. The vessel at that moment passed out of the deadly electrified tentacles and began rising up into the vast dome-shaped interior of the jellyfish.

Knotrauf turned and eyed Mitchell with unmasked irritation.

"What are you doing up here Mitchell? I thought I had made myself clear," he growled.

Mitchell put on his most convincing smile and spoke telepathically, *No worries mate. I just wanted to take a bit o' a look-see. Blimey! You blokes actually live inside this thing?*

Knotrauf frowned, *"If you must know, yes, we live in this place,"* he said curtly and then waved one of his crew over. Shokkeel was a rather voluptuous serpentine mermaid who had a hard look to her. Unlike the others in the crew she was of the eel race of Aquans. She had more reptilian facial features, human like torso and arms, and a long slender tail of an eel.

"But we will not live here for long if we allow someone to see you. Shokkeel! Return this air breather to the hold and keep him there!"

Shokkeel nodded her obedience and gave Mitchell a lecherous look as she moved in.

Mitchell was suddenly held stupefied as he simultaneously saw the mermaid coming for him and received a hard jolt through his telepathic connection with Clifford Tuttle. He quickly recovered and managed to steal one more look through the vessel's windows before Shokkeel grabbed him.

Through the windows he could see that they were

approaching a check point at the edge of a floating mass of habitat buildings. Stopped at the checkpoint was a vessel made up of a disorganized mishmash of containers. In the last second before he was pulled away, Mitchell thought he saw two small, legged figures swim out from the jumbled cargo and make for the edge of the buildings. A third emerged and stopped close behind a row of Aquan onlookers.

An instant later Mitchell was pulled roughly back into the hold. At once a solid door panel closed off the glowing view and cast the hold into the dim light emitted by the naturally phosphorescent radiance of the vessel's walls. As he cast his eyes on his guard, Mitchell's mind raced through a shock of desperate thought. To his surprise Shokkeel was smiling at him.

"We are alone at last, Mitchell." Shokkeel murmured in a deep, sensuous voice as she moved sinuously toward Mitchell.

Mitchell looked thunderstruck. *What!?*

Clifford treaded water just behind the driver and three inspectors as they watched the approach of the same terrifying vessel that had earlier captured him and his friends in the open sea. As he stared, Clifford received a foreign telepathic voice. *Hide you bloody drongos!*

Clifford stiffened from the power of the message and spun around to see that Christa and Marco had also gone stock still. In a burst of adrenaline charged energy, Clifford darted to his friends' sides. He shoved them both into a cranny sized alley between two closely spaced buildings. From there he could see the inspectors hadn't moved or even noticed their movement. There was, however, an excited gathering of Aquan pedestrians close by who were gesturing and pointing in their direction. Clifford spun on his startled friends.

What in the heck are you guys doing!? he yelled through his mind, *now they've seen us!*

The inspectors?! Christa's mind shrieked.

Clifford turned and pointed at the opening at the end of the alley, *No! Them!*

Marco cringed. *What'll we do now!?*

Insanely frustrated, Clifford reached up and grabbed a handful of his flowing black hair. His mind reeled in utter panic.

We're separated from Tasha, Shelly and Sack again! If we don't move fast we're going to loose them for good!

From the telepathic distance Shelly's voice crackled in. *Should we come to you?*

Clifford released the grip on his hair and without rational thought, rushed the stunned group of onlookers. The startled crowd darted off in every direction. Clifford quickly regained his composure, stopped short of the open water and watched as the distracted inspectors nodded some agreement between them and began to move off in the direction of the incoming Angler fish vessel. Slowly Foulstik's ponderous wreck of a vessel lurched forward.

Clifford's command blasted out to all telepathically

listening minds. *Tasha! Shelly! Sack! Stay where you are! Marco! Christa! Make for that Vessel! Go!*

Inside the darkened hold of the angler fish vessel, Mitchell's body went rigid as Clifford Tuttle's decisive command blasted his mind.

Shokkeel let out a squeal of torturer's delight, *"What's the matter, Mitchell? Did I squeeze too hard?"* she purred, relaxing her constrictor grip on Mitchell's body. *"I wouldn't want to break you... too soon, little man. We've barely begun."*

Mitchell's eyes smiled through his goggles. *"Me ninety-eight year old grandmum gives harder hugs."*

Chapter Forty
Shark Bait

Before the amazed eyes of the reassembled group of Aquan witnesses, Clifford and Marco, with Christa in tow, swam for Foulstik's departing vessel. Fortunately for them, Clifford and Marco had made their move just in the nick of time, for as cumbersome as Foulstik's vessel looked, it had managed to gain speed very quickly.

As it happened, it took the three desperate swimmers the entire distance between the check point and the fringe of the electrified tentacles, to overtake the vessel. Still, they may not have made it if not for one final adrenalin-charged effort spurred on by the very real terror of being caught unprotected among the shocking tentacles.

As the vessel sped into the fall of tentacles, Clifford, Marco and Christa pulled themselves into the protected nooks between the vessel's catawampus containers and fell into an exhausted stillness.

Lightning fired over and over as the disturbed

tentacles swapped electric charges, but the vessel and its stowaways remained untouched.

Pushing himself up from his reclined position, Clifford immediately noticed that something was very wrong. Christa, he saw, was out cold, having no doubt, fainted from the shock. (All things considered, Clifford determined she was better off.) Marco was up, but he looked sick and shell-shocked. A growing horror kneaded Clifford's guts as he noticed the water in close proximity to Marco seemed cloudy and darker red in color, more so than the naturally pink light cast by the giant, luminous jellyfish could account for.

Gasping, Clifford moved in close and examined his friend. What he found nearly caused him to faint. Three deep, ragged gashes oozing blood furrowed Marco's cheek. Marco's jump suit had also been torn in several places, exposing more bleeding gashes on his chest and left arm. It was strange that he had not noticed them before.

Clifford shot a telepathic shout to Marco's mind. *What happened? How did you get those terrible cuts?*

Marco waved limply at the cloudy pink water. *Christa. Christa!?*

Marco shook his head slowly as he fought to clear his head. *She's got the talons of a hawk,* he said with a grimacing smile. *Take my advice, mi amigo; think twice before you startle her in close quarters.*

Marco! Are you going to be okay?

Si... sure... I hope so. Ha, I'm bleeding like a stuck pig, Marco replied weakly. *Nothing we can do about it now. Let's just get everybody out of here as soon as we clear the electric, okay Cliff?*

As he spoke these last words, a great disturbance in the water sent the vessel careening out of control. Tentacles all around the vessel exploded in a white blaze of electrical charge.

Foulstik only just managed to wrestle his vessel back into control seconds before a giant dorsal fin struck the vessel slicing it in half. The craft had been severed, separating the section that held the cargo containers from the driver's control pod. Wide eyed with terror, Foulstick swam free of his drifting control pod and quickly assessed the unfolding catastrophe. His vessel was gone, demolished. Searching the surrounding waters for his bundle of cargo containers, he finally spotted them sinking away, far below. And then, before Foulstik's panic stricken eyes, the previously unseen menace revealed its identity as an enormous shark.

Foulstik screamed in high pitched terror and darted blindly off toward the devastated drape of tattered tentacles just seconds before the shark swallowed his control pod whole. As Foulstick and the shark entered the tentacles, lightning renewed its intense strobing fury.

While Foulstik performed his best ever impression of a dancing electric eel, the part of his vessel that held the mishmash of containers was coming unlashed, evicting the stowaways into the open water. Connecting their telepathic bond quickly, the six moved to regroup but with all the chaos going on around them, Clifford and his friends did not catch the first sighting of the shark as Foulstik had, so they were completely unprepared for the creature's next pass.

At first, the reestablished communal mind had feared they had been spotted out after all, and the yet undistinguishable form rushing in on them was the anglerfish-shaped vessel come to recapture them. As the giant fish approached and its outline grew ever clearer, the group wholly wished it *was* the Aquan pirate's vessel and not the terror it really was.

The shark in the movie Jaws would look tiny in comparison to the mammoth scale of the shark that was now bearing down on the six Travelers. Instinctively, the group gathered into a tight defensive knot and then just as the monster was upon them, split off, darting in six different directions. Sack, who had turned black with fear, again expelled his load of black ink as the creature swam past. These spontaneous defensive moves seemed to have succeeded, because the shark veered evasively off and commenced to swim in wide, confused circles around Sack's black cloud and the scattered debris from the vessel.

It smells Marco's blood! It won't take the shark long to find us again!

A great many things happened quickly aboard the anglerfish vessel. As the vessel pulled into the checkpoint, Knotrauf caught a fleeting glimpse of three non Aquans swimming for the shelter of a careening wreck of a scavenger vessel. Simultaneously, a distressed call came in from Makkaw exclaiming that his six prisoners had escaped. Knotrauf put two and two together and steered the vessel into a sudden u-turn, sloshing Mitchell and Shokkeel into an embarrassingly compromised position: a nice relief to the previous mischievously painful torture she had been inflicting on him. The vessel accelerated harshly sloshing them further. By the time the maneuver was completed Shokeel was angry and fit to be tied.

As the vessel launched into pursuit of Foulstik's departing contraption, something big tore through a large section of tentacles setting off a blinding electric charged explosion. By the time the crew's eyes had recovered from the flash, the escaping vessel was in pieces. The pilot veered away from the area of flaring tentacles then stopped a safe distance away.

Shokkeel, cursing an obscene string of oaths, opened the solid dividing door so she and Mitchell could pass into the control area.

Continuous lightning flashed through the fisheye windows as Mitchell's mind was invaded by a bombardment of visions.

Through the telepathic connection with Clifford and his friends, Mitchell virtually swam with the six tiny figures as they emerged from the ink cloud and swam into the sea-filtered light of Aquan's sun. A moment later, in a flash of blue light, the six disappeared.

Within the last seconds of the mind link, Mitchell perceived the echoes of the group's plummet through the black void and passage into the last place in the known universe he would have them travel.

Makkaw swam slowly around the chamber that once held his precious hostages. Three of six holding boxes stood open as did the cabinets that had supposedly held their gear. Something had gone very wrong. For one, he had ordered the Travelers' gear to be locked in the prison's vault, not left in reach of a clever escapee. Second, he had asked to have the hostages confined, each to their own separate boxes. And third, where had the guards been? The more he thought of it the more he smelled a conspiracy.

"Sawren!" he growled.

Makkaw spun around to face the two terrified guards that he *thought* he had assigned to this duty. "Bring Sawren to me now, and I might spare your lives."

This, for the two guards, was worse news yet. Most who crossed the outpost's Chief would willingly opt for death rather than be left to live and face Makkaw's torturous wrath. The two disheartened guards nodded their obedience and exited the chamber leaving Makkaw alone to seethe in his anger, and to lay plans for his revenge against the conspirators.

Suddenly a shadow fell over Makkaw's mind. All the anger and plans of revenge were abruptly smothered in an eruption of unfounded fear. He fought the evil-spawned pull on his mind but the psychic coils tightened still more.

As if walking through a waking nightmare, Makkaw released all of his resistive will, turned and swam through the passage that joined the two chambers that once held his hostages and still held the Horwrath soul eater Kak.

Kak was waiting placidly for Makkaw. As the dazed Aquan Chief swam into the adjoining chamber, Kak opened his eyes

"You have allowed my prey to escape, Makkaw?" Kak snarled in an even toned voice. "That is most unfortunate." Kak idly fingered the top catch on his shirt. "I blame myself as well. Had I recognized the depth of your incompetence, I would have just taken the boy." The first catch popped open. "I've allowed myself to be fooled twice. I have also misjudged Clifford Tuttle's tenacity." A second catch popped open. "Had you done your job I may have let you go. Now, I must have my compensation."

Makkaw heard himself speak as if from deep within the cavernous spirals of a giant conch shell. "Compensation? What compensation do I owe you, Horwrath?"

Kak smiled wickedly as he drew nearer to the clear membrane divider. As he approached, he continued to shed his Horwrath skin shirt slowly, finally exposing the terrifying maw set in the center of his torso.

Makkaw's eyes went wide with terror as Kak simply continued through the membrane as if, for the Horwrath, there was no physical difference between water and air. Too late, Makkaw realized the terrible implications this ability brought to light. As he watched Kak move in, Makkaw's racing heart shuddered through a cadence of irregular beats before his will to fight finally collapsed.

Mitchell reacted quickly to what he witnessed both physically and mentally. *Get this bloody thing moving, Knotrauf!* he demanded telepathically.

The severity of the telepathic order hit the crew like a tsunami. Knotrauf recovered quickly, but by that time, Mitchell was holding a ten inch buck knife against the Aquan's neck.

I'm not a big fan of sushi, mate, but I'd wager there's one whoppa of a shark out there that would just love a bit o' tucker 'bout now," Mitchell said as he allowed the razor-sharp knife to break Knotrauf's first layer of scales.

Although Knotrauf was nearly twice Mitchell's size, he complied meekly to the threat. The pilot quickly swung the vessel back around. In the process, the vessel knocked three inspectors, who had absently approached the vessel while watching the catastrophe unfolding below, head over tails.

The vessel navigated cautiously through the devastated tentacles and out into the open water.

Beaut job, Mate. Now, find me some sun!

Kak swam quickly through the passages and chambers, hot on the residual psychic trail of the escaped earthlings. And though he encountered dozens of Aquans, some actual guards, none came forward to stop his progress. (In an Aquan's mind, instinct told no lies when it came to identifying a dangerous predator.)

Kak arrived at the expansive central chamber that held the Aquan outpost's habitats and looked down upon the flaring chaos below. As he did, Kak perceived another all-too-familiar psychic signature. A vicious smile spread across his face, "Mitchell! My old friend... You are back!"

Mitchell cautiously released his grip on Knotrauf, backed away, and sheathed the blade. *This is where we part ways mates. Now open that hatch,* he demanded.

The pilot and crew at once regained their bravado. *Not a chance, Mitchell!* Knotrauf bellowed as he rubbed the bleeding cut on his neck. *You've just signed your death warrant!*

With their backs to the windows the assembled crew, resolute in their determination for quick redemption, began to converge on Mitchell.

Mitchell casually held up his hands. *No worries mates,* he said evenly. Suddenly his eyes were drawn to the windows.

Seeing what was coming, Mitchell made one more appeal. *Bloody fools! I strongly suggest you dump me here, chucka U-E and get your asses out of here before that bloody shark comes back!*

The crew simply smirked and kept coming.

Mitchell wielded his blade, slicing a nice gash through one of the crew member's forearm. Blood began to cloud the water. They halted.

Knotrauf snarled, *We'll get our asses out of here as soon as you drop that knife, Mitchell.* But it was two late.

The shark rammed the vessel at full speed, shattering the superstructure and sending a mixture of wreckage and the inhabitants swirling through its turbulent wake. Mitchell had just enough time to see that his captors had survived the initial strike before the sunlight delivered him to the void and beyond. *Sad*, he thought. They had a long swim through open water before they would reach the relative safety of the jellyfish outpost and two of them were bleeding. *Bloody fools.*

Safe in the void for now, little did Mitchell know that he was about to be thrown into a much more dangerous situation.

Chapter Forty-One
Cliffhanger

The sensations bombarding Clifford's senses were nearly too much to bear. He had quite suddenly passed from life under water to life in the open air. In addition to this, he had, as suddenly, found himself clinging precariously to a rocky cliff wall.

Clifford's eyes focused first on the gray porous stone six inches in front of his nose. Dreading the need to know more, he forced his head to turn on his nearly petrified neck. As little a move as it was, his balance shifted. His mind swiftly overreacted by running him through an adrenaline charged scenario of gravity induced disaster. His grip, however, held. He opened his eyes and looked at what he could see.

The sun glowed orange from beyond the horizon of a black seascape. He chanced a look down. The act sent his mind into another acrophobic swoon. The rocky, wave battered shore below his feet was, as far as he could guess, four hundred feet down. His involuntarily quivering legs conspired to put him there.

It gave him little comfort to know he was not alone. Through the whooshing of his pulse and the lapping waves below, he caught the cries of his four friends who had found themselves in much the same predicament.

Sack, appearing as a dim white ghost against the black sky, swooped through the air from one stranded Traveler to another. He seemed to be trying to decide who to rescue first. As he approached Clifford's perch Clifford called him over.

"Sack! Is everyone safe? Are we all here?

"Yes. Everyone is here on this terrible place. What is this? I've never seen anything like this before."

"This is a rock cliff, Sack. We have these on Earth, but I don't think this is Earth."

"Is everything this hard on Earth? It hurts to touch this rock."

"Some places are hard, some not so… Except for the water and air, Earth is solid. So… I'm kind of freaking out here! Can you get us off of this cliff or not? Can you lift us?"

"Yes. I lifted you before on the terminal."

"Good. Maybe you should get Christa off first."

"No. I think maybe Marco first. He is very scared. He seems incapable of movement."

Clifford tensed still more. "Marco? Scared? I wouldn't have guessed. I thought Christa-"

"No Christa is Okay. Not scared. She is already climbing up this cliff."

Clifford smiled despite his perilous situation. "Huh. How are Shelly and Tasha?"

"They are climbing too. I think Girls like rock cliffs better than boys." He bobbed in closer and peered at Clifford with his strange compound eyes. *"I will help you first Clifford. I feel you are the most scared."*

It was very selfish of him, but Clifford breathed a sigh of relief as Sack hovered in beneath him, and lifted him from the rock face.

From their vantage point atop the craggy mountain range, the six Travelers could see, to their left, a vast, dark sea, and to their right an expanse of land wearing a patchwork of what seemed to be cultivated land. Rocky mountain ranges cut unnaturally strait lines to the horizon.

"Anyone got a clue of where we are?" Clifford asked.

Marco cast his eyes on the dark landscape far below, "No bro. It's kind of like Earth…"

Tasha was stroking her chin, deep in thought. Her forehead furrowed with worry lines. All at once, her eyes shot wide open. "This could be Drake 2!" she gasped. "I've heard some stories!" She let some breath out making a loose sputtering sound through her lips, and shook her head. "This might not be a very good place to be!"

"And Aquan wasn't?!" Christa exclaimed.

Tasha cast a look toward the cultivated lands below, "Remember that Horwrath soul eater?"

"How the heck wouldn't we?" Shelly put in.

Tasha made dramatic eye contact with each of her

friends before she spoke, "This is where *he* comes from... Drake 2!"

"Oh, nice," Christa said ironically. "We go to all that trouble to get Cliff away from that soul eater, and we land right here on his planet. What else could go wrong?"

Clifford shook his head, "Lots, I guess. Listen. I'm really sorry to have gotten you all into this mess."

Marco shook his head. "Not a problem. It's been a hell of a ride, mi amigo. And hey, we're all still alive, aren't we? Frickin' Travelers all the way!" he cried as he passed out fist bumps.

Clifford smiled despite himself and looked down onto the placid cropland. "Do you think there are Horwraths down there?" His smile faded.

Tasha shook her head. If, and that is a *big* if, this *is* Drake 2, there are three very distinct humanoid societies here. One is called the Phlock, or the Enlightened Ones. That would be their land down there.

"Are they dangerous?" Christa moaned.

"No. Not at all. They are very peaceful, like, you know, 'religious freaks'... so peaceful that centuries ago they split away from the Trunjenn who are the same as the Phlock in every way. The difference is, while the Phlock turned to religion and agriculture, the Trunjenn evolved into the busybody techies of the planet. They're more militarized too. The Horwrath have their particular physiology. Believe me, I've seen it, and it isn't pretty. The planet is supposed to be divided into six sections by mountain ranges– like these. That's why I think, you know... Drake 2," she shrugged.

Shelly smiled and shook her head, "How do you know all this?"

Tasha shrugged again. My mentor took me to Martinez's library once. There are tons of Traveler journals there."

For Clifford, the mention of his own mentor, Martinez, brought on a concussive blast of emotion. It had been a long while since he had thought of Martinez, and his Aunt Gwen for that matter. Gwen had to be hopelessly distraught by now. Clifford tried to count the days since he and his friends had dropped away form Quito, but couldn't.

Marco's voice brought Clifford back to the present, "We should find some place to rest. I don't know about you, mi amigos, but I'm beat.

Clifford and Marco's eyes followed the ridge-top path toward the point where the three mountains that they could see converged. Though it was dark and a distance away, they could make out the silhouette of a structure against the fading sunset. "That looks like something there," Clifford pointed. "Some kind of building, I think."

"Not a soul eater building, I hope!" Christa cried.

Marco shook his head slowly, "I don't think so. But, whatever it is, we should go there. Maybe there's someone there who can tell us exactly where we are. Besides, it looks like we're in for some bad weather."

"I don't know if that is a good plan, Marco. Do not go there until I come back. I will see if there is anyone there. You

should all hide… just in case."

With that said, Sack jetted off skyward, in the direction of the mysterious structure.

The rest hunkered down and finally took the time to rummage through their backpacks for something to eat. It had been ages since any of them had eaten. It was funny though. While their goggle's life support slime was deployed, they had felt no hunger. Now they were all starving.

Sack silently circled the strange structure that was made out of the mountain rock. There was a patchy net covering a quantity of open ground. It looked like someone had been living in the place, but as far as Sack could see, there was no one living there now. Satisfied, Sack returned to his friends and reported what he saw. Soon they were hiking in a single file line along the ridge path.

The terrain was rugged and there were many places where the top of the ridge was only as wide as the trail itself. To either side, sheer drops fell to the land or sea below.

About two hours later they arrived at the structure. As Sack had reported, the place looked lived in, but, for the time, its inhabitants were absent.

Tasha cleared her dry throat and winced, "I don't know about this, guys. For all we know the owner is out on a midnight hunt and could be back at any time," she warned.

"Yup," Christa said as she hitched up her pack, "not

good. I think we should keep going."

The storm bore down hard, launching arks of lightning at the ridgeline as it came. The wind plowed into the huddled group, bringing with it the smell of ozone and coming rain. They turned their eyes to the darkening sky that looked as though it were boiling with pent up fury. Another bolt of lightning slashed the sky, striking a point along the ridge near to where they had gathered after their climb off the cliffs. Thunder followed closely, but hadn't finished its rumbling passage before another bolt struck the summit further away.

"Ohhhkay," Clifford croaked. It's looks like we're going to have to stay."

"Oh… no way, Cliff!" Christa cried, "This rain's going to bring the owner of this place back for sure!"

Tasha shook her head adamantly as another barrage of lightning and thunder rattled the stones around them. "Out in the open, we'll be fried by lightning for sure! Besides do you want to try to walk this trail in the pouring rain and wind? No! This has got to be safer!"

Large, cold drops of rain began to assault them where they stood, just outside the edge of the suspended camouflage netting. Instinctively, they moved under the net's spotty protection.

Marco continued on toward the stone building as the others cowered behind. "I'll check it out. Stay put and alert! I'll be right back."

Marco took a deep breath. He reached out and slowly pulled aside the animal pelt covering the doorway. He peeked in, swept the room with the beam of his flashlight and satisfied the place was deserted, finally entered the domain.

Marco could tell right away that the place had been occupied recently. The main room was furnished with a bed covered in animal fur blankets. There was a fire place that looked as if it had not been used in a long while despite the damp chill the room held. Placed on the mantle were a few very earthlike objects. Marco stuck the small flashlight between his teeth and removed a wooden box and opened the lid. What he saw inside caused his breath to catch. *Goggles?* He turned them over in the harsh beam of LED light and whispered, "An Earth Traveler lives *here?*"

Mitchell navigated the black void through which he had traveled many times before. These days, his travels were controlled maneuvers, requiring a certain degree of planning. Timing, as always, was critical. It was really quite easy to travel between worlds. If properly timed, a Traveler could pinpoint the location of his or her arrival. It had a lot to do with physics and calculus, neither of which Mitchell could give a dingo's arse about. For Mitchell, travel was more about instinct.

After living through years of gonzo travel, counting on his youth to pull him through just about any miscalculated arrival, he eventually decided to seek out a more holistic approach to these maneuvers. He had gone into the Australian Outback on walk-about in search of answers.

During this time he met an elderly Aboriginal who taught him the ways of ancient, celestial travel. This deep knowledge had, to this point, seen him through to a ripe old age with little further mishap.

At this moment, Mitchell knew he was out of control. In desperate pursuit of Clifford Tuttle he had been forced to travel spontaneously to Drake 2. He had no idea where he might arrive. If the trip was truly buggered, he could realistically arrive inside a Horwrath hive, or even land inside one of a million caves that had formed inside the newly born mountain ranges, like so many air bubbles in a loaf of bread.

This dreadful knowledge forced him to consider the fate of Clifford Tuttle and his group. His only comfort came from the fact that he had traveled only a short time after the others. He should arrive, for better or worse, in more or less the same situation. His instincts told him he was about to leave the void, so he braced himself for whatever the result might be.

The Horwrath, Kak, swam directly toward the chaos taking place at the entrance to the Aquan outpost. There was something big and destructive raking havoc on the electrified tentacles and two vessels that had attempted to escape out into the open water. Undaunted, Kak pressed forward.

At the moment, all the trails were fresh: Clifford Tuttle, four other unknown Earthlings, and a Skyloum had just traveled. And, there was Mitchell, hot on the precious Earth child's heels.

Kak reassessed the situation. Unfortunately, all their trails led straight into the heart of the ensuing chaos spread out before him. He grimaced through his thoughts, knowing what he had to do. Despite his exasperation, he had to admit, Clifford Tuttle had a certain quality that made him exciting prey.

As a seasoned Traveler, Kak knew the physics of travel. He knew that the sooner he traveled behind his predecessors the closer he would end up in proximity of their arrival spot. Mitchell had a five minute head start and those before him probably much more.

Kak weighed the information and made a decision. He slowed his pursuit at the edge of the tentacle fall, and tested the echoes of the most recent of the travelers, Mitchell. At once he felt the familiar residual footprint or the waves of the traveler's wake through the void. In a moment he knew exactly where Mitchell was going. Kak opened his eyes and smiled. *I do like a home field advantage,* he thought.

Kak made the necessary adjustments for pinpointing his place of arrival. If Mitchell and Clifford Tuttle were on Drake 2 he would find them. To do this quickly, he first needed to visit the ancient Core, the hive of the Old Ones.

For Kak, fear was an emotion he very rarely felt. The thought of entering the Core constituted one of those few instances of dread.

Mitchell arrived on Drake 2 in the precise spot from which he had left it– sitting uncomfortably on the stone ledge above the grog plant he had harvested just before he was tricked into traveling to Skyloumia. For a moment he wondered whether he had just woken from an exceptionally strong hallucination, but inside he knew he hadn't. He was wearing new goggles and a jumpsuit. The weather was as strong an indicator. This time he was buffeted by stormy winds and soaked in pouring rain. Lightning struck the high ridges with a fierce frequency.

"Oy! Bloody buggers!" he cursed, knowing the climb up would be worse than treacherous. Luckily, his climbing ropes and harness had remained in place. "How'd I get back on this bloody rock?" he grumbled as he belted back into his climbing harness and tested the rope.

Mitchell carefully twisted to look up into the waiting climb. Water flowed down the cliff in rivulets making the hand and foot holds loose and slippery. Torrential rain fell into his face as a sudden and very close lightning strike shook the very rocks he clung to. He began to climb. With any luck he would be back inside the shelter of his watchtower in an hour.

Clifford and his five friends huddled in the dank watchtower staring at the goggles Marco had discovered.

Tasha turned them over in her hands. "They look old school," she commented.

Shelly nodded, "But, how old?"

Clifford took them from Tasha and felt the weight. "Martinez had a pair like these. The Optometrist said they were far outmoded," he continued as he handed them off to Christa.

Christa held them up to her face. They're bigger than ours... a man's I think. Yes, old," she concurred and handed them back to Tasha who looked deep in thought. "Why would someone leave these behind?"

Marco said, "Maybe they're a keepsake. Maybe the owner has gotten new ones."

Tasha nodded, "That's one possibility. The other is that the owner is still here… just away for the moment." Then another thought occurred to her. None of them had explored deeper into the stone dwelling. "These are old, like, Martinez old? Maybe he's, like… dead."

All eyes cast in the direction of the deeper rooms. Suddenly their senses became highly charged. There was a smell about the place, a kind of rotten smell, like spoiled meat.

A cold sweat fought to overtake the dampness of Clifford's clothing. He took the small oil lamp they had found on the fireplace mantle, lit it and walked through the opening to the adjoining rooms. There he found the toilet room and another room that was apparently used for storage. All he found there was some very ripe plucked birds but no half decomposed skeleton.

He finally let out his long-held breath, "There's nothing here but some rotten birds and a bathroom," he reported. He examined the birds. "There're some birds here that look like they were being prepared for cooking. They don't look more than a day old."

Tasha stroked her chin, "Why would someone do that…You know, like just leave food out to rot?" she thought aloud and then looked up into her friend's eyes. "Who ever it was must have left here in a hurry and not made it back."

Christa moaned miserably. "Do you think the soul eaters got him?"

The thought was very disturbing on many levels.

Kak, as he had planned, arrived on the outermost border of the Core's hive lands. He could have placed himself precisely at the gates of the hive but would have been ravaged violently before he could have taken two steps or spoken one word. No, it was much wiser to be invited in.

A strong storm was pushing up over the ridge to the east but the land here had not yet been besieged. Kak sank down to a meditative seated position on the dead, dry ground and waited.

Kak's wait, as he expected, was not a long one. He opened his eyes as five riders approached. He remained seated until the sentry leader dismounted his siven, a soulless horse-like creature. It was black and large with glowing eyes, clawed feet and a mouth full of gnashing carnivorous teeth. The rider, dressed in thick, leather armor approached.

Kak remained seated, eyes cast down at the sentry's feet. He held his empty hands out and waited. He heard the sound of a sword being sheathed or unsheathed. His muscles tensed.

"These are the lands of the Core. What is your business here?" the sentry demanded.

Kak replied without raising his eyes, "I am Kak. I am a Traveler, come from the outer realm of Aquan with news for the old ones."

"Rise Traveler!" he commanded. "I will see your eyes now."

Kak rose to his feet, keeping his empty hands out. He allowed his eyes to make contact with those of the sentry finally. He held the Horwrath's stare with strong confidence.

Kak watched silently as the sentry examined his face and then bowed his head. Kak was a Traveler, held in very high esteem on Drake 2, for there were so few left.

"I must speak of an urgent matter with the old ones at once," Kak repeated. "Take me to the Core, now!"

Mitchell pulled his weary body over the top edge of the cliff and lie with the rain pouring down on him for a long time. He was nackered, starved, hang-over stung, and stressed to the edge of his comfort level. He still had an hour's hike before he would be home. Even then there would be no time for a blow. Clifford Tuttle was somewhere on Drake 2, land of the Horwraths. History was indeed repeating itself. It was a shame the kid hadn't landed on Arris like the time before.

"Why the bloody hell Drake!" he moaned as he rolled

over and sat up.

The only consolation was that there was only one Horwrath Traveler left, as far as Mitchell knew. He had sensed its presence as soon as he came close enough to the jellyfish outpost. His fears were confirmed through telepathic contact with Clifford Tuttle and his fellow Travelers. One of them had actually seen the Horwrath. He would be coming sure as anything. If he wasn't on this ridge already, he would surely be going to the Core.

A dilemma was forced upon Mitchell's reeling mind: go hunt for Clifford and the boy's friends or go hunt the Horwrath Traveler. Truth be known, he hadn't the strength to do either, so he got himself up off the ground and headed for home. There he could rustle up some tucker and catch a little kip. A taste of his homemade grog wouldn't be out of the question either, just a nip or two, to take the edge off.

As unappealing as it seemed, the group's common exhaustion and the damp chill of their shelter eventually drove them all under the warmth of the mangy animal furs piled atop the bed. The five snuggled close together while Sack, who never showed any sign of weariness, hovered at the window opening, dutifully standing watch over his friends. Soon all five had dropped off into a deep sleep.

Kak had been guided swiftly and directly to the Core hive. As the group pulled up, Kak quickly dismounted his siven. As a reward for the beast's swift delivery, Kak produced three hukoo carcasses from the previous rider's game sack. He smiled a grim smile as he tossed them to the siven who ate them ravenously. Kak finally looked each of his escorts in the eyes, then turned, took a deep breath to brace up his withering courage, and entered the Core hive.

Kak had been here before under more tumultuous circumstances. It was soon after the failed insurgency on Arris. The Core had reacted to the defeat most harshly (and with a good degree of insanity). Those remnants of the devastated pool of Horwrath Travelers, who returned to Drake 2, were immediately arrested as traitors and deserters. They were taken to the Core and slaughtered in a frenzied fit of temper. Some escaped the carnage on Arris and Drake 2 by fleeing far and wide into the known universe. Kak himself had returned to Drake 2 on the waning end of the Core's harsh, punishing debacle. By then cooler minds had prevailed. Realizing what they had done, the Core sent Kak out into the universe to hunt down and return the scattered remnants of the once formidable force of Horwrath Travelers.

As his escort ushered him into the hive, Kak remembered how the now quiet and empty passages had looked on his previous visit. The burrowed corridor had been lined with bloody pikes skewering the gruesome heads of a hundred executed Horwrath Travelers. What remained of their rapaciously devoured bodies was piled at the base of each pike. Still, to this day, the ghostly stench of the dead haunted the passage.

In the chamber of the old ones, Kak knelt on his knees before his rulers.

"The Earth child, Clifford Tuttle, has returned to the Traveler's realm, my lords. It is my belief that he has traveled here, to Drake 2," Kak reported.

The five Horwrath elders spoke at once in one voice. The acoustics of the chamber produced a whisper-like echo that, if Kak freed his imagination, sounded as if the entire population of the hive was repeating the elder's words.

"I am the Core. I sense the presence of a power not suffered since the old days. Yessss."

The five old ones drew in a deep, collective breath. Again, Kak's stress induced sensibilities imagined the air in the chamber ebb and flow back in as if the entire hive had taken that same breath. This, of course, could not be possible.

"Long has sustenance been denied the Core. Long has the famine pillaged my strength!"

Again the breath flowed, seeming to pull the air from Kak's lungs. He could feel the Core's pull and the Core's need to feed. Kak resisted with as much strength as he dared expose. He had fed on Makkaw's soul. He knew he was stronger than these five old ones combined. But this strength dare not be exposed. The Core's hunger was great; its will to resist destroying one of their few remaining Horwrath Travelers was weak.

Kak was now seeing a mist trailing off of his body. He knew he was in trouble and if he did not redirect their focus, he would be drained of his soul.

The five focused at once on Kak's eyes.

Kak spoke, clinging precariously to the obligatory eye contact. "Lords, hear me. This child of Earth, Clifford Tuttle... He is special. He has special abilities, abilities the Core could use. We went after him before. We failed. He is back. This time we must not fail for the good of all Horwrath. But I stress to you, the child, Clifford Tuttle must be taken alive."

There came a collective grumble that sent a tremor through the structure of the hive.

Kak continued, "Lords, I offer you this appeasement, there are four other humans and a Skyloum. The Core will feed I assure you, but leave the boy for the future good of the Horwrath."

The misty outpouring from his chest had ceased but he felt the weakness from what he had lost.

The five old ones remained silent for an uncomfortably long moment before they spoke, "I will consider this. I remember the last time. The toll on the Horwrath was great."

Kak knew very well that the toll could have been less, but knew better than to assign blame where blame was due. Instead he urged action.

"My Lords, I must implore you to take swift action. Our opportunity will be lost when this night ends. Clifford Tuttle will travel as soon as his shadow falls before the coming sun. And there is one other problem. The Traveler who calls himself Mitchell has followed Clifford

Tuttle here. We must reach the boy before Mitchell."

"Mitchell! Hunter of Horwrath!? Here!?" The strange communal voice rose. The echo sounded less like words and more like a scream of mixed anger and misery.

"I shall summon the Core. Hunt these humans down! None shall live to see the next sun!" The voice was thunderous. The echo was a writhing cry of fury.

Kak, who had remained on his knees crumpled under the deafening rage. This reaction was not what he had hoped for. In his personal opinion Clifford Tuttle should remain alive, his powers tapped for the good of all Horwrath. Kak had seen many worlds. He had walked among their masses. He had walked even among his own planet's Phlock as well as the Trunjenn, the Horwrath's mortal enemy. The Core had not changed its ways in all the long ages. The Core was blind to all except for their ravenous hunger. Worse still, it made no difference to the Core who they fed on, Phlock, Trunjenn, and their own even.

Kak had been away long enough to shed this Core mentality. There were trillions of souls in the known universe just waiting to be selectively harvested. What Kak saw before him was a way to make the species strong again, but with out Horwrath Travelers, this crop remained forever out of reach. Now he had set before him, an Earth child with the power to take non travelers forth into the known worlds, to harvest, to become strong again. He had before him a second prize, Mitchell, who was equally empowered.

Time was running out. The Core had been released, their leader's murderous order heeded, their hunger unbridled. Kak could feel the ground vibrate beneath his knees and he could feel the Core's communal pull toward action rake his mind and soul.

With the last of his strength, Kak severed the link, bent to kiss the ground before the Old Ones. Without a second's hesitation, Kak assumed his dismissal, rose, and exited the hive.

Kak's commandeered siven was waiting where he had left it at the gate. The guards had since departed with the rest on their murderous mission. Kak mounted the steed and raced out onto the storm battered plains that spread out in every direction from the Core hive.

Kak had no planned destination. At this moment, all he felt was the need to be free of this place. Besides, he had no idea where to start searching for the Earth Travelers. His first instinct was to find high ground, so he spurred the siven and raced for the secret trail that zigzagged up to the top of the towering ridge before him. It had been a long time since he had used the path. He hoped it still existed.

He and the siven found the trail and began the treacherous, rain slicked switchback climb. Half way up they rested. Kak dismounted, stepped to the edge and looked out onto the plains below. What he saw there made his blood run cold. A force of thousands, maybe a million Core Horwraths were advancing across the plain, coming for the very ridge he was climbing. Their foot speed was unrelenting. It was as if they were driven to a panicked stampede under the psychic whips of the soul-thirsty Old Ones. Kak had no time to loose.

Mitchell had walked through a gauntlet of rugged storm battered trails to reach the halfway point in his trek home. The storm had since moved off across the Horwrath plains. The skies above had cleared and blazing starlight illuminated the places below. Mitchell sank heavily onto a rock overlooking the Horwrath plains and the unfolding scene below. He was done in, and first blamed what he saw on a weary mind, but some deep seated instinct told him to trust his eyes. He removed the new goggles from his pack and placed them on his face. Immediately, the goggle's lenses switched to night vision mode.

Shocked comprehension froze his heart. A huge, dark shadow was moving across the Horwrath plains toward the intersection of the two mountain ranges directly below his watchtower. He checked the skies for what might be casting such a shadow but saw nothing.

"That'd be right," he sucked a breath through his gritted teeth, "That's no bleeding shadow! That's a mass of bodies, a bloody Horwrath mob!" he exclaimed as he calculated numbers in the thousands.

Feeling the panic-spawned surge of adrenaline flow to his spent muscles, Mitchell jumped to his feet and began to run.

The nightmare woke Clifford from a dead sleep. In it, a thousand giant cockroaches were swarming over the side of his bed. As he blinked into the dimly lit room, nothing moved except Sack who, hearing Clifford scream, had hurried toward the bed.

Still, the feeling of being overrun by a great mass of creatures remained etched in Clifford's mind. Around him, the others were rousing under the layers of fur covers.

"Get up! Get up now!" Clifford screamed.

At that moment the heavy drape at the entranceway flew open. The inhabitant of the shelter had returned.

Chapter Forty-Two
The Consortium Reports In

Gwen woke suddenly as if Clifford had just screamed out in his sleep. She blinked the fitful slumber from her eyes, truly expecting to find she was back in her own bedroom at her sister's Pittsburgh home. But, she woke in Martinez's home, in the same guest quarters. She got up and hurried across the study to his room. Still, Clifford's bed was vacant. Her tense shoulders dropped as the familiar, empty feeling reentered her soul; a sensation she escaped only in her sleep. She had lost something very precious, something that could never be replaced.

With a heavy heart, Gwen turned away from the threshold and was startled to find Martinez standing in the entry to the hall that connected the rooms to the rest of the house.

Gwen's heart skipped a beat. "Has something happened? Is there any news?" she asked, maybe for the thousandth time since Clifford and his four friends disappeared from the museum court yard two days ago.

Through the windows she could see the world was still cloaked in night and she added, "What time is it?"

Martinez checked his watch. "It is 3:00 am."

Gwen was hopeful. "So... Why are *you* up?"

"The same reason you are, Miss Gwen. Clifford," Martinez said. "The Consortium has called me. Finally, there is news. For certain we now know Clifford is alive."

Gwen breathed a sigh of relief. "I thought I had heard him scream a moment ago... It must have been a dream, but it seemed so real!"

Martinez smiled, "The link between you and Clifford, it is very strong. I have seen this many times before with Travelers and their siblings, spouses, parents, and sometimes with their mentors. These are subtle clues, messages across the galaxies, gifts to loved ones assuring them they are alive."

Gwen's brow knitted, "This was a scream, not a kind, how-do-you-do! Something's happened, something bad."

Martinez approached Gwen. "I will see what this means when I meet with Sovereign, Johanna Rassahmie. All I can say for now is that some kind of contact with Clifford has been made."

Gwen held Martinez's eyes in her glare, "Okay. When do we leave, and don't you *dare* tell me that I can't go!"

Martinez did not back down but looked deep into Gwen's eyes for a long moment. "I wouldn't dream of denying you this," he said finally. "We can leave as soon as you are ready."

Johanna Rassahmie, along with several adult aged Travelers, one of them Gwen's friend Scott Fillmore, greeted Gwen and Martinez in the reception area as they arrived at the museum.

Gwen surveyed the room. She saw that the glass for the picture window looking out on the circular courtyard was still missing and the damage to the plaster ceiling and walls was still apparent. However, the shattered mess on the floor had since been cleared completely away. The buffet table remained but was empty except for a silver carafe of coffee and a tray holding china cups, cream and sugar.

Gwen continued to stare out through the opening, ignoring, for the time, the rest of the attendees in the room. Though it was still dark, she could easily identify the very spot where Clifford had stood just seconds before he disappeared and all hell broke loose. Her stomach knotted at the sight and traumatic memory of it. Her thought was broken by Scott Fillmore's light touch on her shoulder.

Gwen turned and smiled shyly, then gave Scott a hug that she held for a long while. Suddenly, she had needed the feeling of security, and Scott had gladly given it.

"Don't worry Gwen, we'll get him back," Scott assured her.

His voice was sincere, but Gwen could only hope he was right.

Earth's sovereign Consortium leader's voice finally loosened Gwen's embrace. She backed up, feeling embarrassed. But, after seeing the compassion in Scott's eyes, her worries were put to rest.

Johanna spoke politely, "We will meet upstairs in the conference room in ten minutes. Please, help yourselves to some coffee. I will call you when all is ready."

With that, she excused herself.

Scott Fillmore remained at Gwen's side. "How are you holding up Gwen?" he asked with apparent concern.

Gwen's mouth curled up in a small smile, "Better, now." Their eyes met and Gwen could feel the blush rise in her again. "Two full days and this is the first contact. What can I say? How about you? Gotten your powers back?"

Scott shrugged. "I don't know. Some have though, just today. I haven't had the opportunity."

"What do you think this is about? I mean… to get us out at this hour? It has to be that something big has happened."

Scott shrugged, "We'll know soon."

At 4:45 they were all ushered into the Consortium's private conference room on the second floor. Here too, there were signs of damage. Centered in the room was a large, round glass-topped table. This was the only piece of furniture. The walls supported futuristic control panels that appeared modern compared to the technology of the time. To Martinez, this equipment was familiar. To Gwen, she felt as though she had stepped onto a Star Trek movie set.

Gwen's impression was magnified as the space above the table sparkled to life, revealing five holographic figures. Their forms were totally alien and strange.

Sackus Rhue from Skyloumia appeared as a floating bag of air, showing no common earth-like appendages. Sedent O of Arris appeared to be made up of countless crystalline fragments held together by a glowing blue energy source. He appeared in the shape of an enormous head; his face was very human-like, this perhaps only for the earthlings' benefit. Teunnept of Aquan looked like a merman with a horse-like head, human torso and fish tail. Gwen, of course, recognized the Optometrist who was introduced as Sovereign Optomeetruss by name and he was from Cygnus.

The crystalline face of Sedent O regarded the gathered humans. "The Consortium recognizes Sovereign, Johanna Rassahmie of Earth. We must protest the inclusion of the rest in attendance."

Johanna bowed her head in respect. "Sovereign, Sedent O. I will vouch for these in attendance. Some you know as Earth Travelers who have stock in this catastrophe. One is a close relative to the boy, Clifford Tuttle. All here have a right to know."

O hesitated for a moment then spoke, "Very well, Sovereign, Rassahmie." The head regarded the gathering once more, and then continued, "There have been new developments in this volatile situation. First, Sovereign, Optomeetruss will present his report."

All eyes in the room turned to the Optometrist's holographic image.

Optomeetruss grew in overall scale as O's image shrunk.

The Optometrist nodded at Martinez and gave Gwen a stern look that strongly suggested she keep her insolent mouth shut before he addressed Johanna. For Gwen, this warning was not necessary, for she was held in speechless awe by the experience.

The Optometrist gave the gathering one of his small, knowing smiles. "Sovereign, Rassahmie. I have personally sent Mitchell out into the Traveler's realm in an attempt to locate the errant Clifford Tuttle. Mitchell has traveled to Skyloumia, then in pursuit, traveled to Aquan. Correct me Sovereign Sackus Rhue and Sovereign, Teunnept if this is not true."

Sackus Rhue's image enlarged. "Mitchell left Skyloumia exactly one sun behind Clifford Tuttle, from the exact spot the boy and his companions departed. This measure should have placed Mitchell in the exact vicinity of where Clifford Tuttle landed on the next world, Aquan," he said; his head bowed in concerned thought.

Sackus Rhue's image shrunk as Teunnept's enlarged.

"Sovereigns, Aquan has not confirmed that the Earth child, Clifford Tuttle has entered our world. None of the *legitimate* authorities have reported contact. There was however a disturbance reported at one of Aquan's isolated and unlawful outposts."

Teunnept's image shrunk and The Optometrist's grew.

"I have tracked Mitchell's progress and can assure you, my Sovereigns that he did indeed travel from Skyloumia to Aquan. If Mitchell has done this, I believe he is still in pursuit of the wayward child." The Optometrist wheezed a light chuckle. "Clifford Tuttle has proven himself a very resourceful Traveler for one so young. It is also true that this child is not a *quiet* traveler by *any* means! Where Clifford Tuttle goes, there is always calamity, no?"

"This brings us, my Sovereigns, to the next... shall we say 'ripple' in the universal continuum. This disturbance has Clifford Tuttle written all over it, my Sovereigns. It is my belief that Clifford Tuttle's travels have once again awoken an old enemy. It is also my belief that Clifford Tuttle is on Drake 2."

The Optometrist waited as a wave of murmuring rose amongst the holographic attendees.

Gwen looked imploringly to Martinez who was rubbing his face in reaction to the news.

"What, Martinez? Is this bad? What's on Drake 2?"

Martinez shook his head. "Nothing my dear... Nothing."

Gwen squared on him, "Don't lie to me!"

Martinez's chin sunk toward his chest. "Evil lives there... Evil!"

Gwen blinked in reaction to Martinez's blunt response. "Well, don't sugar-coat it... Evil?!"

Si, Miss Gwen. Horwrath. The soul eaters."

"What?!"

The Optometrist was speaking again, "I have contacted Hathah Vaken, Drake 2's self imposed Consortium Sovereign. With the Consortium body's permission, may I invite her to join this conference?"

Sedant O's image enlarged. "By all means, Optomeetruss."

O's image shrunk and there followed a sparkling in the air above the table. Two figures were added to the grouping of holographic figures.

The Optometrist spoke, "Sovereign, Vaken. What news do you have from Drake 2?"

Vaken's holographic image grew in size. She was a handsome, middle aged woman dressed in a Trunjenn military uniform. Her shocking green hair was pulled tight against her head, held back by a length of thick braided hair that snaked over her shoulder. She held a striking resemblance to an Earth, humanoid physique. As her audio came to life, a clamor of back ground voices nearly drowned her own voice out. "My Sovereigns, may I include Heathrobie of the Pflock in our talks?"

O responded in the affirmative.

Heathrobie was dressed in flowing sky blue robes. He was older than Vaken. He had long silver, wizardly hair that covered his shoulders and flowed down his back. His holographic image nodded, but he otherwise remained quiet.

Vaken returned her attention to the conference after an off-screen distraction. Her eyes showed signs of stress. "The Horwrath Core has awoken, my Sovereigns. Their numbers are incredible. Trunjenn is under high alert. We have not, as of now, moved against the Core. We have not yet determined their objective. They are massing at the convergence of their bordering mountain ranges. As you know, the two convergences of the six ranges are the weak points. Because of the Treaty of the Three, the convergence watches have been abandoned for ages," she said looking distressed, for she knew what the next question would be from the Consortium.

Optomeetrus smiled wryly, "So the treaty *has* been broken. How else would you know of this Horwrath insurgence?"

Vaken straightened and regained her steely composure. "We have deployed satellites," she admitted.

Optomeetrus chuckled knowingly, "Indeed."

Vaken appeared to be irritated with Optomeetrus' flippant attitude.

"The Horwrath have been quiet since the time of their failed insurgence on Arris. The number of attacks on Trunjenn and Pflock souls has ceased completely. Their soul eating Travelers have been absent. Never has Drake 2 lived in such peace. But, my Sovereigns, it is in the Trunjenn nature to be curious. Certain questions had to be answered, so we built the satellites and secretly deployed them. Until this day all has been silent in the realm of the Horwrath. Suddenly they are awake! We were startled to find they have grown vastly in numbers. This Core hive alone has spawned a million Horwrath and they are on the move," she concluded and waited. When no one spoke she continued, "Now. Can you blame us for being... curious?

"This news is quite disturbing," Sedant O put in.

Vaken pushed on, "Yes. Disturbing. And how do you explain the fact that suddenly, after all this time, Trunjenn hears from you... just coincidentally as this Horwrath offensive has bloomed? I venture you have been keeping an eye on us as well, which is also in non-compliance with the treaty.

The Optometrist was unmoved by this accusation, "So it is a good thing that we are both... curious. In this non-compliance to the treaty we are not guilty. Our eyes have just recently turned to Drake 2 and all the rest of the known universe for that matter... All of this, for one reason. An exceptional Earth child has once again traveled. I think you can guess, Sovereign Vaken, of whom I speak."

Vaken's eyes widened from skeptical squint to open surprise. "Clifford Tuttle?"

Optomeetrus winked and touched the tip of his forehead, "Clifford Tuttle, I believe, is now on Drake 2."

Just then the noise behind Vaken's image grew, and then fell ominously silent. Vaken turned to her off-holographic colleagues. When she returned her attention to the conference, she appeared shaken to her soul.

"The Horwrath are raising from the seas now... in numbers as great as the ones emerging form the Core hive on land. From the seas! How can this be?" (The implications of this struck home no more severely than on the Aquan Sovereign, Teunnept.)

Sedent O interjected, "What does your satellite surveillance tell you about the pattern of this new threat?"

There was a tense pause as Vaken consulted her colleagues. Then her response came, "They are moving on the same high ridge convergence watch. They are, thus far, ignoring the other borders."

The Optometrist's image grew. "I trust we all now can guess where Clifford Tuttle has landed on Drake 2, No?"

Chapter Forty-Three
Desperation Time

"You're Mitchell," Clifford said as the stranger entered the lamp-lit room.

"Aye, Mate. Been donkey's years, and here we are shin deep in the dog's breakfast again."

Marco had shot out of bed before Clifford had shouted his warning. He was now standing between Mitchell and the three girls who were still in bed.

"You know this guy, Cliff?" Marco asked carefully.

Sack was vibrating with pent-up excitement. His airways sputtered farty sounds not heard for some time now. *"Yes! It is Mitchell, the legend! Remember? I told you!"*

Clifford scratched his head and rose from the edge of the bed. "Yeah, I guess I remember, now. Sorry, stuff just kind of comes back to me. Mitchell... You got me out before, right?"

Mitchell remained planted in space. "That'd be right mate. It mighn't be so easy this time. We have a world of trouble comin' our way, no lie."

Tasha had risen and stood at Clifford's side. "What kind of trouble? Is that Horwrath soul eater coming for us?"

"Ah, yup. He and a couple thousand of his blokes, I reckon."

Christa leaped up. "I told you we shouldn't stop! We need to get out of here!" she cried.

"There's just one problem with that, lass. We need the bloody sun," Mitchell said. He turned to Clifford.

"How long has the sun been down?"

Clifford shrugged his shoulders, "I don't know... a couple hours, give or take."

"Which sun?" Mitchell thought aloud.

"There is more than one?" Shelly asked.

"Aye, lass, there are three. The duration of each night is different."

"So what does that mean?" Shelly asked.

Mitchell cast a glance out the open window. "It means either we'll be overrun before the sun comes up, or not. There's na easy way up these rocks. It will take 'em a bit to get up here, unless they find the trail, that is.

"There's a trail?" they all asked in unison.

"So what do we do, just sit here and hope the sun comes up early?!" Tasha shouted.

"That 'd' be right. Not much else we can do but keep a Captain Hook on the situation."

"Captain Hook? What the heck-"

"This is a *watch* station... so we *watch*. The main point of attack is at the intersection of these two ridges overlooking the Horwrath sector. If they git too close we'll nick off in the opposite direction. We'll need some daylight for that though. That ridge trail is like walking a tightrope compared to the direction we came in from."

"So we just wait? Sounds like suicide to me," Shelly said, voice trembling.

"Na. No worries Sheila. We'll out smart them drongos… somehow," Mitchell lied. "I always planned to cark it here, but I would rather keep hold o' my soul rather then serve it up for a Horwrath's brekkie."

Mitchell regarded the six young Travelers. "Right smart team yuh got yourself, Clifford."

Clifford nodded. "This is Marco, Shelly, Christa, Tasha and Sack."

"Aye… Sack Enestus, son of Ishtabar, I'll wager. Well g' day mates."

With that Mitchell moved past the group and entered the back rooms.

"He is either very brave or completely whacked." Tasha observed. "Can anyone guess how long these nights are here? I mean, I would like to know for sure whether I'm going to be a 'Horwrath's brekkie' before the sun comes up."

Christa was now shivering uncontrollably and blithering, "I s-s-say we follow the grown-up. He got Cliff out before. He seems very brave."

As she said this, Mitchell returned from the back rooms carrying a leather sack that sloshed as he walked. As he passed, the strong smell of fermentation followed him like exhaust fumes. With out a word he pushed out through the skin drape and back into the night.

"Aaa… Was that booze?" Tasha scoffed. "Oh! No way are we letting him get drunk! Not now!"

Marco snorted out through his nose in frustration, "So what are we supposed to do about it? The hombre probably hunts bear with a club. How else could he have gotten all these animal furs? Besides, I know how people are that drink. My Uncle Hernandez would fight anyone to the death if they tried to get between him and his booze." Marco confessed.

Tasha spoke up with uncharacteristic harshness, "I say we let him go. We've gotten this far…haven't we?"

Clifford spoke his mind as he started for the doorway, "At any rate, I think we better get out there, and soon."

The others followed Clifford outside where they were met with the terrible reality of their situation. At once, the angry cries of thousands of soul-hungry Horwraths, borne on the rising wind currents, soared up the mountainside from the plains below, and assaulted their senses. In shocked silence, the five watched as Mitchell slowly walked the circumference of the watch's stone parapet. He had abandoned the booze bag which now sat forgotten on the parapet wall. This, at least, was a good thing. This small feeling of hope was soon snuffed out by the news that Mitchell was about to break to them.

With great effort, the group broke their collective paralysis and hurried to join Mitchell. When they caught up with him, Mitchell was muttering to himself.

G'arn… you're kidding! There aren't supposed to be any bloody Horwraths on this side of the mountain! Ah, Christ! We're all buggered now! Bloody Horwraths from the *sea*?!"

"Mitchell. What's going on?" Clifford's voice broke the trance Mitchell had fallen into.

"What? Right. We need to go… soon," Mitchell muttered still distracted by what he saw over the edge.

Clifford and Marco leaned over the parapet and gasped. Suddenly the cries from below grew louder, as if their little peek over the edge had somehow triggered, in their enemy, a communal knowledge that their prey was close. The base and sides of the cliffs now teemed with their writhing bodies, one sacrificing another, in their blind need to ascend the escarpment.

Mitchell raced to another vantage point and was greeted with the same terrifying reality. The Horwrath were exploding out of the second bordering sea sector. Their numbers were countless.

"Bloody 'ell! All of this buggery, for one boy? The Core must be flippin' mad!"

The six youths had remained at Mitchell's side as he raced from one vantage point to another. Marco finally grabbed Mitchell by the shoulders and spun him around to face the frightened group.

"What can we do Mitchell? Think!" Marco shouted over the stereophonic noise of the climbing Horwrath. The sound seemed to be coming from everywhere at once.

Mitchell threw Marco off like a rag doll. "Nick off,

mate! I *am* trying to think!"

"Do you have any guns, Mitchell?" Shelly demanded.

"Me bloody bush knife's all!" Mitchell shouted back. "Now, give me a fair crack, lass," he dropped his voice to a resigned whisper, "I've never had to face anything like this before!" Then he brightened suddenly. "Me new swag! Me pack! Somebody go grab it!"

Clifford didn't wait. He immediately ran off in the direction of the shelter. He returned in less than a minute.

Mitchell ripped open the pack. "There *was* something…" He pulled out the small lock box and turned it over in his hands. "This was with the swag left for me on Skyloumia. There's na key though. Na place to stick one either. Bloody thing's a mystery," he complained, turning the box over again and holding it out to catch the starlight. All its surfaces were unmarked, smooth and featureless as a solid block of black glass.

The background noise from beyond the parapet was growing in volume and in degree of violence. In their frenzied attempt to climb the cliffs below, the Horwraths continued to inflict great injury and death on each other.

Mitchell's hands were shaking so badly that he nearly dropped the box. As he grabbed for it he flattened his right palm on the smooth surface. Suddenly the face lit up like a control panel. Mitchell lifted it and examined the electronic workings. An illustration of a hand glowed back. At the tips of the fingers dots blinked. Mitchell hesitated for a moment as another scream rose above the din below and then placed his fingertips on the blinking dots. The control screen blinked the words "IDENTITY COMFIRMED." The case hissed as it cleaved in two. Mitchell carefully removed the lid and beheld the content of the box.

The strange object gleamed in the bright starlight. It was not what Mitchell had guessed it would be. What he had hoped for was some kind of powerful, defensive weapon, but it didn't look like any gun he had known. No. It looked like nothing more than a simple wireless computer mouse.

"What is it? Some sort of ray gun?" Tasha asked, eager for good news.

"I'll be daffed if I know," Mitchell said. "I've only had this swag for a day." He carefully removed the object and felt its weight in his hands.

Tasha squeezed in to get a better look. "What ever it is, the thing doesn't look lethal… Mitchell! We need lethal! What else do you have in that pack?"

Mitchell pulled out the remaining climbing gear, 3D mapping device, which he did understand, and the food and water packets.

"Well… we'd be right as rain if we needed to know where we are… but I bloody well know where we are!" he said shoving the mapping instrument and climbing gear back into the pack.

As Mitchell was rummaging in his pack Clifford reached out for the computer mouse-like object. He lifted it and found that it had some weight to it. The object remained dormant.

"This has to do something. Maybe its like, a phaser… you know like on Star Trek." he said as he pointed it away from the group and pressed the center click button. Nothing happened.

"Oy, mate! Put that thing back! This is no time to be playing silly buggers!" Mitchell shouted.

Clifford jumped at the sound of Mitchell's raised voice, "Sorry. I just thought… maybe," he said and replaced it in its case.

"Sorry, Mate. Di' na' mean ta yell," Mitchell said. "No lie. I wish it was a bloody phaser. We could use one of those for cert."

Their attention was drawn away by the sound of falling rock followed by the screams of those below being crushed and thrown from the seaside precipice. The unnerving sound of cracking stone had been close, just beyond the edge of the stone parapet. Collectively, the group stood at once and took several steps back from the edge.

Christa was crying. "That was really close! How could those monsters be that close already?!"

The sound of unseen exertion had drawn very close indeed, and through the sound of close and distant clamoring of thousands below, a more ominous sound had been added. The sound was muffled and deep, rhythmic, thudding.

It was a sound that could only be the synchronized heartbeats of a million Horwraths. "**Thud, thud… thud… thud, thud… thud.**"

Initially, Clifford believed the beating sound was

from his own racing heart but he could hear that too, separately; the whoosh, whoosh, whoosh of blood rushing through his ears. "What's that sound Mitchell?!"

Mitchell's eyes were frozen wide open as he stared at the parapet. It was as if he was expecting, at any moment, to see one dark arm with grabbing hand, flop over the wall, then the other. "The Core," he mumbled. "The hive's hearts are beating as one... Millions of Horwrath hearts beating as one– The Core."

Mitchell appeared to be in shock. Marco grabbed Mitchell again and turned him away from the wall.

At first Mitchell resisted and then he complied. His eyes blinked. He seemed to come back to the present.

"There is a great power. The Core wishes to control our minds, draw us in. Don't be sucked in! Shut your minds to the sound of that heart beat!"

Tasha screamed, "But how?! It's all around me! I can feel the vibration in my chest! I can't just turn it off!"

"Mitchell!" Clifford yelled, "We need to run!"

Mitchell stepped listlessly forward as if he had started his final walk toward the edge. Instead he stopped, knelt down and gathered his pack. He palmed the computer mouse object and stowed the empty box in his pack. To his surprise the mouse began to vibrate. He looked down. *Maybe this thing is a bloody phaser.* he thought. "That'd be right, mate. Run we will. Wish we had some bloody light, but we're liable to have some unwanted company lob in on us right soon."

Mitchell had apparently shed what ever power had

possessed him. His voice sounded more confident and he spoke with more authority.

The sound of sporadic landslides and subsequent carnage-borne screams was coming with more frequency. It was as though the mountain ranges were conspiring to beat back the ascending masses.

Mitchell continued, "We got two ridges that'd be clear. One is impassible. The other is like walking a thousand meter high tightrope in places. There is an old trail down, but that leads straight into the Horwrath sector... not the best shake, but the only other option." He stared off in the direction of the desperately needed sunrise. Still that horizon remained dark.

Mitchell stood in deep thought for a long moment; a moment in which Clifford thought the man had been taken by the Core's spell again. But he snapped out of it quickly.

"Right!" Mitchell barked with resolve, "Thousand meter high tightrope, it is. The Skyloum can carry us across the worse parts. Right, mate?"

"That is correct Mitchell. Thank you. I will do my best to help in any way." Sack said with confidence.

Tasha gave Sack's squishy back a congratulatory pat, "That's my brave boy."

"It is easy for me to be brave, Tasha. I can just fly away from this danger, but you can't. If I was stronger I would fly all of you at once out of this terrible place."

"That you would, mate. No worries. We'll all manage with a little lift here and there. Once we're on that trail and over the rough goes, the dill buggers won't be able to follow. Now, all of you pick up your swag, everyone git yah specs on-"

At that moment they all felt the presence of something hurrying toward them from the direction they had first arrived. The menace was not yet visible but the feeling was as hard as rock.

Mitchell continued, "It's past time we geet a move on."

Suddenly they were there. The first of the Horwraths who had scaled the seaside precipice began to clamber over the stone parapet wall. It flopped limply onto the stone pavement as if every ounce of strength in its body had been spent. Breathing hard, the Horwrath slowly began to rise. Its angry eyes glowed yellow in the darkness.

Instinctively, Mitchell unsheathed his large bush knife with one hand and raised the computer mouse with the other as another thirty Horwraths poured over the parapet like waves breaking over a seawall. Mitchell pressed the mouse clicker button and the thing gave a jerk. A radiant orb shot from the device and bathed the surging Horwraths in blinding white light. There was an initial, nonfatal scream of pain and surprise then a wave of more desperate screams as hundreds of blinded Horwraths plummeted from their precarious grips on the cliff walls.

Clifford and his friends, along with Mitchell, experienced a similar blinding effect, though it was filtered by their goggles' lenses. When their vision returned they were still in the company of dozens of Horwraths who were now writhing on the ground holding their more permanently blinded eyes. Towering above the afflicted was a Horwrath, sitting high on a huge black horse that could never have been designed by anything but a nightmare. As the terrifying equestrian couple approached, the horse's claw-hoofed feet crushed several of the impaired Horwrath's skulls. Each scull cracked open like so many fragile melons beneath the thing's immense weight.

The rider dismounted, setting his feet down in the spreading gore that covered the ancient stone pavement. Ignoring the mess at his feet, he stopped to pat the siven on its jowls who then, permission assumed granted, lowered its head and began to hungrily tear at the flesh of the dead and dying Horwraths sprawled at its feet. The Horwrath rider smiled as he approached the dumbfounded group. Tasha, Mitchell and Sack were the only ones to recognize the Horwrath Traveler, Kak.

Chapter Forty-Four
An Unexpected Ally

The four terrified children cowered behind Mitchell's ridged stance as the two enemy Travelers faced each other down. Beyond, the sound of the continuing assault on the cliffs seemed to die away as their focus landed squarely on the direct threat standing before them.

Finally, Mitchell broke the silent stalemate between him and Kak.

"Big, bloody balls up over one little nipper, Kak," he growled in fluent Horwrath.

Kak stepped two paces to the left in order to study the four youths better. He immediately picked Clifford out from the group. Mitchell followed Kak with his eyes but did not move.

"Clifford Tuttle possesses a power dearly coveted by the Horwrath. The Core conspires to destroy this power," Kak returned in fluent English.

"That's rubbish, Kak. This child is no different. No lie, 'es trouble, but-"

"Clifford Tuttle *is* different, Mitchell. We both know it... and *we* knew it then. The *Core* knew it then!"

"Why destroy him then, if his power is so extraordinary?" Mitchell asked as he moved again between Clifford and Kak.

Kak smirked as a new wave of Horwraths began to reach the top further down the path.

"Clifford Tuttle is a threat to the Core. He wields too much power. If possessed by the Core's enemies—even if the power fell into the hands of his own kind, the balance would be tipped against the Core," he smiled wickedly.

Behind Kak, the siven, who had charged the growing ranks of Horwraths, was now being overrun. There were only seconds left before the Horwrath broke through the fighting siven and were upon them.

"Do it now, Mitchell!" His yellow eyes glared with inner resolve. "You know what that device is!" Kak shouted, indicating Mitchell's left hand. "Use it now, before it is too late!"

Clifford was screaming, "Mitchell! Run! We need to run!"

Sack began to dive bomb the raging mob.

Mitchell spun around to face his terrified charges. "NO! Stick close!" he shouted, then, as well as anyone could in the hissing Skyloum dialect, he commanded, "Ernestus! Come!"

Sack took one last pass at the dozen or so Horwraths who had fought their way past the ferocious siven and then returned to his frantic hovering above his fearfully trembling friends.

Mitchell pointed the device toward the sky and pushed the clicker button. This time nothing happened. He looked desperately at the device and turned it over in his hand. On the back a glowing blue digital clock was counting down from 00:01:16. Instant realization set in. He cursed in some indeterminable tongue and then shouted, "NOW, RUN!"

There was no delay in their adrenalin spurred reaction. All five of them, with Sack jetting over head, took off in full retreat down the path. Kak followed on their rushing heels.

The goggles provided ample oxygen to their supercharged respiration and they soon outdistanced their exhausted Core pursuers, but their retreat was halted by the first of the many "tightrope" sections of the perilous trail.

Marco, who was on point, saw the hazard first and skidded to a stop. The rest plowed into him and they all tumbled into a pile; the last to hit was Kak whose size and weight nearly crushed everyone below him.

Again there was only a handful of seconds before the chasing Horwraths would catch them. Mitchell battled his way out of the mass of frantically flailing limbs and knelt on the stony ground.

The countdown continued from **00:00:29**. Mitchell cursed again then dove for the mass of tangled bodies. He picked out Clifford's pale white hand and dragged him roughly out of the pile. Christa was screaming and Tasha reached in to hug her defensively. Sack landed softly on top of Tasha in an equally desperate gesture of protection.

Kak was quick to regain his feet and grabbed Clifford away from Mitchell by the scruff of his tattered jump suit and held his small flailing body to the sky. "Now! Do it now, Mitchell!"

The Horwraths were slowing their advance, suddenly confused by their prey's abrupt stand. The timer was ticking down

00:00:08, :07, :06, :05.

The Horwraths were less then fifteen yards away and still advancing, yet cautiously.

:04, :03, :02.

All within a twenty yard radius of the toppled group were silent.

:01, 00:00:00.

Mitchell pointed the device once again toward the sky that was just now beginning to lighten on the horizon and pushed the button. The device emitted a brilliant globe of light that shot toward the black space above and then exploded into a sun-bright flash of light. Clifford's shadow fell black across the petrified group, vibrated violently across the surrounding ground and then all went black.

They all fell helplessly through the black void, each not knowing where the others were. Abruptly, the black transitioned to the endless skies of Skyloumia. There was a moment of utter disbelief and then all five of the friends broke out in a cheer of triumph.

Clifford turned around in his flight to take an inventory of his friends. There, to his delight, was Shelly, Marco, Tasha, Christa, and Mitchell. Sack was flying figure eights through the descending group as he checked to make sure all were safe.

Among the familiar Travelers flew the Horwrath, Kak. His presence gave Clifford only a moment's concern only because Kak, above all, had played an important part in their escape.

Clifford extended his arms to right himself and to adjust his trajectory. His slightly tattered arm wings caught the air and he aimed himself toward the glimmering cylindrical form of the Terminal.

Kak adjusted with them and neatly flew up to Clifford's side. He looked over and locked his reptilian eyes on Clifford's.

"Again, your abilities to survive have surprised me, Clifford Tuttle. But know this, we *will* meet again. We will see then if your record will fall."

Just seconds before the Terminal's tractor beam caught Clifford and his friends in its reassuring grip, Kak pealed away and flew out of its field of influence. He continued his now doomed decent as Clifford and his friends watched on with mixed relief and horror. And then, before they had time to think much more about it, they were gently deposited onto the solid surface of the Terminal's shaded arrival deck.

Chapter Forty-Five
Going Home

On the fourth day (Earth time) of Clifford's ordeal, he, Shelly, Marco, Tasha and Christa stood on the Terminal's deck waiting for the moment of their scheduled departure. Despite all that he had been through, Clifford's stomach was aflutter with nervous butterflies. Maybe the anxiety he was feeling had something to do with the strangeness that had fallen between his friends and himself. They were different, distant, and stood apart from him there on the deck. He had tried to talk to them earlier but received only the slightest hint of familiarity from the conversation. Maybe they were feeling anxious as well, but surely something seemed off.

Behind him, Mitchell stood dressed in his beloved Aussie wardrobe. The rough clothing, in comparison to his jump suit, made him look older yet more confident. A faint mist of alcohol breath permeated the air around him.

Off to the side, Sack Earnestus floated next to his father Sackus Ishtabar. Sack seemed much less like the fretful youth he was when they had met just days before in the Terminal apartment. Now he nearly met the height and coloration of his father.

The Optometrist, Optomeetrus, towered over everyone else assembled there as he eyed Clifford with characteristic bemusement.

The last day spent on Skyloumia had played out much as Clifford's friends had first described of their previous travels; clinic time. Though sometimes boring, the quiet time was a gift compared to the stressful events of the past days. Though utterly exhausted, he tolerated the attention.

There were more Travelers from Earth on the Terminal. Apparently what ever had gone wrong in the beginning had now been fixed. It was through these people that Clifford had picked up snippets of information regarding the events of the past days back home and the civil war that had broken out on Drake 2 between the Horwrath and Trunjenn.

To Clifford's wonder, rumors circulated that in addition to the Trunjenn forces, multitudes of Horwraths had raised up against their own Core as well. He wondered if this could all have been his fault, but then coldly determined that even if he had caused all this trouble, he didn't care. He had no love for any soul eater. If the Core was being exterminated by their own kind, that was even better. This also made him think of Kak. What had been his fate?

Clifford spent his last night on Skyloumia alone in Sackus Ishtabar's apartment. By now, the place had been furnished more appropriately for humans so there were more comfortable places to lounge. There was even a facsimile of a TV that showed absolutely incomprehensible programming from Skyloumia. He had walked through the silent, shuttered rooms remembering the brief time he and his friends had spent there, how they had discovered Sack hiding in the closet, and escaped through the secret ducts.

Clifford touched the surface of the door half expecting the rude noise to erupt from beyond, but nothing came. He thought for a moment about opening the door and trying to work out the hidden doorway but just took two steps back. He had had enough clandestine excitement for a lifetime.

In a lot of ways Clifford felt he had gone full circle, returning to the time he first was placed in these rooms. The ache of loneliness had returned and he wondered if his friends would visit or better yet, spend the night in the hammock beds that had remained unused from the time before.

Clifford blamed himself for his current predicament. He guessed his isolation was a punishment decreed by the Consortium, and he wondered what other ramifications would be waged on him.

Now, as the time for departure arrived, Clifford stared straight forward, past the shading canopy and into the wide Skyloumia atmosphere. He recalled his first plunge into this strange world. It had all been real from the first, as he knew it had to be. He took a moment to wonder what would remain of his memories, of these new experiences, once he returned to Earth. Would it all be erased somehow in the coming transition, like the last time? Then a sad realization descended on his heart. His friends hadn't just been ignoring him. That would explain everything.

He chanced another look over his shoulder at the clever Optometrist and wondered still more. *Why haven't my memories of the ordeal been taken?* Like the mental baggage carried by all war weary veterans, some memories would best be left behind in the carnage that born them. He could only imagine the terrifying nightmares to come. After all, he was still just a kid though not so much as he had been before.

It was time. The Optometrist gave Clifford a curt nod and backed away as the platform they were standing on began to glide out toward the waiting sun. Clifford felt a tremendous lump of emotion swell in his throat and a tear brim in his eye. He looked sideways, down the line of his friends. They were all looking back at him in wonder, not each other. In their faces he recognized the same emotions he was feeling. Had there been a spark, an idea, a residual memory behind their eyes that hadn't been there earlier? There, in that moment, Clifford's hope blossomed anew.

Now, it was almost over and what a strange journey it had been. As the sun inched its way toward the tips of his toes, Clifford felt Mitchell's hand fall lightly on his shoulder then, tighten.

Chapter Forty-six
Home

A welcoming delegation of Travelers and relatives of the missing children had gathered in the special wing of the Quito Museum. The lounge room, freshly repaired, buzzed with excitement. Gwen, Martinez and Scott Fillmore sipped cool beverages and picked absently at delicious items from the buffet table. The growing suspense had temporarily taken their appetites.

Gwen swallowed and spoke to Martinez as she remained focused on the circular courtyard, "How can you all be so sure Clifford is going to pop up right here? I thought we had to go looking for him with that fancy truck of yours," her voice quavered with nervous tension.

Martinez chuckled deeply as he chewed, "With all of the trouble these past days, I am certain the authorities on Skyloumia will be extra careful in their calculations. Si, very careful."

Gwen's feet wanted to pace but she stoutly resisted

the pull. Instead, she allowed Scott to anchor her firmly at his side.

"Yeah… I'll believe it when I see it."

Across the courtyard, beneath the arched openings, Travis and his diminished peer group huddled in the shade. Travis had been mortally embarrassed by the events on the day of the solstice. He had not let go of his anger at the pale little prick that had stolen his shadow's power. All this had worked to advance the kid's celebrity even more.

As the time of the arrival drew near, Travis broke away from his group and began to pace the curved corridor like a caged tiger. As he paced, he scowled out at the sun lit ground. Oh, he could have easily walked right out onto those sun bleached stones, in broad daylight, but he wouldn't because unlike many of the others who were similarly robbed of their powers on that rotten day, his powers had not returned, and of this, he wanted no one to know.

Out on the courtyard the air above the paved ground began to waver. Above, a retracted roof began to slide out from two points. The gap of protruding sunlight narrowed as the air inside became foggy. In perfect synchronization, there was a flash as the last sliver of sunlight bathing the stones was extinguished by the closing roof. When the fog cleared, four figures stood up and began to dazedly look around.

Travis, jacked up on rage, was the first to rush out into the open. He stopped short and screamed at the top of his lungs "WHERE IN THE HELL IS TUTTLE!"

Back in the lounge there was a communal gasp of alarm.

Gwen screamed, turned to face Martinez and then grabbed the large man by the collar of his vest and shook him.

"Where is Clifford, Martinez?!"

CPSIA information can be obtained
at www.ICGtesting.com
Printed in the USA
BVOW03s1942281116
469126BV00011B/53/P